SECRET WAR

THE

WAR

S THE ECRET WAR

BO2OK
A JACK BLANK ADVENTURE

Matt Myklusch

ALADDIN

NEW YORK LONDON TORONTO SYDNEY

ALADDIN

An imprint of Simon & Schuster Children's Publishing Division

1230 Avenue of the Americas, New York, NY 10020

First Aladdin hardcover edition August 2011

Copyright © 2011 by Matt Myklusch

All rights reserved, including the right of reproduction in whole or in part in any form.

ALADDIN is a trademark of Simon & Schuster, Inc., and related logo
is a registered trademark of Simon & Schuster, Inc.

For information about special discounts for bulk purchases, please contact
Simon & Schuster Special Sales at 1-866-506-1949 or business@simonandschuster.com.

The Simon & Schuster Speakers Bureau can bring authors to your live event.
For more information or to book an event contact the Simon & Schuster Speakers Bureau
at 1-866-248-3049 or visit our website at www.simonspeakers.com.

Designed by Karin Paprocki and Karina Granda

The text of this book was set in Goudy Old Style Regular.

Manufactured in the United States of America 0711 FFG

2 4 6 8 10 9 7 5 3 1

Library of Congress Cataloging-in-Publication Data

Myklusch, Matt.

The secret war / by Matt Myklusch. — 1st Aladdin hardcover ed.

p. cm.

Sequel to: The Accidental Hero.

Summary: Twelve-year-old Jack may be the Imagine Nation's only hope of fending off
a new Rüstov attack, with the help of his fellow superheroes-in-training, but the virus he carries,
and Jonas's suspicions, provide new complications.

ISBN 978-1-4169-9564-7 (hardcover)

[1. Superheroes—Fiction. 2. Virus diseases—Fiction. 3. Orphans—Fiction. 4. Fantasy.] I. Title.

PZ7.M994Sec 2010

[Fic]—dc22

2010041779

ISBN 978-1-4169-9566-1 (eBook)

FOR JACK,

WHO MAKES EVERY DAY AN ADVENTURE

Contents

THE SECRET WAR

Unintended Consequences

The sun went down on Empire City and Jack locked all the doors to his apartment, then checked and rechecked the locks. He had work to do—*important work*—and he didn't want any interruptions. Not now. Not when he was so close.

Jack entered his lab and cut the lights to half power. He took a deep breath and looked around. Was he really going to do this? Part of him still couldn't believe he was going through with it, but he was short on options and out of ideas. There simply wasn't any other way for him to find out what he needed to know. Jack had learned a great many things since coming to the Imagine Nation, some of which he'd been happy to discover, and some of which he had not. Some things eluded him still, like the key to the secret Rüstov computer virus he'd been working all year to cure.

Jack's powers allowed him to talk to machines, and to control any machine once he understood its inner workings. The more he learned, the more powerful he became. Soon he would be strong enough to stop the Rüstov and their spyware virus once and for all. He was almost there.

Jack was taking on a special research project he'd put off for way too long. Basic engineering and computer-programming studies could take him only so far. Jack needed to study a Rüstov system to figure out the final piece of the virus's puzzle, and he knew exactly where to find one. It just so happened that it was located in the absolute last place he wanted to look. The answers Jack needed were right inside him.

Jack lay down on an operating table and asked all the machines in his lab to please be quiet. At the moment he was interested in one machine and one machine only. Jack closed his eyes, took another deep breath, and let it out slowly. The time to act was now, before he lost his nerve. For the first time ever, Jack used his powers to reach out to his Rüstov parasite. A simple thought was all it took, but the result was rather complex.

Talking to the Rüstov inside him wasn't like talking to other machines, something Jack did every day. With the parasite something felt different. Jack's mind and the Rüstov's mind were connecting on a deeper level than he was used to. He could feel his own heart beat faster as he probed the connection, an eerie reminder that this wasn't some machine separate from his body—it was a part of him. His skin crawled, but he pressed on. The information Jack needed was all there. He could see the parasite's inner workings clearly, everything from the microscopic nanobots swimming through his bloodstream to the root of the infection, buried deep inside his heart. The Rüstov circuit architecture was disorganized, its code language haphazard and chaotic. It made Jack feel dizzy and nauseous, but he kept going, studying the alien system intently, until something broke his concentration.

"Hello? Hello, can you hear me?"

Jack stopped cold. He didn't recognize the voice. None of the machines in his lab were talking. They were all being quiet, just as he'd asked.

"You can . . . ," the voice said. "You can hear me, can't you?"

"Who said that?" Jack asked. "Who's there?"

At first the only answer was silence. Then the voice returned behind a chilling snicker. *"You know who this is. It's about time you and I got a chance to speak. We meet at last, eh, Jack?"*

Jack broke contact with the parasite immediately and sat up with a jolt. The lab was quiet and still. His heart was *racing*. Something inside him . . . something alien . . . had just woken up.

CHAPTER

1

Fighting Gravity

Jack hustled through the streets of Empire City with a baseball cap pulled down low on his head, the brim nearly covering his eyes. He was hoping to avoid being recognized, but he didn't make it five blocks before a woman and her son stopped him on the street.

"Excuse me," the woman said. "I'm sorry to bother you but . . . are you Jack Blank?"

Jack sighed and took off the baseball cap. Some things were no use fighting. "Yep. That's me," Jack said with a weary smile.

The woman clapped her fingertips together as she bobbed up and down in a little happy dance. "I knew it!" she said. "I knew it! I knew it! I knew it!" Jack shot nervous glances to his left and right, looking to see if anyone else had noticed her and, by extension, him. The woman seemed to pick up on this and quickly regained her composure. "I'm sorry, I never do this. Ever. But do you think I could trouble you for an autograph?" she asked. "For my son?"

A redheaded boy about Jack's age, maybe a little younger, smiled eagerly up at Jack and held out a notebook and pen. "Sure," Jack said, reaching out to take them both. The woman and her son looked slightly familiar to Jack, but he couldn't quite place them, so he kept the autograph simple and just signed his name. He handed back the notebook and continued on his way, but the celebrity sighting had not gone unnoticed. Jack had to sign a few more autographs and take pictures with another half dozen or so people before he could finally break away, shaking his head in wonder at how much his life had changed in the past year. He had gone from unwanted orphan to suspected alien spy to national treasure. It still amazed Jack how normal it now seemed to live in a city filled with superheroes, ninjas, androids, and aliens. As crazy as it sounded, he'd gotten used to all that fairly quickly. He didn't think he'd ever get used to fame, though. Especially not his kind of fame, which he considered to be completely undeserved. None of Jack's fans knew the whole story about him.

Jack was grateful for the friends he'd made since coming to the Imagine Nation—people who didn't give him any special treatment. The general public might have already considered him a great hero, but Jack knew he still had a lot to learn on that front. His teachers knew it too, which was why he still had to attend regular classes with his friends, or, in the case of the School of Thought, irregular classes.

School of Thought classes didn't take place in a single building or according to a standard schedule. They were taught by the Inner Circle, the most powerful heroes in Empire City, a group that was also charged with governing and defending the Imagine Nation. Jack's teachers were the guardians of the secret roaming island where all the fantastic and unbelievable things on Earth originated.

They could hardly be expected to run their school according to some arbitrary schedule. Stendeval, the oldest member of the Inner Circle and the only living person who knew all of Jack's secrets, always said that life didn't happen according to a schedule. The world was a classroom. Life was an education. Classes met whenever the Inner Circle called for them, and took place wherever they saw fit to teach. That morning Jack's lessons were being taught in SeasonStill Park.

SeasonStill was the unique park at the center of Empire City where the winds of all four seasons blew at the same time. Jack broke into a slight jog as he made his way there. The simultaneous convergence of all four seasons produced something exciting and unique, even by Empire City's standards: Waiting for Jack in the heart of the park was one of the world's most inviting and alluring wonders—Gravity Grove.

Gravity Grove existed outside of the standard four seasons. The grove was a featherwisp tree orchard surrounded in equal measure by Summershore Stretch, Winterwind Way, Spring Falls, and Fall Springs. The singular temperature created by such a unique enclosure created the one-of-a-kind climate in which a featherwisp tree could grow. Featherwisps were gigantic trees with thick, black trunks curving up into the sky, and long, strong limbs that wove into and around the arms of neighboring trees like fingers in folded hands.

The tree's dark black branches were empty save for the bright fuchsia featherwisp blooms. These very special flowers lined the trees' branches like cherry blossoms, with thick petals that fell up, not down. Featherwisp blooms didn't care much for the laws of gravity and saw that it was suspended in and around their general vicinity. The presence of so many blossoms in one place created a full-fledged antigravity zone in the center of the park. The flowers were attached to the trees in such great numbers that they would have lifted the entire orchard up into the air if not for each tree's powerful roots. Complex networks of strong roots dug into the soil like iron claws. Gravity Grove wasn't going anywhere.

Jack arrived at the center of the park and found the others high up in the trees overhead. He reached up to the lower branches of the closest featherwisp tree. Even the lowest branch was still too high to reach, but the lightest of jumps, just a little flick of his ankles really, was all it took to get up there. Gravity, or a lack thereof, did the rest. At the apex of Jack's first jump, just at the point where he should've started going back down, he kept rising, levitating the rest of the way up to the branch. When he got there, he grabbed the tree's limb with both hands and pushed down. With a whoosh he soared upward toward the others. Featherwisp blooms drifted up into the sky all around him as he flew up to join his classmates.

On his way up Jack saw that today his class would be taught by Hovarth, the warrior king of Varagog Village, and Chi, the sensei Circleman of Karateka. The two Circlemen couldn't have looked more different. Hovarth was a burly mountain of a man, covered with furs and chain mail. He carried multiple swords, axes, and knives. In the grove they all floated weightlessly while strapped onto his back and belt. Chi was a slender ninja with a graceful athletic build who wore a simple karate gi and carried no weapons. A master of countless lost styles of martial arts, Chi was a weapon all by himself.

Jack always looked forward to Chi's and Hovarth's classes. Their tests were generally the equivalent of a superpowered gym class, stressing physical fitness, endurance, and hand-to-hand combat. It was school, but it was fun, too. That was the Inner Circle's trick to keeping students thinking about their lessons long after class was over. The School of Thought followed a demanding curriculum that ran students through a grueling mental and physical gauntlet, but Jack had to admit, it was a pretty exciting ride. School of Thought students got to do a lot of cool stuff, the combination of which taught them not just skills, facts, and figures, but a new way of thinking, a philosophy of heroism that Jack and his classmates took with them everywhere they went.

"Jack! Good of you to finally join us," Hovarth shouted when Jack reached the top of the tree. The Varagog king floated in midair, while Chi and the students all hopped around from branch to branch.

"I'm sorry, Hovarth," Jack said. "I got stopped like six times for autographs on the way here."

"No excuses," Hovarth said. "You should be used to that sort of thing by now. How do you expect to handle yourself battling supervillains if you can't even handle a crowd of starstruck admirers?"

Jack apologized again and went to join his classmates. There was no arguing with Hovarth. Jack had been stopped for autographs hundreds of times over the last year and could have been on time if he'd simply left for class earlier. The real reason Jack was late had nothing to do with his fans. The truth was, he'd been distracted and rattled ever since he'd connected with his parasite. When it came time for this class, he'd almost forgotten entirely.

"No matter," Chi said. "You've penalized yourself with your lateness. You're *it*."

A huge flying object rushed past Jack, sending him spinning head over heels as if he were strapped into a gyroscope. He reached out wildly, struggling for something to grab hold of. When he finally steadied himself, he saw a giant flying serpent with a long, winding body weaving through the trees. It had wild eyes and flowing whiskers and looked like a paper dragon from a parade come to life. The dragon carried a small Asian boy named Zhi Long, a young student from Karateka who had recently been named to a seat in the School of Thought. Zhi was a year behind Jack's class and was the only student admitted in his age group. He had the power to summon seven different mystical Chinese dragons into battle.

"Sorry, Jack," Zhi said, circling back around. "I couldn't help myself. It's not every day you get to buzz the great Jack Blank."

"Hello, Zhi," Jack grumbled. "I didn't realize you'd be in our class today."

"Keep your eyes up, lad!" Hovarth called out from the sidelines. "Always be aware of your surroundings. Don't think you know the battlefield . . . *know* you know the battlefield!"

Jack nodded and looked around, spotting Allegra, the silver-skinned Valorian girl who was probably his best friend in Empire City, and Skerren, the young swordsman from Varagog Village. He also saw Trea, a School of Thought student who was one year his senior. Just like Zhi, Trea was the only student in her year, but in her case it was because the other students in her class had all dropped out. Trea came from Hightown and was something of an "on-demand triplet." She had the ability to split into three separate individuals, each with a different, extreme aspect of her personality. Trea One, who went by T1 for short, was always supersmart but had a huge ego. The second Trea, T2, was incredibly strong but dimwitted. The last one, T3, was a wild card. Jack had seen her be hyper, happy, mean, depressed, silly, and more. He knew that anything was possible when it came to her. Chi was trying to teach her to balance her multiple selves, but so far it seemed she wasn't there yet.

"What do you mean, I'm it?" Jack asked Chi.

The ninja master of Karateka fitted an arrow with a long blue ribbon tied to its end into his bow. He drew back the string and fired the arrow into a tree trunk far below the floating students. "The tree with the arrow represents safety. Students! Your goal is to get to the arrow before Jack can tag you out. Whoever can reach the arrow first, wins." Chi paused and looked at the students hovering in place. "Begin!" he ordered with a clap of his hands.

The moment Chi's hands came together, three more dragons ripped through the grove, looping through the air like roller-coaster cars. They swirled around Jack, each of them missing him by mere inches. Their scaly, snakelike bodies glowed in bright reds, yellows, and oranges. Zhi's dragons did his bidding, and he was using them to throw Jack off his game pretty effectively.

"C'mon!" Jack shouted. "There's nothing up here for me to use my powers on. This isn't fair."

Hovarth laughed. "Combat doesn't care about fair and unfair, Jack. Battles go on either way. You have to be ready for them, with or without your powers."

"Use your environment," Chi said, floating gracefully through the trees. "Adapt. Machine powers are not your only talents. The human body and mind are powerful machines in their own right. If your powers desert you, you still have yourself to rely on."

Jack nodded again and went to work putting Chi's advice into action. He thought of the dragons as part of the environment and grabbed one by the tail as it rushed past him. He held on tight as it pulled him through the air and then whipped around suddenly to shake him loose. Jack let go, and the dragon sent him flying straight at Allegra. She stretched her liquid metal skin to avoid him, but he was going too fast. Jack shot right through her, splitting her in half at the waist. Little mercury-like droplets of Allegra's midsection floated through the air like bubbles.

"Allegra is out!" Hovarth said.

"That was fast," Skerren said.

"What can I say?" Jack asked, smiling as he coasted through the air. "I *am* the great Jack Blank." Allegra shot him a fierce look. "Kidding!" he added, putting up his hands.

"Ha-ha-ha . . . ," Allegra replied as she pulled herself back into one piece. "Don't get cocky. You haven't won anything yet."

Jack drifted into a defensive position, guarding the tree with the arrow. Allegra was right, winning this game was not going to be easy. Skerren, Trea, and Zhi could all use their powers up in the trees, and what's more, they outnumbered him. Still, Jack had one advantage. His opponents weren't working together. Only the first person to reach the tree would win the game, so they had no incentive to help one another. Jack could use that against them and pick them off one by one. He smiled to himself. There was no doubt about it, classes in the School of Thought were *fun*. It was just what he needed to get his mind off things.

Jack went after Zhi next. Chi's young protégé was good, but Jack had a full year of training over him. Zhi was young and inexperienced, and what's more, he idolized Jack. He kept sending his dragons after Jack like he was trying to prove himself by beating him physically, when he should have just flown down to the arrow on the dragon he was riding.

Jack leaped from his tree branch out toward a flying dragon and used it as a springboard to jump to another branch that was higher up and had been out of reach. He grabbed hold of that branch and swung around like a gymnast on parallel bars to land right on the back of Zhi's dragon, mere feet away from the young dragon rider. Zhi took the beast down in a nosedive trying to shake Jack off, but it was too late. Jack was already upon him.

"Zhi is out!" Hovarth said as Jack tagged Zhi and jumped off the dragon. He got off just before it turned around to fly back up, keeping his strategic position between Skerren and Trea and Chi's arrow. So far he was following Chi's instructions about using the environment to his advantage very well. The value of that strategy was not lost on Skerren. Using his swords, he chopped off tree branches and threw them down at Jack, trying to knock him out of the way and clear a path to the arrow.

"Is that all you've got?" Jack said, needling Skerren as he dodged branch after branch. "Don't tell me that's the hardest you can throw!"

Jack knew that Skerren would normally be able to throw the tree limbs much harder, but the zero-gravity effects in the grove were slowing them down and bringing them back up before they could come close to hitting him. Skerren angrily chopped a big, heavy branch off and put all his weight behind thrusting it down at Jack. It came crashing through the trees like a falling piano, breaking off dozens of little branches along the way.

"Is that hard enough for you?" Skerren yelled as Jack jumped out of the way, just barely avoiding the branch. The branch would have knocked Jack out if it had connected, but instead it turned out to be just what Jack needed. When the branch changed directions to float back up, Jack saw it was big enough to hide behind. He rode the branch up, concealed beneath it, and jumped out at Trea, surprising her as he passed her by. She had just enough time to use her powers and split into three identical versions of herself before Jack tagged her out.

"Trea is . . . one-third out," Hovarth said after some deliberation.

The Trea that had gotten tagged kicked the large severed branch in frustration, hard enough to crack it in two. Judging from the damage her foot had done to the massive tree branch, Jack knew he had tagged out T2, her strong version. That meant that the supersmart and wildcard sides of Trea were still left. He wondered who the wild card was going to be this time.

Meanwhile, Skerren was making his way down to the arrow. Jack grabbed one of the severed branches and threw it at Skerren, which sent him floating back up the tree. Jack scampered down the tree trunk he was closest to and reclaimed the low ground, guarding the tree with the arrow. "You're gonna have to do better than that," he told the other students.

"We have to work together," one of the Treas, presumably the smart one, told Skerren.

"Only one of us can win," Skerren replied.

T1 shook her head back at Skerren. "Oaf," she muttered. She looked over at her other self. "T3," she called out. "We're awfully high up, don't you think? I'd hate to think what would happen if for some reason gravity suddenly came back and we all fell. . . ."

A look of intense fear came over the wild-card Trea's face. "Could that *happen?*" she asked.

"Anything's possible," the supersmart Trea replied. "In fact, I heard that one time up here . . ." T1 leaned over and started whispering into the ear of her wild-card self. A look of pure terror came over T3's face as T1 recounted what Jack assumed was some horror story about falling from the trees and dying.

It was all T3 needed to hear. She started rushing down the tree, not caring about the arrow, not caring about getting tagged out by Jack . . . not caring about anything but getting down. It appeared that T3's most prominent personality trait this time was fear. Perhaps an extreme fear of heights. She rushed down recklessly, slamming right into Jack and knocking him off balance. She was tagged out, but Trea was still only two-thirds out of the game by Hovarth's count. It was a good move by Trea, sacrificing part of herself to take Jack out.

Jack floated up helplessly until he could grab hold of another tree branch. Meanwhile, T1 and Skerren used the opportunity to head for the arrow. They were both well past Jack by the time he regained his footing. Trea had the lead on Skerren. She was about to grab the arrow when the wind blew the ribbon tied to its end up toward Jack. He grabbed hold of the ribbon and ripped the arrow out of the tree, pulling it skyward. Allegra and Zhi cheered from the sidelines as Jack grasped the arrow and stabbed it into the tree behind him. "Hey!" Trea shouted. "You can't do that."

"Why not?" Jack asked. "Chi said the tree with the arrow represents safety. He didn't say it had to be *that* tree."

Skerren and Trea were speechless.

"Very good, Jack," Chi said. "Very good indeed. Skerren! Trea! If neither of you can reach safety, Jack wins the day. Do you concede defeat?"

Skerren straightened up. "Never," he said. "Never in my *life*."

He and Trea were both down below Jack, who floated in front of the arrow. Once again they had to come through him, but it looked like this time they were going to try something different. Trea pulled Skerren close and talked quietly, covering her mouth so Jack couldn't hear.

Skerren appeared to hesitate, then nodded, agreeing to follow her plan.

Skerren and Trea came up at Jack together, but from opposite sides of the grove. "Some fights you can't win, Jack," Trea said. "This is one of them." It didn't take Jack long to realize what she was talking about. He was going to have to choose between them. Guarding the tree in the center, he would eventually have to commit to either going right or going left. Whomever he went after, the other one would easily reach the arrow. He couldn't win. The only question was, which one of them did he want to beat? Jack had to hand it to Trea—that T1 side of her was every bit as sharp as Skerren's swords. He wanted to win, but if he could beat only one of them, he wanted to beat her. The upperclassman. It didn't happen that way, though. On the way up Skerren slipped while jumping off a branch and got turned around, completely missing the next branch he reached for. He sailed upward, out of control.

Jack couldn't believe it. Skerren? Slipping? He was like a monkey in those trees and as agile as a cat everywhere else. Before Jack even had a chance to react, Skerren was all over him, coming in on his right. Jack grabbed him. "I got you, Skerren," he said, steadying his friend. It was just the opening Trea needed to come in from the left and touch the arrow tree. Game over.

"We have a victor!" Hovarth said, clapping. "Trea! Trea wins!"

"Of course I did," Trea said, clutching the arrow like a trophy. "I'm older."

Skerren frowned. "By a *year*."

"That year made the difference," Trea replied.

"Right," Jack said. "That and the fact that Skerren slipped."

"What are you trying to say?" Skerren snapped at Jack.

"Uh . . . nothing," Jack replied. "I was going to tag her out until you got in the way. That's all."

"Don't feel bad, Skerren," Chi said, joining the students in midair. "Sometimes a sacrifice is the only move one can make. In chess, pieces are regularly surrendered so that others might advance. It's simply good strategy."

"Right, pawns are sacrificed for queens," Trea said with a smirk.

Chi looked at Trea, lecturing her with a stare. "Trea,"

he said after a moment. "Clearly you still need to work on balancing your multiple personalities. Otherwise you wouldn't be lording your victory over someone who helped you win."

Trea's smile vanished. "Yes, Master Chi," she said, looking down.

Skerren looked back and forth between Trea and Chi. "I didn't help her win," he said. "I slipped."

"Of course you did, lad," Hovarth said, patting Skerren on the shoulder. "That's not important. The important thing is you had a common goal and worked together. I'm proud of you."

"I'm serious," Skerren protested. "I slipped!"

Jack couldn't help but smile. As much as Skerren had loosened up around him in the last year, he remained as competitive as ever. Especially when it came to Trea. Jack was about to tease him about it a little more when his powers picked up on an airship approaching from the west in the skies over Winterwind Way. "Guys, we're about to have company," he said as the ship flew into place, hovering above the grove. Jack watched as a small door on the bottom of the ship opened and a lone figure jumped out . . . without a parachute. Seconds later Blue's massive frame came crashing through the treetops, breaking branches left and right.

"Look out below!" Blue shouted on his way in.

Jack and the other students scattered out of the way as Blue came busting into their outdoor classroom. He barreled down through the trees like a truck that had driven off a cliff, but the antigravity field caught him in its invisible net. Seconds later he was drifting up through the featherwisps, lighter than air.

"Sorry to drop in on your class like this," Blue said to Hovarth and Chi. "I didn't mean to distur—ah, who'm I kiddin'? I love this antigrav stuff. Couldn't help myself."

"Blue, are you crazy?" Jack said. "You could've gotten killed jumping out like that for no reason."

"It wasn't for no reason," Blue said, looking around for his sunglasses and finding them floating in the air next to him. "It was for fun. Besides, this forest has been fighting gravity as long as I can remember. It ain't giving up on my account." Blue smiled and put his sunglasses back on. Both lenses were cracked. "Oh, man," he said, taking them back off and examining the damage.

Hovarth cleared his throat loudly, impatient for Blue to explain the meaning of his interruption.

"Right," Blue said, turning his attention back to the two Circlemen. "Like I said, sorry to just barge in on you guys, but I need to borrow Jack, Skerren, and Allegra. If you're all through here, that is."

"What's going on?" Jack asked Blue.

"We got trouble in the Real World, kiddo," Blue replied, jerking a thumb up toward the airship. "Gotta fly."

CHAPTER

2

Sidekicks

The ship Blue had jumped out of belonged to a veteran superhero called Midknight. He was a well-known vigilante detective who had operated out of Hightown for years and was a major player in the greater Empire City crime-fighting scene. His ship was called the *Knightwing*. It was jet-black with a silver bottom and shaped like a boomerang with a pod-like bulge at the center. Jack thought it looked like a sleek, futuristic stealth bomber. Seated inside the *Knightwing*, Jack looked out the window as the aircraft raced through the sky at supersonic speeds.

Only Jack, Skerren, and Allegra had followed Blue into the ship. They took most of their classes with Zhi and Trea, but this was something different. Jack and his classmates were participating in a kind of work-study program for second-year School of Thought students, "sidekicking" for established superheroes that the Inner Circle thought they could learn from. Skerren was assigned to Midknight, Allegra got Ricochet, a British heroine with energy rebound powers who often worked with Midknight, and Jack was partnered up with Blue, who had recently quit the police force after finally getting fed up with all the paperwork.

Allegra was sitting in the chair next to Jack, looking uncomfortable as she did her best to sleep through the flight. She morphed her body to fit the contours of the chair and started to doze off. Skerren was sitting silently in the captain's chair, with the *Knightwing* flying on autopilot. No one was talking. This was a big step for all of them. It was their first mission to the outside world. Jack knew it was the first time Skerren and Allegra would be setting foot outside the Imagine Nation, period. People from the Imagine Nation called it "the Real World." Jack used to call it home. It was a place he hadn't seen since coming to the Imagine Nation a year ago.

Jack had some knots in his stomach, but he told himself he'd be fine. This might have been his first mission outside Empire City, but it was far from his first mission. He had been sidekicking with Blue a few months now, and it wasn't like he was lacking in combat experience. Last year he'd been a key player in the biggest battle since the Rüstov invasion, when he'd killed Revile, the unstoppable Rüstov supersoldier and possible future version of himself. Jack pushed that last part out of his mind, as always. If he could deal with that battle, he could deal with this mission, whatever it was. He was a student in the School of Thought. He was supposed to be able to take it.

The *Knightwing* had been flying for a couple of hours, long enough to cross several time zones on its way out of the Imagine Nation. It had been light out when they'd left Empire City, but the sky was pitch black wherever they were now. A quick conversation with the ship's navigation system told Jack they were flying somewhere over the American Southwest. The local time was 11:58 p.m.

Jack could have gotten exact coordinates from the ship's nav-computer, but he was less interested in those details than he was in how being back home made him feel. He was thousands of miles away from where he had once lived in New Jersey, but it was still his home. Jack might have been born in the Imagine Nation, but this was where he came from. This was his country too, and it was a part of him. If there was trouble here, Jack was glad that he'd be here to do something about it.

Miles away, he felt a train approaching in the desert below. It was still too far out of range for the *Knightwing's* detection systems to pick it up, but with nothing else around for miles in any direction, Jack couldn't miss it.

He got up from his seat. Allegra was now sleeping comfortably on the chair next to him, but Skerren was still up, keeping watch at the helm. Jack walked over to him. "They're out there," he said. "We're about to get a ping on the radar."

Skerren gave Jack a surprised but not entirely skeptical look. He leaned forward toward the windshield, ignoring the radar screen on the dashboard. "Are you sure? I don't see anything."

"I'm sure," Jack said. "I can hear it coming."

Sure enough, a red blip appeared on the radar screen a moment later, drawing the attention of the ship's owner.

"What have we got?" Midknight asked the two boys. His voice commanded instant respect. It was as if every word he spoke was infused with a lifetime of crime-fighting experience, which wasn't too far from the truth. Midknight wore a black mask that covered most of his face, but the character lines around his mouth told Jack there was at least a fifty-year-old man underneath it. That was the only giveaway. In his dark bulletproof supersuit and silver body armor, Midknight looked every bit as strong and fit as any young superhero Jack had ever met. Jack had seen Midknight fight, too. The old man hadn't lost a single step to the passage of time.

The red blip pinged on the radar again, and Skerren turned his eyes to the dashboard. "Supervillains, sir. Dead ahead," he said, tapping the radar.

"Yup," Blue said, leaning into the conversation, his massive bulk crowding Skerren as he looked out the forward windshield. "There they are. Right on schedule."

Way out on the horizon, a speeding bullet train came

into view, winding its way through red-rock canyons in the barren landscape down at ground level. It was late at night, but the moon was bright enough to reveal a few shady-looking passengers on the roof of the train.

"Looks like your source's information was spot-on," Ricochet told Midknight. "Again," she added. Jack turned to see the stylish Englishwoman patting Midknight on the shoulder.

"Looks that way," Midknight agreed.

"We're going to have to meet him someday," Ricochet said.

Midknight rotated his head slowly. "He's shy," the professional hero replied.

"What's the deal here?" Jack asked, indicating the speeding train down below. "We got a train to catch?"

"Something like that," Midknight answered. "I got tipped off about a gang of supervillains robbing this train. Don't know what's on it yet, but it's got to be something important for them to come all the way out here." Midknight fastened the chin strap on his helmet. "I'll tell you something, kids, your class is seeing way more supervillain action than even I'm used to. I don't know if you should be grateful for the experience or worried about what it all means."

"Grateful," Skerren said. "Definitely grateful."

"Right," Blue said to Skerren. "Leave it to you to be happy about sidekicking in the middle of a supercrime wave. Here they come now," he said, pointing. "Jack, you think you can stop that train so we can get this party started?"

"No problem," Jack said, opening his mind to communicate with the train. "Just give me a minute to—whoa." Jack stopped himself, surprised by what he'd found. He'd spent a considerable amount of time studying all kinds of engines and countless other machines to better master his powers, but this train was way more advanced than anything he'd ever encountered, even inside the Imagine Nation.

"I'm sorry. That is *not* a normal engine in there," Jack said. The mysterious high-tech train wouldn't talk to Jack, and was being a real jerk about it too. There was nothing Jack could do to slow the train down. Well, almost nothing. "I *could* make it throw a wheel and crash, but—"

"Not until we know who or what's on board," Midknight said. "Hmn," he grunted. "Guess we can't do much from up here, can we? Somebody wake up Allegra. I'm separating the *Knightwing* and taking us down. Jack, I assume you can still keep both halves of this ship on track once we get down there?"

"Yes, sir," Jack said instantly.

"All right, then," Midknight replied. "Look alive, people. We're going to have to do this one the hard way."

Blue let out a laugh. "You're tellin' me there's some *other* way to do things?"

Midknight just smiled. It was time to go to work.

The whole team moved to the *Knightwing's* lower half. The top and bottom halves separated, and the outer shell remained up in the air with room enough for one pilot flying solo in the captain's chair.

Jack steeled his nerves as the open-air glider descended on the supervillains below.

"All right, kids, you know the drill," Midknight shouted. "You see an unfriendly, you call 'em out. Let your teammates see what you see. Let 'em know what you know." Midknight always assumed the leadership role on operations because he had been doing this kind of thing longer than anyone else in the group. Jack knew calling out hostile supers on sight was a good strategy. It let your teammates know exactly who and what they were up against. As Jack heard the names called out, his mind flashed back to the hundreds of mug shots, code names, and abilities he had memorized back in his intro-level supervillainy course.

"Backstab!" Allegra shouted. *ShadowClan ninja with knifelike fingers charged with psychic energy.*

"Pain!" Blue yelled. *Superstrong and nearly invulnerable. Size and strength increase in proportion to the amount of pain he inflicts upon his enemies.*

"Fugazi!" Skerren called out. *The crystal man. Refracts light through his body to blind opponents and make them see things that aren't there.*

As the glider swooped in, Jack saw that the bad guys were ready for a fight. It was jarring to see them out in the Real World. Back in Empire City they blended right in with everyone else, but out here they seemed larger than life. The Real World landscape was like a black-and-white picture that the supervillains were scribbling on in 3-D, glow-in-the-dark fluorescent crayon.

Backstab, Pain, and Fugazi were positioned all along the train, keeping lookout on the roof. Jack scanned the area for any more superpowered rogues and saw a teenage girl with dark purple hair, dressed all in black. She was speeding along on an open AirSkimmer on the other side of the canyon, keeping pace with the train. Jack didn't recognize her. He assumed she was one of the bad guys, even if she didn't seem to be involved or interested in the heist. She was busy typing away on her phone. Jack's powers picked up the messages; she was texting her friends!

Jack was about to tell the others about the mysterious girl in black when a dark blur that was buzzing around the last few train cars slowed down enough for Jack to make it out. This one there was no question about: *Superspeed. Razor-sharp claws. Bad attitude.*

"Speedrazor!" Jack yelled.

Jack gulped. He had a history with Speedrazor, a super-fast psycho who had been bad enough back when he'd been on the right side of the law. Jack was certain Speed-razor still held a grudge against him. Jack and Jazen, his late android friend who had brought him to the Imagine Nation, had taken the speedster out when they'd broken into SmartTower last year. Like a lot of Jonas Smart's former soldiers, Speedrazor turned to supervillainy after the

Peacemakers were decommissioned. Jonas Smart, Jack's old nemesis, took no responsibility for that, but Jack thought the number of Peacemakers who went bad said a lot about the kinds of people Smart used to hire. Speedrazor was the worst of a bad lot, and these days he was heading up a gang of supers who were just as crazy as he was.

"I found what we came for!" Speedrazor told his cohorts while running alongside the train. "It's in the last car. Pain, get back there and help me load it onto the AirSkimmer! The rest of you," he added, sizing up Jack and the others, "take care of these *heroes*."

"Hear that, gang?" Blue said. "Speedrazor and the B-List All Stars are going to take care of us!"

"Oh, are they?" Ricochet chimed in. "My, my. That is going to be embarrassing. Whatever shall we do?"

Midknight grabbed two nightsticks from holsters on his legs. "Might as well get it over with," he said with a grin. He ran across the wing of the glider and leaped onto the roof of the train. The other heroes and sidekicks all followed close behind.

"Allegra and Jack, find out what's in the last car,"

Midknight ordered. "Secure that cargo and don't let Speed-razor get out of here with it! Everybody else," he added with a slight shrug, "take out some bad guys already."

Skerren didn't need to be told twice. Jack could tell he was itching for action, as always. He'd already matched himself up against Backstab. The beautiful but deadly ninja drew herself up into a fighting stance, cutting quite the imposing figure as Skerren approached. Backstab wore a dark crimson leather suit and mask. Her sharp, clawlike fingers glowed bright white and crackled with psychic electricity. Skerren spun his swords with dizzying brilliance and settled into his own ready position.

"Impressive, boy," Backstab said. "But all that swordplay is just that. Play." She lunged at Skerren with her claws, and he crossed his swords in front of his body, blocking her attack. Her white-hot claws stopped inches away from his face. "They don't let you kill in that school of yours, do they?" Backstab asked with a sinister smile. "Your blades are nothing without the will to truly use them."

Skerren pushed the villainess back and went on the offensive, thrusting his swords at her. "I don't have to kill you," he said, swinging away. "I just have to distract you."

Backstab dodged each of Skerren's blows and then connected with one of her own, knocking Skerren to the floor. "Distract me?" She laughed. "From what?"

From his knees Skerren swung one sword out across his body, moving Backstab back. He brought his other sword down to her left, forcing her to the right. She dodged the blade easily before slamming right into a large cactus that was growing out of the canyon ledge. She caught it right in the face at one hundred fifty miles per hour.

Skerren laughed. "From that."

Half a train car away, Fugazi bent the moonlight through his body to create five more images of himself to guard the injured Backstab. Jack blinked, and Skerren was surrounded, mostly by mirages. With no way of knowing which Fugazi was real, Skerren fought them all, swinging his swords through illusions instead of pressing his advantage against the evil ShadowClan ninja.

Meanwhile, Ricochet and Blue headed after Pain, who was working his way back to the last car on the train. Jack and Allegra followed after them, trying to beat the bad guys to the last car and the train's mysterious cargo. Jack went slowly as they moved across the roof of each car. He was still using his powers to control both halves of the *Knightwing*, which took a lot of concentration, especially with the train going so fast. Jack wanted to get a closer look at the engine and figure out why he couldn't do anything to slow the train down, but he had enough trouble trying to fly Midknight's ship and pay attention to the superfight at the same time. As a result, he nearly got cut in half when Speedrazor ran up the side of one of the train cars and rushed by him with his claws out. Jack fell back and grabbed the top rung of a ladder that ran down the side of the train car he was on. He held on tight as Speedrazor ran by him again. That time Jack would have been a goner if Allegra hadn't gotten in front of him and formed a shield.

"Don't worry, Jack, he's not getting through me," Allegra said.

Jack breathed a sigh of relief. He didn't even see Speedrazor coming, but he knew he was safe as long as Allegra was there with him. Her shape-shifting Valorian body had saved his life before, and she was a lot better at being indestructible these days.

"Stay out of this, little girl," Speedrazor warned Allegra.

"Me and Jack have some bad blood between us. Only way to get rid of that is to spill it!"

"You stay back!" Allegra shouted, morphing her liquid metal body to flash out with sharp, spiky quills. "You make a run at us like that again and you'll regret it."

Speedrazor didn't have any answer for Allegra. If he ran by her when she was shaped like that, he'd get ripped to shreds. From the look on the speedster's face, Jack could tell he knew it too.

"Good thing for me you don't scare so easily anymore," Jack told Allegra.

"The only one who's got anything to be afraid of is him if he comes back here," Allegra replied, loud enough for Speedrazor to hear.

Speedrazor scowled and went back to running along-side the train. "Pain!" he yelled, looking up toward the roof. "What's taking so long up there?"

Jack got to his feet and saw that Ricochet and Blue had caught up with Pain. Jack and Allegra would get to the back of the train first as long as those two could keep Pain occupied. The villain was outnumbered, but he evened the odds with a punch that knocked Ricochet clean off her feet. Ricochet became a dark blue streak as she went flying through the air, bouncing off the canyon walls like a rubber ball. Jack and Allegra kept moving as the blue streak that was Ricochet started glowing, picking up speed and energy as she went. Pain looked down at his fist. Even with his face hidden by the creepy skull mask he wore, it was clear he had no idea what had just happened.

"Wondering why you didn't get a power upgrade from that hit?" Blue asked as he delivered a devastating punch to Pain's midsection, driving him back. "Simple. You didn't hurt her any," he explained as he hit Pain again. Blue continued to lay into Pain like he was the punching bag at a gym. "See," he said, pounding away, "Ricochet absorbs that kind of energy. She builds it up into more, and then turns it back against you."

At that exact moment Ricochet fired back in toward Pain, landing a flying elbow to his jaw, cracking his skull mask and knocking him flat on his back. "Like so," she said in a calm voice as she landed softly back on the train. "Any questions?"

Pain's only answer was an agonized groan. Unlike Backstab, Pain received no assistance from Fugazi when

42

he went down. Having determined the difference between man and mirage, Midknight was able to splatter the real Fugazi with oil-slick capsules, one of the many items he carried in his utility belt. With Fugazi's ability to create illusions ruined, he had to direct his full attention to fighting Midknight hand to hand. Fugazi's hands were solid crystal, so he was by no means helpless, but Midknight, whose superhuman abilities made him stronger, faster, and even smarter as the night went on, was currently at the height of his power. Given the lateness of the hour in their present location, Fugazi didn't stand a chance.

Speedrazor was left to access the cargo in the last train car by himself. Unfortunately for him, Jack and Allegra were now in his way. Jack managed to get ahead of Pain and down to the passenger level of the car. He used his powers to open the cargo-car doors but couldn't read the encrypted cargo manifest. It wouldn't talk to him.

"What is it with this train?" Jack said, frustrated that his abilities kept getting stymied.

Speedrazor also seemed frustrated that a thirteen-year-old girl was keeping him away from his big score. Allegra swiped at him with machete blade arms, forcing him to keep his distance from the car. "Pain!" Speedrazor screamed. "I'm *waiting.* . . ."

Up on the roof of the train, Pain was still getting beat down by Blue and Ricochet. "*You're* waiting?" he yelled back. "Where's Lorem? We're getting our butts kicked up here!"

Speedrazor looked up and over at the girl speeding on the AirSkimmer. When he saw her typing away on her phone's keypad instead of helping, he absolutely lost it.

"Are you kidding me?" Speedrazor cried out. Unable to do anything more with the train's cargo, Jack watched Speedrazor run up the canyon wall and come out on the ledge next to the AirSkimmer. "Lorem!" he shouted at the girl as he ran alongside her. "We didn't bring you along for your sparkling personality, you know. Are you planning on joining us, or what?"

"In a minute," the girl replied, waving him off with one hand while texting her friends with the other.

In a flash Speedrazor was on the AirSkimmer. He snatched her phone away with his superfast hands and threatened to drive a claw through it. "Now," he said.

The girl rolled her eyes at Speedrazor and shook her

head. "Fine," she said, standing up on the speeding aircraft. She stretched lazily for a moment, and then leaped onto the moving train. She executed a dazzling acrobatic routine, flipping over and around Blue, Ricochet, and Skerren. The girl tagged them all before they even knew what hit them.

"Lorem?" Midknight said when he saw her flying through the air. "Lorem Ipsum? Is that you?"

The girl touched down in front of Midknight, who had taken most of the fight out of Fugazi. She dove at him instead of replying. Midknight rolled backward, barely evading her touch. He counterattacked with his nightsticks, trying to keep her back, but she was even faster than he was. Jack was impressed by her grace and agility. Midknight was one of the best fighters he'd ever seen, and he couldn't lay a hand on her. Midknight clearly shared Jack's admiration for his opponent's skills. "Lorem," he told the girl sadly as she ducked underneath his fist, "you had such potential."

"Ugh," the girl scoffed. "Spare me." She jumped up and flipped over Midknight's head, reaching down toward him as she went.

Although Midknight's bulletproof supersuit protected him against most physical attacks, when Lorem's fingers skidded across the helmetlike mask he wore to hide his face, her pinkie finger grazed his cheek, and that was it. The fight was over.

Midknight opened his mouth and said, *"Lorem ipsum dolor sit amet . . . Consectetur? Adipisicing elit! Sed!"*

Lorem Ipsum just laughed. "You can say that again," she replied.

"Do eiusmod tempor!" Midknight continued, struggling to speak. *"Incididunt ut labore et! Dolore magna aliqua!"* He seemed unable to say anything but gibberish.

It was the same for the other heroes, too. They were all disoriented and unable to communicate with one another. It was just the opening Speedrazor and his super-powered hijackers needed.

Backstab got up and plunged her synapse-scrambling fingers into Midknight and Skerren. Fugazi ripped a headlight off the train and shined it through an oil-free hand, blinding Ricochet and Blue. Pain took the opportunity to slow down the train in a way Jack had never thought of trying. He threw Blue underneath it.

46

As Blue's massive frame tore up the tracks, the cars all careened into the canyon walls, making a horrible screeching noise as the train ground to a halt. Sparks shot out everywhere as Pain ran back to the last car, shoved Jack and Allegra to the side, and ripped apart the coupling that connected the caboose to the crashing train.

Speedrazor grabbed hold of the cargo car and told Pain to forget about loading it anywhere. He started running the car down the tracks in the other direction, with his superstrong legs pushing it along easily. As he ran he told his cronies to take the AirSkimmer and get out of there. Allegra and Jack were powerless to stop them.

"Jack, he's getting away!" Allegra yelled. "What do we do?"

"What *can* we do?" Jack asked. He threw his hands up, exasperated. He had one job on this mission—to keep that cargo out of Speedrazor's hands. Right now he was failing at it, but he had an idea. "There is one thing . . . ," he said, trailing off.

Allegra looked at Jack. "What one thing?"

Jack shook his head.

"Do it!" Allegra shouted. "Whatever it is, just do it!"

Jack hesitated. He didn't know how this would go over with the others, but he couldn't ask permission. The mentor heroes couldn't even talk. Jack didn't know what Speedrazor had in that train car, but whatever it was, Jack couldn't let him get away with it. He had one chance to stop him. He was still controlling both halves of the *Knightwing*, and the top half, the one still up in the air, was armed to the teeth.

Jack fired a series of shots from the *Knightwing* gunship. The cargo car that Speedrazor was running off with exploded in a fireball, and when the smoke cleared, the former Peacemaker's unconscious body was sprawled across the train tracks. As the rest of Speedrazor's gang escaped in the AirSkimmer, Jack got a good look at their shocked faces. They couldn't believe what he'd just done. Lorem Ipsum was laughing like it was the funniest thing in the world. She was definitely a strange one. The villains sped out of sight, leaving their ringleader behind, and Jack and his friends turned their attention to the wreckage of the train.

Later, when Lorem's gibberish touch wore off, the adults told Jack he'd done the right thing, and he'd done the wrong thing. "It's good that you stopped the heist," Midknight told him. "But you destroyed the cargo in order to save it. Doesn't make much sense, does it, son?"

"No, I guess not," Jack admitted, feeling pretty foolish.

"We don't even know what was in there," Ricochet added. "It could have been anything."

"I'm sorry," Jack said. "Really. It seemed like a good idea at the time."

Blue gave Jack a pat on the back. "Don't beat yourself up too much, partner. You're learning. That's what this is all about. Besides, no one got hurt except Speedrazor. You knocked him into next week, and that's always a good thing." Blue put up a fist for Jack to bump.

Jack smiled and gave Blue's fist a pound. "Thanks, Blue. I just wish I'd been able to get Pain in there with him. I mean, the guy threw you under a train. That's not cool."

Blue rubbed his neck and turned to look over at the mangled train cars. "Forget Pain. We've got other stuff to worry about," he said, wincing. "Check it out."

Jack looked over at the wrecked bullet train and the flabbergasted people who were slowly staggering out of it with their mouths agape. They were people from the Real World. People who weren't supposed to know anything about superheroes, supervillains, or any other residents of the Imagine Nation.

"Blue," Jack said, "we don't have any cover out here."

"Tell me about it," Blue replied grimly. "This is a job for the Secreteers."

3

The Clandestine Order of Secreteers

After the crash about thirty-five people stepped off the wrecked train in a state of total, wide-eyed shock. No one appeared to be seriously injured, but they had all seen way too much. Some of them were even taking pictures with their cell phone cameras. That kind of thing wasn't a concern when Jack and his friends fought the CyberRaiders in Machina, or when they ran the Doppelganger Gang out of Hightown. People were used to superfights in those places.

"What happens now?" Jack asked. "Are we going to get

in trouble for this?" It was the first time Jack had ever had to deal with Real World witnesses. So far he didn't like it. One of the first things Jack learned about in the School of Thought were the laws of intervention and secrecy. They were the two guiding principles that governed any and all contact the Imagine Nation had with the outside world. Jack and the others had clearly violated at least one of them.

The law of intervention maintained that interfering with the lives of normal humans was permissible only in order to help them. This law was strictly enforced by the heroes of the Imagine Nation, and regularly broken by the villains they met in battle. The law of secrecy decreed that no direct proof of the Imagine Nation's existence was ever to be left behind in the Real World. Real Worlders weren't ready to know about the Imagine Nation or the extraordinary wonders and dangers within it. For more than five hundred years, the Clandestine Order of Secreteers had made certain they didn't, usually by cleaning up messes like the one Jack and his friends currently found themselves in.

"Don't worry," Midknight assured Jack. "This kind of thing comes with the territory. Besides, we're out in the middle of nowhere right now. This is containable."

"It's *quite* containable," Ricochet said, agreeing with Midknight. "But it doesn't really matter where we are. We don't get to plan out the emergencies we respond to, Jack. We do our part to save lives and defend justice. That's our job. Covering our tracks is someone else's responsibility."

Jack nodded slowly, giving Ricochet a curious look. He agreed that saving lives and upholding the law had to be prioritized above all else, but her carefree attitude toward the witnesses took him by surprise. Allegra apparently felt the same way.

"Ricochet, I don't mean to be rude, but . . ." Allegra paused and looked up at her mentor, unsure if she should continue.

Ricochet turned to her sidekick with an understanding smile. "It's perfectly all right, Allegra. You never have to be afraid to ask me anything."

"In that case," Allegra continued, "aren't we being a little casual about all this? What about the laws of secrecy?"

"Forgive me, I don't mean to be so cavalier," Ricochet replied. "The laws of secrecy are very important, and I certainly don't wish to make more work for the Secreteers. I'm simply saying that we have to focus on our job and allow them to focus on theirs. You may think I seem overly calm about all this, but it's only because they're so very good at what they do."

"How exactly are they going to do what they do?" Jack asked. "This isn't the kind of thing these people are going to forget anytime soon. Shouldn't we at least call the Secreteers and tell them what's going on here?"

"You don't call Secreteers, Jack. They just show up," Blue replied. "Trust me, they know to come here. They know everything." Blue tugged on his collar and looked around, hunching his shoulders with an uneasy look on his face. "Creeps me out, to tell you the truth."

"Really?" Jack asked. He was surprised to hear Blue admit that he got creeped out by anything, let alone the Secreteers, who were supposed to be good guys.

"The Secreteers have dedicated their lives to guarding over the Imagine Nation's secrets," Skerren said. "Are you saying that you—"

"I'm saying that I don't *like* secrets," Blue said, interrupting Skerren. "It's hard to trust people who keep secrets. Especially people who keep as many as they do."

Jack froze up at Blue's comment. He shifted from one

foot to the other, hoping that someone else would back up Skerren's point, because he wasn't going to touch it. Fortunately, Midknight chimed in and broke the silence.

"Easy, big fella," Midknight said to Blue. "You're just not used to working with them yet. When you've been through as many of these Real World jobs as Ricochet and I have, you'll see it's no big deal. The Secreteers are harmless. We just have to take care of these people until they get here." Midknight clapped his hands and started giving orders again. "Let's go, team. First aid kits are on board the glider. Let's break 'em out and make sure everyone's okay."

At Midknight's direction, Jack and the others tended to the train's wounded passengers while they waited for the Secreteers to arrive. Everyone was pleasantly surprised to find that the train's crash-safety measures were just as advanced as the engine Jack couldn't talk to. A few ugly bruises and scrapes aside, the riders were all doing fine. Almost too fine. They were all well enough to work their cameras and were snapping pictures and recording video like tourists in a theme park. Having grown up as a comic book fan in the Real World, Jack sympathized with their desire to take away some proof of an encounter with costumed superheroes, but he figured the Secreteers had enough to clean up already. He used his powers to delete all the pictures as they were taken. Jack was amazed that the Secreteers managed to keep the Imagine Nation hidden, with all the high-tech gadgets people had these days. He was excited to finally see one and find out how they did it.

Once all the passengers were taken care of, Skerren pried open one of the broken shipping crates that had been thrown off the train in the crash. "'Intelligent Designs,'" he read off the stylish blue and white boxes that spilled out and piled up at his feet. "What's that?" he asked Jack.

Jack picked up one of the boxes and examined its sleek corporate logo. He knew the brand well. "They're a big company out here," he told Skerren. "They make computers. High-tech toys. Things like that." Jack looked around and saw more of those very same toys scattered around the crash site. There were smart phones, desktop computers, laptops, and more. Were these what Speedrazor's gang had been trying to steal? That didn't seem right.

"What's wrong?" Allegra asked Jack, picking up on his puzzled expression.

Jack shook his head. "Nothing. I'm just surprised the train's technology was so advanced. Intelligent puts out some real high-end stuff, but this train . . . this was another level. Either they're way ahead of themselves or I'm falling behind."

Allegra nodded. "I guess that explains it."

Jack turned to look at Allegra. "Explains what?"

"You getting frustrated and going nuclear out here. When I told you 'just do it,' I didn't think you were going to blow up the whole train."

Jack tilted his head and smirked at Allegra. "I didn't blow up the *whole* train," he replied, smiling. "I just blew up the most valuable thing on it."

Allegra laughed. "Right. That's *much* better."

Jack laughed along with her. "I had to do something. My powers were getting me nowhere on this mission. It was embarrassing."

"You want to talk about embarrassing?" Allegra replied. "I slept through Midknight's mission prep! I can't believe you guys didn't wake me up for that."

"There wasn't any mission prep," Jack replied. "It was just: 'Jack, can you stop the train? No? Okay, we're going in.'"

"You know, if you'd fired on the train tracks, that would have made more sense," Skerren said. "Speedrazor couldn't have pushed that car across the desert sand. Not fast enough to escape, anyway."

Jack had to admit Skerren had a point. Midknight had been preaching patience and strategy to him ever since his apprenticeship had begun. Skerren had clearly been paying attention. "Thanks, Skerren," Jack said. "Where were you when I needed you?"

Skerren put his hands up. "I specifically told you to *'lorem ipsum dolor sit.'* It's not my fault you don't listen."

"Right," Jack said. "I'll try to work on that." It always took him a little extra time to realize when Skerren was making a joke. It wasn't like Skerren's jokes were bad or anything; they were just so unexpected that it was hard to tell when he was kidding. A sense of humor was a relatively new development for him.

"Hey, who was that girl with the gibberish touch, anyway?" Jack asked Skerren. "Lorem something? She was incredible."

"She *was* very good," Skerren agreed.

"She was an evil witch," Allegra said harshly. Jack and Skerren both looked at her, surprised by her reaction. "What?" Allegra asked them both. "Maybe I'm not as quick to compliment supercriminals as the two of you."

"Nothing wrong with giving credit where credit's due, Allegra," Midknight said, joining the conversation. "And she wasn't always a supercriminal, either. She used to be just like you. Her name is Lorem Ipsum, and she was a student in the School of Thought."

"She was in our program?" Jack asked. He could hardly believe it. "What happened?"

"I wish I knew," Midknight replied. "I'm not in the Inner Circle, so I never really got all the details. I *can* tell you she was slated to be my sidekick at the end of her first year, but she dropped out before she ever got that far." Midknight frowned. "Had some issues with her father. A very controlling man. He wanted to handle her training himself."

"That obviously worked out great," Allegra said.

Midknight shrugged. "I like to think things could've been different, but who knows? The right influence is important, but in the end it's up to the individual. Seeing her here now, running with Speedrazor's gang . . . it's a shame. Makes me wonder if we're giving you three enough independence. The time is going to come when you have to make your own decisions about things. You won't have any experience with that if we keep holding your hands all the time." Midknight rubbed his chin, turning the matter over in his head. "No, I'm sure of it," he said at last. "We need to have you each take on a solo mission this year."

Skerren's head snapped around. "A solo mission?" he asked. "Really? What kind?"

"Whatever kind of caper you can get yourself involved in," Midknight replied. "There's certainly enough super-crime to go around these days. It'll be interesting to see how you kids go about taking the bad guys on by your-selves. And it'll be good to have you out there. We're prac-tically outnumbered as it is."

Jack couldn't argue with that. The Imagine Nation's heroes had been so busy dealing with supervillains lately that they hardly had time to pay attention to the Rüstov anymore. Fear of a second invasion didn't grip Empire City the way it used to. It had taken a backseat to more immediate concerns. That was partly a good thing because it meant less pressure on Jack and the Rüstov infection he carried. It was also a bad thing because of the Rüstov spyware virus that only he and Stendeval knew about. The biological virus that the Rüstov parasites used to infect living creatures and take them as host bodies was bad enough. Their *computer* virus posed a whole other threat to Empire City's Mecha population and, by extension, the world at large. The spyware virus let the Rüstov see and hear everything an infected system came in contact with. They could even override an infected Mecha's programming and use it like a puppet. Jack found out that that was how the Rüstov got past Empire City's defenses back during the invasion. The virus was still out there, and no one was dealing with it except him.

Blue and Ricochet discussed the matter of the solo projects with Midknight and agreed that the sidekicks should each take on a case of his or her own. Their fellow students, Trea and Zhi, would fill in as sidekicks in the meantime. Allegra raised her hand with a question. "Does that include Jack, or does the project he already has count toward this assignment?" she asked.

Jack tried to wave Allegra off as she was talking, but it was too late. She'd already said it. Jack put his palm to his forehead and groaned.

"Sorry, I figured they knew," Allegra told Jack, realizing the three mentor heroes didn't have any idea what she was talking about. They stared at her with inquisitive eyes, and she felt compelled to explain further. "There's some secret project Stendeval has Jack working on," she said reluctantly. "We don't know what it is."

Blue looked at Jack. "Secret project?" he asked. "What's that about?"

"It's nothing," Jack lied. "Just stuff I work on in my lab. You know, I work on machines. I build things. It's part of how I'm supposed to develop my powers."

"How come we never see any of these things?" Skerren asked.

"Trust me," Jack said. "After tonight I'm going to start busting them out on missions. I need all the help I can get out here." Jack hoped his explanation would satisfy everyone's curiosity. The last thing he wanted to talk about was what went on in his lab.

Before anyone could ask any more questions, the wind

started to pick up, coming out of nowhere and blowing hard enough to overtake everyone's attention. Jack and the others squinted and turned their backs into the breeze as sand whipped into their faces.

"Is that it? Is that them?" Jack asked, thankful for the interruption. He put up a hand to shield his eyes and craned his neck to look up at the sky. Dark clouds were gathering around the moon. There was a flash of lightning and a crack of thunder, and then a large flying boat burst out from the clouds. The massive ship just appeared out of thin air, directly above the train wreck.

"It appears our Secreteer is here to tie up loose ends," Ricochet announced.

"Whoa," Jack said, genuinely impressed by the ship's stunning, sudden appearance. "I wasn't expecting that."

"Nobody does, Jack," Midknight replied, patting Jack on the back. "Nobody ever does."

It was truly a fantastic sight. The large wooden ship was decorated with shiny gold fixtures, ornately carved figureheads, and stained-glass windows that basked in the glow of gas lamps and the full moon's light. It was the kind of ship that Jack would have expected a pirate to go sailing around in, only in place of the mast and sails, the ship had a giant hot air balloon. A massive fabric envelope fashioned in a dynamic mosaic of colors was covered over with thick webbing and strapped tightly to the ship's railing. At the rear of the ship, a large iron cauldron filled with purple flames pumped hot air into the balloon and kept the vessel afloat among the clouds. Standing at the helm was a figure in a black cloak. The Secreteer's appearance was exactly what Jack had expected, but the ship he'd arrived in was anything but. Jack had lived in the Imagine Nation a full year without seeing a Secreteer. Now he wondered how he could possibly have missed them.

"They fly around the world in these things and nobody notices?" Jack asked. "I thought Secreteers kept a low profile."

"They can fly around in anything they want," Blue said. "Secreteers have memory powers. Nobody can remember anything about a Secreteer unless the Secreteer wants them to. You'll see."

Jack did his best to do just that, but from his angle below the ship he couldn't make out much. The Secreteer made no effort to address the heroes. Jack watched as the mysterious figure briefly surveyed the scene before turning and leaving the wheel of the ship. The Secreteer's black cloak twirled up behind him and flapped in the wind as he vanished from sight. Seconds later twin streams of dark purple smoke dove out over the railing and shot down like missiles. They didn't hit the ground, but rather spun out in spiral patterns, swirling through the air. The smoke spread quickly as the wind began to howl, and in an instant everything was pitch black. Thick, murky vapors filled the area, and Jack couldn't see anything, not even his friends right there next to him.

Now Jack could understand why the Secreteers creeped Blue out.

Jack heard yelling. The train's passengers were scared. He didn't blame them. If he hadn't known what was going on, he'd have been terrified himself. He called out his friends' names and heard his own called back from a dozen different directions. It was no use. The wind was so strong he could barely open his eyes. Still, he did try, and for a split second he was able to glimpse the Secreteer flying around, camouflaged by the smoke. It was only for a second, but it was enough. The black cloak fluttered in the wind, and Jack drew focus on the elusive Secreteer. He got a good look at her. *Her*. Apparently, he was a she—a tall, dark woman with long, thick dreadlocks tied back behind a beaded headband. Jack locked eyes with her for the briefest of moments, and in that short time span he saw the Secreteer's eyes narrow with an intense focus. The next thing he knew, the smoggy fumes seemed to single him out and attack him personally. He felt around in front of him, coughing hard. He couldn't see Allegra; he couldn't see Blue. . . . It was like being stuck outside in a hurricane. And then suddenly it wasn't.

As quickly as the smoke storm had appeared, it was gone. There was one last strong gust of wind, and the air was calm and clear. The flying ship was gone, and so was the Secreteer. Jack, feeling dizzy and disoriented, leaned on Blue, struggling to keep his feet below him. As he looked around, he saw the train passengers were even more out of it than he was.

"Time to get going," Midknight said to the group.

Jack regained his balance and motioned toward the witnesses stumbling around like they'd just gotten off a merry-go-round that was spinning at warp speed. "What about them?" he asked. "They look worse than they did before we patched them up."

"They'll be fine," Midknight said. "They all came out of this relatively unscathed, and I've already called emergency services in the nearest city. Help is on the way, and we need to be gone before it gets here. Right now the norms over there are still in a daze," he said, pointing at the people who could no longer be referred to as witnesses. "That's our cue to leave, before they snap out of the funk they're in."

Blue grabbed Speedrazor by the collar and started dragging his unconscious body toward the *Knightwing* glider. Jack, Skerren, and Allegra followed after him and helped tie Speedrazor up in the back of the ship. After that, Jack took the glider up to reconnect with the other half of the ship, which was hovering in the skies overhead, and handed the controls back to Midknight. As Jack, Skerren, and Allegra strapped in for the flight home, the encounter with the Secreteer was the main topic of conversation.

"Well, that was different," Allegra said as she buckled up.

"Yeah, it was," Jack agreed. "The Secreteer wasn't anything like I expected. Coming in on a flying pirate ship like that? That was crazy."

"Pirate ship?" Allegra laughed. "What are you talking about? The Secreteer came in on a sleigh. I saw it. It was being pulled by a team of flying horses with huge wings."

"You two need to get your eyes checked," Skerren said, sitting up in his seat. "The Secreteer showed up on a flying carpet. I was looking right at it. I saw it perfectly."

Jack looked back and forth between Skerren and Allegra like they were crazy. *Flying carpet? Winged horses?* What where they talking about? "Did you guys hit your heads in the train crash?" he asked them. "It was a flying boat with a huge hot air balloon. You couldn't miss it."

"I don't think so," Allegra said, shaking her head.

"I know what I saw," Jack told her. "You don't forget a thing like that."

"Don't be so sure," Ricochet said. She and Midknight smiled at each other, snickering. Jack didn't like not being in on the joke. Apparently, neither did Skerren.

"What's so funny?" Skerren asked, frowning.

Ricochet leaned forward in her chair. "Ask yourselves this, all of you. Do you have any clear memory of what the Secreteer looked like?"

Ricochet waited patiently as Jack, Skerren, and Allegra all fell silent. Jack racked his brain trying to picture the Secreteer's face. He couldn't do it.

"Don't waste your time trying to remember," Midknight advised everyone. "It's not going to happen. The Secreteer didn't just alter the memories of the witnesses on the train. She altered our memories too. They always do."

"What?" Jack asked. "Why?"

Midknight motioned with his hands. "I don't ask that question anymore. The Secreteers like to play their cards close to their vests. It's just the way they are."

"It's because they're paranoid," Blue called out. "Makes *me* paranoid."

"Don't worry," Midknight said. "They might get a little extreme about how they stay anonymous, but really, we're all better off this way. The less people know about the Secreteers, the easier it is for them to do their jobs. We trust them to keep our secrets, and so far no Secreteer has ever abused that trust."

"Yeah, as far as you can *remember*," Blue grumbled. Midknight gave Blue a you're-not-helping look. "Hey, I tell it like it is," Blue told him.

"I don't get it," Allegra said. "If they're going to mess with our heads, why do it this way? Why make us all remember different things that are still wild and unusual? If they're going to alter our memories, wouldn't it be easier to just wipe them clean like they did those people back there?"

"They just like to mess with us," Blue grumbled. "This is exactly what I'm talking about with these guys. I hate this feeling. You can't even trust your own memories around Secreteers."

"I think I do remember something, though," Jack said. "The Secreteer . . . I'm pretty sure I saw her in the smoke."

"Her?" Allegra asked.

"It was a woman," Jack confirmed. "A beautiful woman with dark skin."

"Jack . . . ," Blue said with a laugh. "If you really think you can remember a Secreteer's face, you're reading too much of your own press. Nobody gets close enough for that. Nobody."

Speedrazor, who had woken up at some point during

the conversation, found that extremely funny for some reason. He started giggling like a maniac, but Blue shut him up with a quick smack to the back of the head. "What's so funny?" he asked. "Your big score is down there in a flaming wreck, and your gang left you to take the heat for it. I wouldn't be laughing if I were you."

Jack looked out the window at the blown-up cargo car. He couldn't get any reading from whatever had once been inside it. His powers didn't let him talk to dead machines.

"I still can't believe you blew it up," Allegra told him.

"I just hope whatever that train was carrying wasn't some one-of-a-kind treasure," Blue added. "As it is, you're gonna hear it from your old buddy Jonas Smart when we get back to Empire City."

"Jonas Smart?" Jack repeated. "What's he got to do with any of this?"

"Intelligent Designs," Blue replied. "It's a front company for SmartCorp out in the Real World. Whatever you just blew up belonged to him."

"No way," Jack said. Blue gave him a look that said he wasn't kidding. Jack leaned back in his seat and let out a heavy sigh. "Great," he said. "That's just great."

Jonas Smart, a man who had once tried to have Jack executed and dissected because of his Rüstov infection . . . a man who was probably the last person left in Empire City who still thought of Jack as a Rüstov spy . . . he was the owner of the coveted cargo that Jack had just blown to bits. Ricochet was wrong. The Secreteers hadn't tied up every loose end on this mission after all. Jack was going to have to answer for what he'd done on that train, and Jonas Smart was going to be the one asking the questions.

CHAPTER

4

The SmarterNet

As it turned out, the self-proclaimed smartest man in the world didn't even wait one full day before he had Jack called before the Inner Circle, charged with the willful and malicious destruction of SmartCorp property. It was a ridiculous claim. Jack knew that SmartCorp had front companies operating out in the Real World, but he'd had no way of knowing that Intelligent Designs was one of them. The extent of the Imagine Nation's involvement in the Real World was as much a mystery to Jack now as it had been back when he'd lived there. Still, Smart never let facts get in the way of his campaign against Jack, and this was no exception.

Jack stood in the pit of the Inner Circle's sphere, staring up at empty chairs and waiting for the Circlemen to arrive. He wasn't as nervous as he'd been the first time he'd been there, back when Smart had wanted to dissect him. Things were different now. Gone were the days when Smart could just say "Rüstov" and scare everyone into doing whatever he wanted, but Jack knew how quickly that could all change, and he wasn't about to underestimate Jonas Smart. That was why, even though Jack's friends regarded this hearing as little more than a time-wasting nuisance, he was still hounded by a tiny, nagging morsel of doubt. It sat there in the pit of his stomach like an ice cube that refused to melt.

One by one the Circlemen began to file into the sphere. Stendeval was the first to arrive, materializing in an orange-white flash up at the ceiling. The red energy particles that swirled around him faded down to nothing as he lowered himself into his chair. "Hello, Jack," he said, getting comfortable in his seat. "In trouble again, I see," he added with a reassuring smile.

Jack shrugged. "I guess so," he replied. "What else is new, right?"

"Indeed," Chi said from across the table.

Jack's head shot up, startled by the sound of Chi's voice. One second ago his seat had been empty. Now the sensei Circleman of Karateka was sitting in his chair, calm and still, as if he'd been there all along. He put his hands together and bowed his head slightly. "Jack," he said in greeting.

"Master Chi," Jack said, returning the gesture.

The appearance of the next two Circlemen was far less sudden. First there was Hovarth, the warrior king of Varagog Village, who grunted and grumbled as he stomped his way down the tunnel. Then there was Virtua, the glamorous light projection of artificial intelligence that governed the robotic borough of Machina. Jack heard the buzzing whirr of Projo, the mechanized orb who carried Virtua's holographic image to the unplugged world, as they approached the sphere.

Jack looked up at the empty chairs on the circle, knowing that the Galaxis seat would remain unoccupied that day. Prime, the leader of the alien borough, was off-world on a diplomatic mission to Caltec, execu-world of the Calculan Planetary Conglomerate. Prime had gone there hoping to forge the first link in an intergalactic alliance against the Rüstov. He would be reaching out to all possible allies. Even the hated Draconians, longtime enemies of Prime's former planet of Valor, would be offered a seat at the table. Prime's mission highlighted the Imagine Nation's clear shift in strategy for dealing with the Rüstov threat. There was now a willingness to try to set aside differences in favor of a common goal, a willingness that hadn't existed when Jack had first arrived in Empire City.

After witnessing Jack defeat Revile, the Rüstov soldier whose very existence personified the enemy's invincible strength, the people of the Imagine Nation were suddenly feeling hopeful and confident about the future. They were no longer going along with the politics of fear and division, and the old wedges that Jonas Smart had once used to drive people apart just couldn't seem to find a foothold anymore.

As a result, Smart arrived in the sphere wielding considerably less power than he had when Jack had first met him. After persecuting Jack as a Rüstov spy so fiercely,

Smart had ended up looking very foolish when Jack defeated Revile and became a hero in everyone's eyes. A year later Jack was still a beloved figure in Empire City, and Smart's policies were a thing of the past. When Jonas Smart entered the sphere, he didn't get to sit up in his old Hightown seat. He had to stand next to Jack and wait around like everyone else.

Jack looked up at the tall, grim figure. Smart didn't say hello to him or even bother to insult him. He just peered down at Jack with scornful eyes and blew a sharp snort of air out through his nostrils before looking away. Jack knew it was killing Smart to have to stand there with him as an equal. They waited in awkward silence as the footsteps in the tunnel leading from Hightown grew louder. After a lengthy wait Circleman Clarkston Noteworthy finally emerged from the shadows and took his place in Smart's old chair. He was a tall, handsome man with slick blond hair and expensive clothes. Circleman of Hightown was the first job he'd ever held in his entire life. Jack didn't know Noteworthy all that well. He was an Inner Circle member and School of Thought teacher, but he was hardly ever seen by the students. He taught Jack and his classmates even less than Smart used to, if such a thing were possible. All Jack knew about Clarkston Noteworthy was what people said about how he'd won the Hightown election—he'd bought it. Jack thought it was believable enough. In Empire City the Noteworthy name meant one thing and one thing only: money.

Smart scowled at the man sitting in his old seat. "You're late, Circleman Noteworthy," he said.

"Be thankful I'm here at all," Noteworthy replied. "I wasn't made aware that we would be entertaining your particular brand of nonsense in this meeting until well after my morning tea." Noteworthy looked to his fellow Circlemen. "I'm here now. Shall we get on with it?"

"By all means," Smart replied.

"He was talking to the other Circlemen," Jack said.

"It's fine, Jack," Stendeval said, heading off a rebuke from Smart. "Being a guest in this sphere is a new experience for Jonas. It's only natural that it should take some getting used to." Stendeval turned his attention to Smart. "Jonas, you asked that this hearing be added to our agenda today, arguing that the matter could not wait. Out of respect for our past association, we have honored your request. Now, perhaps you could share with us the details of your grievance?"

"Gladly," Smart said. He smoothed out the front of his customary black suit. "I'm here today to discuss a matter of great urgency. Something that, I'm sad to say, none of you seem overly concerned with anymore. Namely, the security of the Imagine Nation and the protection of its people."

Jack rolled his eyes and groaned. A few Circlemen joined him. "Are you serious?" Jack asked.

Smart looked at Jack like Smart was actively resisting the urge to strangle him. "I am deadly serious," he said. "Interrupt me again, and you'll see for yourself." Smart turned back to the Circlemen and continued. "Last night, while operating under the cover of a training mission with his fellow students, Jack Blank took the opportunity to destroy a very valuable piece of SmartCorp technology, a one-of-a-kind machine that was on its way here to the Imagine Nation. Given the specific nature of the technology in question and the purpose it was meant for, I can only conclude that Jack destroyed it with the intention of weakening the Imagine Nation and making us more vulnerable to attack."

"Oh, c'mon!" Jack said. "I stopped Speedrazor from getting away with your property. That's what I did. That's *all* I did! I don't even know what your contraption was."

"Don't insult my intelligence," Smart said. "You control machines. You talk to machines. That train was running in the Real World. I placed no nullifiers on board. You had to have known it was carrying the key component in a device that would help fend off the Rüstov."

"I couldn't understand anything on that train. It was too complex," Jack interjected.

"You *knew* it would bolster our defenses against your Rüstov brethren, and you destroyed it!" Smart continued, talking over Jack.

Jack threw his hands up in disbelief. "Here we go again. Congratulations, you made it a full minute before you brought up the Rüstov this time."

"One day it's going to be the last time," Smart shot back. "Don't make the mistake of thinking I've gone soft like everyone else. Unlike the Inner Circle, I've yet to slow down when it comes to the Rüstov."

"No arguments here," Noteworthy said, and grinned. "How's that working out for you, Jonas?"

Smart narrowed his eyes at his successor on the Inner Circle. "I may have paid the price for maintaining a level of vigilance that has fallen out of fashion, but I have no regrets. I do what is necessary. No one else in this city cares to remember the events of the Rüstov invasion. No one else in this sphere cares about the ongoing Rüstov threat! I'm still watching for enemy agents. I'm preparing for the day their armada returns, and when that day comes, you'll all see that I was right about this boy."

Tired faces stared down at Jonas Smart from the Circlemen's table. His fiery passion for the subject of Jack's loyalty was starkly contrasted by the Inner Circle's exhausted patience for the topic. "Still holding a grudge, I see," Virtua said. "Bitterness doesn't become you, Jonas. The smartest man in the world should at least know when to quit." Jack knew Virtua had a grudge of her own against Smart for the way his Peacemakers had run Machina at the height of his power. Jack wasn't about to complain about Virtua's grudge.

"Jonas, please," Hovarth pleaded. "Haven't we been through this enough times already? Jack's given us no reason to suspect anything close to what you're suggesting.

Og's blood, the boy bested Revile in single combat! Hasn't he proven himself by now?"

"A *lot* of people fought Revile, Lord Hovarth," Jack chimed in, very eager to share the credit for that victory. "You were there too. You all were."

"But you finished him," Hovarth countered. "You won that battle." He turned back to Smart. "Jonas, can't you just admit that you were wrong about Jack? I have."

Jack forced out a weak smile. He appreciated having the support of the Circlemen, but it always made him feel uncomfortable whenever one of them would commend him for defeating Revile. They wouldn't be singing his praises if they knew the truth. What if they knew it was his face behind Revile's mask? That he might grow up to be Revile one day?

"Hovarth, I mean you no disrespect, but I am simply stating a fact when I say you are not known as a great thinker," Smart said. "You're the one who's wrong about Jack. You all are. The whole of Empire City might love this boy, but I see right through him. Jack is hiding something. I know he is."

"Hiding what, exactly?" Chi wanted to know.

Jack held his breath, hoping desperately that Smart was not about to reveal the secrets Jack had been guarding so closely all year. Smart glared up at Chi and paused a moment before answering. "I don't know . . . yet," he said at last.

The members of the Inner Circle shook their heads. Only Smart would have the audacity to accuse Jack of treason with absolutely no idea what form the alleged treachery took. Jack was relieved when he heard Smart admit he was still in the dark. Smart was playing the Rüstov card, but he didn't have any details to come after Jack with. For the new-look Inner Circle, that wasn't going to fly.

"Do we really have to devote so much time to this?" Noteworthy asked, checking his watch. "I have a luncheon to attend this afternoon with some very important people in Hightown society. I don't want to be late." The comment struck Jack as odd. Noteworthy's peers on the Inner Circle were arguably the most important people in all six boroughs of Empire City, and he clearly didn't mind showing up late to their meeting. Jack noticed a few Circlemen shooting disparaging looks in Noteworthy's direction. The newest member of the Inner Circle seemed unfazed by their disapproval, if he noticed it at all. "It's obvious what's going on here," he went on. "Circlewoman Virtua has already hit upon it. *Former* Circleman Smart is bitter. We all know his business has suffered now that he no longer has the Peacemakers to act as his enforcers, or his SmartCams to spy on his competitors. This city has changed, and his inability to change with it has cost him. Rather than admit that to himself, he's content to go on blaming this ruined boy. It's sad, really."

Noteworthy's words surprised Jack. *"Ruined?"* he asked. "What do you mean, ruined?"

"Yes, Clarkston . . . what are you talking about?" Virtua asked, echoing Jack.

Noteworthy appeared to be surprised that his comment required any explanation at all. "Let's be frank," he explained. "Whatever good this boy might do in life, he'll always remain infected. . . . He'll always be tainted by an association with the Rüstov. Add to that a low-class upbringing in the Real World of all places, and you have a series of stains that no reputation can overcome." Noteworthy turned to Jack and added, "No offense to you personally, Jack. It's simply a fact."

84

Jack frowned. *Sure. No offense,* he thought.

"That 'fact' means very little here," Chi told Noteworthy. "We don't all measure a life's worth with the same ruler used in Hightown society."

"There you go again," Smart chimed in, shaking a finger at Chi. "Ignoring the truth about Jack. Ignoring the danger he represents."

"So you keep telling us, Jonas," Hovarth said. "But I daresay that your position seems more personal than anything else. A year ago you voted Jack into the School of Thought, and yet ever since you were voted out of office, you've done nothing but try and tear him down."

"Meanwhile," Virtua added, "your NewsNets spend all day telling everyone who is willing to listen—and even those of us who aren't—how the new Inner Circle has done nothing but make the Imagine Nation less safe."

"What did you expect?" Smart shot back. "You discontinued my policies. Policies that kept everyone safe for twelve years."

"At what cost?" Stendeval asked. "Do the ends justify the means, Jonas?"

Smart scowled at Stendeval. "My policies may not be very popular anymore, but I don't remember anyone complaining at the time."

Virtua's image flickered and then grew intensely bright. "No one was complaining because they either didn't know about your policies or they were afraid to speak out! Like with the case of your secret prison in the Outlands of the Imagine Nation, and the brutal interrogations of innocent Mechas!"

"We're getting off topic and delving into the realm of unsubstantiated rumor," Smart said. "I don't wish to validate these wild accusations, but I can assure you that if I *did* have a secret prison, no 'brutal interrogations' would have been conducted there. There perhaps would have been 'prisoner interviews' that utilized 'extreme motivation techniques.' Things like power deprivation, circuit-boarding, and other perfectly legal procedures. But that is all beside the point. The point is, we weren't attacked by the Rüstov during my years on this Circle, and for that I will never apologize. I'm still working to make sure things stay that way, and I refuse to believe it's a coincidence that Jack destroyed my means of doing so."

Noteworthy studied Smart for a moment. "First of all, we *were* attacked during your tenure as a Circleman, Jonas. I seem to recall several incidents last year, including a battle with Revile that took place on the roof of your own building. Second, what is this Rüstov defense system you're talking about?" he asked. "You have a bad history with this sort of thing. Forgive me if I'm not exactly comforted by the thought of you hard at work on something new. What exactly did you have coming in here from the outside world?"

One by one each member of the Inner Circle agreed that they, too, wanted to know more about what Smart was up to. Jack was impressed by how deftly Noteworthy had just turned the focus of the entire meeting onto his main political rival's closely guarded plans.

"What's going on here?" Smart asked. "I'm not the one on trial. Why are you questioning me instead of Jack?"

"This isn't a trial," Stendeval said. "It's a complaint you are bringing against a fellow citizen that we have agreed to hear and pass judgment on. But you raise a fair point. We're getting ahead of ourselves. We still need to hear Jack's side of the story. Tell us, Jack, did you purposely destroy Jonas's property?" Stendeval asked. "If so . . . why?"

As always, Stendeval's voice was kind and comforting. It put Jack at ease.

"I *did* purposely destroy Smart's machine," Jack confessed. "But I didn't break it because I thought it was some kind of anti-Rüstov system. I didn't even know it was his until after I destroyed it. I was just trying to keep whatever it was out of the wrong hands." Jack looked up at Smart, trying to find some middle ground. "It was probably a bad idea to blow it up, I'll give you that. But at least the bad guys don't have it right now. That's gotta count for something."

Jack went into the details of the mission, describing for the Inner Circle how it all went down. When he was finished, the Inner Circle agreed it was the same story that Midknight, Ricochet, and Blue had each told them earlier in their reports. After a brief discussion they found Jonas Smart's complaint against Jack to be without merit. Jack was free to go.

"You're making a grave mistake," Smart admonished his former colleagues. "The Rüstov threat hangs above all our heads like an ax ready to fall, and you do nothing."

"To be honest, Jonas, I'm more concerned about this anti-Rüstov system you're working on than anything else," Virtua said. "You misspoke before when you said we merely discontinued your policies. The fact is, we condemned them. I think we need to know more about this new invention of yours."

"Gladly," Smart replied. "It's called the SmarterNet, and it launches as soon as I can rebuild what Jack destroyed last night. His sabotage has set my schedule back somewhat, but I will not be deterred."

"I told you, I didn't sabotage anything," Jack said.

"Quiet, Jack. Adults are talking," Noteworthy said. "Just what does this SmarterNet of yours do, Jonas?"

Smart just shook his head. "The SmarterNet has been compromised enough already. I'm not going to jeopardize it further by going into unnecessary detail here, but I will share with you something the project has already uncovered." Smart removed a handheld holo-computer from his pocket and held up the device for all to see. "I have in my hand a communication between an enemy agent here on Earth and Rüstov high command. It was intercepted just this morning."

A jolt of nervous energy shook up Jack's spine, and a hush fell over the room. Suddenly Jonas Smart had everyone's undivided attention. He was easily dismissed when trying to stir up fears using vague allusions to faceless threats, but if he had real, tangible evidence to share . . . that was something else entirely. The members of the Inner Circle leaned forward, but Smart made them wait as he basked in the glow of their anxious concern.

"I'm afraid I'll have to play you the raw data," Smart told the group. "I don't have an alien-language translator with me."

"Of course you don't," Noteworthy said. "I suppose you expect us to just take your word for what this so-called message says?"

"No," Smart replied. "Since you all trust Jack so much, you can take *his* word. Jack speaks Rüstov. Don't you, boy?"

All eyes turned to Jack. He didn't like the position Smart was putting him in. "I see what you're doing," Jack said. "Trying to get me to vouch for whatever it is you're going to use against me next? Forget it. That's not going to happen."

Smart sighed. "The message isn't about you, Jack. If it were, you would have heard it long before now."

Jack realized that what Smart said was probably true. Still, he wanted no part in whatever this was. "That doesn't matter," he told Smart. "I'm not helping you. And I don't *speak* their language, by the way. I just understand it when they talk."

Smart gave Jack a smirk. "Splitting hairs, aren't we?" he asked. "So be it. Even your limited abilities would serve our purposes here today, but if you'd prefer to help cover up Rüstov activity rather than shed light on it, that's fine. We'll simply do this later, without you."

Jack frowned. That was no good either. He didn't want to be the mouthpiece for Smart's latest attempt to reignite fears about the Rüstov, but if he wanted to stay in the loop, he was going to have to play along. He didn't have much choice. Jack had been covering up Rüstov activity ever since he'd first learned about the spyware virus, and this was his chance to find out if Smart knew anything about it. He agreed to translate the Rüstov transmission for the Inner Circle, and Smart pushed a button to launch the holo-computer's audio player.

Jack listened intently as Smart played the intercepted message. Everyone else heard only the techno-organic clang of Rüstov speak, but Jack understood every word, as clear as a bell:

Glave to command. Glave to command. Report: Operation proceeding as planned. Phase one complete. Now in position. Risk level: zero. Moving forward with phase two. Inform the Magus that his loyal subject stands ready to strike a crippling blow against the Imagine Nation. In five days Empire City will belong to him. Long live the Magus. Long live the empire. Glave out.

The message tied Jack's stomach into a Macedonian knot. Five days until the Rüstov controlled Empire City . . . On its face such a claim seemed impossibly ambitious, but Jack knew better. The Rüstov had maintained a low, almost nonexistent profile since the Revile incident last year, but Jack knew the dangers that were lurking beneath that peaceful facade all too well. Was now the time to tell everyone about it?

"Well?" Noteworthy asked Jack. "We've heard Jonas cry wolf about the Rüstov before. Tell us. Was this more of the same, or was it real?"

Jack looked up at the Circlemen. The fear in his eyes

was unmistakable. The members of the Inner Circle all leaned forward, trading nervous glances with one another.

"It's real," Jack admitted. "That was definitely a Rüstov agent talking."

A concerned murmur ran though the Inner Circle. From the look on Smart's face, Jack knew he was taking a creepy sense of pride in the tension he'd helped create. Jack didn't like letting Smart use him this way, but he had to tell the truth. For one thing, it was written all over his face, and for another, if he lied, Smart would eventually play the translated message and Jack would be found out anyway.

Jack translated the message, and the sphere fell silent as each Circleman paused to consider the hidden Rüstov threat.

"People need to hear about this," Hovarth declared.

"Hovarth!" Noteworthy blurted out, casting a reproachful eye toward his fellow Circleman. "Do you want to cause a panic? *No one* should hear about this. Not yet. There isn't any proof the threat is real."

"Not real?" Smart shot back. "Empire City's favorite son just confirmed it was. You all heard him."

"I heard no such thing," Noteworthy countered. "Jack confirmed it was a genuine Rüstov transmission. He didn't say anything to validate its content. How could he, unless he knows something about the Rüstov's plans that we don't?" Jack gulped. He felt like he was sinking in quicksand. Up in the Cognito seat at the Inner Circle's table, Stendeval made a subtle, almost imperceptible motion for Jack to keep quiet. Smart opened his mouth to speak, but shut it once again without saying anything. Noteworthy seized the opportunity to keep going. "Of course the Rüstov *think* their plan is unstoppable," he continued. "If they didn't, they'd form a different plan." The socialite Circleman shook his head. "No, until we're presented with concrete evidence to back up these claims, it's nothing more than hearsay. And it's dangerous."

"I find myself agreeing with Circleman Noteworthy," Stendeval announced.

"You can't be serious!" Smart said. "The only danger lies in ignoring these warnings."

"We will ignore nothing," Stendeval said. "We have a responsibility to maintain order and peace in the Imagine Nation, and we will do so." Stendeval turned to his fellow

Circlemen. "We must investigate this Agent Glave and his plans, each of us through our own channels. We must bring all possible resources to bear, but treat the matter with the utmost discretion. If word of this were to get out . . ."

"It would be hysteria," Noteworthy said. "I second Stendeval's motion. Anything less would be irresponsible."

"Agreed," Virtua said. "I've seen what fear of the Rüstov does to people in this city. I've no desire to see it again."

Chi pressed his fingers to his lips in silent deliberation. "We must be swift," he said, raising his head after a moment. "Five days is hardly any time at all."

"And who is swifter than the ZenClan ninjas?" Stendeval asked. Chi nodded in agreement. He was on board with Stendeval's plan. "Hovarth?" Stendeval asked, turning to the Inner Circle's last member. "What say you?"

The giant king of Varagog rubbed his beard. "I am unsure about this," he said. "But until I am sure, I will stand with the Circle." Hovarth rapped his knuckles on the table and nodded toward Stendeval. "Aye."

Smart shook his head and stuffed his pocket holocomputer back inside his jacket. "Fools," he spat. "Blind fools, all of you! Lucky for the people of this city, I'm not without my own resources. I have my own work . . . my own 'channels,' as you say. Know this: I intend to conduct my own investigation. The truth will come out," he said, turning to look down at Jack with a hard stare. "I won't rest until it does."

Jack swallowed hard. *You and me both*, he thought. These days the truth was what kept Jack up at night.

CHAPTER

5

In Cognito

When Jack's business with the Inner Circle was con-
cluded, he left the sphere and started walking home
across Hero Square. Huge crowds of people recognized
his famous face along the way. After the meeting he'd
just had, Jack wasn't in the mood to shake hands and
take pictures, but then, he never was. Jack dealt with the
horde of people as best he could and pressed on toward
the border of Cognito, where he was able to break away
from the crowd.

Jack's fame was part of the reason his home was in a

new place these days. After the incident with Revile last year, the owners of the Ivory Tower had offered to let him stay there rent free for as long as he wanted. The Ivory Tower loft was a fantastic place to live, located in the wealthiest district of an already rich borough, but it wasn't for Jack. Not anymore. Everything in the apartment made Jack think of Jazen and how maybe if he'd done things differently a year ago, his friend would still be alive today.

Shortly after entering the School of Thought, Jack had asked Stendeval if he could help him find a new place to live. The wise Circleman had been glad to help, and had set Jack up among the hideouts and secret lairs of Cognito, where he could have a fresh start and all the privacy he wanted.

Jack got back to Cognito a few hours before the daily shuffling of the streets. Home was in a different place for Jack in more ways than one. He was on his way back to an apartment that had literally moved on from where he'd left it the day before. Somehow, Jack still knew which way to go. He didn't have a special map of Cognito, and no one had ever told him the secret of how to navigate its shifting streets, but he always knew how to find his way home. He even knew the precise hour at which the borough's streets were scheduled to move. It happened at different times each day, and that day it was scheduled to take place a few hours before sunset. Jack had meant to ask Stendeval how he could have known stuff like that, but he was always so busy with the School of Thought and his work on the virus that he never got around to it. Jack remembered that Jazen had once told him that only the locals knew their way around Cognito. Maybe it had something to do with the fact that, thanks to Stendeval, he was now a local too.

Cognito was the perfect place for Jack. He needed a hideout every bit as much as he did an apartment. He needed a place to escape the unwanted attention and admirers he'd picked up as the hero who had defeated Revile. No one in Cognito ever made a big deal about Jack and his exploits. No one in Cognito was ever around to begin with. The entire borough was made up of heroes and villains who were trying to maintain secret identities, as well as other, more cryptic, groups of people like the Secreteers and the Mysterrii. The Secreteers were never seen on the streets of Cognito, so Jack didn't think they really counted as neighbors, even if they did own most of the property in the borough. The Mysterrii, on the other hand, were always out and about, but kept completely to themselves, so Jack decided they didn't count either.

Jack didn't know much about the Mysterrii other than that they were the native population of Cognito. He passed a small band of them on his way back to the apartment. They were all no more than three feet tall, dressed in white clothing with red cloth bandages wrapped tightly around their heads, feet, and hands. Bright yellow eyes glowed behind the red wrappings that covered their faces. Jack thought they looked like mini mummies. As always, they scattered as soon as they saw him. Crimson strands of bandages flew wildly in the air as the Mysterrii sprang into action. *"Hup hup!"* one of them said as it jumped on another one's shoulders and then scampered up over a wall. *"Ho-pahhh!"* said another Mysterrii as it used its hands as a springboard to launch a friend through a high window and safely away. They executed backflips and front flips, darting away in every direction. The last few disappeared into an open manhole. Before Jack even had a chance to say hello, they were gone. He didn't take it personally. They did that to everybody.

Jack walked in the door of his apartment and collapsed into a chair. From the outside his building looked like every other structure in Cognito—white stone walls with no markings of any kind, and open windows carved out in random, irregular places. Inside Jack's apartment it didn't look much different. He had put up no decorations, and the apartment was barely furnished. Jack didn't waste time setting up creature comforts in the living area of the apartment, since he spent most of his time downstairs in the lab.

The mission to the Real World combined with the Inner Circle meeting had completely wiped Jack out, but he felt guilty just sitting there in his chair. Jack never felt like he had the right to be tired, not when there was so much work to be done and he was the only one who could do it. He looked over at the door that led down to his workshop and thought about the project that was waiting for him downstairs. The real secret project that Allegra had nearly spilled the beans on—finding a cure for the Rüstov spyware virus. Jack knew he should really head down to the lab and get some work in, especially after hearing what the Rüstov agent Glave had said, but he couldn't bring himself to do it. Not after what had happened the last time he'd been down there. Jack looked away from the lab door. His body was weary and his eyelids were heavy. He drifted off without even trying and slept peacefully in his chair until the rumbling of the changing streets woke him up.

The roaring din of entire city blocks grinding their way into new positions was impossible to sleep through. Jack shot up in his chair as his whole apartment started shaking and rotating counterclockwise. He went to the window and watched as the Cognito landscape did its daily exercises. Whole buildings spun around and sank into the earth, while others rose up out of it, climbing higher into the sky. Bridges separated and reattached to new end points, and street signs scrambled their letters. Roads flipped over and turned around so that dead ends became intersections and intersections became left turns. As the final pieces settled into place, Jack looked over at the building that was coming to rest next to his. It was a crooked tower with plain white walls, just like every other dwelling in the borough, but Jack recognized the handprint slapped over its front door in bright orange paint.

"Stendeval!" Jack called out his window, hoping his friend was home. "Are you in there?"

Moments later Stendeval appeared at his window and smiled. "Jack!" he said. "What a pleasant surprise. It's not often that the day brings me an old friend for a new neighbor. And this saves me the trouble of coming to you. We need to talk, you and I. I was just about to have some tea up on my roof. Please join me."

Jack started to say he'd be right there, but before he even managed to get the words out, there was a flash of light and he felt himself being lifted off the ground. The next thing he knew, he was standing next to Stendeval on his roof deck. Red energy particles twirled about in the air above him and blew away in the breeze. Teleportation used to make Jack queasy, but he was used to it now.

"Have a seat," Stendeval said, motioning to a table and chairs next to a small garden that had not been watered in some time. "Let us enjoy the view for a moment." Jack thanked Stendeval and took a seat. The garden wasn't much to look at, but the sun was setting behind Mount Nevertop, and the crystal mountain bent the falling light out in odd, wonderful angles that lit the skyline of Empire City from behind like a halo. It was another beautiful evening in the Imagine Nation.

"The day is nearly done, but I think I should have enough power left to provide us with some music," Stendeval told Jack. He had a certain amount of energy available to him each day that he could use to do almost anything. Some things took a little bit of power, some took a lot, and some were beyond even his reach. When his pool of energy ran out for the day, he was just a normal man like anyone else.

Stendeval held his hand out over the dried-up garden, and the flowers began to bloom. The withered brown stems grew into robust, luscious greens, and vines sprang out of the flower beds, weaving their way up and around the trellis that Jack and Stendeval sat beneath. Every inch of the vines blossomed with brilliant orange and yellow flowers. They were incredibly fragrant, filling the roof deck with an intoxicating aroma like gooey cinnamon cakes dipped in honey.

"Wow," Jack said, marveling at the exotic blooms. "That was great. But where does the music come in?"

"These flowers are called harmonias," Stendeval explained. "Their scent should help attract a belcanto bird, whose song will be pleasing to us. They live in the hills beyond Empire City. I didn't have enough power left to find one and bring it here, but the harmonias will take care of that for us. Sometimes we all need a little help to get what we're after."

"Help from flowers?" Jack asked.

"Help is help," Stendeval said as he poured the tea. "It can come from all kinds of places." Stendeval and Jack sipped their cups in silence and watched the sun move slowly down toward the horizon.

"We were lucky today, Jack," Stendeval said after the sun finally went down. "If the message Jonas played for us in the sphere had mentioned the spyware virus, we would have had to come forward with what we know. I've held off telling the Inner Circle this long to avoid causing a panic, but there's no point in keeping a secret if the secret is already out."

Jack sipped his tea, nodding slowly. "I know," he said.

"I almost wish they had talked about the virus in that message. Then at least I wouldn't have to worry about keeping it quiet anymore. I hate this, Stendeval. It's like Smart said, I feel like I've got an ax hanging over my head all the time and it's ready to drop at any moment."

"I know it's not easy," Stendeval told Jack. "But you know what would happen if the truth came out too soon, just as well as I do."

Jack studied his reflection in his teacup, then pushed it away. He knew exactly what would happen. The new atmosphere of togetherness and unity in the Imagine Nation was too fragile a thing to weather the truth.

"I know. It would stir up everyone's fears again. We'd spend all our time trying to make sure the Mechas didn't end up dismantled and shredded." Jack shook his head. "We don't have time for that. Not anymore. I mean . . . five days? That's all we've got left?" He threw his hands up in frustration. "That Rüstov message didn't mention the virus by name, but that had to be what Glave was talking about."

"That was my conclusion as well," Stendeval said.

"How am I supposed to solve this thing in five days?" Jack asked.

"When last we spoke you said you were on the verge of a breakthrough."

"Right," Jack replied. "A break*down* is more like it. I haven't done anything in a week."

"A week?" Stendeval said, sitting up in his chair. He placed his teacup on the table next to Jack's and leaned forward. "Jack, what happened? Tell me everything."

"I heard a voice," Jack told Stendeval.

Stendeval squinted at Jack. "I don't understand. What voice? When?"

"Last week," Jack said. "I was doing research. I realized I needed to know more about Rüstov systems to finish the cure-code, and I decided to study the one inside me. I reached out to my parasite with my powers. I knew it was a bad idea. . . . I knew it. I put off doing it for the longest time, but I wanted to finish this, so I did it anyway. I heard a voice, Stendeval. My parasite's voice. It knows my name."

Stendeval looked concerned. "I see," he said, leaning into his fist. "Are you still hearing it?"

"No, but something's different now," Jack said. "It's awake. I can feel it getting stronger. I think I made a big mistake here."

Stendeval didn't say anything at first. A pained look came over his face, but he dropped it as the belcanto, a great blue bird with yellow-tipped wing feathers, landed on the roof. The bird had a proud, majestic bearing and a large orange beak. It breathed deeply of the harmonia flowers' scent and began to sing. More birds arrived soon after to enjoy the garden's pleasing aroma and to lend their voices to the chorus. Stendeval took a brief moment to listen to their song as he turned the matter over in his mind.

"This changes things," Stendeval said. "I bought us time in the sphere today, hoping that you were . . ." Stendeval trailed off and shook his head slightly. "So be it. Whenever you encounter a problem in life, it simply means your situation has changed," he said, regaining an optimistic tone. "You need to take steps to deal with the new situation. Are you prepared to do that, Jack?"

"I haven't been prepared to do anything in more than a week. I've been too freaked out."

"Then, perhaps it's time to bring others into the fold after all."

"What?"

Stendeval motioned with his hands as if what he'd said were the most obvious thing in the world. "Our time is short and your progress has stalled. You need help," he said. "Don't you?"

"From who?" Jack asked. "If you tell the Inner Circle about the virus, you'll have to let Smart go public with Glave's message. We just got done saying why that can't happen. If you tell them I'm hearing voices too, it'll be even worse."

"That's true," Stendeval replied. "But I never said I was going to tell the Inner Circle anything."

Now it was Jack's turn to squint at Stendeval. "What are you talking about?" he asked.

Stendeval got up from the table and went to stroke the neck of a singing belcanto bird. "It's not easy keeping things from those you care about. Believe me, I know. You feel disconnected from the people you should feel close to. You spend all your time fixating on the different angles, worrying what people will think if they find out about this, but not that. That, but not this. It gets hard to keep the story straight sometimes. I once met a very witty American writer who grew up on the Mississippi River.

He said: 'If you tell the truth, you don't have to remember anything.'" Stendeval smiled as if he'd just remembered something funny. "Of course, this was the same gentleman who said, 'I don't care what people say about me, as long as they don't tell the truth.'"

"I don't understand," Jack said. "I thought you just said we *couldn't* tell anyone. Who am I supposed to—"

"Your friends, Jack," Stendeval said. "Tell your friends what's going on."

"My friends?" Jack repeated. "What can they do? Computer viruses aren't exactly their area of expertise."

"If nothing else, they can share your burden and help you find a way to move forward," Stendeval replied. "You're under too much pressure trying to do this all alone. When you first started working on the cure-code, you were making such great progress. That was part of the reason I encouraged your silence, but I can see you've carried these secrets too long. It's affecting your work. With five days until the Rüstov strike, and you stalled on a cure, we no longer have the luxury of absolute secrecy. Like Jonas said earlier today, it's only a matter of time before the truth comes out."

Jack let out a heavy sigh. "I know. I was thinking that too. If this SmarterNet of his can pick up Rüstov spy transmissions, it's only a matter of time until he picks up something about the virus."

"I'm afraid that Agent Glave, whoever he is, is not the only possible source here either," Stendeval said. The birds finished their song and began to fly off. Stendeval returned to the table, his hands clasped behind his back. He did not sit down. The grave look on his face had returned. "After you left the sphere, our next order of business was a trial. A real trial . . . for Speedrazor. He pled guilty in exchange for leniency, and revealed that the information his gang had gotten on Jonas Smart's business had come from a most unusual source."

"An unusual source?" Jack repeated. "Who?"

Before Stendeval could answer, Jack felt a strange broadcast signal fly across the airwaves, forcing itself forward like a battering ram. It was a pirate signal. Jack felt it taking over the holo-screen in his apartment next door. He saw the same thing happening on floating billboards that were hovering nearby. Screens on the sides of buildings that were playing NewsNet broadcasts got hit too, and everywhere Jack looked, he saw moving pictures cut to static. Someone was hijacking every screen in Empire City.

"Speedrazor got his information from someone people trust to keep secrets," Stendeval told Jack. He scrunched up his face with chagrin as the static all around was replaced by images of a cloaked figure with glowing eyes. "If I had to guess, I'd say that's him now."

CHAPTER
6
The Rogue Secreteer

Jack looked up at the holo-screen. The face on it was hidden behind bandages that covered the nose and mouth. A hood covered the person's head, his glowing eyes hanging in the black shadows beneath it like lanterns in the night.

"This message is going out across all known Imagine Nation broadcast channels," the figure on the pirated holo-screens announced. Despite the bandages that covered his mouth, his voice came through crystal clear. It was practically hypnotic. "I do apologize for the intrusion.

What I have to say is very important, and the truth is, there is no proper way to do what I am about to do. My name is Obscuro. I am a Secreteer."

Jack put his hands on his head and clutched at his hair. "A Secreteer?" he said. "A Secreteer is telling secrets?"

Stendeval didn't answer. He just put up a finger, telling Jack to wait. He was intently focused on Obscuro. Jack had never seen him like this. He looked worried. More than worried. Jack turned back to the holo-screen and listened quietly.

"I have been a Secreteer for as long as I can remember," Obscuro continued, his voice echoing throughout the city. "It has been both a privilege and an honor. The greatest honor of my life. For hundreds of years the Clandestine Order has hidden the Imagine Nation from the Real World . . . a world that doesn't understand us. A world that isn't ready for us. It has been our sacred duty to ensure that the Imagine Nation remains unknown until such time that the Real World can finally welcome it back." Obscuro paused a moment and looked down. His glowing eyes dimmed. "I'm sad to say that day will never come."

Jack and Stendeval exchanged nervous looks, then turned back to the broadcast.

"It is with a heavy heart that I share this with you," Obscuro declared. "It goes against everything that I am, and was by no means an easy decision on my part. People like myself with psychic powers—memory powers—we train for years for the right to perform the order's sacred duty all over the world. It is hard work. It's lonely work, but we do it without complaint. I remind you all of this only so that you will not doubt my word," he explained. "By controlling information, Secreteers maintain order in the world, and in the process, we gain knowledge. Sometimes we discover things that we would rather not know. This is one of those times. It has come to my attention that the Rüstov are coming back, and this time . . . this time they are going to win. In five days, starting this morning, the Rüstov are going to take over Empire City, and there's nothing we can do to stop them."

Jack slid his hands behind his head and paced around in a small circle. "I don't believe this," Jack said. "Tell me this isn't happening."

"I cannot in good conscience keep this information

from you," Obscuro went on. "There will be no beating the Rüstov this time. This is a fact. You all deserve to know at least that much. The enemy penetrated our defenses long ago, even before the invasion. Their agents are here now, even as we speak. They have been laying the groundwork for their takeover all year. I could tell you what I know of their plans . . . of their master spy . . ." Obscuro shook his head. "It would do no good. The Rüstov plot goes all the way up to Empire City's greatest heroes, and their work is all but done. Better I give you all the choice and the chance to escape before it's too late. I advise you all to pursue any means necessary to save yourselves. That is what I intend to do. I stand before you today, ready to break every vow I ever made to the Clandestine Order. I am selling my secrets—*all of them*—to finance my escape from this planet.

"Empire City, I make you the following offer: Those of you who have money to spend and wish to know what I know, make your intentions known and I will find you. If, like me, you are leaving this place, seek me out for information you feel might aid in your escape. If you choose to stay here, seek me out for information you've always wanted to know before you die. All the knowledge I possess can be yours for a price. The combined secrets of the Secreteers—all the mysteries of the world—are for sale. Those of you who wish to engage my services, do not delay. Those of you who wish to stop me, do not waste your time. Believe me when I tell you there isn't much left."

Jack stared out in a nearly catatonic state as the holo-screens on the floating billboards and the sides of buildings all returned to static, then one by one flipped back to their regular programming of news and advertisements. Jack realized he'd been holding his breath for half the transmission. He let it go once all the screens were back to normal.

"It appears we're going to have a panic on our hands after all," Stendeval said, frowning. "Jonas Smart now has the confirmation he requires. There'll be no keeping him quiet after this."

"They both mentioned the same five-day deadline," Jack said, nodding up at the screens. "Obscuro is worried about the same thing Glave is working on," he said, connecting the dots as he spoke. "It's the virus. It has to be."

Stendeval looked at Jack. "We have to stop it."

Jack didn't reply at first. His mind was racing. He thought about how the Rogue Secreteer's actions were going to spook the city, and shuddered. Then an idea struck him and he realized a potential silver lining to the dark cloud that was Obscuro's warning. "Maybe we can stop it," Jack replied. "If we know what he knows, we can. That's the key, Stendeval. Forget the virus for a second—if we can find Obscuro, we can find Glave. We find Glave . . . and we shut him down."

Stendeval shook his head. "That won't be easy. Every Secreteer in the Imagine Nation will be looking for Obscuro after tonight. They'll kill him for this betrayal."

Jack sighed and shook his head. "Then I guess we'd better get moving."

7

The Circle of Trust

By the time Jack got back to his apartment, stories about the Rogue Secreteer had already begun to dominate the NewsNets. It didn't even matter that none of them had any new facts to report. Speculation about Obscuro's mysterious Rüstov threat was more than enough to keep the coverage going all night long. Jack's powers being what they were, the media frenzy was tough to avoid. He meant to watch only a little bit but ended up listening to interviews and scanning cyberspace for reactions half the night. Every cybersite on the Net was buzzing with frightened comments. A Secreteer selling secrets was completely unprecedented, a real hero-robs-bank kind of story. Sometime after midnight Jack remembered to call Allegra and ask if she could get Skerren and come by his place first thing in the morning. Fear was gripping the city, and Jack was one of the few people who knew exactly what there was to be afraid of. Membership in that very exclusive club was about to go up by two.

The next day Skerren and Allegra arrived at Jack's apartment just after breakfast. By that time Jack had been watching the NewsNets for twelve hours straight. He barely said hello to his friends as they came in. He just nodded at them with a vacant look and quickly turned back toward the many holo-screens he had up and running in his living room. The members of the Inner Circle were all putting out statements, each of them addressing Obscuro and his grim predictions for the future. Skerren and Allegra got there just in time to catch the end of Stendeval's speech:

"I reject as false the idea that the Rüstov have somehow taken our city without so much as firing a single shot," Stendeval told the people of Cognito. "We are monitoring Rüstov activity inside our borders, just as we have every day since the invasion. The Rogue Secreteer's actions, and this notion that all hope is lost, run contrary to everything we stand for. Here in the Imagine Nation, we *always* believe that tomorrow a better day will dawn. Here in the Imagine Nation, we fight for that day. An old English statesman I knew years ago once said that wars are not won by evacuations. I urge all citizens of the Imagine Nation to remain calm and, above all, remain here. We're going to need one another before this is over."

"This is unbelievable," Skerren said, motioning toward the screen. "A Secreteer selling off secrets because he's afraid of the Rüstov? This didn't even happen when Revile came back."

"It's crazy," Allegra said. "The launchpads in Galaxis are already backed up with ships full of people who want to follow Obscuro's advice and get out of here."

"I know," Jack said without taking his eyes off the screens. "I've been watching. It's the same in Hightown. Noteworthy tried to downplay Obscuro's warning, but he got drowned out by SmartNews." Jonas Smart's personal NewsNets were running nonstop the Glave transmission he'd intercepted.

Jack flicked his wrist, brushing away the holo-screen with Stendeval on it, and reached out with his other hand to pull another screen forward. He put both hands together and then separated them like he was pulling an invisible string at both ends. The holo-screen expanded to three times its original size, displaying an image of Jonas Smart being interviewed on SmartNews.

"The Rogue Secreteer is a hero," Smart told Drack Hackman, his NewsNet's lead anchor. "If not for Obscuro, I would still be bound by the Inner Circle's order to keep this information classified. Thanks to him, I am free to act—free to give Empire City a fighting chance."

"But what about those who say this warning comes too late?" Hackman asked Smart. "If even the Secreteers are convinced the Rüstov are going to win, shouldn't we all be afraid? Clearly, this Secreteer knows something we don't."

"Without question," Smart agreed. "But only for now. There's no cause for concern as long as the Inner Circle gets out of my way and lets me do what is necessary to protect this city. The do-nothing Inner Circle stopped paying attention to the Rüstov long ago, but as my successor, Clarkston Noteworthy, is fond of saying, I am no longer associated with that venerable institution. For the last year I have diverted a significant amount of SmartCorp resources away from my existing, lucrative enterprises and focused all my time and energy on a device that will tell us exactly what the Rüstov are up to. It's called the SmarterNet," Smart announced. "It would have launched already if Jack Blank hadn't destroyed a key component the night before last, but have no fear. It *will* launch before the deadline Obscuro warned us about. Once the SmarterNet goes live, the Rüstov will never be able to hide from us again."

Allegra shook her head. "Amazing how he never misses a chance to get in a dig at you," she said to Jack.

"He's been saying stuff like that in every interview," Jack said. "Right now you're probably one of about five people who care. Smart's Instant Polling numbers are way up. Look." Jack snapped his fingers, and a small data screen appeared. It read:

Jonas Smart, Current Favorability Rating: 65%. (Margin of error: 97%)

Jack grimaced. Yesterday Smart's posturing would have drawn the ire of Jack's many supporters throughout the

Imagine Nation, but not today. Today people had other things on their minds.

"Jack, you look awful," Allegra said. "Did you sleep at all last night?"

Distracted, Jack stared at the screens a few more moments before he realized Allegra was talking to him. "What?" he asked. "Oh, yeah. I think so. Yeah, I passed out for a little while there. Definitely."

"You've been watching this all night?" she asked.

Jack rubbed the back of his neck. "I didn't mean to, but yeah . . . I guess I have been. I kind of got sucked in."

"Maybe it's time for a break," Allegra suggested.

Jack's eyes darted around at the screens and the relentless noise that was coming out of them, passing itself off as news. He looked at Allegra and waved his arm like he was clearing off a table with one clean swipe. The screens all blinked out, and the sudden silence came as a relief. Watching the NewsNets all night hadn't helped Jack learn anything new; it had served only to stress him out.

"That's better," Allegra said.

"Yeah," Jack agreed. "Yeah, I think so."

Skerren took a seat on the arm of Jack's couch. "So?"

he asked. "You watched everything the news has to say. What do you think? Is this for real?"

Jack collapsed into his chair and looked up at his friends. "It's real," he said. "I know it is. That's why I asked you guys to come here." He stopped and took a breath. Jack knew he had to tell his friends what was going on before they could help him, and thanks to Glave and Obscuro, he needed help now more than ever. That didn't make coming clean any easier. He could guess how his friends were going to react to what came next. "The thing is . . . ," Jack began, "I know more than just what's on the news. I know what's got the Rogue Secreteer so scared."

Jack's apartment reached new levels of quiet as Skerren and Allegra stared at him in disbelief. Skerren got up off of the couch. "What?" he asked Jack. "What do you mean, you *know*?"

Jack put his hands up. "Just . . . hear me out. I'll tell you guys everything, but first you have to promise it stays between us. I'm bringing you guys in on this because I need your help, but it has to be *your* help. You can't tell anyone else. Not yet."

"Why not?" Allegra asked.

"Because I'm afraid of how other people might react," Jack said. "What I'm going to tell you is a secret. You have to promise not to tell anyone else. Trust me, you'll understand."

Allegra crossed her arms and gave Jack a slightly annoyed look. "We better," she said. Jack stared at Allegra, waiting for her to say the words. "Okay, I promise," she said.

"What about you, Skerren?" Jack asked. "In or out?"

Skerren stood there cracking his knuckles with one hand and studying Jack with suspicious eyes. When he was finished cracking the knuckle on the last finger, he made a fist and stared at it for a brief moment. Eventually he looked up at Jack and nodded. "Let's hear it," he said.

Jack figured that was about as positive a response as he could hope for from Skerren. "Not here," he said to Skerren and Allegra. He pointed at the steps going down to his basement. "Down there. In my lab."

Jack asked the lights in the basement to turn on as his friends followed him down the steps and into his workshop. The fluorescent bulbs flickered on to reveal a no-frills wreck of a computer lab if ever there was one. It was the exact opposite of the pristine, bright white facilities that Jonas Smart used for his experiments across town in SmartTower. Jack's cramped, tiny lab looked like an auto-body garage run by the greasiest of grease monkeys. Old computer hardware components were stacked up on boxes and crates that were being used for makeshift workstations. Burned-out hard drives, memory chips, and circuit boards were piled high on shelves until they could fit no more. The lab was as untidy, chaotic, and disorganized as they came.

"Ewww," Allegra said, scrunching up her face as she looked around Jack's lab. She frowned at the countless old fast-food containers that looked like they should have been thrown out weeks ago. "This place is disgusting."

"At best," Skerren agreed, using one of his swords to flick an old slice of half-eaten pizza across the room into an open garbage can. He picked up a stripped-down Mecha skull as he walked around, checking the place out. "What's going on, Jack?" he asked. "What is all this?"

"This is what I've been working on all year," Jack said, motioning to the different models of android hands, heads, and more that hung from his ceiling like pots and pans over a kitchen island countertop. Half-assembled Mecha body parts seemed to cover every inch of his lab. "This is my *real* secret project. But before I tell you about it, I have to tell you how it all started. It's a long story, but just bear with me. This is going to be kind of hard for me to say." Jack took another deep breath as Skerren and Allegra leaned in to listen. *Here we go*, Jack thought, and he opened his mouth to speak.

"You guys already know that last year Jazen Knight and I broke into SmartTower to find out the truth about who I am. What you don't know is that we didn't go in there on a hunch," Jack told his friends. "We had proof. I had proof that Smart knew all about my family *and* my name. He'd been lying to me from day one. He'd been lying to everyone, all so he could use me to stir up fear about the Rüstov. As long as I was a mystery, I was a potential threat to this city, so that's what he made me out to be. For a while there it worked pretty well."

"Hang on, I don't get it," Allegra cut in. "Why didn't you tell anyone about this? Why didn't you tell us?"

"We didn't have time," Jack replied.

"You didn't have time?" Skerren repeated. He sat down, and Allegra sat next to him. "You had a whole year."

"I mean back then," Jack explained. "I convinced Jazen we didn't have time. It's complicated. I had proof that Smart knew all about me, but I didn't know what he knew. I wanted to hack his files before he realized we were on to him. I didn't want to give him the chance to delete that info before I found out who I was."

Allegra and Skerren nodded. So far Jack was making sense, it seemed.

"Also, we thought Smart might have been the real Great Collaborator," Jack added.

Skerren and Allegra sat up in their chairs. Any ideas they'd had about Jack making sense just went out the window.

"Jonas Smart?" Skerren asked, nearly breaking into a laugh at the very idea. "You thought *Jonas Smart* was the Great Collaborator? Really?"

"How did you figure that?" Allegra asked, dumbfounded.

"Jazen put that part together," Jack said. "He didn't have to sell me too hard on the idea, though. It made sense at the time. We thought about how Smart consolidated power after the invasion, and how much he'd gained from getting everyone so riled up about me," Jack explained. "He was the only one benefiting from any of that. Also, the Rüstov were after me, and we knew that someone on the inside was tipping them off. Smart was one of the only people in Empire City who always knew where I was and when. We figured maybe he was playing both sides against the middle for his own gain."

"And was he?" Skerren asked.

"No," Allegra answered for Jack before he even had a chance to speak. "If he was, Jack would have said something about it before now, proof or no proof. Right, Jack?"

Jack nodded grimly. "You're right," he said. He was now at the hardest part of the morning's ugly confession. "It wasn't Smart tipping off the Rüstov. It was Jazen."

"*What?*" Skerren and Allegra blurted out again. This time their outburst was even louder than before.

"It's not what you think," Jack said. "There's a reason it's taken me up until now to say that sentence out loud. It wasn't Jazen's fault. He was infected."

"Infected?" Skerren asked. "What do you mean? He was a Mecha."

"The Rüstov have another virus," Jack said. "A spyware sleeper virus that affects Mechas. It's undetectable, but it's real, and Jazen had it. The Rüstov saw everything he saw. They heard everything he heard. That was how they always knew where I was."

Jack stopped for a moment to try to keep his emotions in check. He didn't like talking about this, and the look on Skerren's and Allegra's faces made it worse. Silence blanketed the room. Jack would have wrapped himself up in it and gone to sleep for a hundred years if such a thing were possible, but it wasn't.

"What happened to Jazen?" Allegra asked.

"Did you have to kill him because he was infected?" Skerren asked.

Tears welled up behind Jack's eyes. "No," he said. "Jazen died just like I said." Jack swallowed, determined to get through this without crying. "He died saving my life. He wouldn't even have been there if it hadn't been for me, and I'm standing here now only because of him. Jazen was stronger than the Rüstov. He beat their virus. He overpowered it and ran two Rüstov Left-Behinds out through the tallest window in SmartTower, and he went down with them just to make sure they didn't get away." Jack wiped away teardrops before they escaped his eyes. "I've been trying to find a cure for the virus ever since."

"By yourself?" Skerren asked Jack, more angry than sympathetic. "Who else knows about this?"

"Stendeval," Jack said.

"Just Stendeval?" Skerren asked. "What about the rest of the Inner Circle? What about Hovarth?"

Jack shook his head. "Just Stendeval."

Skerren made an astonished grunt. "You mean all this time, the virus has been out there spreading and you never said anything? How many are infected?"

"I don't know," Jack said. "But it's probably a lot if Obscuro thinks there's no way to stop the Rüstov from taking over the city in five days."

"Four days now," Skerren corrected Jack.

Jack gave a tired nod. "Four days," he agreed.

"Where are you on the cure?" Allegra asked. "Are you at least getting close?"

"Yes and no," Jack said. "I'm working on a cure-code. I have a prototype model to test it on, but it's not ready yet." Jack looked away from his friends, over at a dark corner in the rear of his lab. "I thought I'd have this cured by now. I really did, but I . . ." Jack trailed off. For a second he thought about telling his friends the whole truth. How he'd heard the voice of his parasite waking up the last time he'd worked on the cure. That second came and went. "I've hit a wall," Jack said. "It's a problem."

"A problem we need to tell people about," Skerren said. "I can't keep this from my king!"

"Skerren, you promised," Jack said. "You can't tell anyone. You gave me your word. This secret would tear the city apart."

"What do you think the infected Mechas are going to do four days from now?" Skerren asked. "And what are *we* supposed to do to stop them? In case you haven't noticed, I'm no computer expert."

"Skerren does have a point," Allegra said. "What do you expect us to do?"

"Help me find Obscuro," Jack said. "We need to find the Rogue Secreteer."

Skerren and Allegra looked at Jack like he'd just told them he wanted to find a raindrop hiding in the ocean.

"You're out of your mind," Skerren said.

"Why?" Jack asked. "Why is that so crazy? We can do this."

"Find a Secreteer?" Skerren replied. "It's impossible."

"Nothing's impossible. We do the impossible every day here."

"How is finding Obscuro going to help stop the virus?" Allegra asked.

"This guy knows something. About the virus *and* Glave. If we put whatever he knows together with the work I've already done, maybe I can finish the cure-code." Jack tapped Skerren on the shoulder, ready to drive the point home. "Or if the Rogue Secreteer can lead us to Glave, then we can finish *him.*"

Skerren locked eyes with Jack. Jack knew he was always on board with anything that involved killing Rüstov. There had been precious few opportunities to do that over the last year.

"We have to do this ourselves," Jack said. "No one can know about the spyware virus. Not yet. After what people have already heard from Obscuro and Glave, the truth about the virus would put them over the edge. It'd be chaos, and that's not gonna help stop the Rüstov."

Skerren rubbed his chin, thinking. "It's not a *terrible* idea," he admitted. He looked like he was starting to come around. "And we do have to take on solo projects for the School of Thought," Skerren said, thinking out loud. "Can you imagine the look on Trea's face if the three of us bagged a Secreteer?" He grinned.

"How are we supposed to do that?" Allegra said. "Nobody can find a Secreteer who doesn't want to be found. Nobody."

"Actually," Jack began. "I've got an idea where to start looking."

"Where?" Skerren asked.

"In your part of town," Jack told Skerren. "Varagog Village."

CHAPTER

8

The Flying Shipyards

The idea came to Jack out of the blue. He didn't know much about Secreteers—no one did, really—but what little experience he'd had with them had led him to believe he could find one in Skerren's backyard. After taking a few moments to rummage through his lab and gather supplies, Jack, Skerren, and Allegra headed south to Varagog.

Like all parts of the Imagine Nation, Varagog Village was a fascinating corner of the world. The medieval borough of Empire City had a mystical quality that went far beyond simply mirroring the culture and lifestyle of a centuries-old era. Varagog Village didn't just *look* like the Middle Ages; it was actually *in* the Middle Ages.

The walls of Varagog surrounded what can best be described as a pocket in time. Inside those walls it was forever the year 1404. Time in Varagog repeated in an infinite loop. It snowed and rained on the same days, year after year. Flowers bloomed and died on the same days, year after year. The only things that changed in Varagog were the people who lived there, and the people who lived there were not fond of change.

As Skerren led Jack and Allegra down the cobblestone streets of his home borough, Jack marveled at the view. He passed grand castles, towers, and other stately manors that had been built over winding stone streets. He climbed great stone stairways lined with shacks, shanties, cabins, cottages, and inns. Varagog was a true old-world village. The people who lived there had jobs like blacksmith, tanner, miller, jester, knight, squire, and king. People of every class were packed into every inch of Varagog. They were all very much attached to their medieval ways and held fast to them despite the availability of modern conveniences that could be imported from the neighboring boroughs.

Varagog was a magical place. Technological devices didn't work inside the walls, but the people got along just fine without them. There were no NewsNets in the village, but countless magic mirrors reflected SmartNews broadcasts using sorcery that Jack couldn't begin to understand. In addition to the medieval nobles and peasant townsfolk, the borough was inhabited by all manner of magical creatures from the English realm of Faerie, the Russian Thrice-Ten Kingdom, and countless other places. Secret passageways to the old enchanted lands could be found all throughout Varagog Village if one knew where to look. Jack would have loved to spend hours exploring for such things if he ever had the chance, but he rarely made it down to Empire City's medieval district. The people of Varagog still had yet to warm up to Jack, and thanks to the Rogue Secreteer, the villagers' attitude toward him at present was hostile at best and violent at worst.

"A pox on ye, Rüstov!" an old lady yelled at Jack from the window of an inn, and a bucket of dirty dishwater splattered down, just missing him. Jack looked up to see who had poured it out. The perpetrator, a middle-aged woman, made no effort to hide.

"Fool! You missed him!" her ancient neighbor scolded from across the street. It appeared that the recent newscasts had gotten the villagers a little extra worked up.

"Jack, try not to walk so close to me," Skerren said with a chuckle. "I don't want to get drenched the next time someone throws their dishwater at you."

Jack brushed off the water that had splashed onto him and gave Skerren a hard look. "Laugh it up," he said. "That was hilarious."

"Calm down," Skerren replied. "It's only water." He kept walking.

There were no more dishwater attacks as the children made their way through the village, but groups of little kids did pop out of alleyways to whip pebbles at Jack and then run away, until Skerren finally scared off his tormentors.

"I can't get over how the people here are still so blatantly unfriendly toward Jack," Allegra said. "Even with Obscuro getting people all worked up about the Rüstov again . . . it's got to be the only place in Empire City still like this."

Skerren shrugged. "People here are set in their ways."

"People here live in the past," Allegra said.

"That's true as well," Skerren said with a wry grin. "Don't worry. I'm not expecting any more unpleasantness. My warning to those halflings back there should take care of that."

"They treat you like royalty here, Skerren," Jack said, noting how all the pestering passersby had stopped bothering him and were now making way for him. Many of them were clearly trying to get Skerren to notice how helpful they were being. "*Are* you royalty?" Jack asked after considering the situation for a moment.

Skerren's reply carried an uncharacteristic air of modesty. "No," he said, almost appearing embarrassed by the question. "But Hovarth has no children, and his opinion of me is well known. These people just honor my word out of respect for their king."

Jack nodded silently, putting together for himself what Skerren was apparently too humble to say out loud. The general consensus in Varagog was that Hovarth would one day name his sword-wielding protégé to succeed him on the throne. Varagog had countless kings, dukes, counts, and earls, but the one who held sway over all was Hovarth, warrior king of Clan Varren. It was a comforting thought.

Jack knew that as long as he followed Skerren through the winding streets of Varagog, he was under Hovarth's protection as well.

As the group approached the south side of Varagog, Jack could tell Skerren was not entirely sold on the possibility of finding a Secreteer hiding out in his hometown. He led the group up a stone staircase to an arch on the borough's great wall before stopping. "Here we are," Skerren said, motioning out past the village's stone border. "I still don't know what we're doing here, though. Secreteers live in Cognito, not Varagog. Everybody knows that."

"Skerren, I already told you," Jack said. "You're not going to find anything wandering around the streets of Cognito. No Secreteers, no nothing. I've lived there for a year now, and I've never even met one of my neighbors except Stendeval. But I did see a Secreteer on our last mission."

"No one knows what we saw on our mission," Allegra told Jack.

"I do," he replied. "That's why we're here."

Jack reached the top of the staircase and stepped out onto the great wall. He could see everything from up there.

It was a beautiful late afternoon. The sun was dipping down behind large puffy clouds with gray tops and pink cotton-candy bottoms. Rays of light shot out from behind them like the golden glow that shines out of a treasure chest with an open lid. Varagog sprawled out beyond the great wall and up to the cliffs of the Imagine Nation. The land in between was covered with the modest workaday homes of peasant villagers and the thriving port district Jack had come to see—the Flying Shipyards.

It was the first time Jack had ever laid eyes on the shipyards. They stood in stark contrast to the futuristic spaceport stations across town in Galaxis. The two ports differed in every way one could possibly imagine. Instead of rocket launchpads and sleek steel runways with perfectly aligned landing lights, the Varagog shipyards had wooden docks and boardwalks lit by gas lamps and tiki torches. Rickety wooden decks, long ago hammered together by hand, jutted out over the cliffs of the Imagine Nation and ran far out into the open air.

The Flying Shipyards catered to seafaring vessels of a special sort. All along the docks, ships from dinghies to clippers were lined up and tied off on pylons like they would be at any marina, except that these ships were floating in midair. Just like the flying boat Jack had seen appear in the desert skies of the Real World, these ships had hot air balloons in place of the mainmast and sails. Big and small, the vessels filled the sky like pirate zeppelins. As Jack, Skerren, and Allegra descended the steps toward the shipyards, a giant multidecked galleon passed over them, sailing up into the clouds. Small flaps extended out from the hull on either side so it could catch the wind and steer. It was an impressive sight, but it wasn't the ship Jack was looking for.

Jack led the way out onto the docks. It was not at all the kind of place anyone would expect to find a member of the Clandestine Order, but Jack knew that if he could find the ship he'd seen, he'd find the Secreteer that sailed it. The memory he had of it was too clear in his head to be a fake. After about twenty minutes of walking the docks looking for the Secreteer's ship, Jack realized that that was going to be more difficult than he had expected. There were hundreds of ships in the port. So far none of them resembled the one he was looking for.

"I told you this was a waste of time," Skerren said.

"There was no flying ship in the air after our mission. You just remember it that way. You saw what the Secreteer wanted you to see."

"No," Jack maintained. "I saw it too clearly. I can still see it."

"I have a clear picture in my head too," Skerren said, "of the Secreteer showing up on a flying carpet. You don't see me taking you guys out to shop for rugs, do you? I should have known better than to listen to you about my own borough. What was I thinking?"

"That you want to catch a Secreteer and impress Trea," Jack said.

"That's not why I'm doing this," Skerren said a little too quickly.

Skerren started toward Jack, but Allegra got in front of him. "Skerren, take it easy," Allegra said. "Let's just agree that we're here because we don't know where else to look, okay? Unless you have any better ideas . . ."

Skerren grumbled something Jack couldn't quite make out, but Jack got the gist of it just the same. If Jack didn't find the ship in the next five minutes, Skerren was gone. Skerren had grown a lot during the last year, but when push came to shove, Jack knew he was just as head-strong as ever. That didn't mean he didn't have a point, though. Jack was starting to wonder if Skerren was right and the flying ship was just a false memory implanted by the Secreteer. He scanned the last few boardwalks on the dock, looking for the Secreteer's ship, but the port was so busy with all the people, packages, crewmen, and cargo bustling about, it was impossible to be sure if the ship was there or not without walking every inch of the shipyards. Skerren definitely wasn't going to stick around for that. Jack was about to give up when something familiar caught his eye. Little people wearing white suits with red ban-dages. The Mysterrii. Three of them, in fact, all making their way to the far end of the docks in a big hurry.

"This way," Jack said, taking off after them. Skerren and Allegra followed Jack and the Mysterrii along a cir-cuitous route that ran up ladders, down staircases, over barrels and crates, and on through to the very last slip on the westernmost dock in the shipyards. The ever-acrobatic Mysterrii weren't easy to keep up with. They zigzagged through the crowded docks, weaving their way around people like mice scurrying through a maze, but they led

Jack and the others to exactly where they wanted to go: a large wooden ship decorated with shiny gold fixtures, ornately carved figureheads, and stained-glass windows. There was a massive multicolored balloon tied to the deck, and a crew of Mysterrii was working feverishly to fill it with hot air. Standing at the back of the ship, near a large purple bonfire, was the cloaked figure Jack had come here to find. The Secreteer. Jack recognized her by her dreadlocks. She locked eyes with Jack once again, and beneath her hood he saw an eyebrow rise in surprise. This time she resisted the urge to fire clouds of smoke at Jack and his friends. Instead she smiled.

"Hello again, children," she said with a wave of her hand. "Congratulations. I'm officially impressed."

9

Hypnova

"Razza frazza!" the agitated Mysterrii shouted at Jack and his friends. *"Razza frazza! RAZZA FRAZZA!"*

Jack, Skerren, and Allegra stopped short a few feet away from the boat, their path to the Secreteer's ship blocked by a pack of Mysterrii. They were hopping around, shouting gibberish, and waving sticks to keep them back.

"Friendly little buggers, aren't they?" Allegra said to Jack.

Jack shook his head. "I've never seen them in such a frenzy. I've never even seen them stay in one place long enough to get this worked up." He put up his hands to show he meant no harm. "Easy, fellas! We're not looking for any trouble."

"But we know where to find it," Skerren said, reaching for one of his swords. It was clear that the Mysterrii had no intention of getting out of the way.

"Stay your hand!" the Secreteer called out from the aft deck of her ship. "If you want to keep a single memory in your head after you leave this place, you'll keep that sword in its scabbard."

Skerren dropped his hand back to his side, empty. "I was just going to scare them," he said.

The Secreteer gave Skerren a reproachful look before turning to the Mysterrii. "Concern yourselves with the bonfire and making those flames hotter," she told her miniature crewmen. "We need more hot air or we'll never get past the falls." The Mysterrii grumbled and turned away. Over at the fire they sprang into action, prying open large barrels of purple powder and shoveling it into the large flaming cauldron. "You'll have to excuse my crew," the Secreteer said to Jack and Allegra as they approached the edge of the dock, with Skerren lagging behind. "The

Mysterrii have been in the service of the Secreteers for ages. They're very passionate, but they've yet to develop any sense of manners or social grace."

"That's okay," Allegra replied. "We've got the same problem with Skerren." She chuckled and gave Skerren a friendly shove. He replied with a sour smirk and a sarcastic "Ha-ha-ha." Jack watched a smile form on the Secreteer's lips. He wondered what a mysterious woman who had already shot smoke down his throat for daring to look in her direction knew about manners and social grace. He looked over at the fidgety Mysterrii, who were still hopping around and grumbling, and decided it was all relative.

"How much longer?" the Secreteer asked the pint-size crewmen, who were busy stoking the flames in the blazing cauldron beneath the ship's balloon.

"*Zavva-zaazza. Frezza-fap!*" was their unintelligible reply.

"Very well," the Secreteer said. She turned back to Jack and his friends. "Allow me to introduce myself. My name is Hypnova. It appears my ship will be ready for takeoff in less than ten minutes. If you wish to speak with me, I can give you until then." A gloved hand emerged from the folds of the Secreteer's cloak and untied a golden rope on the railing. A wooden staircase lowered itself down to the dock. "This way," the enigmatic ship captain said, motioning for Jack to come forth.

Jack climbed on board, but just as his feet hit the deck, Hypnova stepped forward onto the top step, blocking Skerren and Allegra's path. "Not you," she said to Jack's friends. "Just Jack."

The children all traded surprised looks. "No way," Skerren protested. "We're a team."

"Hypnova . . . ," Jack said. "Skerren's right. We're together on this thing."

Hypnova gestured in the direction Jack had come from. "You can stay or you can go," she replied. "The choice is yours."

Jack was about to argue, but Allegra waved him off. "Just go, Jack," she said. "We'll wait out here. It's okay."

Jack grimaced. "Guess I'll see you guys in ten minutes?"

"Guess so," Skerren said. "Thanks a lot."

"This way," Hypnova told Jack as Skerren and Allegra went back down the stairs to the dock. Jack felt bad leaving his friends behind, but he knew he couldn't walk away from a meeting with a Secreteer. Hypnova was their only lead on Obscuro.

Jack followed Hypnova belowdecks to a modest-size cabin decorated with pictures and souvenirs from her travels all around the world. She motioned to a set of hand-crafted wooden chairs arranged around some food and drinks and invited him to have a seat. Jack's guilt gave way to a surge of excitement as he entered. He was inside a Secreteer's hideaway. She was going to speak with him. Voluntarily! Jack doubted many people in the Imagine Nation ever got this close to a member of the Clandestine Order's inner sanctum. Fewer still had ever seen a Secreteer's face. She was even more beautiful than Jack remembered.

A loud sound flapped through the cabin as the Secreteer removed her cloak, shook it out, and hung it on a hook. Beneath her flowing black shroud the Secreteer was young and vibrant. She had dark black skin and hazel eyes that didn't glow without her hood, but still glistened in the soft light of the cabin. Hypnova cut an energetic, stylish figure in a bright green and gold outfit. With knee-high boots on her feet, a golden saber on her hip, and a shining cape on her back, she looked like a dashing buccaneer or some kind of pirate queen. A *gorgeous* pirate queen.

Jack stared, speechless, transfixed by her stunning appearance. Hypnova laughed. "Jack, please," she said. "Relax. Help yourself to some refreshments."

Embarrassed, Jack quickly shook himself out of the minor trance he'd lapsed into. He grabbed some fruit from the buffet platter and hurried into a chair. Trying to recover, Jack started to introduce himself, but the Secreteer cut him off.

"I know who you are, and why you're here," she said. "Though I'm afraid you've wasted your time in coming."

Jack nearly choked on a piece of star-shaped fruit he didn't know the name of. "What do you mean, wasted?" he asked. "I haven't even told you what I want to know."

"You don't have to, Jack Blank," the Secreteer said. "Your plight is no secret to someone like me. You want to know how to find the Rogue Secreteer."

Jack stared on in wonder. "How did you know that?" he asked.

"I am a Secreteer myself," his host replied. "We find things out. It's what we do."

"I thought Secreteers just protected secrets people told them," Jack said. "I've never heard of them working to seek them out."

"We do both," Hypnova replied. "And we do more. Guarding over secrets is just another way of collecting them, wouldn't you agree?" Given that he himself was full of secrets, Hypnova's answer made Jack squirm in his seat.

"Are you the one who wiped all our memories after the fight with Speedrazor's gang?"

Hypnova was intrigued. "You remember that, do you?"

"It's how we found you," Jack said. "I could only barely remember your face. What little I saw of it anyway. But this ship . . ." Jack tapped his head. "It's in there."

Hypnova nodded slowly. "Impressive," she said. "I'm shocked you were able to retain even a vague memory of me or this ship. You were not supposed to be left with even that. Unless . . ." Hypnova paused to ponder Jack's surprisingly strong memory. "Ah," she said, snapping her fingers. "Unless those details are lodged in the *Rüstov's* memory."

Jack sat up in his chair. "The Rüstov's memory?"

"Indeed," Hypnova replied. "Perhaps that's something

153

you're able to draw on because of your rather unique relationship with your alien parasite. I'm curious, what else do you two remember?"

"Nothing," Jack said. "And there aren't two of us over here. There's just me." The thought of sharing memories with his parasite made Jack's skin crawl. He wondered if their connection had always been that strong or if it was a new development. The thought of losing control of his body to the Rüstov inside him terrified Jack. He hoped more than anything that the parasite wasn't gaining ground.

Hypnova shrugged. "Have it your way. I ask only because you and I have met before."

Now it was Jack's turn to be intrigued. "We have? When?" He thought back, trying hard to recall where he might have encountered Hypnova before this. Nothing came to mind. Bits and pieces of memories fluttered around in his brain like butterflies, all of them just out of reach.

"It was when you went to live in Cognito," Hypnova revealed. "At Stendeval's request I arranged lodging for you and implanted in your memory a map-plan of the changing Cognito streets so that you could get around the borough without difficulty. It's something we Secreteers do for all the people who rent hideouts in our borough. Did you never wonder exactly how you could navigate the ever-changing labyrinth of Cognito without any help?"

"I did, actually," Jack said.

Hypnova raised a hand. "Now you know," she told Jack. "I didn't feel you needed to remember that meeting. Odd that your parasite doesn't seem to remember it either."

Jack tugged at his collar. Most likely, his parasite didn't remember that meeting because it had taken place before he'd reached out to it. Before he'd woken it up. "Why are you telling me all this but you won't tell me what I came here to find out?"

"Good question," Hypnova replied. "The answer is because you're a special case, Jack," she said, taking a seat across from Jack and putting a hand on his knee. "The truth is, I feel partly responsible for the predicament you find yourself in with Obscuro. It's why I let you in here to begin with."

"Responsible?" Jack repeated. "What are you saying?"

Hypnova motioned with her hands. "I'm saying, back when I was implanting map-memories in your head, I may have . . . *glimpsed* your secrets. So you see how I know why you're here today and what you're worried about as well."

"Wait a minute," Jack said, taken aback by the revelation. "What do you mean, *glimpsed* my secrets? You mean you snuck around in my head?"

Hypnova nodded.

"You raided my memories?" Jack asked. He couldn't believe his ears. He felt violated.

"I admit I was a bit nosy," Hypnova replied. "All Secreteers are. It's just part of who we are, I suppose."

"*That's* what you say?" Jack shouted. "It's who you are? No apology?"

"Would an apology make you feel better?" Hypnova asked.

Jack stood and threw his hands up. He couldn't get over how Hypnova was telling him all this like it was no big deal. As far as he was concerned it was anything but. "So you know *everything*?" he asked.

"Everything," Hypnova confirmed. "It's quite a conundrum you find yourself in. Don't worry. I won't reveal any of the details. I am bound not to by the rules of my order. Secreteers don't tell secrets. They keep them."

"Yeah, a Secreteer telling secrets . . . that'll *never* happen."

"You have a right to be upset," Hypnova allowed.

"Oh, good. I'm glad you're all right with it," Jack replied. "How does Obscuro know anything about me if *you* were the one who snooped? Did you tell him?"

"Yes and no," Hypnova said. "This is not commonly known, but every secret that a Secreteer collects is eventually uploaded, for lack of a better word, into a shared memory bank that all members of the order can access. It seems Obscuro was so unnerved by what I found in your head that he has opted to betray the order and sell as many secrets as it will take to finance his escape from this planet. But you know that already."

"Obscuro's got it all wrong," Jack said. "He knows about the spyware virus, but he doesn't know what I've been doing to stop it. He thinks the situation is hopeless, but it isn't. He's jumping the gun. I need to know what he knows about Glave and the virus." Jack snapped his fingers. "Wait a minute," he said. "If you guys share secrets, then you know what Obscuro knows. Please tell me. If we work together, we can stop the Rüstov before they attack."

"Even if I wanted to, I couldn't tell you that," Hypnova said. "Obscuro has not uploaded anything into the memory bank in quite some time."

Jack sighed. "Then tell me how to find him. He obviously isn't shy about talking. He'll tell me, won't he?"

"I'm sorry, Jack, but the Rogue Secreteer won't be telling any more secrets after tonight," Hypnova said. "He has to pay for what he's done. Because of our connection to one another, we Secreteers must have absolute trust that none of us will reveal any of the secrets we protect. If even one of us breaks the vows of secrecy, our entire order could collapse."

"What does that matter if the Rüstov take over?" Jack asked. "Isn't stopping them more important? You said this was a special case," Jack argued. "It's your fault this is happening in the first place! Can't you make an exception?"

"I already have. The fact that it's a special case means you get to have this conversation with me," Hypnova said. "I'll even let you all remember this encounter after the fact, something my brethren would certainly never allow. I'm simply trying to give you some closure. I know you better than you can imagine, Jack. I know your search for me and for answers about the rogue would continue endlessly without it, and you need to focus on other things. Don't you?"

Jack opened his mouth to respond, but Hypnova put up a hand to stop him. "Please, I know you have good intentions, but believe me when I tell you I've heard it all before. Pleas from secret-seekers looking for answers . . . assurances that the source of those answers would never be revealed, come what may. A Secreteer who caves in to such arguments is not worthy of the name."

Jack slumped back into his chair and threw his half-eaten fruit back onto the buffet. "You weren't kidding when you said this was a waste of time."

"No, I wasn't," Hypnova told Jack. "Try to see it from my point of view: A secret that everyone knows about is worthless. It isn't even a secret. This is the currency Secreteers trade in. We can't very well be expected to devalue it. People trust us with the job of keeping things quiet for the simple reason that we can be *trusted* to keep things quiet. I can't tell you anything more. If word got out that *another* Secreteer was talking out of turn? No one would trust us with anything ever again."

"A little late to worry about that, isn't it? In case you haven't noticed, Obscuro's already ruining your reputation."

"Which is why we are going to make an example of him," Hypnova replied. "His actions threaten everything the Secreteers stand for. We'll see to it that he's punished for what he's done, and we will restore the natural order of things."

There was a knock on the cabin door, and three Mysterrii poked their heads in. *"Hup-hup-hup!"* the three of them said in unison. Hypnova nodded toward them, and they left.

"I'm afraid our time is at an end," Hypnova said. "For what it's worth, I'm sorry I couldn't help you more." Hypnova stood up from her seat, reached for her cloak, and shook it out. The ends of the black fabric extended outward, transforming into dark smoke that filled the room with a loud whoosh. The next thing Jack knew, he was standing on the dock with Skerren and Allegra. Hypnova's ship was rising up into the sky. Jack had no memory of how he'd gotten there.

"She did it again," Jack said to himself. It took another moment or two before he realized Skerren was holding him by the shoulders and shaking him back and forth.

"Jack . . . Jack!" Skerren said. "Snap out of it! What did she say?"

Jack shook the cobwebs out of his head and backed out of Skerren's grip. "They're going after him," he said. "They're going to kill him."

"What?" Allegra said. "Who? Obscuro?"

Jack nodded, watching helplessly as Hypnova's ship drifted away from the dock. "We have to follow her," he said. "Allegra, are you strong enough to carry all three of us? Please tell me you are."

"Carry all three of us? What are you talking about?" Allegra asked.

"You need to stretch out and hook on to Hypnova's ship before it's too late," Jack said. He pointed to the flying ship slowly sailing off into the sunset. "We can follow her to the Rogue Secreteer. That's where she's going now. This might be the only chance we get."

Skerren and Allegra traded harried looks. Whatever they'd been expecting Jack to say when he stepped off

Hypnova's ship, this wasn't it. Allegra shook her head and wrapped one of her arms around Skerren and Jack several times. She stretched her other arm way out past the dock's edge to latch on to the back of the airborne vessel. "Hang on tight," she said. With a daring leap the trio of children went flying through the air.

Allegra held on as tightly as she could, her steely grip the only thing between her friends and the falls below. Slowly she retracted her arm to pull the group up to the bottom of the ship's hull, and then shape-shifted into a pocket large enough to safely hold both Skerren and Jack. Hypnova's ship sailed on, ignorant of the three stow-aways who were now on board. Jack and his friends rode away from Empire City in silence without anything even resembling a plan.

CHAPTER

10

Hostile Environment

Hypnova's ship sailed west beyond the borders of Empire City and on through the clouds for more than an hour until it was alone in the sky. The whole way, Jack looked down from his perch below the ship, watching quietly as the landscape rolled away beneath his feet. The ship sailed over the small towns and villages that were scattered across the hills of the Imagine Nation, heading deeper and deeper into the Outlands.

The Outlands was the name given to the far reaches of the floating island, an untamed, strange wilderness that made up almost half of the Imagine Nation's landmass. Until that night they were just undeveloped badlands that Jack had heard much about but never seen firsthand. Jack was a stranger to the Outlands, but only because Empire City was the kind of place a person could live his entire life and still not see everything. Between Jack's work, classes, and other daily distractions in the Imagine Nation's capital city, he'd yet to have any real time or reason to strike off into the island's uncharted territories. As the ship began its descent into Gravenmurk Glen, it was clear that he now had both. Given the right reasons, Jack had made the time.

Gravenmurk Glen was a thick forest that started in the mountains behind Empire City, sprawled out across the hills, and ran up to the cliffs on the island's north edge. The tall trees of Gravenmurk stood over a long, deep ravine that was cut by a river running down from the mountaintops and out into the ocean. Gravenmurk Glen's trees were packed together so tightly, and the foliage overlapped to such a degree, that any attempt to look into the forest from outside was pointless. A fine white mist coasted slowly over the treetops, the trailing ends of a much thicker fog that snaked between the precious few gaps that did exist among the trees. Despite the strength and weight of the fog in the forest, the landscape was perfectly clear beyond the woodland's edge. The tall trees seemed to pen in the hazy smog, refusing to let it escape. Jack knew that people who entered the dark woods of Gravenmurk Glen alone often suffered the same fate. He was glad he had his friends with him.

Above, the Mysterrii rigged the sails to catch the headwind, slowing the ship down as it neared the center of the forest. Jack heard Hypnova give the order to prepare to drop anchor. They had reached their destination. A hatch opened directly below Allegra, and a Mysterrii emerged with an anchor that was tied to a massive chain. If the Mysterrii looked up for just a moment, he would spot them.

"We have to get off this ship," Jack said.

Skerren pointed up at the crew of Mysterrii on the ship's railing. "Can't let them see us," he said. Skerren turned to Allegra. "HALO jump?"

Allegra nodded. "HALO jump."

Jack groaned. A HALO jump was a High Altitude Low

Opening parachute drop characterized by a prolonged rush toward the ground and a last-minute opening of the lifesaving chute. It was a strategic infiltration maneuver that was once routinely employed by Valorian women to get into position before battle. It was a dangerous stunt to pull with all three children jumping at once, but the less time they spent in the air, the less likely they were to be noticed. Allegra put a finger to her lips and, without any further warning, released her hold on the bottom of Hypnova's ship. Jack's stomach jumped into his throat, and he resisted the urge to scream as they fell away into the night.

Jack and his friends plummeted from the flying vessel and fell for three full seconds before Allegra morphed her upper body into a parachute that opened with a loud whomping noise. Jack's body jerked upward painfully as Allegra's shape-shifting halted the trio's descent with an abrupt and forceful jolt. Her new form slowed them down just in time to keep them alive. Jack and Skerren hit the treetops at half speed and fell through into the forest. Branches broke under Jack's body, and twigs whipped against his face as he tumbled down through the unforgiving brush and finally slammed down against the cold, hard earth.

Jack rolled over and grunted. It hurt, but he'd live. The others would too. Their entry into the glen hadn't been comfortable or easy, but arriving in comfort and ease hadn't been the goal. Times like this reminded Jack of just how impressed he was with how strong Allegra had become.

Jack stood up and looked around. It took a few minutes for his eyes to adjust, and when they did, he didn't see much. Night had fallen and the thick canopy overhead blocked out the moonlight almost completely. The weak moonbeams filtering through the trees served only to give the fog an eerie, supernatural glow. The thick, greenish-white fog was everywhere, making it almost impossible to see more than a few feet in any direction.

"I can't see a thing down here," Skerren said. "Did Hypnova tell you where she was going?"

Jack shook his head. "No."

"What did she say to you exactly?" Skerren asked.

"I told you," Jack said. "She said they were going to take care of Obscuro. That they were going to make an example of him. Tonight."

"That's it?" Skerren asked. "That's all she said?"

"Give me a break, Skerren. You saw me. I don't even remember getting off the ship." Jack actually remembered much more than that, but he didn't want to get into what Hypnova had said about his sharing memories with his parasite. He was worried enough about what that meant. He didn't need Skerren adding to his troubles on that score.

Skerren exhaled noisily and started climbing a tall tree without another word to anyone. Allegra used her stretching powers to help him reach some of the highest branches. Jack couldn't feel the presence of any machines in the forest except the ones he was carrying in his bag. He was glad he'd taken a minute to grab them before leaving his lab, because once again he was stuck in a place where his powers weren't likely to be of much use. Skerren's powers were another story. The children couldn't see where Hypnova's ship was heading until Skerren sliced through the trunk of the tree he was clinging to.

"Skerren, don't!" Allegra shouted, but it was too late. Skerren's sword chopped off the top of the tree like it was the head of a broccoli stalk. The treetop fell to the ground, revealing a starry night sky and Hypnova's ship dropping its anchor up ahead.

Skerren quickly hopped down from his lookout point to relay what he'd seen. "The ship looks to be stopping north of here," he said, pointing. "That direction."

"I thought you were just going to climb up the tree and look out over it," Allegra told him. "You shouldn't have done that."

Skerren turned toward Allegra. "Done what?" he asked. "Figure out which way to go?"

"No, cut into that tree," Allegra said. "We learned about this place in our Imaginature class, remember?"

Skerren scrunched his eyebrows and chewed his lower lip like he was trying to recall the lesson. Jack helped him out. "This forest wasn't always here," Jack said. "It grew up over old burial grounds. It's sacred." Jack motioned at the severed treetop. "You don't treat sacred ground like that."

A thorny vine crept across the ground and wrapped itself around Skerren's ankle.

"Not unless you want to deal with the Gravens—," Allegra said, pointing at the slithering vegetation, her eyes wide. The vine jerked Skerren off his feet and started dragging him across the ground.

"Og's blood!" Skerren called out. "It's alive!"

Allegra and Jack ran over to Skerren and grabbed him tightly underneath his arms, giving him time to cut himself free.

The severed vine snapped loose like a broken rubber band, shooting backward. The vine sank into the earth like a snake's tongue retracting into its mouth after a long hiss. The ground bulged at the spot where the vine had disappeared. A little mound of dirt started rising up there and very quickly turned into a big mound of dirt. Something was coming out of the ground. Jack looked down and saw more earth cracking and crumbling all around him. Everywhere he looked, roots and rocks were bursting up from below. Something down beneath the earth was digging itself out—a lot of somethings, by the looks of it.

"Here we go," Skerren said. "Get ready. Back-to-back formation."

"Hey, look who cares about strategy all of a sudden," Jack said.

"Not now, guys . . . ," Allegra told them both.

Jack took a deep breath as scores of dark, dirty creatures pulled themselves up out of the ground, surrounding him and his friends. The first one out opened its mouth and moaned. The air blowing through the mud in its gaping maw sounded like a sick person wheezing through mucus. It wasn't a person at all. The Gravens weren't subterranean monsters pulling themselves up from underground. They were the underground itself, rising up in the form of people. They looked like ecological zombies, made up of roots, moss, and muddy earth. Some had vines for arms, and some had hands made of soil and clay. None of them had eyes. They just had deep pockets burrowed into the dirt where their eyes should have been. Each one was at least six feet tall, and they towered over the children as they trudged forward, step by muddy step.

"Jack, keep behind us," Allegra said. "Your powers won't work out here."

"I can handle myself," Jack said. "It's like Chi said, if your powers desert you, you still have yourself to rely on, right? I planned ahead this time around." Jack dug into his bag, looking for something specific. "Here we are," he said. Jack took out a pair of heavy metal gloves and slipped them on.

"What's that?" Skerren asked.

"Just a little something I've been working on," Jack replied. "Nuclear Knuckles." Jack punched his hands together and the gloves started heating up. His hands lit up with energy as the gloves emitted a sizzling yellow glow. "Check it out," Jack said as he waved his hand over the ground at his feet. The earth ruptured beneath his palm as if he'd dragged a spike through the dirt, even though he hadn't even touched it.

"Whoa," Allegra said.

Just then a Graven wrapped a vine around Jack's waist and pulled him close. Jack closed his eyes and swung as hard as he could, his gloved fist hitting the Graven square in the chest. Mud splattered everywhere, and the vine's grip on him loosened instantly. Jack opened his eyes and saw that all that remained of the Graven was a pair of legs. He had knocked off the Graven's entire upper body.

"Nice!" Jack said. The Graven's legs collapsed into a heap of mud on the ground before him. "I've been looking for something I could really hit with these things," he told Skerren and Allegra. "Only so much you can do in the lab, you know?"

"You can do as much as you want out here," Skerren said. "Here they come!"

A wave of fresh Gravens closed in on them from every angle, and Jack, Skerren, and Allegra lashed out, pushing them back.

Skerren spun his swords in his hands and sprang forth, slicing Gravens in half with big, sweeping cuts. Allegra morphed her fists into sledgehammers and started splattering the Gravens with hard hits. Fighting with their backs to one another offered Jack and his friends the most protection possible against the green monsters, but they were greatly outnumbered. Allegra had just reduced one of the Gravens to a pile of moss, dirt, and rocks when another one broke through the circle and came at her from behind.

"Allegra, look out!" Jack shouted as a thick, muddy arm with roots running through it like veins wrapped itself around Allegra's neck. The Graven pulled Allegra down to the forest floor, where hands grew out of the ground and started tugging on her body. Jack and Skerren were too busy fighting their own battles to get to her, but Allegra liquefied, turning herself into a flowing stream of silver that ran through the Gravens' grimy fingers like water. She reformulated behind the Graven with a hand shaped like a large ax.

"It . . . it was trying to pull me under!" Allegra shouted with a little hitch in her voice. She threw her arm down and chopped her attacker in half. "Don't let them get too close to you!" She made her other hand into an ax and stepped away from the circle, spinning around with her arms extended, carving out some breathing room.

Allegra's move cleared up space on Jack's left flank, but more Gravens poured in on his right. Jack clapped his hands together, sending a shock wave into the midsection of the Graven in front of him. Mud and pebbles splattered everywhere. Jack pressed his forehead into his shoulder to wipe his brow and kept right on throwing punches and thunderclaps. Thanks to his Nuclear Knuckles, the Gravens went down easily, but there were so many of them. Jack was getting out of breath, and the Gravens were still coming by the dozen.

Hands grew out of the earth to grab at Jack's ankles.

One of them got ahold of him and pulled his foot underground. He was in up to his shin before he was able to swat the Graven hands away with his energized fists. He and his friends couldn't keep this up forever. They were holding their ground for now, but it wouldn't be long before the ground was holding them—for good. There was an endless supply of Gravens . . . and they were getting smarter.

Jack was pounding Gravens left and right when a few of them teamed up and joined their bodies together to form a giant super-Graven. The creature rushed at Jack, and he swung. Mud sloshed over his hand as it got stuck in the super-Graven's stomach. The mossy muck bubbled around the energy from Jack's Nuclear Knuckles, but the super-Graven stood there and took it. It grunted out a terrible laugh that smelled like pollution and sounded phlegmy. The creature jumped back, and there was an ominous slorping sound as it pulled the metal glove off Jack's hand. Jack's eyes bugged out as he looked at his bare hand, then up at Skerren and Allegra. More super-Gravens were coming.

Skerren's jaw hit the floor. "Fall back!" he shouted.

He sliced out a clear path in the woods behind him and pointed with a muddy sword. "Go! Now!" Jack and Allegra ran through the clearing Skerren had just made, and he followed. They ran through the forest as fast as they could, desperate to put some distance between them and the Gravens. Ahead they spotted a rocky outcropping and sprinted to the top, hoping that the Gravens couldn't come up through stone.

"These things are tougher than I thought," Jack said once they'd stopped running.

"We've got to get out of here," Skerren said.

"Which way?" Allegra asked, pushing aside some shrubs on the top of the rock and looking as deep into the forest as she could. "I can't see anything out here." The mist was blocking the view in every direction.

Skerren and Jack looked around too. The only thing thicker than the fog in the forest was the forest itself. Gravenmurk Glen was overrun with a thorny under-growth of small trees and bushes.

"I don't know . . . ," Skerren said, thinking. "This way!" he decided, and started down the other side of the rock.

"Wait a minute," Jack said. "We can't just pick a direction and go. Who knows where we'll end up?"

Skerren scowled at Jack. "What do you suggest we do? Stay here?" The wind carried gurgling moans through the air. The Gravens were coming.

"I just don't want us to make the situation any worse than it already is," Jack said. "We can't go running off half-cocked."

"A little late for that, don't you think?" Skerren asked. "You're the one who pushed us onto that ship without a plan."

"Don't put this on me, Skerren," Jack said. "I'm not the one who invited the Gravens to this party."

"Both of you, stop it!" Allegra said, getting in between Jack and Skerren before things escalated any further. The Gravens were at the base of the rock. They didn't have time to argue. "Listen," Allegra said, putting up a finger. "You hear that?"

Jack and Skerren both shut their mouths. After a few seconds Jack heard the sound of running water. "The river," he said.

"It flows into the sea on the northern border, right?"

Allegra asked. "Hypnova's ship is north of where we are . . ." She trailed off, waiting for the boys to put it all together.

"We follow that sound to the river, and we follow the river to Hypnova's ship," Skerren said, finishing Allegra's thought.

"And we let the river take care of the Gravens," Jack added.

Allegra nodded with enthusiasm. "We use our environment to *fight* our environment."

"Now, *that's* strategy," Jack said, giving Skerren a light shove on the shoulder.

Skerren didn't smile. Allegra did. "We better get moving," she said.

Jack, Skerren, and Allegra struck off in what appeared to be the direction of the river. It wasn't easy getting there. They had the sound of running water to lead them and Skerren's swords to cut a path through the dense thicket, but the forest fought them tooth and nail (or, more accurately, thorn and smog) the whole way. The eerie luminescent haze that filled the forest got thicker and more opaque with every step they took. It seemed to be hugging the trees, pooling up around their trunks, and purposely obscuring prickly briar patches filled with spiky barbs, slowing them down. That was something they could ill afford, as the Gravens didn't let up. They dogged the children's steps with a vengeance and were almost upon them when Jack, Skerren, and Allegra broke through a thorn bush and discovered that there was nothing on the other side but air.

They fell straight down into the river, narrowly escaping the grasp of two super-Gravens who were right behind them. Jack plunged deep into the water, and when he came up for air, one of the Gravens who had fallen in behind him was clutching at his shoulders. Jack screamed as another Graven's vinelike arms wrapped around his legs and pulled him under the water, but the grip wasn't strong. Not like before. Jack kicked his way free and looked below him. Through the darkness he could make out the sight of the Graven dissolving into a floating pool of moss, weeds, and mud. When Jack came up for air a second time, he saw the that Graven that had grabbed his shoulders and pushed him down below was slowly breaking apart in the water. Its vacant eye sockets stared at

Jack, and the creature snarled out a growl that drowned in bubbles as its head slid apart in the water.

Jack looked across the river and saw that Skerren and Allegra were both okay. He sighed with relief and turned around to float on his back as the current carried him and his friends safely away.

CHAPTER

11

The Battle of Gravenmurk Glen

The river shallowed out and the current slowed as Jack, Skerren, and Allegra approached the area below Hypnova's ship. The group came up on an empty riverbank and got out of the water. Jack stood and turned his messenger bag upside down on the ground. All the electronic devices he'd brought along, including the remaining Nuclear Knuckles glove on his left hand, were shorted out. Ruined. "So much for my bag of tricks," he said to himself.

"This way," Skerren said, heading off toward a light that could be seen off in the distance.

"C'mon," Allegra said to Jack, and followed Skerren.

Jack hustled after his friends as they hiked up the ridge. He caught up with them, and rubbed up and down on his arms to warm up as they walked along the river's edge. He felt chilled to his bones. It was a cold night in the woods, and being soaked from the river made it worse. The creepy, dark forest oozed out a feeling of mysterious dread. Jack didn't like it there, but it was exactly the kind of place he'd expected Secreteers to gather. The three of them kept following the river toward Hypnova's ship. Sure enough, he heard what sounded like voices up ahead. A lot of voices, in fact.

Jack, Skerren, and Allegra quieted down as they closed in on a rocky crag that the river ran over as it headed out of sight. The voices were coming from the other side. Inch by inch Jack and the others crawled toward the lip of the stone ledge and took cover behind a row of thorn bushes. They looked down on a clearing in the forest. The land before them fell away with a steep decline, and the river narrowed into a tight stream that ran through a rocky gorge. The rock walls on either side of the river had smooth grooves that lined their stone faces with long, straight rows, the kind of erosion that was the work of years and years. The trees were all set back from the gorge, and the fog lingered back with them as if an invisible fence were keeping it in place.

Without any fog there to muddle his view, Jack could see at least two dozen robed figures standing atop the ridge walls on both sides of the water. The soft glow of the Gravenmurk mist lit the figures from behind, turning them into silhouettes with glowing eyes that seemed to float in the darkness beneath the hoods of their cloaks. There was no question who they were. Secreteers. Lots of them. Jack doubted anyone had ever seen so many in one place.

"There," Skerren whispered, pointing at a shadowy figure a hundred yards away. He was standing on a natural stone bridge that connected the two rock walls of the gorge. All the Secreteers were watching him. Moonlight twinkled like glitter on the surface of the water beneath his feet as it shone down to reveal his shape and size. He wore the same robes as the other Secreteers, only his were open. A golden clasp at his collar held the dark purple cloak in place, and the enveloping shroud seemed impossibly large as it fluttered in the breeze. Beneath his vestments he wore all black. His hood was up, and a mask covered his mouth and nose. Unknowable eyes stared out from the blackness within. The children all looked at one another in silence. There was no mistaking him. . . . It was Obscuro.

Moments later the row of Secreteers on the right parted at the center, and a person who appeared to be their leader stepped forward. "Traitor!" she called out. "Do not attempt to flee this place. You are outnumbered and overmatched. Your time of judgment is at hand."

The head Secreteer threw back her hood, revealing an angry face with smooth, graceful features, pale skin, and flowing white hair.

"Oblivia," Obscuro said, giving a formal bow. "So good of you to come. It's an honor." His voice sounded positively reptilian.

"You seem almost glad to see me," Oblivia said.

"Of course," Obscuro replied. "I would have taken offense if anyone other than the matriarch of our order had dared to try to apprehend me."

A murmur ran through the contingent of Secreteers, no doubt bristling at Obscuro's nerve and ego. Oblivia silenced them all with a wave of her hand.

184

"You know better than that, Obscuro," she said. "We have not come to 'try,' and we are not here to 'apprehend.'"

Oblivia nodded to her fellow Secreteers, and they slowly advanced on Obscuro's position.

"For hundreds of years the Clandestine Order has guarded the hidden truths of this planet," Oblivia declared. "Your betrayal threatens not only our sacred mission but also the very existence of our order. Your selfishness and cowardice are unacceptable. You cannot be trusted to keep the real secrets of this world—to hold the line between the imaginary and the real." As the Secreteers closed in on Obscuro, blocking off his exit on both sides of the bridge, Oblivia prepared to render her final judgment. "For breaking your vows and violating the most sacred tenets of our order . . . for the damage you have already done to our cause and our good name, your life, Obscuro . . . is forfeit."

Obscuro let out a terse laugh. "All life on this planet is forfeit, Oblivia. The Rüstov are going to win this war. You know that as well as I."

"I know of no such thing," Oblivia replied.

Obscuro waved his hand. "Have it your way, then.

185

Your decision is final? Your mind made up?"

"The only choice in this matter was yours, Obscuro. You've sealed your own fate, and your lack of remorse leaves me with no regrets," she told her former acolyte. "Take him!" she ordered.

Allegra grabbed Jack's hand. This secret gathering was about to turn into an execution. "What are we going to do?" she whispered. "We can't just let them kill him!"

"How do you propose we stop them?" Skerren asked. "Obscuro broke his vows. He knew what he was getting himself into."

"If they kill him, we're back at square one," Jack said. "We need to know what he knows. He's the only Secreteer who'll tell us anything about Glave and the virus."

"I know, but how are we supposed to save him?" Skerren asked. "I count at least twenty Secreteers down there, and there's only three of us. Four, if you count Obscuro, who doesn't even know we're here or what our intentions are."

Jack grumbled to himself. Skerren had a point.

The Secreteers closed in on Obscuro's left and right flanks, and he jumped down from the bridge, landing on the stone riverbank. They followed him down, surrounding him.

"There's no escape," Oblivia said. "Don't make this any harder than it has to be."

"I'm afraid I have to if I want to go on living," Obscuro replied. "My continued survival is quite important to me. That *is* the reason behind all of this, you know. It's also why I brought *them*."

"Them?" Oblivia asked.

The Rogue Secreteer clapped his hands, and a legion of supervillains stepped out of the mist on the ridge walls, taking up positions in the places the Secreteers had just vacated. Obscuro was no longer outnumbered and overmatched. If anything, he'd just outwitted his pursuers, luring them down to his level on the riverbank while his henchmen took the high ground above them.

"I'd like you to meet some of the people I've been forced to associate with as of late," Obscuro told his fellow Secreteers. "I know it's nothing to be proud of, but I've had to make certain sacrifices to avoid being sacrificed myself. I'm ready to leave this world, Oblivia, but not the way you have in mind."

Jack, Skerren, and Allegra stared on, aghast at the stunning turn of events.

"Supercriminals," Allegra said. "There's so many of them."

"He must have been selling secrets for a while now," Jack whispered.

"That would explain the crime wave," Skerren agreed. "And look who's here," he added. "Some old friends." Skerren pointed out Pain, Fugazi, and Backstab among the throng of supervillains that had emerged on the scene. Jack looked over the rest of the superpowered felons, noting some former Peacemakers and straight-up bad guys there as well. Jack saw Tiki Man, Albatross, Celsius, Arsenal, Fist, Battlecry, and Onyx, just to name a few. They were all heavy hitters. The one villain he did not see was Lorem Ipsum.

Despite the sudden evening of the odds, Oblivia remained undaunted when Obscuro's mob emerged from the fog. One fierce look from her was all it took to make the villains closest to her step back. "You've been expecting us," she said to Obscuro.

"I knew you'd come calling sooner or later," Obscuro

admitted. "As a precaution I've altered the memories of a few clients here and there. The way they remember things, their job is to protect me. They think they're part of my gang." Obscuro shrugged. "I suppose in a way that's true now, isn't it?"

"It won't save you," Oblivia replied.

Obscuro flipped back up onto the stone bridge and raised his hand in a bring-it-on motion toward Oblivia. "Do your worst," he said.

Oblivia and her Secreteers did exactly that. They attacked with artful deception and a complete lack of mercy, wielding bats, clubs, and staffs. Hidden safely behind the thorn bushes, Jack, Skerren, and Allegra watched eruptions of smoke run through the gorge in waves as Secreteers vanished and then reappeared, blindsiding their enemies over and over. They moved like ninja ghosts, striking hard and fading away fast, only to reappear again moments later in clouds of smoke, attacking from new angles.

Obscuro and his supervillain cronies met the Secreteers blow for blow. Obscuro's brainwashed allies returned fire with a diverse array of creative violence. Onyx, the giant black stone man, swung away with his large, powerful fists. Keystone, who had the power to break his enemies into hundreds of equal-size pieces with a single touch, was dismantling every Secreteer he could get his hands on. Tiki Man, a tribal shaman wearing a large wooden mask and grass skirt, was throwing cursed weapons at the Secreteers from a satchel he carried over his shoulder. His bag of tricks seemed positively bottomless, and dozens of other villains were there, every one of them attacking with equal ferocity.

Jack didn't know what to do next. Everything was happening so fast. "Now what?" he asked the others. "If we help the Secreteers, we make it easier for them to kill Obscuro. If we help Obscuro . . ." Jack shook his head. "What are we going to do, fight alongside supervillains? We can't do that."

"Maybe we're better off sitting this one out," Allegra said. "Take our chances with whoever's left standing."

Skerren shook his head. "I've got unfinished business with some of the villains down there. I'm not sitting anything out. This is what we train for."

Jack thought about that for a second. Skerren was right

again. "I say we help the Secreteers," he said. "Maybe if we help them, they'll help us."

"If we go in there now, we're just as likely to get attacked by one side as the other," Allegra said.

"We can't just stand by and do nothing," Skerren said.

"Let's see what I can do from up here before we rush into anything," Jack said. The inventions he'd brought with him might have been gone, but there were plenty of supervillains down there with powers he could mess with just by thinking about it. "Just give me a minute," Jack said, looking over the battlefield for a target.

First came Albatross, the living tank. Jack remapped his weapons systems to target supervillains instead of Secreteers. A few people in the battle down below seemed surprised when one of Albatross's missiles crashed into Pain, but the Secreteers didn't miss a beat. They stopped attacking Albatross straightaway. As long as he was taking out his own teammates, they were happy to let him do it. Next came Fist and Battlecry, two more Peacemakers who had gone bad. Jack used his powers to short out the controls on Battlecry's sonic weaponry, causing him to blast his allies. After that, Jack took control of Fist's oversize bionic arm and made him punch himself in the face a few times.

Unfortunately, the more Jack used his powers, the more obvious it became that there was a hidden player on the battlefield. Arsenal, a supersoldier-mercenary who carried every sort of weapon imaginable, furrowed his brow when one of his laser guns misfired. He switched to a new weapon and looked around, curious. When that one didn't work, he threw it away and went for another.

Jack enjoyed frustrating Arsenal's efforts as he grabbed gun after gun. The man was an infamous assassin, rotten to the very marrow of his spine, and Jack was thrilled to be using what he'd learned in class on him. Jack had learned loads about machines and weapons over the past year. He was a force to be reckoned with, using his powers to save the Secreteers' lives, but he wasn't paying attention to the little details. He realized too late that as Arsenal fired each new weapon, trying to shoot Secreteers, he wasn't really aiming. Arsenal was looking around the forest each time he pulled the trigger.

"Jack . . . ," Allegra began. "Something's wrong. He's not looking where he's shooting."

"Who, Arsenal?" Jack asked, only half paying attention. "Good. That means he's not hitting anybody."

"No, Jack," Allegra said. "It means he's not looking at his targets. He's looking—"

"For us," Skerren said as Arsenal turned and focused on the three of them.

"Down!" Allegra yelled as Arsenal took out throwing knives, something Jack couldn't manipulate with his powers, and threw them with deadly accuracy. She morphed into a shield, blocking the daggers.

"There!" Arsenal called out, pointing up at the thorn bush that Jack, Skerren, and Allegra were no longer hidden behind. The battle ground to a halt for a split second as all eyes turned to look up at the children.

"Get them!" Obscuro screamed at his minions.

"You heard the man," Arsenal shouted. "Get the kids! We're gonna need hostages if we want to get out of here!"

With that, the entire focus of the fight turned from the Rogue Secreteer to Jack, Skerren, and Allegra. Bursts of smoke blasted out of the ground all around Jack and his friends as the Secreteers rushed to them. One of them grabbed Jack off his feet and pulled him close. "What are you doing here?" she screamed. "I told you we were going to handle this!" Beneath the shadows of her hood, Jack could see it was Hypnova. Oblivia appeared at her side almost immediately.

"What's he doing here?" the matriarch demanded. "Did they follow you?" It wasn't so much a question as it was an accusation. Oblivia gave Hypnova the kind of look that could turn a person inside out. It was clear to Jack that he'd put Hypnova in a bad spot. A really bad spot. She set him back down without another word. The villains converged on them, looking for hostages. Pain grabbed through a liquefied Allegra while Skerren dodged Keystone's probing fingers.

Jack wasn't so lucky. He was snatched up by Arsenal while Hypnova was busy pushing back against his cohorts. Jack fought back as the heavily armed mercenary tried to carry him off, but it was no use struggling—at least not physically. Arsenal had the clear advantage in size. Luckily, even though Arsenal wasn't using his tech-based weapons against Jack, he was still carrying them. With a thought, Jack blew up the stores of ammunition and explosives in Arsenal's belt. Flames shot out of Arsenal's waist as little compartments blew up one after the other. He scrambled to take his belt off, and Jack squirmed free. Before Arsenal could recover, Jack activated a cartridge of knockout gas the mercenary had loaded into a wrist cannon and pushed Arsenal's hand up toward his own face.

Arsenal went down, and Jack jumped back into the melee. Skerren was fully in it, slicing away at Backstab, doing his best to take her in a rematch. Allegra was wrapping her arms around Onyx's legs, tripping him up while the Secreteers pounced on him in ever-increasing numbers. Not wanting to miss out on the action, Jack looked around for something to hit, and he found it in Tiki Man, who was throwing fire from his satchel down onto the Secreteers on the riverbank. Jack ran up and jumped off a rock, launching himself into Tiki Man's back and knocking him over the edge. Jack landed squarely on his feet and looked down with pride at the sight of Tiki Man jumping into the river, trying to escape the very flames that he himself had thrown. When Jack looked up, he saw Hypnova staring down at him with a disapproving look.

"I know you didn't want our help," Jack began. "But you have to admit, we are making a difference. Maybe you guys can pay back the favor when we're done."

Just then a barrage of rapid-fire smoke blasts blinded Jack, and the next thing he knew, he saw Obscuro holding Skerren and Allegra up by their necks.

"There'll be payback," Hypnova said to Jack with a bitter edge in her voice. "You can count on it."

"This ends now!" Obscuro shouted. Skerren dropped his swords at his feet. He looked like he didn't recognize what they were. Allegra looked dazed as well. It appeared that Obscuro now had his ticket out of the glen.

"No!" Jack shouted. "What did you do to them?"

"Nothing yet," Obscuro said. "So far I've only made them forget how to use their powers. I'm walking out of here, Oblivia. Either that or I'll wipe their minds clean forever."

"How do you know I wasn't going to do that myself?" Oblivia asked. "I've done far worse things to punish interlopers for nosing into our affairs. These children are not my concern, and they are not my responsibility. You are."

"Oblivia!" Jack shouted. "You can't let him do it. They're my friends!"

A few tense seconds passed in silence. It was a high-stakes standoff, but Oblivia blinked first. Obscuro almost seemed to be smiling underneath his mask. "Nice try," he told his former leader. "But you won't sacrifice innocents. No matter how stupid they were to interfere."

Oblivia said nothing. Jack realized Obscuro was speaking the truth, and he was at least partially relieved, but his friends weren't out of the woods yet. If anything, they were going in deeper than ever. Obscuro backed away slowly, and then rushed off into the mist, taking Skerren and Allegra with him.

.

12

The Days of No Tomorrow

Forced to let Obscuro go, Oblivia and the other Secreteers quickly turned their attention to the supervillains in the area, hoping to at least prevent their escape. Jack, on the other hand, was still intently focused on the rogue who had disappeared into the murky haze with his friends.

"No," Jack said through gritted teeth. "Not again." He darted into the woods after his friends. He had gotten them into this mess, and he was determined to get them out of it. He couldn't lose them, too . . . not like he'd lost Jazen.

Jack ran through the fog, trying to follow the sound of Obscuro and his friends. Jack heard them nearby and could see a muted light moving through the shimmering fog up ahead. He realized it was coming from Obscuro's glowing eyes, shining in the haze. The glittering light in the faded olive vapors left an illuminated trail for Jack to follow. He ran hard after it, plowing through pricker bushes and blindly rushing across uneven terrain. Eventually he caught up to Obscuro, just as he was about to escape into a cave near the end of the river. The entrance was camouflaged by thick ivy and weeds. Jack found the Rogue Secreteer pushing the cave's leafy cover to one side.

"Obscuro!" Jack called out as he sprang out of the brush and back onto the river's edge. The Secreteer stopped and looked back to find Jack running up behind him. Jack stopped a few feet away from Obscuro and put his hands up in the air. "I'm alone," he said in between gasps of air. "Please . . . let them go."

Obscuro studied Jack for a moment. "Jack Blank," he said. "What are you doing here?"

Jack, still catching his breath, didn't answer right away, but he thought the answer should have been obvious. "I need to talk to you," he said, gasping. "You don't have to do this. You don't have to sell your secrets or run away. We haven't lost yet. We can still stop the Rüstov."

Obscuro looked around to make sure there wasn't anyone else lurking in the mist, and then released his hold on Skerren and Allegra. "No, Jack," he said. "The Rüstov are the future. You of all people should know that. And you know they've already laid the groundwork for that future, deep within Empire City."

"The spyware virus," Jack said. "I know all about it. It's not invincible. There's still hope."

"I wish I could believe that," Obscuro replied.

"It's true," Jack said. "You don't know what I'm doing to stop it."

"What *are* you doing?" Obscuro asked. "It can't be all that much if you're out here chasing after me."

Jack swallowed hard. Obscuro had him there, but he wasn't about to admit that. "I can beat them," Jack said. "But I need your help. Please, tell me what you know. You have to give me a chance to shut down their virus."

"It's not just the spyware virus that concerns me, Jack. It's you. It's the virus in you."

Jack was taken aback. "What?"

"Surely you understand that the Rüstov will never let you go," Obscuro told Jack. "They have more invested in you than you can possibly imagine."

"What are you talking about, let me go? They don't have me."

"Don't they?" Obscuro replied. "I knew about the spyware virus long before I saw what you had in your head, Jack. The virus is just the enemy's plan. Over the years I've seen a thousand evil plots from a thousand supervillains. That's not enough to make me do what I'm doing."

"Then why?" Jack asked.

"Because of what the future holds," Obscuro said. "After what I learned from you? About Revile?" The Rogue Secreteer shook his head as Jack drew in a sharp breath of air and looked over at Skerren and Allegra. Luckily, they were both still too dazed by the effect of Obscuro's memory powers to overhear. "These are the days of no tomorrow," Obscuro told Jack. "The war is already over. There's nothing left to hope for. It's destiny. It's fate."

"I don't believe in fate," Jack said. "I make my own destiny." The words came to Jack quickly; he didn't even think about them. He had been telling himself that every day for a year now. Most days he even believed it.

"Of course," Obscuro said. "The future isn't written yet. Your will is strong. You're not going to succumb to the Rüstov inside you. Is that it?"

"That's right," Jack said.

"Let me ask you this," Obscuro said as he motioned for Jack to come closer. Jack leaned in, and the Rogue Secreteer dropped his voice to a whisper. "Heard any voices lately?"

Jack's stomach dropped. "How do you know about that?"

"I think I've made my point," Obscuro answered. "I'm sorry, Jack, but I'm afraid you're already lost. That means so are we. Please don't think poorly of me. I didn't create this situation; I just happen to be one of the few people who know enough to profit from it. My secrets are only worth something here in this place. I can't sell earth-bound secrets out in space to people who don't care to know them, and I can't very well leave here with nothing. I've grown accustomed to a certain standard of living." Obscuro motioned toward Skerren and Allegra, who were still in a daze. "Your friends are fine," he said. "I was just doing what I had to in order to escape. We all do what we have to. You will too. There's no avoiding this, Jack. You can't fight the future." Obscuro stopped to think, and then turned toward Jack. "Unless . . ."

"Unless what?" Jack asked.

"You could come with me."

Jack took a step back from the Rogue Secreteer in shock. "What?"

"Come with me," Obscuro repeated. "I could hide you from them. From the Rüstov. You know you'll never be safe here. Not really. Come, Jack, now," he said again, this time reaching his hand out toward Jack. "We don't have much time."

Jack didn't entertain Obscuro's offer for a second. "I'm not running from them," he said. "This is the first real home I ever had. I'm not leaving it because of the Rüstov."

"This is just a place, Jack," Obscuro replied. "A home is where your family is." The Rogue Secreteer leaned in close to Jack again. "Don't tell me you wouldn't like to see your father again. . . ."

Jack froze. Obscuro's words hit Jack like a bolt of lightning to the heart. His world completely stopped spinning. "What?" was all he could say.

Obscuro turned his palms up. "I know a great many secrets, Jack Blank. There's a whole universe out there . . . other worlds and more. There are things I could share with you, but you have to come with me."

Obscuro reached out a hand to Jack. Jack wanted to hear more about his family, but he hesitated. "How do I know you're telling the truth?" he asked. "You say my father's still alive? What do you mean see him *again*? Where is he?"

"You have to trust me. Your father's out there," Obscuro said, pointing up at the sky. "I can take you to hi—" He stopped abruptly when an intense spotlight shone down on him from above.

"There!" a voice called out from high in the sky, and Jack looked up to see the *Knightwing* hovering overhead. The ship had separated, and Midknight, Blue, and Ricochet were riding down toward them on the lower half. A glowing Chinese dragon was following close behind with Trea and Zhi on its back. Obscuro grunted angrily as he watched the heroes approach.

"Think about it, Jack," Obscuro said as he backed away slowly. "Just don't take too long. The clock is ticking faster than ever." The Rogue Secreteer dove into the nearby cave opening, leaving Jack dumbfounded. He stuck his head in after him, but saw nothing. Nothing at all. The Rogue Secreteer had vanished.

Jack was still trying to wrap his head around what Obscuro had just told him, when his classmates and the mentor heroes touched down.

"Jack? Jack! What's going on here? Who was that?" Midknight demanded.

"Midknight?" Jack said, confused. "What . . . what are you guys doing here?"

"What are we doing here?" Midknight repeated. "We're tracking down a lead on Speedrazor's gang. What are *you* doing here?"

"I'll tell you what he's doing," Oblivia cut in as she came up behind Jack with a very angry group of Secreteers in tow. "Ruining our best chance to end the Rogue Secreteer's madness!" The matriarch of the Clandestine Order was absolutely livid. Jack looked again at the cave Obscuro had escaped into. He frowned. Something about the cave felt off. Before he could put his finger on what it was, Skerren and Allegra came out of their Secreteer-induced trances and immediately barraged everyone with questions.

"Why are you all here?" Skerren asked, looking around at Midknight and the others. "What happened? Where's Obscuro?"

"Obscuro?" Ricochet exclaimed. "The Rogue Secreteer? That was him?"

"Yes," Oblivia said curtly. "And thanks to your side-kicks, he got away."

"Got away?" Skerren cried. "When? What's going on? How did we get out here?" He was getting ready to blow at any minute. Allegra was a bit more composed.

"Jack," Allegra said, placing a hand on his shoulder. "What happened?"

"Are you okay?" Blue asked. "Jack, what was he saying to you before we got down here? Before he took off?"

Everyone was talking at once. Jack was overwhelmed. Just getting the words out of his mouth was going to be a struggle; he could hardly believe them himself. But he wanted to believe. He wanted to more than anything.

"He said," Jack began, finding his voice at last. "He said he knows where my father is. He said he can take me to him."

"Your *father?*" Blue replied. "Really?"

Jack nodded and looked over the faces of the many Secreteers who kept arriving on the scene one after the other. Oblivia, Hypnova, and all the other members of the Clandestine Order were furious, and the fact of the matter was they had every right be.

"That's it?" Skerren asked. "*That's* what you talked about? You could have asked him anything, and you asked him about your father?"

"I didn't ask him," Jack said. "He just told me. He didn't even . . ." Jack trailed off midsentence. His head was all over the place. "Hypnova, if Obscuro knows secrets about my father, doesn't that mean you know them too?"

"You can't be serious," Hypnova shot back. "Do you honestly think I'm going to tell you anything now? After what you've done? Do you have *any* concept of the position your actions here tonight have put me in?"

"Jack. Focus," Midknight said. "This information about your father is interesting, but the Obscuro situation is important. What are you doing out here? What's got you three hunting the Rogue Secreteer through the Outlands by yourselves?"

Jack tried his best to look innocent. "What do you mean?" he asked. "You said we had to take on solo missions."

"Don't play games, Jack," Midknight countered. "Something else is going on here, I can tell. What did Obscuro say to you? What do you know about this Secreteer business that we don't?"

Jack stared up at the old vigilante detective's penetrating eyes. He had to hand it to Midknight, the man didn't miss a thing. He was a real pro. Blue, Ricochet, Trea, and Zhi all started looking at Jack the same way, wondering what he wasn't telling them.

"What's Obscuro scared of?" Ricochet asked. "Did he say?"

Jack shook his head. He wished Stendeval were there to help with this.

"Jack, just tell them," Allegra said. Jack felt his head snap around to look at her. Allegra didn't know what she was asking. She didn't know what Obscuro had just said about his future.

"What is this, Jack?" Blue asked. "Tell us what?"

Jack had a hard time looking Blue in the eye. This wasn't how he wanted to tell Blue about Jazen. He didn't know how on earth he was going to tell everyone what Obscuro had just said about Revile.

"It's okay," Allegra insisted. "Just tell them about the virus, Jack. We have to."

Jack thought for a moment. Allegra couldn't have known it, but she'd just given him an idea. *Just tell them about the virus,* he thought. He looked up at his friends' surprised and expectant faces. They were his friends. He could trust them with that much. He'd have to. He certainly had to tell them something now. Jack looked at the Secreteers. They already knew everything, but they were sworn to secrecy. They wouldn't say anything if Jack happened to leave part of the story out.

"Okay," Jack said to Midknight and the others. "But you have to promise not to tell anyone else." One by one Midknight, Blue, Ricochet, Trea, and Zhi all agreed to Jack's terms, but Blue looked especially disappointed. "If this gets out," Jack said, "the whole city's going to be at risk. Even more than it is now."

"I don't like this, Jack," Blue said. "I told you how I feel about secrets."

"I know, Blue," Jack said. "I didn't have any choice. Trust me, you'll understand after you hear what I have to say." Jack cleared his throat and looked up at his friend and mentor. "I hope you'll understand."

After not talking to anyone about the spyware virus for more than a year, Jack was about to tell the story for the second time that day. He opened his mouth and started talking. It wasn't any easier the second time around.

CHAPTER

13

The Lost Boy

The next morning Jack woke up to find Stendeval sitting in his living room reading a copy of Cognito's local paper, the *Cipher*.

"Good morning, Jack." Stendeval smiled, looking up from the newspaper. "I hope you don't mind, I let myself in. I didn't want to wake you. I understand you had something of an eventful evening last night."

Still groggy, Jack ran a hand through his messy hair and squinted at Stendeval. "Yeah, you could say that," he said after a moment. He went to the refrigerator and took out a pitcher of juice that glowed with a bright electric-blue light. "What's going on? Is something wrong?" he asked. As Jack gulped down his juice, he realized what a ridiculous question that was. "You know . . . ," he added. "Other than the fact that the Rüstov are coming back in three days and we're all going to die."

Stendeval didn't answer right away. An article on the front page of the paper had all his attention. When he was finished reading, he frowned and folded the paper in half. "You should read this."

Jack winced. "Do I have to? I was actually going to try and avoid the news today. The other night I stayed up watching the NewsNets for hours. Didn't learn anything and just ended up making myself crazy."

Stendeval got up out of his seat. "I'm afraid it can't be helped," he said, bringing the paper over. "I can't promise this won't add to your troubles, but at the very least you'll learn something new."

Jack put his glass down and leaned on the counter. "I'm afraid to look," he said as he took the paper from Stendeval. He dropped it onto the kitchen counter a few feet away from him like it was a three-day-old piece of fish.

Stendeval slid the paper back across the countertop toward Jack. "Ignorance and avoidance make poor solutions to any problem," he said. "Better that you should know what's going on and arm yourself with information. As a highly trained military unit I once fought alongside used to say, knowing is half the battle."

"Got it," Jack grumbled. "Thanks." More good advice from Stendeval's peers in the impossible-role-model club. That was *exactly* what he wanted to hear.

Jack opened up the paper with a loud flap and saw articles written in every direction imaginable: top to bottom, bottom to top, right to left, and left to right. There were even articles written diagonally, and all of them were filled with jumbled letters that were splattered across the page in nonsensical gibberish.

"How's today's riddle?" Jack asked. "Is it a hard one?"

"It's fitting," was all Stendeval said in reply.

Fitting? Jack thought. That was an odd thing to say. He turned back to the front page and read the one line of text that was laid out in proper order: the daily riddle. That was what made the *Cipher* such a one-of-a-kind publication. It wasn't enough just to buy Cognito's local paper—you had to solve the daily riddle to unscramble its stories. There was no other way to make the paper give up the news of the day. Sometimes they were clever riddles, like: What falls but never breaks, and breaks but never falls? (Night and day.) Sometimes they were tricky riddles, like: Who can jump higher than the mountains? (Everyone. Mountains can't jump.) And sometimes they were logic-game riddles, like: The boy is afraid to go home because the man in the mask is there. Why? (The boy is playing baseball. The man in the mask is the catcher.)

Today the riddle was a logic riddle. When Jack read it, he saw that Stendeval was right on the money. It was fitting. A little too fitting, in fact.

A judge tells an accused boy,
"If you lie, we will hang you.
If you tell the truth, we will shoot you."
What can he say to save himself?

Jack put down the paper and looked at Stendeval. "What is this, some kind of joke?"

Stendeval shook his head. "Riddles are often humorous, but I don't think this one is meant to be. Think about it," he said. "The answer's right there in front of you."

Jack leaned over the paper and looked back down at the riddle. He turned the question over in his head a few times, but he couldn't think of anything at all. "The boy can say, 'I'm taking the Rogue Secreteer up on his offer and getting the heck out of here.'"

Stendeval peered over at the paper to see if the letters had begun moving themselves into the correct order. "I don't think that's the answer, Jack," Stendeval said without cracking a smile.

"You know he offered to take me with him, right?" Jack asked. "He said he could take me to see my father."

"I know," Stendeval said. "I spoke to Midknight after he brought you and the others home. He also said you turned Obscuro down. You're not changing your mind, I hope."

"Don't worry," Jack told Stendeval. "I'm not going anywhere. Not yet anyway."

Stendeval appeared relieved. "Good. How did Blue take the news about Jazen and the virus?"

Jack just stared down at the paper. "Not well," he said.

Stendeval nodded but didn't say anything. There was nothing to say about that.

Jack gave the paper's riddle one more try, but it was no use. His head was overloaded from what Obscuro had told him the night before, and he was no closer to solving the *Cipher's* conundrum than he was his own. The riddle of the day felt like the same question Jack had been asking himself for the better part of a year, and he was tired of searching for the answer. He pushed the paper away in frustration and told Stendeval, "I give up. You tell me what the boy says, because I obviously don't know. If I did, I would have said it a long time ago."

Stendeval sighed heavily at Jack's defeated tone. "The boy can tell the judge, 'You are going to hang me.'"

Jack sat motionless at the table, looking at Stendeval. At most, he might have raised an eyebrow. "Not really seeing how that helps the situation."

"Think about it," Stendeval said again. "If they hang him, he told the truth. They should have shot him. If they shoot him, he lied. They should have hung him." Stendeval sat back in his chair and waved a hand as if to say "There you have it."

The letters and words in each article began rearranging themselves, dancing across the pages and spinning back into a proper, legible order. Stendeval watched them as they worked, looking quite amused. Jack always liked watching the *Cipher*'s letters move back into place, especially since they were printed with real ink on real paper, but he didn't share his teacher's appreciation for the riddle's so-called solution.

"I still don't get it. How does that help the boy?" Jack asked.

Stendeval put his hands up. "He leaves the judge with no options. Based on the rules that he himself set up, the judge can enforce neither punishment. He's stuck in an infinite loop." Stendeval smiled. "The boy's managed to lie and tell the truth at the same time. He's beaten him at his own game."

Jack still wasn't clear on how that helped the boy in the riddle. "Sounds like a *great* plan," he told Stendeval. He looked down at the unscrambled story on page one and frowned. "I think I like my solution better."

It wasn't hard to see why. The *Cipher*'s front-page headline read, JONAS SMART OFFERS ROGUE SECRETEER FIFTY

MILLION CREDITS FOR JACK BLANK'S SECRETS. Jack felt like a spider was crawling up his back as he leaned forward to read the story on page one:

FORMER CIRCLEMAN MAKES BID TO SAVE EMPIRE CITY

By Drack Hackman

(on special assignment for the *Cipher*)

This morning Jonas Smart called out Obscuro, the Rogue Secreteer, urging him to stop selling secrets to supervillains in the shadows and come forward with what he knows about the looming Rüstov threat. It's a claim the former Circleman is backing up with his wallet, offering fifty million credits for information he believes is vital to the Imagine Nation's defense. With just three days left until the Rüstov strike, has Empire City finally found the savior it so desperately needs?

"If the rogue's only concern is money, I still have plenty of that," Jonas Smart said in a statement outside his SmartCorp offices. "I'll gladly pay whatever it takes to learn the truth about this Rüstov threat." When asked what brought on this bold move, and what Jack Blank's connection to the Rüstov invaders might be, Smart revealed that his SmarterNet project had intercepted a new, chilling transmission from the Rüstov agent Glave (translated from the Rüstov language below):

"Glave to command. Glave to command. Report: Operation remains on schedule. Making use of all available Left-Behind operatives, and have established contact with Khalix. In three days the infinite war will return to Earth. The Lost Boy will fulfill his destiny. Long live the empire. Glave out."

This morning in an exclusive interview, Jonas Smart made it clear exactly who he believes "the Lost Boy" to be, and this reporter is inclined to agree with him. "Whatever it is that's coming, Jack Blank is involved, and I want to know how," Smart said. "For the last year the Inner Circle has held this boy up as a hero while deliberately dismantling security provisions that once kept the Imagine Nation safe. I may not be Circleman of Hightown any longer, but I've never stopped working for the people of this city. Rest assured, all of you, if your elected officials on the Inner Circle won't protect you ... I will."

With a second Rüstov invasion mere days away, it's clear that at least one citizen of the Imagine Nation is doing everything he can to fight back. Jonas Smart has just put the ball squarely in Obscuro's court. If the Rogue Secreteer is still on our team, this is his chance to prove it.

Once Jack's eyes reached the bottom of the page, he scanned the article again, rereading the worst parts. He couldn't take his eyes off the paper. He felt dizzy with dread, like the walls of his apartment were closing in on him. If this kind of talk kept up, Jack really was going to have to take Obscuro up on his offer and grab a seat on his spaceship out of town. The article read like a SmartCorp press release. Jack had come to expect that from the biased and dogmatic SmartNews broadcasts, but this was the *Cipher*. Jack could hardly believe his own eyes. Then he noticed the word ADVERTISEMENT printed in tiny letters way up at the top of the page.

"Wait a minute," Jack began. "This isn't an article. . . . It's an ad. No wonder Hackman was the reporter!" Jack shook his head. "Special assignment . . . yeah, right," he said, and grunted. Jack looked up at Stendeval and slapped the paper with the back of his fingertips. "The *Cipher* sold the front page to Jonas Smart."

"Not just the *Cipher*," Stendeval said. "All the city papers. The *Datafeed*, the *King's Herald*, the *Comet*, the *Ninja Scroll* . . ."

"The *Empirical*, too, I bet," Jack guessed, naming the Hightown major daily. "They probably ran it for free. That's all I need. Every paper in the city offering fifty million credits for what I know." Jack grimaced. "Obscuro just wants money—he'll jump at that. Once Smart finds out about Revile and the virus, he'll put it out in every paper. He'll tell the story his way, just like this, and turn the whole city against me again," Jack told Stendeval. "The worst part is, he's right," Jack added. "I *am* the Lost Boy. Obscuro said so."

"What are you talking about?" Stendeval asked. "Midknight didn't mention—"

"Midknight told you everything *he* knows," Jack said. "I didn't tell him everything *I* know. Obscuro's not worried about the virus. He's worried about me. He knows all about Revile and the future. He says the virus is just how we get there."

"Jack, that's fantastic," Stendeval said.

Jack's face contorted. "How is that fantastic?"

Stendeval raised his hand as if the answer were a given. "It tells us that Obscuro's concerns about the Rüstov are misplaced," Stendeval replied. "They're not based on facts about the viral threat, but rather on irrational fears about one possible future. It tells us the virus is beatable."

"What if Revile is more than just a possible future?" Jack asked. "Maybe Obscuro is right and the virus is just one more thing I can't stop before I lose control."

"You're not losing control, Jack."

"Maybe I am. I don't know," Jack said. "I *should* be able to beat this virus, Stendeval. I should be done by now. My powers are way stronger now than back when I started. I know a ton about machines. . . . I'm even building my own inventions, but I don't know if I can do this anymore. All of a sudden I'm hearing voices, and I just found out I'm sharing memories with my parasite! That wasn't the case before I woke it up." Jack shook his head. "Now Smart comes out with this," he said, holding up the paper. "I should have just told them about Revile last night. If Smart comes out with that first, it's going to look like I really am the sleeper agent he always said I was. . . . It's gonna look like I kept quiet about the virus because I want to help the Rüstov with their plan."

"That's precisely why you can't tell anyone about Revile yet," Stendeval said. "Everything you're saying right now is true. What's also true is that you are the single best chance we have of stopping this virus before it's too late. We can't afford to lose you, Jack. There's a reason I kept the truth about Revile hidden so long, even from you. If people find out about your connection to Revile now, in this climate . . ."

"But what if Smart tells everyone about me before we can stop the virus?"

Stendeval shook his head. "People will be scared either way. You need to give yourself every opportunity to finish the cure-code before that happens."

Jack nodded. Stendeval was right. He couldn't go public with his connection to Revile any more than he could with the spyware virus. Jack was just like the Mechas. If people knew the truth, they would think he was dangerous and that he couldn't control himself, even if it wasn't his fault.

"I know this isn't fair to you," Stendeval told Jack. "It's my nature to be mysterious, not yours." He put his hand on Jack's shoulder. "Unfortunately, sometimes people aren't ready for the truth, and we don't have any choice but to keep it from them."

"How do you know when they're ready?" Jack asked.

Stendeval put up his hands. "You just know."

There was a knock at the door. "That'll be Trea," Jack said. "Last night I told her how to get here. She's going to help me work on the virus today. Which is good, because I don't know how I'm going to focus on it now. I can hardly bring myself to go into the lab as it is."

"Trea won't be alone," Stendeval said. "The lady Virtua is coming with her to check on your progress. That's the other reason I'm here this morning."

Jack spun his head around to look at Stendeval. "You told Virtua about the virus?"

Stendeval nodded. "My fellow Circlemen and I have yet to turn up anything in our search for Glave. I told you earlier, we no longer have the luxury of absolute secrecy."

Jack was already opening up the door. Stendeval's logic made sense, but Jack wished he'd at least given him a heads-up about it. "How did she take it?" he asked.

The door swung open all the way, and Virtua's image-caster, Projo, whizzed in. The floating orb projected

Virtua's image into the room next to all three Treas, who followed Projo inside one after the other. The Circle-woman looked down at Jack with a stern face.

"Not well," Stendeval said. "Not well."

CHAPTER

14

Lab Partners

Trea's supersmart version, T1, looked around at Jack's filthy laboratory. The old fast-food containers that Allegra had turned her nose up at a day earlier were still there. "Seriously. Gross," she decided. "This big secret Smart is after . . . ," T1 said, turning to Jack, "is it the virus you told us about last night, or the fact that you have no sense of smell?"

T3, Trea's wild-card self dared to look inside one of the ancient Styrofoam containers, and gagged. "Ughhk!" She was blinking and rubbing her eyes like her retinas were on fire. "Honestly, how do you get any work done down here?"

"I was just wondering the same thing," Virtua said, clearly not encouraged by the state of Jack's lab. "You really have made a mess of things, haven't you, Jack?" From her tone of voice it was clear she was talking about more than just the mess in Jack's workshop.

"I'm working on it," Jack said. "It's not easy. I've been trying to clean this up all year."

"Have you?" Virtua asked. She drifted around the room, looking over the many unfinished side projects and random inventions that were strewn about the lab. There were things like Nuclear Knuckles, Air Grabbers, Magna Lock boots, and more. "Tell me, which one of these wondrous devices is the one that's going to save my people?"

Jack grimaced. "None of them," he admitted. "That doesn't mean I haven't been working on the cure-code, though. I work on these when I'm blocked or out of ideas."

Virtua cast a sideways glance at Projo, who squawked out a sharp beep in reply.

"I once met a talented puppeteer who said he had no idea where ideas came from, but when he was working well, they simply appeared," Stendeval told Virtua. "It's just a matter of figuring out how to receive the ideas that are waiting to be heard."

Virtua looked at Stendeval. "What's your point?" she asked.

"We're not here to judge Jack's creative process . . . just the results," Stendeval replied. "You can't force inspiration. Lightning strikes the earth in its own time."

"That's the problem, isn't it?" Virtua replied, clearly in no mood for the old Circleman's wit and wisdom. "There *aren't* any results as far as I can see, and we don't have time to wait for the thunderbolt to come. We wouldn't need to force anything if you two hadn't kept the virus to yourselves. We could have had Empire City's brightest minds working on a cure all year long."

"Right, like Jonas Smart!" the dim-witted T2 said. She was serious, too.

T1 shook her head, embarrassed by her physically strong but mentally weak side. Jack suppressed a smile. T2 probably didn't know it, but she'd just done more to justify his silence with four words than he could have done with a two-hour speech.

229

"We wanted to cure the virus before we came forward," Stendeval told Virtua, driving the point home. "I think you know that Empire City's brightest mind would have used this information to advance a very different agenda."

Virtua continued to float around, inspecting the lab and looking cross. "You could have told me at least," she said. "Both of you."

"That would have put you in the position of having to lie about the virus," Stendeval replied. He shook his head. "I stand by my decision. I wouldn't have told you anything at all if it weren't for Glave's deadline."

"It's not that we didn't trust you, Virtua," Jack said, trying to sound a little more apologetic than Stendeval. "It's just that I couldn't tell who was infected and who wasn't. We were worried you couldn't trust yourselves."

Virtua scoffed. "I've heard that argument before," she said.

Jack was stung by the truth of Virtua's words. He really was in the exact same boat as the Mechas. The only difference was that Virtua had publicly backed him up when other people had said the same thing about him.

"How about now?" T1 asked Jack. "Can you tell who is infected and who isn't?"

"Yes and no," Jack said. "Sometimes I can tell virus code from regular code, but not always. I *can* recognize a corrupted system if it's transmitting, though. Transmissions to Rüstov command look like glitches. You don't have to worry. So far it looks like Circlewoman Virtua is clean."

"So far!" Virtua repeated. "Wonderful!" She looked at Projo and shook her head. Her image-caster replied with a series of indignant beeps. "Let me be sure I understand this correctly," Virtua said to Jack after Projo had finished talking. "The Rüstov have a secret virus that allows them to take control of Mecha systems, and you've spent the last year working to stop it."

Jack nodded. "That's right."

"And this . . . *this* is the secret that convinced Obscuro to turn rogue?" Virtua asked.

Jack nodded again. *It's one of the secrets*, he thought.

Virtua crossed her arms, her image flickering. "Your progress on the cure-code must be astounding," she said.

"Virtua," Stendeval said. "That is not fair."

"It's okay, Stendeval," Jack said. More and more he was coming to understand that concepts like fair and unfair didn't count for much. Virtua probably knew that better than most. "I'm working on a test subject," he said. "It's back this way. I'll show you." Jack hit a button on the wall behind him, and the wall slid back to reveal another room. In that room was a long metal box on what appeared to be an operating table. "That's it," Jack said. "The virus-free prototype."

Stendeval, Virtua, and the three Treas followed Jack into the lab's hidden room.

"What's it doing in here?" T1 asked Jack, looking around at the previously concealed portion of Jack's lab.

"And why does this room smell even worse than the other one?" T3 added, waving her hand in front of her nose.

Jack ignored T3's fussiness. "I have to keep the prototype sealed off until I'm ready to test it," he said. "I can't risk it getting contaminated by the spyware virus before then. I don't know how the virus spreads. I don't think it's gone Wi-Fi, but I can't chance it. The prototype's safe in there, though. I designed that box myself. No signal gets in or out of the coffin."

"The coffin?" Virtua asked.

"That's what I call it," Jack said. "It's a dead zone. When I'm ready, we'll open it up, and hopefully the cure-code will work. If not, I've got a fail-safe backup just in case." Jack patted his hand down on a ramshackle contraption with a small satellite dish and a large red button. A strip of masking tape was stuck to the base with the letters EMP written on it in black marker.

Projo beeped and shot over to the lab door, getting as far away from the fail-safe machine as possible. Projo's trepidation didn't go unnoticed by T2. "What does 'EMP' stand for?" she asked Jack.

"Electromagnetic pulse," T1 answered. "If Jack's cure-code fails and the test subject is still infected, he can hit that button and fry it."

"Fry it?" T3 asked.

"As in beyond repair," T1 replied.

Projo zoomed back in and unleashed another barrage of angry beeps and whirring noises, right in Jack's face. Jack let him finish, resisting the urge to swat the feisty little Mecha away.

"Isn't that it, then?" T2 asked. "Can't we just light that

pulse across the city and fry the virus everywhere, all at once?"

"What about my people?" Virtua asked. "Do you intend to fry them, too?"

"This is exactly why I never said anything," Jack cut in. "This is why I did what I did. I kept it all quiet to protect the Mechas."

"Protect us?" Virtua exclaimed. "What you've protected is the Rüstov's secrets. You've made me an accomplice to their plans!" she argued. "My circuits! Jonas has been right all this time. We *have* been letting the Rüstov threat flourish." Jack had never seen Virtua so upset.

"If the Mechas are infected, who protects us from *them?*" T2 asked.

T1 gave her muscle-brained side a shove. "Stop it," she said.

"What did I say?" T2 asked.

"Just be quiet," T1 replied. "You're embarrassing us."

"Where do you stand on a cure, Jack?" Virtua asked.

"I'm close," Jack said. "But I'm not there yet. That's why Trea's here, to help me finish. I didn't mean to make things worse," Jack told Virtua. "I was just trying to protect your people from Smart while I worked out a cure."

"And yet your decision has left me trapped between two executioners," Virtua replied. "The Rüstov on one hand, and Jonas Smart on the other. I'm sorry, but I have to leave. I have the answers that I came here for. Now I have a few decisions of my own to make," Virtua said. "Good day, all of you. Projo, come!" she barked, and blinked out of sight. Projo whipped out of the room and up the stairs, leaving behind only awkward silence and tension.

"Well, that went great," Jack said after Virtua was gone.

"Don't worry, Jack," T1 said. "I'm here now, and I haven't met a computer code I couldn't hack my way around. Let's see what you've done so far."

"We're going to have to do something about this work space first," T3 said, looking around at the mess.

"Don't mind her," T2 said to Jack. "T3 is a bit of a neat freak this morning."

"Really," Jack said. "I hadn't noticed."

Stendeval left Jack and the three Treas to work on the virus. An hour later T1 was still going through Jack's notes while he waited. T3 passed the time organizing things around the lab, and T2 helped. Jack had expected to start by going over the latest version of his cure-code with the supersmart T1, but she didn't want to talk to him about that until she was completely caught up on all his earlier work. She buried her nose in Jack's notebooks, completely ignoring him. That gave Jack plenty of time to think about what had happened to him the last time he'd been working down in his lab. He didn't like being down there one bit, and just in case his parasite's awakening hadn't brought enough stress to the table, now he had Smart's offer to the Rogue Secreteer to worry about. Every now and then Trea would laugh to herself as she read through his binders, writing in the margins. "Oh, this is all wrong," she muttered, crossing out entire pages with a red pen. It was absolutely driving Jack up a wall.

"What is it?" Jack asked, getting fed up. "What's wrong?"

"I'll show you later," T1 said without looking up. "I want to read through everything you've already tried so we're not duplicating efforts here. The good news is, while I'm going over your work, I should be able to correct all your earlier mistakes."

Jack's back stiffened. "What makes you so sure I made mistakes?" he asked. "You haven't even asked me anything about my work."

"She doesn't need to," T3 replied. "She's supersmart."

"Thank you, T3." T1 smiled. "Don't worry, Jack. I'll figure this out," she said. "You can help too, though," she added, smiling. "Maybe you can get me a drink or something. How's that?"

Jack frowned. "A drink?" he repeated. "Are you kidding?" He didn't like what was apparently Trea's impression of her role in this project, riding in on a white horse to save the day and do what he couldn't. Jack would have been fine with her finishing the whole thing by herself, but Trea's attitude, or T1's attitude, about the whole thing was so irritating. "You and I are the only ones here who know how to do this stuff, and you want me to go get drinks?" Jack asked.

"I'd be further along if this place weren't so disorganized," the supersmart Trea replied. "It's more efficient to use SmartPaper, you know."

Jack shook his head. SmartPaper was the tangible digital paper invented by Jonas Smart. It was a Hard-Light

Holo projection as thin as regular paper, but each sheet had all the functionality of a laptop computer. "I don't use any SmartCorp products if I can help it," Jack told T1. "I don't trust them."

The three Treas rolled their eyes at one another. "Someone has trust issues," T1 said, and then went back to scribbling comments in Jack's notebooks.

"You do have a lot of secrets," T3 agreed. "A secret project you work on in a secret box in a secret room?"

T2 shook her head as if she were saying "tsk-tsk-tsk." "I don't know how you keep it all straight," she said. "I couldn't do it."

It took Jack a second to decide which Trea he was supposed to answer first. Talking to the three of them at once was never easy. "That room isn't a secret," he said to T3. "It's a dead zone, like the coffin. I have to take the prototype out of the box to work on it, don't I? I seal off the room first so that I don't contaminate my work."

"Jack. Relax," T1 said. "She was just making an observation. You don't have to get defensive. Look at him, he's getting defensive."

"He is," T2 said.

"Very defensive," T3 agreed.

"All right, stop it," Jack said. The three Treas were giving him a headache. "This isn't working for me. Can you pull yourself together?" he asked. "It's really distracting to try and talk to you like this."

The three Treas looked at one another and shrugged. T1 marked her place in Jack's notes and closed the binder. "I suppose we could take a little break," she said.

"Promise me you'll finish cleaning up this lab after I'm gone," the ultrafastidious T3 told the others. T1 and T2 agreed to follow through on the cleanup, before zipping back into one, an action that made a sound like air being sucked into a vacuum. Jack was relieved. It was really just Trea's smart side that he found so grating. That side was arrogant and severe with no social graces whatsoever. It wasn't an issue when her three sides were combined, but when she was split up . . . it was no wonder Chi was always preaching balance in her School of Thought lessons. A Trea divided against herself was something Jack could not stand.

Still, Jack couldn't deny he needed Trea's help. That

much was obvious as he scanned through what she'd written on his notes, while she went upstairs to get her own drink. The notes she was reading through were from another time, back when Jack had been sure he'd crack the cure-code any day. It seemed like so long ago that he had written them. What little Trea had done that afternoon looked better than what he'd done all month. Maybe T1's ego wasn't so misplaced, Jack thought. He couldn't deny he was burned-out on the project. Maybe a fresh set of eyes was exactly what the job needed.

"What we need is more information about the Rüstov to help us fight this virus," Trea told Jack when she came back downstairs. "I was wondering, could we study your infection somehow?"

"What, you want to dissect me?" Jack asked, joking around. "I've already been down that road with Jonas Smart, you know."

Trea laughed. "No, nothing like that. I thought it was something you could do. You know, with your powers. Your parasite is a living machine—you could use your powers to try and connect with it. You could learn from it."

"No," Jack said instantly. "I can't do that."

"Can't or won't?" Trea asked. "I haven't come across anything like that in your notes yet."

"It wouldn't be in my notes," Jack said. "Just forget it, okay, Trea? I don't want to talk about it. Not my favorite subject, you know?"

Trea furrowed her brow. "This from the guy who doesn't have a lot of secrets." Trea paused to gulp down a glowing green energy drink. "Fine. Have it your way, but we're going to need to get something else to work off of. We need a Rüstov. We need to get a Left-Behind or some other kind of Rüstov tech to compare against all this standard Mecha tech you have."

"No argument here," Jack said. "But where are we going to get a Left-Behind?"

"Wrekzaw Isle?" Trea suggested.

"I'm not going back there," Jack said. That was where he'd left Revile, burning in the heart of an Infinite Warp Core engine. His future self was still there, melting and reforming, over and over. Jack didn't want to chance running into him again. For all Jack knew, showing up on

Wrekzaw with his recently revitalized parasite might just inspire Revile to work harder on finding a way out.

"Where else are we going to look?" Trea asked.

Jack rubbed the back of his neck, thinking. "Smart used to have pieces of Left-Behinds all over his lab, but that's no good either," he said. "He'd never share that stuff with me, and I'm not about to break back into SmartTower to get at it. Even if I wanted to, these days he's got power nullifiers all over that building. My powers cut out every time I walk past the place."

"It's too bad we can't work with Smart," Trea said. "I don't like him any more than you do, but you have to admit he *is* brilliant. He's forgotten more about chasing down the Rüstov than you or I will ever know. If we were able to join forces with him, I'm sure we'd figure this out. We'd at least have access to the data we need for our work."

"We can't trust Smart with our work," Jack replied. "You know what he'd do with this information just as well as I do. His priority wouldn't be solving the problem. It would be solving *his* problem of how to get back on top. It's not an option, Trea."

"Jack, I'm not suggesting—"

"And another thing," Jack interrupted, pointing a finger at Trea. "I don't trust this SmarterNet he's using to 'chase down the Rüstov.' I mean, really, what does it do? Why won't he say? How come no one's asking about that? Smart's got his secrets just like everyone else, you can count on it. He's just better at hiding them than I am."

Trea shook her head, not even trying to argue with Jack about Smart. "If you would stop for a second and *listen*," she told Jack, "you'd realize I'm not talking about actually working with Smart. I'm just saying it's too bad we can't. It's a wasted opportunity, that's all I'm saying. I'm not foolish enough to expect a fair shake from a man who kidnapped Mechas and kept them in a secret prison."

"Secret prison?" Jack repeated as an idea that was stuck all the way in the back of his brain suddenly screamed out for attention. "Trea, that's it!" he said. "That's where we'll find our Left-Behind!"

"What are you talking about?" Trea asked. "Smart's secret prison? Jack, they call it that for a reason. No one knows where it is."

"I think I might," Jack said with growing enthusiasm. "Yeah, I think I've got a pretty good idea, actually." Jack fired up a holo-screen on one of his computers and started scrolling through maps of the Imagine Nation until he found what he was looking for. "There," he said. "There's gotta be something out there for us. Smart must have had some Rüstov locked up in that prison too. It can't have been *all* Mechas, right?" Jack asked.

Trea put her hands up. "How should I know? If you really think you know where it is, let's go find out. How are we getting there?"

"Not we," Jack told Trea. "Me. You gotta split back up and keep working on those notes. We've gotta work this from a couple different angles."

"Jack, I'm not staying here while you run off looking for some abandoned prison on your own. What if you find it and there *are* Rüstov in there? Real, live, hostile Rüstov? You can't go in there alone."

"I won't," Jack told Trea. "I'm never alone."

"Right," Trea said. "You, Skerren, and Allegra . . . you're like the Three Musketeers, aren't you?"

Jack looked over at the operating table where he'd tried reaching out to his parasite a week ago. "Yeah," he replied. "That's it. I'll take Skerren and Allegra with me." Although that wasn't what he had originally meant at all.

CHAPTER

15

Family Business

By lunchtime Jack, Skerren, and Allegra were speeding across the plains of the Imagine Nation on Allegra's open AirSkimmer. The flying raft moved almost twice as fast as Hypnova's ship and got them to their destination in nearly half the time. It wasn't long before Jack looked down over the railing and saw mist-covered treetops spread out far and wide. They were back in the skies over Gravenmurk Glen.

"That way," Jack said, pointing toward the back end of the woods and the cliffs on the island's north face.

Homing in on the machine signal he'd picked up in the cave the night before, Jack was leading the group back to the same place where Obscuro had escaped, and possibly somewhere new as well: Jonas Smart's secret prison.

"You don't think he'll still be there, do you?" Allegra asked.

"Who, Obscuro?" Jack said. "No. He hasn't stayed hidden this long by being careless. Even if he was using that cave as a hideout instead of just an escape route, he would have had to abandon it after last night."

"You and Obscuro really just talked about your father last night?" Skerren asked. "That's all?"

Jack cleared his throat and looked out over the railing. This was the second time Skerren was asking him that. "Pretty much," he said.

"Pretty much?" Skerren pressed. "What does that mean?"

Jack turned to face his friend. "Where's this coming from, Skerren? You don't trust me anymore? Don't tell me Smart's ads are getting to you already."

Skerren shrugged. "It's not just that," he replied. "There's that Glave message about 'the Lost Boy' that went out this morning too. You can't blame me for being a little suspicious. You have been lying to us all for a year now."

"I never lied to you guys," Jack said. "I just didn't tell you everything."

"What's the difference?" Skerren asked.

"There's a big difference," Jack claimed.

Skerren's eyes narrowed, examining Jack like he was trying to spot something out of place. "Just tell me," he said. "Is this it? Is this the only secret you were keeping from us?"

Jack could feel Skerren's righteous eyes boring into his head like lasers. He didn't want to lie, but everything Stendeval had said earlier that morning was still true. Jonas Smart's news machine was reawakening people's old fears about him. Jack couldn't tell anyone the whole story just yet. Not even his friends.

"Give it a rest, Skerren," Allegra said. "Jack wouldn't keep anything else from us now. Glave's attack deadline is too close to take any chances."

"Thanks, Allegra," Jack said. "I appreciate that." Allegra nodded like it was no big deal. Jack cleared his throat again and walked to the front of the AirSkimmer.

"We're here, guys. Bring us down over there, Allegra. Just past the clearing in the trees up ahead."

"I see it," Allegra said. "Here we go, boys. And, Sker-ren?" she said, turning her head. "Try not to cut any trees down this time around."

Allegra landed the ship on the ridge overlooking the river. They'd have to walk from there. The woods looked a lot less scary in the daytime. The fact that a horde of Gravens wasn't trying to drag Jack and his friends down into the earth didn't hurt, either. As Jack led Skerren and Allegra back to the spot where Obscuro had vanished, he also walked them through the theory that brought them back to Gravenmurk Glen in the first place.

"When Trea mentioned the secret prison this morn-ing, it all clicked," Jack explained as he followed the river through the woods. "It got me thinking about how when Obscuro got away, I felt something funny in that cave he ducked into. Machine signals. They came out of nowhere, like someone just flipped a switch. We were in the middle of the forest with no machines anywhere, so at first I thought it was just the *Knightwing* pulling in overhead."

"How do you know it wasn't the *Knightwing*?" Skerren asked.

"Because I should have felt that ship coming half a mile away," Jack replied. "I think someone *did* flip a switch. There's no way I would have missed it otherwise."

"You really think someone was using power nullifiers out here that night?" Allegra asked Jack.

"Not just anyone," Jack said. "Smart. Trust me, I've been hit with those things enough times to know. I didn't put it together at the time because I was still in shock over what Obscuro said about my father, but it felt just like it does when I walk past SmartTower. My powers cut out, and then they come flooding back later, when I get far enough away. Smart puts those nullifiers on all his stuff nowadays. . . . He'd definitely put them on his secret prison."

"Here's the part I don't get," Skerren said. "You think Obscuro escaped through there, but stopped to shut off the power nullifiers on his way out? Why would he do that?"

"Don't ask me," Jack replied. "Maybe it was an accident. He could've been trying to turn on a light, for all I know. Or maybe they just shorted out. We'll have to see."

"That we will," Skerren replied, gently pushing a bothersome thorn bush from his path as he hiked along. "We'll find out soon enough. Smart's secret prison *has* been rumored to be hidden somewhere in the Outlands, so I suppose it's possible. It's just too bad you didn't think of this last night when it would have made a difference."

Jack grunted as a prickly branch whipped him in the face. "Give me a break, Skerren," he said. "Like I said, I wasn't exactly thinking straight when this all went down."

It was the understatement to end all understatements. "Not thinking straight" was one thing, but Jack's brain had practically folded itself in half when Obscuro had started talking about his missing father. Almost a day later it still wasn't back to normal. Even with everything that was going on, Jack was well aware that turning Obscuro down might have meant giving up his only chance to be reunited with his family. Jack couldn't believe he'd done that without even thinking about it. But he couldn't just run out on the Imagine Nation and leave his friends to deal with the Rüstov alone. He could stay and fight, or he could run and hide. Those were the choices that Obscuro had really offered him, and no matter how badly Jack wanted to find out about his father, he knew he couldn't go out like that. Of course, that didn't stop the back of Jack's brain from grabbing on to Obscuro's offer and refusing to let go.

"It's all right, Jack," Allegra said. "The important thing is you thought of it now. It can still make a difference."

"Let's hope so," Jack said as they closed in on the entrance to the cave. "Otherwise, this whole trip is just a big waste of time."

As soon as Jack stepped inside the cave, he knew it wasn't. The cavern was brighter in the light of day, but that hardly even mattered. It could have been darker than the dirty swamp water back at St. Barnaby's, the New Jersey orphanage in which he'd grown up, and the machines that were built into the cave's fake rock walls still would have been calling out to Jack like blinking Christmas lights. Microchips and motherboards—*thousands of them!*— were buzzing away like a vibrating phone on a glass table. There was no doubt about it. This was more than just an ordinary cave.

How could I have missed this? Jack asked himself, already knowing the answer. Jack shook his head as he found a seam in the wall, cursing himself for being so clueless.

Skerren was right—if only he'd been more focused back when it had mattered, maybe Obscuro wouldn't have gotten away.

"This is it," Jack said, feeling out the edges of a hidden door with his fingers. Jack knew he had to shake off his disappointment and keep moving forward. Allegra was right; it wasn't too late to make a difference.

Unfortunately, the front door of Smart's secret prison was in no mood to cooperate. Jack asked it very nicely to open up for him, and it responded with a comment so rude that Jack flat out refused to repeat it in front of Allegra. "Oh, that's how it's gonna be, huh?" Jack replied, not budging an inch. The door's aggressive attitude was exactly what he'd needed to get his head screwed on right and get ready for action. Jack didn't take that kind of lip from any machine, with or without a mouth.

Jack took a step back so he could take a look at the big picture. Using his powers, he reached out to the door with his mind and looked through its inner workings. "Let's try this again," he said once he had everything he needed. "You should know that I'm only asking you to open up nicely because I have manners. I don't need your permission. You're an X-15 model SmartLock door with a DeadVolt-brand electroshock deterrent added on. The power nullifiers are off, and I know your systems inside and out. I can take you apart in my sleep, and if I really want to teach you a lesson, I can use whatever power is left in that DeadVolt battery to fry your CPU while I'm at it," Jack warned the door. "So what's it going to be? Are we gonna do this the easy way or the hard way?"

The door slid back into the wall like a frightened puppy running off with its tail between its legs.

Jack smiled at Allegra and Skerren. "Open sesame."

"That was awesome," Allegra told Jack.

Jack shook his head like it was no big deal. "Security systems always think they're so tough. C'mon. Let's go see what's in there."

The three children walked through a short tunnel and emerged into a massive underground chamber that was carved deep into the rock caverns below the forest. The air was cool and moist in the vast, empty space. The floor beneath their feet was nothing more than a small platform anchored to the wall, overlooking a huge vertical shaft that went down hundreds of feet. Jack felt like he was standing on the inside of a gigantic well.

To his left Jack saw a small metal staircase leading down from the platform to a highway-size ramp that wound itself around the walls and down like a spiral staircase. A giant freestanding tower of video screens stood in the center of the shaft, rising up off the ground floor and climbing all the way up to the ceiling. Countless monitoring stations wound around the video tower from top to bottom, circling it in unbroken loops. The monitoring station chairs were all empty. No one was watching the screens anymore. They were all shut off, burned-out, or cracked. It was clear this place had not been active in quite some time, but when it had been open for business, it definitely had been a major operation.

"I don't get it," Skerren said. "I cut off a treetop last night, and we get mobbed by Gravens. How did Smart manage to build this place?"

"The Gravens are responsible for the earth," Allegra said. "I guess that means the rocks are on their own. My question is, how did he keep something this big a secret?"

"He buried it, for one thing," Jack said. "After that it's just 'deny, deny, deny,'" he added from experience. "I'll tell you one thing, I doubt we'll find anything here with the SmartCorp logo on it."

Jack started down the steps to the main ramp, and Skerren and Allegra followed close behind. As they went, they noticed several other small doors like the one they'd entered through, all scattered about the walls of the pit with their own crooked stairways leading up or down to the main ramp. Abandoned guard stations were posted near each door and set up behind empty gun turrets that were mounted into the walls. It was dark, but rings of emergency lights lined the interior walls all the way down to the ground, giving off a dull fluorescent glow. The cavernous facility felt cold and industrial, and the faded lighting made everything look worse.

At the bottom of the staircase, Jack saw a battered computer kiosk with a smashed screen and keyboard. He wondered if Obscuro had done that and somehow shorted out the nullifiers in the process. There was no one to ask. The deserted prison was as quiet as a grave. Jack tried using his powers to turn on the tower of screens and see if they could tell him anything. A few sets flickered on briefly to reveal rows of open cell doors, empty hallways, interrogation rooms, and guard stations, but the images quickly blinked out. There wasn't enough power left to run the giant surveillance tower anymore.

"Imagine being a Mecha forced to stay here for no reason," Allegra said.

"Not necessarily for no reason," Skerren corrected. "There is the Rüstov spyware virus."

"Doesn't excuse what Smart did here," Jack told Skerren. "He didn't even know about the virus."

"That doesn't mean he didn't take any infected Mechas prisoner," Skerren replied. "We'll never know, one way or the other. They're all gone now." Skerren looked around and listened to the silence. "This place is deserted. It doesn't look like there's any trace of Obscuro, and I don't think we're taking any Left-Behinds home with us either."

"Maybe not *live* Left-Behinds," Jack said. "There might be something down there we can salvage. If Smart had any Rüstov locked up here, that is. Let's see if I can narrow things down."

Jack walked up to the busted computer kiosk and tried to connect with the prison's cameras, map-finder programs, and anything else he could think of, but everything was either broken-down or not hooked up to a live power source. The best he could do was light up three tunnels that split off from the main path. They were positioned at the top, middle, and bottom of the winding down-ramp and ran deep into the rock walls. The children agreed that they needed to check out what was in there.

"We should split up," Skerren said. "We'll cover more ground that way."

"That makes no sense," Allegra disagreed. "There's a reason we came here together. This place is dangerous."

"This place is empty," Skerren countered. "This is just a salvage operation now. We're not going to come across any live Rüstov. Jack already said as much. If they were here, he would have sensed them."

Skerren and Allegra both looked to Jack for confirmation on that. It was true; if there had been any live Left-Behinds in the area, Jack would have picked up on it. "I think it's safe to split up," Jack said. "But we should stay in contact just in case." He went into his messenger bag and took out two bracelets. "I made these a few weeks ago. Here, take one," he said, offering one of the bracelets to Allegra.

"What is this?" Allegra asked.

"I meant to give one of these to you a while back," Jack said. "I guess they got buried under all the junk I have in my lab. I totally forgot about them until I was in there with Trea this morning."

"You made bracelets?" Skerren asked.

"They're two-way communicator bands," Jack said. "Kind of like mobile phones you wear on your wrist, only they're just hooked up to each other. If you get in trouble, just call me." Jack showed Allegra how her bracelet worked, and put the other one on his wrist.

"Thanks, Jack," Allegra said, looking over his gift. "This is really cool. I even like the design."

"Do you really? I hoped you would."

"Yes, they're very nice, Jack. Very impressive," Skerren said. "I can't help but notice that you didn't make me one."

"What?" Jack replied, caught off guard. "No, I have more back at the lab. I just didn't think you'd want one. I mean . . . it wouldn't even work in Varagog."

"It's fine," Skerren said. "You're right, I don't need it. I just thought it was funny. That's all."

Jack gave Skerren a curious look. "I'm still not used to your sense of humor, Skerren."

Allegra slid the bracelet onto her wrist. "It fits," she said. "Check, check," she added, speaking into her wristband's microphone.

"Copy," Jack said, speaking into his own. "All right. Should we get going?"

"Absolutely," Skerren said. "Now that we're all wearing the proper accessories," he added with a grin.

The three children split up, with Allegra taking the first tunnel, Skerren taking the second, and Jack taking the last one all the way down at the bottom. It was darkest down there at the base of the ramp, with the emergency lights glowing just brightly enough for Jack to see where he should put his next step. When Jack reached the bottom, he saw a row of footlights leading from the end of the down ramp to the mouth of the tunnel. Beyond the light's edge was an endless void, a sea of blackness that anything could be hiding within. Jack didn't even know for sure if there was a ground out there. He didn't stray from the path but went straight into the tunnel and down the long hallway.

Most of the way down, it didn't seem like there was anyone else there. Jack followed the tunnel past empty interrogation rooms that reminded him of the places Smart had used for his stress tests a year earlier. The drip, drip, drip of leaky pipes above Jack's head created puddles beneath his feet that brought him back to the watery basement at St. Barnaby's. They were both bad memories. Jack was starting to think that memories were all that was left in the prison. He didn't see any Left-Behinds, and he certainly didn't see any trace of Obscuro. That was a major disappointment. The outside chance that he might somehow get a message from his father was still nagging at his brain, even if he did know that he was supposed to be focusing on more important things.

Jack passed through a set of gates and found himself in a guard's break area. There was a large kitchenette filled with boxes of prepackaged instant meals, the kind of food that people put in bomb shelters because it never went bad. Looking around, Jack saw something funny. Someone had recently washed the dishes. A set of plates and silverware were stacked neatly in the drying rack, still wet. Was this where Obscuro was staying? Maybe he was still here after all? Pressing on, Jack found a locker room and barracks in the back. Countless bunk beds with bare mattresses filled the room, but one of them was made up with sheets and a comforter. It had been slept in recently.

"Can I help you?" a voice asked from behind Jack.

Jack jumped, spinning around to see Lorem Ipsum standing in the doorway behind him. She was leaning against the door frame, keeping one eye on Jack and one eye on the phone in her hand. Jack instinctively went for his wristband communicator to call Allegra, but Lorem leaped into action like a cat. Before Jack could even blink, she had her hand in front of his face, threatening him with her gibberish touch.

"If you want to go on speaking English . . . don't," she told him. "I'm not bothering anyone here. Don't give me a reason to bother with you."

Jack moved his hand away from his wrist, and Lorem dropped hers to her side. She walked past Jack to her bed, where she sat down and plugged a set of headphones into her phone. She stuck one earbud in her ear and let the other one hang down over her shoulder. *She isn't here to fight,* Jack thought, intrigued. That was good, because Lorem was a couple of years older than Jack, and he was no match for her speed. Luckily, she was content to just type away on her phone, looking disinterested and very cool.

"What are you doing here, kid?" Lorem asked. "Looking for me?"

"No," Jack replied. "I'm here for Rüstov parts."

Lorem scrunched up her face. "Rüstov parts?" she asked. "Why?"

"Either that, or Obscuro," Jack added, looking around. "Have you seen him?"

"Who?"

"Obscuro. The Rogue Secreteer," Jack clarified. "He came through here last night."

Lorem shook her head like she didn't know what Jack was talking about, and raised the free, hanging earbud up toward her ear.

"It's really important," Jack said. "He definitely came through here. Are you sure you haven't seen him?"

Lorem Ipsum stopped just short of sticking the additional earbud into her left ear. She looked annoyed. "It's a pretty big place. You can see that, right?"

Her answer left Jack frustrated and curious. "Yeah, I can see that. What are you doing in it?"

263

"I *live* in it," Lorem said. "At least I have been recently. Second time around for me in this place. I lived here before, too, but in a much smaller room."

"You were a prisoner here? A prisoner of Smart's?"

Lorem nodded. "This was my home for way too long back when the place was active. This is where he kept me. You know. Off the books."

"Really?" Jack asked. "I thought he only kept Mechas here. People he suspected of Rüstov stuff." Lorem Ipsum just shrugged. "Why'd he put you in here? Was it because you're a supercriminal?"

Lorem burst out laughing. When she finally stopped, she said, "Oh, that was good. Really. I needed that."

Jack didn't see what Lorem found so funny. "If you're not a supercriminal, what are you doing running with Speedrazor's gang?"

"Please," Lorem said. "I'm not in Speedrazor's gang. I just wanted to hit back at SmartCorp. I owed the old man that much." Lorem got up and looked around the sad, empty barracks. "My life was supposed to be different. Way different. I was in the School of Thought too, you know."

"I know," Jack said. "Midknight told us you had to leave because of . . . your father." Jack paused a moment, trying to remember Midknight's exact words. He had called Lorem's father a very controlling man. Jack thought about what Lorem had just said about wanting to hit back at SmartCorp. The sound in her voice when she'd called Smart the "old man." "Smart's your father?" he guessed.

"Close," Lorem replied. "He's my manufacturer." Lorem pulled back her sleeve to reveal a UPC bar code and a SmartCorp logo tattooed on her wrist. "I was grown in SmartCorp labs. I'm Lorem Ipsum Smart, lab test 212973, genetically engineered to have a specific power. 'Daddy' was going to grow his whole Peacemaker army that way, so he wouldn't have to recruit questionable sorts like Speedrazor. He cut me loose when he couldn't control me. Or more accurately, he locked me up."

"I don't believe it," Jack said. "Well, I do believe it, but seriously . . . he locked you up? That's crazy."

Lorem shrugged. "I wasn't supposed to have a personality. That was the one flaw in the experiment." Lorem pulled her sleeve back into place. "What do you expect?

You don't get sentimentality from a man with no heart. I don't have to tell you that, do I, Jack?"

Jack didn't know what to say. Lorem clearly knew who he was and all about his bad blood with Smart. He wanted to tell her that he thought her story was far worse than his own. That every time he didn't think Smart could sink any lower, he did. The man was constantly inventing new ways to be less of a person. But before Jack had a chance to say any of that, there was a crackle-static noise on his wrist, and Allegra's voice broke the silence.

"Jack . . . Jack, do you read me?" Allegra asked over the wrist communicator. "My tunnel hallway looped in with Skerren's. Neither of us found anything. We're heading back to the entrance. Do you want to meet us there, or should we come to you?"

"You call them down here, and I'll be gone," Lorem warned, raising a finger toward Jack. "And you'll be incomprehensible."

Jack's back stiffened. "Why?"

"It's bad enough you're here," Lorem told him. "The last thing I need is more people knowing where I live."

Allegra called Jack's name again. "Jack. Jack, do you

read me?" Jack didn't reply. He was busy thinking. "Jack, are you okay?" Allegra's voice asked, sounding concerned.

"Better get going," Lorem told Jack. "Don't want to keep your girlfriend waiting."

"Allegra's not my girlfriend," Jack said quickly.

Lorem raised an eyebrow. "Okay," she said with a smile. "You're funny."

"Jack, do you need us to come to you?" Allegra asked.

"No," Jack said into his wrist, holding down the talk button on his bracelet. "No, this is Jack. I'm fine. I'm on my way back too. Don't come to me. I'll be up in a minute." Jack let go of the talk button and looked up at Lorem Ipsum. He didn't move an inch. Regardless of what he had just told Allegra, he wasn't ready to head back just yet. Jack thought about Smart's fifty-million-credit offer and what would happen if Obscuro sold him out. By some crazy stroke of luck, he was standing three feet away from his best chance of stopping that from happening.

"Lorem, how long does your gibberish-touch power last?" Jack asked.

Lorem almost looked intrigued, but not quite. "As long as I want," she replied.

"As long as you want," Jack repeated. *Perfect.* "Lorem, we're after the Rogue Secreteer. He's telling everyone's secrets, causing trouble. He's about to cause *me* a whole lot of trouble."

Lorem shrugged for what seemed like the hundredth time. "And?" she asked.

"And I was thinking . . . ," Jack said. "What if he couldn't talk? What if every time he opened his mouth, nothing came out but gibberish?"

"Wouldn't that be something?" Lorem asked. "What's in it for me?"

Jack turned his wristband all the way off. "How about a guarantee that it'll drive Jonas Smart absolutely crazy?"

Lorem Ipsum smiled. "I'm listening."

CHAPTER

16

Secret Alliances

Stendeval had told Jack earlier, "Whenever you encounter a problem in life, it simply means that your situation has changed. What you need to do is take steps to deal with the new situation."

With a little help from his friends, including some new and unexpected friends, Jack was now doing exactly that. A plan was starting to come together in his head. He didn't have all the moves mapped out just yet, but he had the players. If Trea liked working alone, maybe that was for the best, Jack thought. Considering where his head was at lately, she had a much better chance of curing the virus than he did. Having Trea's help on the virus also freed him up to go after Glave and to try to keep Obscuro quiet. If everything went perfectly, there was even a chance he could be reunited with his father when this was all over. Unfortunately, if Jack's plans were going to work, some very big pieces of the puzzle were going to have to fall into place at exactly the right time, and that was something that rarely ever happened. For Jack it had never happened, and it wasn't about to start now.

Jack, Skerren, and Allegra got back to Cognito in time to find out why. They entered Jack's apartment and found Trea still there, watching a SmartNews broadcast on Jack's holo-screen. Her eyeballs were glued to the set, and the news anchors commanding her attention looked especially excited. That was never a good sign. As Stendeval might have put it, Jack's situation was about to change once again.

"What's going on?" Jack asked Trea.

"I don't know," she answered. "I just turned the screen on as it cut to a special report. Looks like something big, though. Something about Smart."

"Again?" Jack asked. He groaned and turned his eyes toward the holo-screen. Jack knew he wasn't going to like anything he saw there, but Stendeval was right—he was better off knowing what Smart was up to.

"Welcome back," Drack Hackman began, smiling into the camera. "We're just moments away from going live to Hightown, where we're told former Circleman Jonas Smart is getting ready to make a major announcement. No word as of yet regarding the subject matter of his statement, but whatever it is, you can bet it's going to be exciting. And important."

"I know I'm excited," Hackman's blond, cold-eyed coanchor agreed. Jack scowled at the screen. The woman looked like a snake wearing a wig. "Jonas Smart recently revealed that since being voted out of office, he's spent nearly all his time and a large amount of his personal fortune on a powerful defense system called the SmarterNet. Is he finally ready to tell us all about it? SmartNews has the story."

"The SmarterNet," Hackman repeated. "I get chills just thinking about it. Hang on," he added, touching a finger to his ear. "I'm being told Jonas Smart has left his

271

office and is about to take the stage at SmartTower. Let's go there now."

Jack and the others watched as an image of Jonas Smart striding confidently toward a press conference stage overtook the screen. Flashbulbs went off as he worked his way through a sea of microphones, reporters, and loyal supporters. He took his place at the lectern and prepared to address the crowd. Jack noted that Smart didn't bother to thank anyone for coming to hear him speak.

"Good evening, Empire City," Smart began in his usual grim tone. "As everyone within the sound of my voice already knows, my name is Jonas Smart, and I am the smartest man on the face of the Earth. But what concerns me tonight, and should also concern you, is what we *don't* know. With just over forty-eight hours left before the Rüstov strike, I have yet to be contacted by the Rogue Secreteer regarding Jack Blank's secrets."

Jack breathed a momentary sigh of relief.

"While I wait, my Real World business concerns have been raided once again," Smart revealed. "No doubt the work of Rüstov spies trying to sabotage the same key components of the SmarterNet that Jack Blank destroyed once already," he said. "The raid was unsuccessful, but it is still indicative of a greater problem. Our enemies move freely about the world at large, and nothing is being done to stop them. Meanwhile, here at home"—Smart tapped the lectern a moment and grunted—"a disturbing development in Machina has just been brought to my attention."

Jack traded apprehensive looks with his friends. Machina? What was going on there? Were infected Mechas succumbing to the spyware virus ahead of schedule?

Smart cued in a holo-screen for the crowd, and the SmartNews producers cut to an image of the Hightown-Machina border. What Jack saw on the screen surprised him—a giant wall was being built around the Mechas' borough.

"What the . . . ," Jack began.

"The Mechas are sealing off their borough!" Smart's voice called out over footage of the wall's construction. "Days before an attack, they are fortifying their position in this city and refusing to explain why!"

Jack and the others watched the holo-screen as it played footage of Virtua overseeing construction of the wall. "No comment," she told the SmartNews reporters on the scene, turning away to avoid their cameras. "No comment," she said again as her security detail moved in to block the frame.

"Yeah, *that's* not going to freak anyone out," Trea said.

"Virtua, what are you doing?" Jack wondered aloud.

A concerned murmur ran through the tightly packed crowd assembled before Smart. He nodded in agreement with them, gaining momentum from their heightened state of fear. "I want to know what's going on behind that wall!" he declared. "What do the Mechas know about the coming attack that we don't? Who is this Glave? *Where* is he? Who is his partner, Khalix, and what is their plan? We cannot afford to have these mysteries!" Smart pounded a fist on the lectern. "That is why as of this moment, I am doubling my offer to the Rogue Secreteer. That's right . . . one hundred million credits."

The figure drew more gasps from the crowd. And from Jack. "A hundred million credits?" Jack exclaimed. "This is crazy!"

"No doubt you will all say this gesture goes above and beyond my duty as a private citizen," Smart continued. "In these trying times, I say it is still not far enough. Whatever Rüstov plot has the rogue scared enough to betray his order—whatever dark secret their Lost Boy, Jack Blank, has refused to share with us—I will uncover it, one way or the other."

The crowd at SmartTower cheered Smart on, loud and angry. It was plain to see that Jack didn't have any friends at that gathering. Public opinion was starting to turn, just as he'd feared. The mood of a city was a fickle thing, something Jack knew better than most. A year ago Empire City's mood had shifted in his favor overnight. Jonas Smart was doing his best to flip that switch back in the other direction. If the reaction in Hightown was any reflection of how this speech was playing in the rest of the city, Jack's days of signing autographs were all but over. He could practically see the wheels turning in people's heads, the renewed curiosity about what he might be hiding. . . . It reminded him just how powerful people's fear of the Rüstov was. There was an atmosphere of paranoia still lurking under the skin of Empire City like a scab waiting to be picked at, and Jonas Smart had only just begun to scratch at the wound.

"The end of the Imagine Nation could be mere days away, and still Jack Blank remains silent," Smart railed from the pulpit. "The Inner Circle has done nothing to protect you. If anything, they have worked hard to make you less safe! I say, 'No more.' I have found a way to safeguard all of you against the Rüstov while still complying with the Inner Circle's newfound sensitivities for our enemy. The Rüstov operate globally, free to work their machinations in secret. From me they shall receive a global response. People of Empire City, have no fear. If these Rüstov interlopers expect to achieve their goals in the next forty-eight hours, then I will act decisively to stop them in the next twenty-four! Starting tomorrow my SmarterNet will deploy in the outside world, and it will hunt down these Rüstov invaders before they ever reach our shores!"

Thunderous cheers rang out from the audience. Smart bared a row of teeth in a chilling smile as the noise grew louder and louder. The applause wasn't stopping, so Smart kept going, talking over the crowd's ovation. "You are all invited to witness the launch of the SmarterNet tomorrow at Hero Square," Smart shouted. "I promise you, one and all, the next time the sun sets on the Imagine Nation, you will be able to rest easy. Take comfort in the knowledge

that Jonas Smart is watching the world at large and keeping our enemies at bay."

The throng of Hightowners outside SmartTower roared with vociferous approval as Smart turned and left the lectern. Jack was loath to admit it, but it was as good a speech as Smart had ever given. The Jonas Smart faithfuls in the Hightown crowd simply ate it up. The SmartNews anchors did as well. Not interested in hearing Drack Hackman say any more on the subject, Jack shut the holo-screen off with a thought. The light from the screen blinked out, and the blaring, abrasive NewsNet vanished from sight. The void left by its sudden absence made the room seem unbelievably quiet. All eyes turned to Jack for his reaction.

"A hundred million credits," Jack eventually said, breaking the silence. "I can't believe it."

"What do you think Obscuro is waiting for?" Skerren asked. "He can't be holding out for more. I didn't think Smart even still had that kind of money anymore."

"I'm not sure he does," Trea replied. "Everyone knows his business hasn't been the same since he lost the SmartCams and Peacemakers. Rumor has it he sank everything he's got into the SmarterNet."

"Am I crazy, or did he still not say what the SmarterNet actually does?" Allegra asked.

Jack grimaced. "You're not crazy. I think it's pretty clear what it does, though. It finds out secrets that people try to keep quiet. What he didn't say is *how* it does it."

Jack ran his hands through his hair, his problems feeling big and impossible all over again. He was feeling claustrophobic, stuck there inside his apartment. He had to do something to take back some breathing room.

"We need to find Obscuro again," Jack said.

"Obscuro?" Trea asked. "You already tried that. He didn't tell you anything."

"So we'll try again," Jack said. "And we can't let him tell Smart about the virus."

"*Everyone's* going to find out about the virus unless we stop it," Trea said. "We need to focus on the cure."

"If Obscuro tells Smart the truth about me," Jack began, but stopped himself because it sounded so suspicious. "You know, about what I knew and when," he explained. "If Smart finds that out . . ." Jack drew his finger across his throat. "When he's through with me, no one will trust any cure that I had a hand in."

Trea shrugged. "That might be true, but—"

"Who says Obscuro won't tell us anything?" Skerren cut in. "If we can find him again, I'll *make* him tell us what he knows about Glave. We'll take care of this problem at the source."

"Let's get real here," Trea said. "Finding a Secreteer is a once-in-a-lifetime thing. You guys already had your chance, and you blew it. You couldn't even find us a Left-Behind to work on. Or do you have one stuck in your pockets that you haven't told me about yet?"

"That's not my fault," Skerren shot back. "Smart's prison was deserted. None of us found anything in there."

"Right," Jack said, his voice cracking just a bit. "The place was empty."

"Empty?" Trea asked.

"Empty," Jack repeated. "Totally empty."

It was, of course, another lie.

Jack didn't like lying, but he was learning to live with it. If he was harboring any doubts about the deal he'd struck with Lorem Ipsum, they were rapidly evaporating after hearing Smart's speech. He needed to keep the Rogue Secreteer quiet while Trea worked on the cure-code. Lorem

279

Ipsum was the only person who could buy him the time he needed. But first he had to find the Rogue Secreteer.

"We need to talk to Midknight," Jack said. "He's the detective. He'll have some ideas about how to find Obscuro."

"Let *them* go," Trea said, pointing at Skerren and Allegra. "You're supposed to be working on the virus with me."

"Wait, now you want my help?" Jack asked. "This morning you wanted me fetching cold beverages."

"That was T1 talking," Trea said. "You know how she gets."

"Yeah, she gets pretty hard to work with," Jack said.

"She also gets results," Trea said. "We made it through your notes. We even organized the files and uploaded them to your hard drive. I've been waiting for you. I have questions for you. We don't have time to waste here." Jack made a face. "What are you looking at me like that for?" Trea asked.

"Sorry," Jack said. "It's just . . . after this morning I thought maybe you could work on this while I did something else. Something that didn't require me to be stuck in the lab like I have been all year."

"Like what? Run off on a wild goose chase?" Trea asked. "You said yourself we're the only people who know how to do this."

"I know, but . . ." Jack let out an exasperated sigh. It figured that Trea had picked this exact moment to realize she wanted his input. Going down to his lab and crunching numbers at a desk was the absolute last thing Jack wanted to do. "Really, you're better off without me, Trea. I can't work on this right now. Between this thing with Smart, and Obscuro bringing up my dad . . . my head is all over the place. You keep going, and when I come back, we'll look at *your* notes. Then we'll work together, okay?"

Trea grumbled, "Fine, but you're pulling an all-nighter with me when you get back. No excuses. Deal?"

"All right," Jack replied. "Deal."

Less than five minutes later Jack took off for Hightown with Skerren and Allegra.

Riding Allegra's open AirSkimmer, Jack, Skerren, and Allegra quickly made it to Midknight's apartment complex. Like most of the buildings in Hightown, it was nice. Maybe not Ivory Tower nice, but still very nice. The people they passed along the way were another story. Jack's famous face got plenty of attention as he flew through the wealthy borough with his friends. People stopped, stared, and pointed. Random Hightowners gave him dirty looks and made rude comments. It was hard to believe that just a few days ago Jack had walked these streets as a hero. Smart was taking full advantage of the paranoia that the Rogue Secreteer's behavior had inspired. As usual, he was playing it perfectly.

Allegra suggested taking the wind out of Smart's sails by confirming the rumors about his secret prison, but Jack convinced her otherwise. There was still a chance that Obscuro might go back there, but only if he thought the place was 100 percent off the grid. Before leaving, Jack had convinced the machines in the prison to signal him if Obscuro returned. It wasn't the only deal Jack set up before leaving Smart's prison, but that was the other reason he didn't want to go public with what they knew. He didn't want to put Lorem Ipsum out of a home.

Skerren thought it was something they should talk about with Midknight. It was a tough call, especially since they were out of leads on Obscuro, but Skerren was certain his mentor would know the right thing to do. Midknight was Empire City's greatest vigilante detective. He'd been at the hero game a long, long time. If anyone could help them figure out their next move, it was him.

The doorman in Midknight's building recognized Skerren as the local hero's sidekick and let the children into the elevator without bothering to call upstairs. Jack, Skerren, and Allegra got in and rode the car up to the top floor. A bell dinged, and the doors opened directly into Midknight's penthouse apartment.

The luxurious penthouse stood in stark contrast to the ultramodern, minimalist designs that were common to most of Hightown. It had a spacious foyer with high ceilings, fresh flower arrangements, and a decorative marble floor. Through an arch on the far side of the foyer, Jack glimpsed the rooms beyond filled with dark brown mahogany furniture, plush leather couches, and walls decorated with books and pictures. Softly lit lamps bathed the entire penthouse in an amber glow that gave the classic, elegant home a comfortable and welcoming feel.

"Right on time for once, eh?" Jack heard Midknight say as he approached the foyer. "Usually you're at least ten minutes late. I hope that's not nerves getting to—" Midknight stopped short when he turned the corner. "You?" he said, surprised. "What are you kids doing here?"

Midknight appeared to be in the middle of suiting up for action. He had his mask on and was busy tightening the straps on his battle armor. From the look on his face, it was clear that now was not the best time to have dropped by unannounced.

"Sorry we didn't call ahead," Jack said, suddenly feeling uncomfortable about being there. "We didn't mean to just barge in like this."

"The guy downstairs let us up," Allegra explained.

"I hope it's not a problem," Skerren told Midknight. "You always said I should feel free to come here if I ever needed help with anything. I just assumed . . ." Skerren trailed off as Midknight stared at him blankly.

"We can go," Allegra offered, taking a step toward the door. "Yeah, I think that's a good idea. We'll come back later."

"Wait," Midknight replied, snapping out of whatever daze he'd been in. "Please, forgive me. I don't mean to be rude, it's just . . . I was expecting someone else. You surprised me. I'm afraid this isn't a good time, kids. I have some very pressing matters to deal with this evening."

"We just need some advice," Jack said. "It's really important."

"We promise not to take too long," Skerren added.

"Please?" Allegra threw in for good measure. It seemed to do the trick. Midknight checked his watch and took a breath.

"Okay, but we have to make it quick," the veteran hero said. "Through there. Have a seat in the living room."

Midknight ushered Jack, Skerren, and Allegra around the corner and into the comfy sofas and club chairs that were laid out in his sitting room. While Jack and the others took a seat, Midknight called downstairs and asked the doorman if he could do him the courtesy of announcing his next guest. The bookshelves and walls in Midknight's living room were loaded with holograph pictures and digital newspaper clippings commemorating a lifetime's worth of adventures and more. Thanks to his powers, Midknight aged only during the day, which made for an impressive run at the hero game. His career had already lasted several decades longer than the average crime fighter's career.

Jack looked over the many pictures, keepsakes, articles, and awards. Midknight had certainly seen his share of victory and defeat over the years. Jack found it odd that he kept memories of both on display in his home. An article about Midknight receiving the key to the city was hanging on the wall right next to one of the old posters from his failed political campaign. Midknight had run against Smart and Noteworthy for Circleman of Hightown in the previous election. Unfortunately, he didn't win.

"I'm surprised to see you here, Jack," Midknight said. "I thought you'd be holed up in that lab of yours, working on that virus you warned us about."

"Trea's there now," Jack said. "She's working on it."

"Is that right?" Midknight asked. "Figured the problem could benefit from some fresh perspective, eh?"

"I'm working another angle," Jack said. "Trea's going to take care of the virus."

"She didn't say that exactly," Skerren said.

"I said I was going to help her later tonight, Skerren," Jack replied, getting a little testy. "Besides, Stendeval told Virtua about the virus yesterday. She's working on it too."

"She is?" Midknight asked, intrigued. "Hmn . . . I suppose that explains that wall," he said, rubbing his chin. "I've been working this case from another angle too," he said after a few moments of thinking and rubbing. "It's taking longer than I expected. Good thing you kids are all working solo right now. We can't afford to leave any stones unturned here."

"That was no accident," Skerren said. "You're the one who assigned the solo missions."

"Right," Midknight agreed. "Guess I was thinking ahead. The point is, it's good we're talking now, because I might not see you three again until after this invasion deadline passes."

"Why not? What are you doing?" Allegra asked.

"Don't worry about me. I'll be fine," Midknight replied. "You three came here for my help. The question is, what can I do for you?" he asked. "Quickly, please."

Jack was surprised to see Midknight acting so rushed. "We wanted your advice on how to catch the Rogue Secreteer," he told Skerren's mentor.

"Obscuro?" Midknight asked, giving Jack a curious look. "You sure you're not thinking about taking him up on his offer, Jack? Hitching a ride on his spaceship out of town and going to see your dad?"

"I'm not running," Jack said. "We need Obscuro to tell us how to find Glave." *And I need him to keep his mouth shut about me,* Jack thought but didn't say.

"We're out of ideas," Allegra added. "I thought we might try to ask Hypnova again, but—"

"You don't want to do that," Midknight cut in. "There's no telling what she'd do to you. She got in big trouble after what happened with you guys in the Outlands. Word round the campfire is that she got put on probation by the Clandestine Order. She may even be getting kicked out."

"Serves her right," Jack said. "None of us would even be in this mess if she hadn't decided to go snooping around in my brain."

"That's a little harsh, isn't it, Jack?" Midknight asked him. "Kind of like blaming a scale for the weight, or a mirror for its reflection. Hypnova didn't create this situation, she just found out about it. But never mind that now," Midknight said, waving a hand in the air. "That's a topic for another time. I don't want to get sidetracked here. Focusing on *your* problem, you don't need Hypnova to track down Obscuro. After today that should be simple. Assuming you heard Smart's speech, that is."

"We heard it, all right," Jack said.

"Then you know all you need to know," Midknight said. "Your lead on the Rogue Secreteer is Jonas Smart. The Secreteer wants money. Smart has it. He's court-ing the rogue. This SmarterNet of his—whatever it is—is launching tomorrow, so you know where he'll be. . . . Just stay on Smart. Sooner or later he and Obscuro are going to cross paths. You can bet on it."

Jack snapped his fingers. *Of course,* he thought. It was so simple. The best ideas usually are, at their core. Some-times that's what makes them so hard to think of.

A ringing videophone announced an incoming call, and Midknight snapped his fingers to open up a holo-screen with an image of the doorman. "Your guest is here, sir," the doorman said.

"Thank you," Midknight replied, and quickly shut the screen. "Ten minutes late," he said, checking his watch again. "I'm afraid we're out of time, kids. Right now I have a meeting."

"Who is it down there?" Jack asked.

"I'm glad I was able to help you out," Midknight said, getting up and leading the children out of the apartment. "Good luck. I think we're all going to need it." The next thing Jack knew, he, Skerren, and Allegra were all in the elevator going down.

"Okay, that was weird," Allegra said after the doors closed.

"I know," Skerren agreed. "Midknight seemed . . . tense. That's not like him."

"What do you think he's working on?" Jack asked. "I mean, what angle of this case doesn't involve Obscuro, Glave, or the virus?"

"I don't know." Skerren shrugged. "But Midknight connects dots other people don't even see. That's what makes him so good. I've spent enough time as his sidekick to learn not to doubt him."

"Still," Jack said. "I wonder who he's meeting with."

As the elevator car raced toward the ground, another one flew up in the opposite direction alongside it, and Jack got his answer. Jack's head spun toward the wall, and then turned up toward the ceiling, following the path of an elevator car no one else even knew was there.

"What is it?" Allegra asked Jack.

"I just saw him," Jack said. "Through the security camera in the elevator car next to ours. He's going up there now. It's Clarkston Noteworthy."

"Noteworthy?" Skerren and Allegra both blurted out.

"What's he doing meeting with Noteworthy?" Skerren asked.

"I don't know," Jack said. He raised a hand and stopped the elevator in place. Then he motioned up toward the ceiling, bringing the elevator back up until it reached the level marked FACILITIES. Jack spread his hands apart, and the doors opened. "Let's go find out."

Jack led the others past the building's furnaces and boilers to the emergency stairwell. If he'd thought something weird was going on with Midknight before, he was sure of it now. He didn't know what to make of this secret meeting between old political rivals. Jack dug into his bag at the foot of the staircase as Skerren came through the door behind him. He looked up at the stairs. They snaked up around the walls, going up level after level.

"Jack, what are we doing in the staircase?" Skerren asked. "The penthouse is a hundred floors up. They're going to be done talking before we get halfway there."

Jack found what he was looking for in his bag. "Not if we use this," he said, pulling out an electronic device with a round lens on the front.

"A camera?" Allegra asked.

"No," Jack said. "It's something else I've been working on. We're going to do a Laserline jump."

"A what?" Skerren asked.

Jack clipped the device to his belt buckle and switched it on. The lens on the front turned red. "Quick, Allegra, wrap us up," he said, motioning for them to grab on to him. The three children huddled close together, and Allegra wrapped her silvery arms around everyone several times. Jack hit another button, and a red light shot out of the contraption on his belt, firing a laser beam all the way up to the ceiling. The Laserline beam was solid, another Hard-Light Holo. It hooked into the ceiling and retracted. Jack, Skerren, and Allegra zipped up through the vertical corridor, the floors racing by them as they flew up the shaft. It was like bungee jumping in reverse. The line pulled Jack and the others up to the ceiling, where they stopped just short of crashing into it. A computerized voice on Jack's belt said, "Laserline jump complete." But it wasn't quite complete. Jack and his friends were still dangling from the ceiling a hundred floors up.

"Now what?" Skerren asked.

Jack looked below him. It was a long way down. "Now . . . Allegra pulls us over to the stairs and I turn this thing off," he said.

Allegra grumbled and stretched out an arm. She pulled the three of them over the railing of the steps to the top floor. Jack turned off the Laserline, and they dropped down onto the landing. Jack rolled down a few steps before catching on to the banister. Once he stopped moving, he took the Laserline projector off his belt and looked at it. "Wow, that thing really worked."

"A little warning next time would be nice," Allegra said. "If I'd gotten scared and liquefied, I could have dropped you both."

"I never doubted you for a second." Jack smiled. "Besides, the Laserline was attached to my belt. You would have only dropped Skerren," he added with a wink. Allegra laughed.

"Ha-ha-ha," Skerren said from the penthouse's stairway door. "Midknight's door is locked," he said, trying the knob unsuccessfully. "I don't think I should be cutting through it. I shouldn't even be out here like this. I'm his sidekick."

Jack's head shot up like he'd just heard a noise. "We don't have to go in," he said. "The *Knightwing*'s engine just turned on. They're on the roof."

Jack, Skerren, and Allegra ran up one more flight of stairs and out onto the roof of Midknight's building. The *Knightwing* was parked nearby with its entrance ramp lowered. Midknight and Noteworthy were standing in front of it arguing. They were such an unlikely duo. Jack and his friends crept quietly toward them, taking refuge behind power generators, air-conditioning units, and other equipment on the roof as they went.

"And you're certain this is the only way left for us to proceed?" Jack heard Noteworthy say to Midknight once he got close enough to hear.

"Relax, Clarkston," Midknight replied. "Last time I checked, I was the one taking all the risks here. You don't have to worry about anything."

"Don't I?" Noteworthy asked. "If you get caught, people are going to want to know who helped you. I can't afford that kind of exposure with Smart stirring people up again. You've seen it out there—paranoia is the order of the day." Noteworthy shook his head. "It's amazing what that ignorant rabble will swallow. After everything that's happened, they still don't know anything."

"Can't argue with that," Midknight said. "They voted for you, didn't they? You're right, though. . . . They don't know anything, and they won't even know *that* much until it's too late. That's why we're here now."

Noteworthy grumbled something Jack couldn't make out, so he inched closer to hear what was being said. Jack put his weight on the generator in front of him as he leaned in to eavesdrop. It creaked under the strain, and Noteworthy jumped when he heard the noise. His hand lit up with energy. "Who's there?" he demanded. "Show yourselves!"

Jack recoiled from the generator. "Let's get out of here!" he whispered to Skerren and Allegra. They all broke for the door to the stairs, running as fast as they could. Jack could hear Noteworthy running across the roof behind him, but he didn't dare look back. He was the last one to the door and was almost through it when a flash of light whizzed by his face and dug into the door frame. He paused to look at the blazing disklike blade that was jammed into the wood. It had three sharp, slender protrusions that flared out like tongues of green electric fire. Skerren's face appeared in the doorway to check it out. The two boys marveled in silence at the energy weapon in silence as Noteworthy's footsteps grew louder.

"What are you two doing?" Allegra said. "He's coming!" She grabbed both of them and held on tight. "Hope you guys are up for another HALO jump." She didn't wait for an answer. She just stepped up onto the railing and leaped over the side. Seconds later the three children were all down on the ground and running out the front door of Midknight's lobby. They ran for several blocks before they finally felt like they were in the clear. They sat down on the curb and took a minute to catch their breath.

"I don't believe it," Skerren said, breathing heavily. "Do you realize what we just saw?"

"I don't know what we just saw," Allegra admitted. "What part of it are you talking about?"

"Noteworthy's powers," Skerren clarified.

"Yeah, the energy blade," Jack said, panting. "Pretty cool. I thought he was just superrich."

"You don't understand," Skerren said. "I recognized Noteworthy's weapon. I've seen them in Varagog."

"So?" Jack asked. "What's so important about Noteworthy's weapon?"

"Everything," Skerren said. "It's an old-style blade, but it has a name you know. A name everybody knows." Skerren gulped. He looked like even he couldn't believe the words he was about to say. "It's called a glave."

17

Midknight Marauders

"No way," Jack said. "You don't think . . . Noteworthy is Glave?"

"I don't know what to think," Skerren said. "You heard them up there. Tell me that didn't sound suspicious."

Jack and Allegra looked at each other, then back at Skerren. Jack couldn't deny that Midknight and Noteworthy's conversation had sounded fishy, but no way had he expected Skerren to suggest what he was suggesting.

"You're serious about this," Jack said. "You really think Noteworthy and Midknight might be Glave and Khalix?"

"There's gotta be some other explanation," Allegra said. "What kind of spy uses a code name that's the exact same thing as his powers? Isn't that a little obvious?"

"Maybe that's the point," Skerren replied. "It's so obvious that people dismiss it as *too* obvious. Obscuro did say Glave was a master spy."

Jack mulled that over for a second. "He also said the Rüstov plot goes all the way up to Empire City's greatest heroes," Jack said. "I thought he was talking about me and what I knew about the virus, but if Midknight's involved . . . that does make more sense."

"You think of yourself as one of Empire City's greatest heroes?" Skerren asked.

"No, but other people do," Jack said. "At least they did."

"Guys, Noteworthy is in the Inner Circle," Allegra said. "You don't really think he could hide out under the Circlemen's noses and fool them every day, do you?"

"The Inner Circle!" Jack said, touching a hand to his temple. "I almost forgot."

"What?" Skerren asked.

"When Smart came out with the first Glave transmission, it was Noteworthy who convinced everyone to keep it

299

a secret," Jack revealed. "It was only when Obscuro started selling secrets that Smart was able to go public with that."

Jack watched his friends' eyes widen as the dreadful realization hit them at the same time.

"We have to follow them," Skerren said. "The *Knightwing* has a cloaking device, Jack. Can you still track it?"

"Cloaks only work on other machines," Jack said. "They don't work on me."

Jack, Skerren, and Allegra headed back to Allegra's AirSkimmer, still perched close to Midknight's building. Allegra revved up the AirSkimmer. "Let's go," she said. They jumped onto Allegra's ride and struck off after Midknight and Noteworthy. As it turned out, tracking the *Knightwing* was even easier than Jack had expected. Midknight and Noteworthy hadn't even left Hightown. They had taken the ship only as far as Empire City's Securamax Prison, located fifty blocks straight down into the guts of the borough, affectionately known to the locals as Lowtown.

Securamax was a monolithic structure built at the lowest point in Lowtown. It looked like it had been forged out of a single piece of black iron; a giant domino without any white dots. The prison had no visible doors or windows, and no roads ran into it. MagLev highways curved around and away from the prison as if compelled by some unseen force as they wound their way up toward the more respectable sections of the borough. The chic towers of Hightown obscured Securamax as they reached toward the sky, leaving it behind like something better off forgotten.

Jack, Skerren, and Allegra came to a halt on a MagLev down ramp overlooking the prison. Midknight and Noteworthy had the *Knightwing* running silently in the shadows nearby. In its cloaked state the ship was invisible to the Securamax detection sensors, but not to Jack.

"Securamax," Skerren said. "Doesn't Smart run this place?"

"Smart doesn't run it," Jack said. "The Circleman of Hightown does."

"Look!" Allegra said, pointing up at the foundation of one of Hightown's finer towers, where the *Knightwing* was parked. A lone figure came flying out of the shadows. Only, he wasn't flying, he was falling . . . gracefully. It was Midknight. He was holding a miniature glider as he dove toward the prison. When he was halfway there, he released the glider and let the winds carry it up and away as he continued his descent toward the side of the building and a very solid wall.

"What's he doing?" Skerren asked. "He's going to crash."

But Midknight didn't crash. He passed right through the wall as if it were a mirage. Skerren and Allegra were dumbfounded. Only Jack knew what was going on.

"He had the phase frequency," Jack said.

"The what?" Skerren asked.

"The phase frequency," Jack repeated. "Securamax doesn't have any doors in or out. You need to know the frequency it's vibrating at to get in. If you have the right equipment, you can match the signal and walk right through the walls. Someone fed Midknight the frequency."

"Let me guess . . . ," Allegra said.

"Noteworthy," Jack said with a nod.

"Or should we say Glave?" Skerren added.

Jack reached out to the prison's other defense measures with his powers and found that Noteworthy's assistance didn't stop at the prison wall. "He's overriding the system," Jack said. "He's running the security cameras from the ship."

"Don't they have people inside watching the monitors?" Allegra asked. "Can't they tell something's up?"

"Noteworthy's being smart about it," Jack said, shaking his head in admiration as he looked through the cameras inside the prison. "He's just tightening up the range of the cameras as they sweep the halls. Midknight's moving in their blind spots. I can almost see him in the corner of each one, but not quite."

"What about the Keepers?" Skerren asked, referring to the Securamax guards.

"What about them?" Jack asked. "This is Midknight we're talking about."

"Jack's right," Allegra said. "It's getting later," she added, holding up the clock on the comm-bracelet Jack had given her. "Midknight's getting stronger by the minute. It's going to take every Keeper in the prison to bring him down."

"I don't get this," Jack said. "What's he doing breaking *into* prison?"

"The question is, who's he breaking out?" Skerren asked.

Jack nodded. That was the real question. He intended

to find out the answer. He wondered who it could be. Another Rüstov collaborator? A squad of Left-Behinds? Jack kept a figurative eye on Midknight, tracking him through the prison by following the hijacked cameras. Noteworthy was turning them all away from Midknight as he moved through the prison. He was also feeding Midknight positions of Securamax's Keepers so he could incapacitate them as necessary, or avoid them altogether. The Circleman of Hightown was clearing a path for his partner straight to the maximum-security level and a single electro-cell. Jack was surprised to find out who it belonged to.

"I don't believe it," Jack said. "It's Speedrazor. They're busting Speedrazor loose."

"Speedrazor?" Skerren asked. "That doesn't make any sense."

"None of this makes any sense," Jack said.

"But Midknight helped us put Speedrazor in there," Skerren replied.

"Maybe that's not what that mission was about," Allegra said. "Don't forget, we only got Speedrazor because Jack nearly blew him up."

"He's typing in the access code for the cell," Jack told the others. "He's almost got it open."

"That's far enough, then," Skerren said. "I don't know what they're doing, but they can explain it to the Keepers. Sound the alarm, Jack."

"Yeah," Jack said. "This is over. Now."

Jack reached out with his powers and tripped the alarm. There was a loud noise like someone had thrown a massive switch, and suddenly the entire prison was awash in light. Sirens wailed at earsplitting volumes, and through the security camera lenses, Jack saw Midknight turn in surprise as two Keepers clad in jet-black super-suits sprang out of the wall next to Speedrazor's cell. The bulky Keepers rushed him, and two more followed close behind, gang-tackling Midknight like linebackers on a football field. Outside, searchlights swept the area looking for intruders, and Jack helped them out by deactivating the *Knightwing*'s cloak and turning the spotlights onto its location. Noteworthy hastily backed up the ship, bumping into the surrounding buildings before turning around and fleeing the scene.

"Noteworthy's bugging out," Skerren said.

"Some partner," Allegra noted.

"There's nothing he can do for Midknight now," Jack said. "Securamax is on full lockdown. The phase frequency is set to shift every ten seconds. He can't get back out through the walls the same way he went in."

But when Jack turned his attention back to the interior security cameras, he didn't see Midknight being taken into custody. Instead he found a mound of unconscious Keepers piled up outside Speedrazor's cell. Seconds later an explosion blasted through the face of the prison, and Midknight dove out into the night sky. He fired a grappling hook into the bottom of a MagLev highway and swung out into the air.

"Then again . . . ," Jack said.

Midknight sailed away from the prison as no fewer than fifty superhuman Keepers flew through the walls after him. Every one of them had superstrength and flight powers, but if Midknight was concerned about the odds, it was impossible to tell. He released the cable he was swinging on and went right at his pursuers, throwing himself at the nearest Keeper. Midknight latched on to a prison guard in midair and flipped over, using his weight and downward momentum to send the Keeper hurtling back into one of his comrades. Another guard came flying at him head-on, but Midknight got his hands over the Keeper's shoulders and forced him down. He stepped hard on the back of his assailant's head to keep him down, and sprang up to deliver a devastating uppercut to another Keeper who was flying in from above.

"Man, he's good," Jack said. He watched Midknight take a punch across the face from one Keeper just as another one lowered his shoulder and rammed into him, knocking him through the air like he'd been shot out of a cannon. The vigilante detective regained his bearings midflight and turned to deliver a flying kick at a guard who was flying in to collect him. As Midknight continued to fall through the air, he looped a line of cable around the leg of yet another Keeper and used him to swing onto a MagLev overpass directly above Jack and his friends.

Keepers swarmed him from all sides, and he fought them in the street, dodging HoverCars and LaserBikes as they sped down the road. No matter how many Keepers came at him, he always seemed to be in control.

"Forget what I said about every Keeper in the building," Allegra said. "That might not be enough."

No sooner had Allegra finished talking than Midknight paused mid-punch and started scanning the roadways beneath him. "I think he heard you," Jack said to Allegra. Jack's suspicions were confirmed as Midknight barreled into a throng of Keepers and ran them off the side of the road. They fell into the street next to Jack, Skerren, and Allegra, causing traffic to come to a screeching halt.

"Hey, kids, fancy meeting you here," Midknight said.

"Midknight, we—we—," Skerren stammered.

"I hate to do this to you guys, but don't worry," Midknight interrupted. "They'll let you go. Eventually." Midknight's hands moved like lightning as he went to his utility belt, detached three pellets, and threw them at the children. Before they could even think about dodging, each capsule hit its target, and Jack, Skerren, and Allegra were each enveloped by a fast-growing sticky green substance.

"Jack, do something!" Allegra shouted as the rapidly spreading goo covered her body. She was stretching to escape it, but it was no use.

"I'm trying!" Jack said. "It's not mechanical!"

"Nope, it's organic," Midknight said. "An organic wrap," he added with a short laugh. He jumped off the down ramp, flipping over and up onto another MagLev road, where he hijacked a LaserBike. "I'm really sorry about this," he told the driver. "I'll make it up to you, I promise."

The last Jack saw of Midknight, he was climbing onto the stolen LaserBike and speeding off into the shadows. As Midknight's wrap covered Jack's body up to the neck, he fell to the ground, where he had a sideways view of a mob of Keepers' feet as they touched down on the road, one after another. Jack heard them talking to one another, but he couldn't make out too much of what they were saying. "Looks like Smart was right about this one, eh?" one of them said clearly enough.

"What are you doing?" Jack asked. "He's getting away!"

"Quiet," the Keeper replied. "Jack Blank, you're under arrest."

CHAPTER

18

The Prisoner's Dilemma

The Keepers took Jack, Skerren, and Allegra into Secura-max and brought them all to different interview rooms. Several hours later Jack didn't know where Skerren and Allegra were, but he was still stuck inside his room, sitting across from the same interrogator, going over the story.

"I already told you ten times," Jack said. "We weren't here to help Midknight break into this place. We were here to stop him. I don't know how many other ways I can say it."

Jack's interrogator sat there staring at him and tapping his fingers on the table in between them. The man's face was even less expressive than the four barren walls surrounding him and Jack. After what felt like an eternity, he snorted and shook his head. "You three can certainly keep your stories straight, I'll give you that much," he said. "But you must think we're really stupid if you expect us to believe it." Jack's interrogator leaned over the table and locked eyes with him. "Every security measure we have looked the other way when Midknight broke in. I'm supposed to buy that the kid who controls machines didn't have anything to do with it? Come on."

Jack put his head down on the table and sighed heavily. He was tired and had no idea how long he'd been in that room. "You don't know what you're doing, keeping me here like this," he said. "I have things I need to get to. Important things." Jack looked up from the table. "How much longer are we going to do this?"

"Until we get to the truth," Jack's interrogator replied. "We know you were working with Midknight. The Skerren boy in the next room is his sidekick, for crying out loud. What were you doing here tonight? Why were you trying to break Speedrazor out of prison?"

Jack put his head back down and gently banged his forehead against the table. This conversation was going nowhere . . . slowly.

"How did you get to Midknight?" the man asked Jack, pressing harder. "We couldn't see his face. . . . Is he infected? Does he have a Rüstov scar underneath that mask?"

Jack grumbled into the table. "There's no point talking to you. You're not listening to a word I say."

"Just answer the question, Jack."

Jack sat up and pushed himself away from the table. "No. I'm done with that. This isn't right. You can't keep me here like this all night."

"I'm going to keep you here until the administrator of this facility says otherwise."

That actually made Jack laugh. "You mean Noteworthy?" he asked, making a big show of looking around. "Where is he? Let's get him out here. I'd love to talk to him."

"He's *coming*," Jack's interrogator insisted. The man shifted uncomfortably in his seat. "I don't know what's taking him so long, but he's coming," he muttered. "Jonas

Smart would have been here hours ago. I voted for him, you know."

"No kidding," Jack replied. "That's a real shocker. Here's another: Noteworthy's not coming anywhere near this place. I told you, he was the one working with Midknight. He bolted as soon as I set off the alarms."

"Then you better get comfortable," the man across the table told Jack. "Because we're going to be here for a long, long time, just you and me."

There was a knock on the door, and another Keeper poked his head in. "Jones, take a break," the man said. "Someone's here to see the kid."

Jack's interrogator, the man called Jones, sat up straight and twisted around to face the door. "But, sir!" he said. "I'm not finished with my—"

"Take a break," the man repeated. "Now."

Jones scowled but didn't argue any further. Instead he got up in a huff and stomped out of the room like a child. Once he had squeezed his way around whoever was waiting for Jack out in the hall, the man who had interrupted Jack's interview put up a fist and said, "All yours, big guy."

A massive blue hand came into view and bumped the fist in return. "Thanks, Chief," a familiar voice said, and Jack felt a huge swell of relief as his friend and mentor entered the room.

"Hey, kiddo," Blue said, grabbing a chair and turning it around to lean forward against its back. "Can't seem to stay out of trouble, can you? Secreteers? Prison breaks? Maybe you oughta keep it simple and stick to blowing up trains."

"Blue," Jack said, still shocked by his friend's sudden appearance. "What are you doing here? How'd you even know to find me in this place?"

Blue waved Jack off like it was no big thing. "I've got plenty of friends in this joint from my days on the force. They tipped me off that you and your friends were here."

"And you came just like that," Jack said, leaning back with relief. "Does this mean you aren't mad at me anymore?"

Blue shook his head. "I was never mad at you, Jack. I was *surprised* when you told me about Jazen and the virus, sure. . . . I needed some time to wrap my head around it. But I wasn't mad. More than anything, I hated that you felt like you had to keep the truth from me. You didn't have to do that, Jack. You didn't have to make it so hard on yourself."

Jack gave Blue a tired grin. "You're telling me there's some other way to do things?"

Blue tilted his head and returned the grin. "Fair enough," he said. "All right, tell me. What's going on? What are you doing here?"

Jack told Blue everything that had happened that night. He told him about the shady meeting between Midknight and Noteworthy. How they'd followed them both to Securamax, and how they'd stopped Midknight from busting Speedrazor out of jail. He even told Blue how they suspected that Noteworthy and Midknight were actually Glave and Khalix.

"Noteworthy?" Blue exclaimed. "*Midknight?* No way. Those two hate each other."

"That's the perfect cover," Jack said. "I'm telling you, Blue, I know what I saw. What else could they have been talking about on that roof? And what were they doing here, breaking into Securamax?"

"I know, but Midknight . . . ," Blue said, shaking his head. "I just can't believe it."

"Maybe he's infected," Jack said. "When was the last time you saw him without that mask?" Blue rubbed his face, thinking back and considering the possibility that Jack could be right. "And how about Noteworthy?" Jack asked. "Isn't he supposed to be here? He runs this place now. Where the heck is he?"

Blue nodded. "The warden here has been trying to reach him for hours. So far, nothing."

Jack put his hands up as if to say, "There you go."

"All right," Blue said. "I'll circle the wagons and see what kind of help I can get tracking them both. We'll see if there's anything there. First we gotta get you outta here, though. I can't spring ya. We need a Circleman for that."

"Blue, I can't stay here much longer," Jack said. He leaned in and lowered his voice. "Obscuro's gonna sell my secrets to Smart. If I'm still stuck in here when that comes out, they'll never let me leave."

"Don't worry," Blue said. "I had 'em make a few more calls when they couldn't get Noteworthy. Trust me, I know we gotta get you outta here and back to work on that virus."

Jack pinched the bridge of his nose. "The virus," he said. "I was supposed to go back and work on it with Trea tonight, and I end up getting arrested instead. She's going to kill me."

"She'll live," Blue said. "It'll all be fine once you get back there and start pitchin' in. You're gonna do your part—she knows that."

"I don't know, Blue," Jack said. "I'm so burned-out on this thing, I don't know if I can."

"No time to lie down on the job, partner. You gotta push yourself. You owe Jazen that much."

Jack rubbed the back of his neck and looked down at his shoes. He knew what he owed Jazen. He knew it all too well. "I'm sorry I didn't tell you about him," Jack told Blue. "I was protecting his memory as much as anything else. You've got to believe me."

Blue nodded. "I believe you, Jack. I just wish you'd told me sooner." Blue reached over to mess up Jack's hair. "It's going to be okay," he said. "Jazen already beat this thing once, right? That means it's not invincible. You'll beat it too."

"Okay," Jack said.

"I mean it," Blue said. "But you gotta focus. You gotta buckle down. I know what's going on in that head of yours, Jack. You can't let what that Secreteer said about your dad distract you. This is the most important thing. This right here. Okay?"

Jack nodded silently. Blue knew him so well. What Obscuro had told him about a message from his father had been rattling around in his brain like a lone penny shaking around in an empty tin can. Before that night in the glen, Jack had basically given up all hope that his parents were even still alive. Obscuro's offer was hard to ignore.

"You know, Jack, I was curious," Blue said. "The other night when you told us about the virus, you said that you and Jazen broke into SmartTower last year to get some information about who you were. You never told me what ended up happening with that. Did you ever find out anything about your past?"

Jack swallowed hard. He'd known this question would come sooner or later. The simple answer was yes. He had found out way more than he had ever bargained for that night, about both his past and his future. Telling Blue about it wasn't quite so simple, especially in a room that he knew was bugged. It wasn't a subject Jack liked to think about, and it certainly wasn't anything he wanted to talk about. In the end, he didn't have to. Blue knew Jack too well. The look on his face gave it all away.

"I hate to see you like this, Jack," Blue told his sidekick. "I can tell just by looking at ya, you're all wound up. It's not just this virus, either, is it?" Jack said nothing, so Blue just kept talking. "Jack, if there's something else you're worried Obscuro might say about you, even if it's something you haven't told me yet, that's okay. I'm not gonna be mad. I just want to help you get out in front of this thing." Blue put his hand on Jack's shoulder. "Whatever it is, partner, you can tell me. I've got your back. Think about it. . . . If you give up your secrets, they're not secrets anymore. You sure there isn't anything else you wanna tell me?"

Jack gave Blue's words serious consideration. He knew his friend was sincere, and he didn't want to lie anymore either, but the weight of the secrets Jack carried was like a sack of bricks on his back that even now he didn't know how to properly set down. Jack was still deciding what to tell Blue, when the door opened up and Projo flew in.

"I certainly hope there's nothing else," Virtua said. "I don't think my people can take any more of Jack's secrets." Jack clammed up as Virtua's holographic eyes judged him from across the room. "Up, Jack," she said. "You're free to go. Come join your friends outside. They're waiting for you."

Virtua turned to leave, and Blue rapped his knuckles on the table as he got to his feet. "To be continued," he told Jack. Jack got up and followed Blue and Virtua out of Securamax, hoping against hope that he wouldn't be back anytime soon.

Skerren and Allegra were waiting for Jack outside the main gate, but Virtua wasn't done with him yet. "Can I have a word with you, Jack?" she asked. The tone in her voice conjured up memories of Jack's days at St. Barnaby's and getting sent to H. Ross Calhoun's office. He nodded and followed Virtua a few feet away from the others, where they could speak in private. Projo, Virtua's orb-shaped image-caster, kept bumping into Jack's head as they walked. Jack could tell he was doing it on purpose.

"I'm sorry, Jack, but I am very concerned about your apparent lack of progress on the virus," Virtua began. "Even more so with your lack of focus."

"That's not how it is, Virtua. I—"

"Let me speak," Virtua said, putting up a finger in a manner that shut Jack up immediately. "I don't think you fully appreciate the position I am in. I have been made party to an imminent threat to the Imagine Nation, a threat that involves using my own people as a weapon. Even worse, I can't even warn this city of the danger at hand without inviting disaster into the lives of the very people I mean to protect."

"I hate to be the one to say it, but I don't think building that wall without telling anyone why did anything to ease the tension," Jack said.

"That wall is for everyone's protection," Virtua replied. "And you are hardly one to lecture me about being open and honest."

"I know that," Jack said. "Don't you think I know that? That's why I'm trying to make sure the Secreteer doesn't tell anyone about the virus."

"If you had simply focused on curing the virus, the

other Secreteers would have dealt with Obscuro on their own. You might have found a cure by now. This brings us to the heart of my dilemma. I cannot rely on you to solve this problem, Jack. While you are scattered, trying to figure out your priorities, the enemy advances unchecked. In the past I would have dismissed Jonas Smart's paranoia as just that, but we both know the threat is real. Obscuro's warning, coupled with the Glave and Khalix communications, tell us that this virus is about to go live. I have to plan for that contingency, Jack. I want a copy of all your research on the spyware virus to date."

Jack looked up, alarmed. "My research?" he asked. "But what if you get infected? The Rüstov would know how close we are to a cure. They might adapt the virus."

"What's the matter, Jack? You don't trust me?"

"No, I do," Jack said. "I do, it's just . . ."

"I need that information," Virtua told Jack. "It would be one thing if you were working on it, but—"

"I *am* working on it."

"Are you?" Virtua asked. "It looks to me like you're letting Trea do all the work while you go chasing after the Rogue Secreteer. I wonder about your fixation with him. . . . Is it because he knows your secrets, or because he knows your father?"

"Is that what you think I'm doing out here?" Jack asked. "Obscuro's offer has nothing to do with me avoiding my lab."

"So you *are* avoiding it, then."

"No," Jack said. "I didn't mean it like that. Don't put words in my mouth." Jack looked away. He could guess how selfish he must have looked in Virtua's eyes just then, but he couldn't tell her the real reason he was so freaked out about the prospect of working on the virus. "I'm not avoiding the problem," he said. "It's just that I can do more *outside* the lab right now."

"My IP address is 239847230987230984," Virtua told Jack, unmoved. "Can you upload your files to that location from here or not?"

Jack sighed. "No, it's too far away. But Trea uploaded all my research to the lab computers. If you can send a signal to my mainframe in Cognito, I can tell it how to get there and add an authorization code for the data transfer."

"Good enough," Virtua replied. She created an info-light data package, a buzzing concentration of computer code stored in a glowing ball of pink light. Jack pressed down on it with his fingers to enter in the access codes to his mainframe. The info-light was hot to the touch. Jack released the data package, and it zipped away through the air like an oversize digital firefly.

"That'll give you everything I have," Jack said. "It's a lot of work, it really is. It's just lately, I've been . . ."

"Distracted," Virtua said.

"I have help now," Jack told her. "I'm going to get back to it. There's still time."

"I hope so, Jack," Virtua replied. "I truly do."

Jack could tell that Circlewoman Virtua remained unconvinced. She blinked out, and Projo zipped away as Jack's friends came over.

"What did she have to say?" Skerren asked.

"Nothing I didn't deserve," Jack replied. "Did you guys tell her about Noteworthy and Midknight?"

"We told her," Allegra said.

"Good," Jack said. "She'll tell the Circle."

Rays of light started peeking in through the foundations of the Hightown towers that were built over the prison. The sun was coming up.

"Two more days," Blue said. "I'll see what I can dig up on Midknight before tomorrow. Hopefully, I can get Ricochet to help me."

"She's not going to like that," Allegra said. "Ricochet and Midknight are tight."

"I know." Blue frowned. "What about you kids? What's your next move?"

"We never got any Rüstov tech to help crack the cure-code," Jack said. "We need Obscuro. He's got to know something that can help us. He's still here, I know it."

"How are you going to find him?" Blue asked.

Jack shook his head. "As crazy as it sounds, we can follow Midknight's advice for that," Jack said.

"You mean follow Smart," Skerren said.

"Obscuro's not going to leave a hundred million credits on the table," Jack said.

"Kind of putting all our eggs in one basket, aren't we?" Allegra asked. "What about the virus?"

"We still have time," Jack said, trying to convince himself as much as he was the others. "Blue, can you drop me off in Karateka? I need to talk to Zhi before tomorrow."

"Today is tomorrow," Blue said, opening up the door to his HoverCar and sliding over to make room for Jack. "I hope you know what you're doing, partner."

"Me too," Jack said. "Me too."

CHAPTER

19

Betrayal Most Foul

Jack was both tired and hungry but couldn't afford the luxury of eating or sleeping. After he left Karateka, he had time for one quick stop in the Outlands, and then it was straight to Hero Square. He arrived just in time for the SmarterNet launch, and found that half of Empire City was there too. Thousands of people had turned out to get a look at Jonas Smart's big project. People from every borough filled the square in numbers that reminded Jack of the Rededication Day celebrations.

Smart was holding court nearby, next to a SmartNews

remote broadcast desk that had been set up for the occasion. Words sailed through the air around the SmartNews set, thanks to digital projection signage that called out the NewsNet's many slogans and catchphrases. Advertisements that read "SmartNews: Our opinions are your facts" and "SmartNews: Information for the *real* Imagine Nation" were impossible to miss, especially for Jack.

"We all know that Jonas Smart is a tireless defender of the Imagine Nation and its people," Drack Hackman said as he came back from a commercial break. "But even now, with his business struggling and him being out of office for nearly a year, still doing his part to protect us from the Rüstov?" Hackman shook his head in awe. "That's more than we can say for our current Circleman."

"A lot of our viewers have been saying that very same thing," Hackman's cohost agreed. "Speaking of which, the SmarterNet isn't the only big story today. Last night there was a break-in at Hightown's Securamax detention center. As of this morning, prison authorities *still* haven't been able to locate Clarkston Noteworthy to discuss the security breach."

"No surprises there," Hackman said. "He's probably

sitting on a launchpad in Galaxis ready to blast off right now."

"Oh, it gets better, Drack," the cohost added. "Smart-News has confirmed that local adventurer and former Jonas Smart campaign rival Midknight was the one actually breaking into Securamax . . . helped along by our old friend Jack Blank, no less."

"Really!" Hackman exclaimed as if this exchange hadn't been rehearsed a dozen times before the cameras had started rolling. "Three people that Jonas Smart warned us about, all somehow involved in this prison break?" he asked his cohost. She threw up her hands as if she couldn't believe it either. "That's astounding," Hackman marveled. "You know, looking at the turnout we're seeing here today, I have a feeling that elections in Hightown might go a little differently next time around. You can't keep Jonas Smart down for long."

"No, you certainly can't," Hackman's cohost agreed with a hearty laugh.

Jack's eyes narrowed as he looked over at Smart. His face was stretched across giant holo-screens as he talked with Hightown's high rollers, shook hands, and smiled.

The man with no heart looked practically giddy with excitement for the launch of his latest invention. Jack had to admit, Smart was pushing all the right buttons. The way he worked the crowd was nothing short of masterful, and his popularity was on the rise once more. He was stoking the fires of people's worst fears while simultaneously assuring them that everything would be all right because of him, and the crowd in Hero Square was only too happy to thank him for it. *How quickly they forget,* Jack thought. A week ago the pervading feeling in the Imagine Nation had been one of hope for the future. Using a combination of Rüstov spies and the Rogue Secreteer, Smart had seized his opportunity to turn that sentiment around completely. Jack realized fear was like a fuse waiting to be lit. All it takes is someone coming along with the right match. If no one blows it out, sooner or later . . . boom.

Jack spotted Skerren, Allegra, and Zhi near the Inner Circle's sphere and was headed in that direction when he got ambushed. "We thought we'd find you here," a pair of voices said in unison just as Jack approached the sphere. Jack looked up and saw two-thirds of his lab partner blocking his path. "What's going on, Jack?" T2 asked him. "You never came back to the lab last night."

"We heard you got arrested," T3 added. "What's *that* about?"

"Hey, guys," Jack said. "Sorry about that. Last night got a little out of hand," he explained. "I'll be back there later today; I just have some stuff I gotta do first. It's still early." Jack pushed around the Treas and kept walking.

"Not cool, Jack," T2 said, keeping pace with Jack until he reached the others. "Not cool at all."

"T1's on her way to Cognito now," T3 added, coming up behind him. "I can't believe you're not there. This is ridiculous. She's been practically living at your lab— *we've* been practically living at your lab! Where've you been? Nowhere, that's where. You haven't done a thing to help yet!"

"Let me guess. You're Trea's temper, aren't you?" Skerren asked T3.

"Shut up, Skerren!" T3 hollered back at him. "Don't try and change the subject! What are you guys doing here? Is this about the Secreteer again?" Jack looked around uncomfortably as T3 laid into him. She was causing a scene. "You said you were going to put some time in and help us! I swear, we should just walk and leave you to deal with this mess on your own. We would, too, if it weren't so important."

"This is important too," Jack shot back in an angry whisper. "It's all connected. You just can't see how yet."

"Maybe you should fill us in, then," T3 said.

Jack frowned. "I'll be back later today," he said. "We've still got all of today and tomorrow. There's still time."

"T1 said if you aren't going to help her, we're going to help ourselves," T2 told Jack.

"What does that mean?" he asked.

"What do you care?" T3 shot back. "If you want to find out, stop slacking and come down to the lab for a change. We're out of here," she said, grabbing T2 by the arm and dragging her off in the other direction.

Over at the event stage, it was time for the big ribbon cutting. Smart was nearing the end of another long, impassioned speech about his selfless nature and ingenious vision for protecting the Imagine Nation. When he was finished, he tapped a few keys on his pocket holocomputer, and a large tangital console with a hand-size power button materialized on the stage before him. Smart declared the Imagine Nation to be under his protection once more, and hit the button.

There was a flash of light, and suddenly the air was filled with streamers, confetti, and fireworks bright enough to be seen in the morning sky. The crowd cheered for the spectacle, but Jack saw it for what it was: a lot of showmanship to make up for the fact that the SmarterNet was not actually on-site in Hero Square. Jack figured the device was somewhere far away in an undisclosed location, doing who-knows-what. There was no real payoff for hitting that button that could be seen with the naked eye, but Jack felt the effects of the SmarterNet launch almost instantly. He felt new information flying through the airwaves, but couldn't read any of it. There was an encryption code with a weak nullifier signal mixed into the transmission that locked Jack out. As far as he could tell, nothing bad was happening as a result of the SmarterNet's launch, but there was definitely something in the air.

As the crowd continued to applaud, Jonas Smart checked his watch and then gave one final wave before ducking into his HoverCar to leave. Jack looked over at Skerren, Allegra, and Zhi. It was time to go to work.

Jack, Skerren, Allegra, and Zhi raced across Hero Square toward Karateka, where their next move was less likely to attract attention. They found a quiet, near-empty park with a pond surrounded by cherry blossom trees. It would have to do. Smart's HoverCar was already almost out of sight, exiting Hero Square at the southwest corner.

"We're gonna lose him," Skerren said.

"I don't need to see him to track him," Jack replied. "We want a little distance between us or he might catch on."

"There's distance, and then there's *distance*," Skerren told Jack.

"I'm not gonna lose him," Jack said. "Zhi, everything set for today?"

"Just like we talked about," Zhi replied.

"Good," Jack said, hoping that everything would play out according to plan. If things didn't work out, it wouldn't be for a lack of trying on his part. "Let's do this."

Zhi bowed his head and pressed a fist into his palm. He spoke, soft and low, in an ancient language Jack didn't understand, and then there was a flash of light, a sound like thunder, and a strong gust of wind that brought Zhi's dragons flying into the park. Jack counted four of the seven mystical Chinese dragons Zhi had at his command. Glowing with the light of the supernatural, the spirit dragons flew through the air, their long, snakelike bodies weaving over, under, and around one another. They were fierce creatures with large talons, wild eyes, sharp fangs, and horns. Each dragon had a thick mane of hair running down its back, and long, flowing whiskers that ran out like mustaches. With a single word from Zhi they all landed, stretching out their front legs and lowering their heads in submission.

"Go ahead," Zhi told the others. "Get on. They'll let you."

"Will they listen to us?" Allegra asked. "I don't speak Chinese."

"Don't worry," Zhi said, climbing onto the back of the orange dragon. "Just pull on their mane in the direction you want to go. They'll understand. Oh, and hold on tight," he added as he called out another command in Chinese, launching his dragon mount up into the sky. Zhi and the orange dragon shot high up into the air, looped into a spiral dive, and swung out over Jack and the others. "What are you waiting for?" Zhi called out. "Let's go!"

"You have one of these things for everybody?" Jack asked Zhi.

"Just like we talked about," Zhi said again. "I told them to follow their riders' orders without question."

"Okay," Jack replied as he climbed onto the green dragon. Allegra chose the blue, and Skerren the red. Seconds later they were all up in the air, riding the spirit dragons and holding tight to their manes. It was exhilarating. The wind whipped through Jack's hair as he soared over the tiered rooftops and decorative wooden arches of old-town Karateka. As the group flew away, Jack looked back to see the tail of a purple dragon swinging down into the park they had just left.

Okay . . . good, Jack thought.

"Which way now?" Skerren wanted to know.

"Where did Smart go?" Allegra asked.

Jack closed his eyes and felt out the area with his powers. "Follow me," he shouted as he took the lead, heading south toward Galaxis. Jack drove his dragon hard and fast through the heavily trafficked alien borough, dodging starships, LaserBikes, and HoloTrains as he zipped down the busy HoverCar-filled streets.

"How are you tracking him?" Allegra asked Jack, pulling up alongside him. "I thought Smart always used his power nullifiers against you."

"He does," Jack said. "This time I'm using them against him."

"What are you talking about?" Skerren shouted.

"The power nullifiers are *how* I'm tracking him," Jack revealed. "Smart puts them on all his machines and buildings. He even carries a portable nullifier with him everywhere he goes to cancel me out. What he doesn't realize is that from my point of view, that portable nullifier creates a moving dead zone that sticks out like a sore thumb, especially here in a high-tech borough like Galaxis. It's like a pocket of nothing that can only be filled with one thing: Jonas Smart. This way!"

Jack led the others through the intergalactic borough quickly, heading right up to the very edge of Empire City where the spaceport's launchpads and landing strips jutted out over the cliffs of the Imagine Nation. Sure enough,

Smart's empty HoverCar was parked there on a runway. "There!" Zhi yelled, pointing at a small ship that had just taken off near the abandoned vehicle. It was headed for a luxury launch platform that hovered in the air off the coast of the island.

Jack looked at the ship intently for few tense moments as it flew toward the platform, one of several ships that were blasting off from the spaceport launchpads. The aliens of Galaxis were taking Obscuro's advice and leaving town in a hurry. "He's on that ship," Jack confirmed. "Let's go, but slowly. Use the other starships for cover as much as you can. We don't want to give ourselves away."

Jack's voice crackled through Allegra's communicator bracelet as he spoke. Skerren asked Jack if he'd meant to do that, and he replied that he must have hit the talk button on his wristband by accident. The group moved on, chasing down Jonas Smart, and hopefully Obscuro as well.

Jack and his friends crossed the sky carefully on their way over to the floating platform Smart's ship had just disappeared into. It was a large crescent-shaped structure with a flat top that served as a launchpad for a handful of very expensive ships. The platform was an exclusive spaceport reserved for luxury starcruisers and wealthy aliens looking for something a little more sophisticated than the crowded docks in Galaxis proper. Jack and the others pulled up to the main hangar and dismounted by jumping into the station and leaving their dragons outside. Smart's empty ship was parked inside next to a few equally flashy AirShips. The station attendants, dressed all in white, were so busy waxing the ships in the bay that they hardly took notice of the children's entrance.

"Can you still track Smart in here?" Allegra asked Jack.

"As long as he's wearing that nullifier I can," Jack answered as he reached out with his powers. It was as if there were a small black hole moving through the station, a place where, for all intents and purposes, there were no machines to talk to. Jack knew better than that, and as a result, he knew which way to go. "That way," he said, pointing toward a sign that read PRIVATE HANGARS 10-19. "Easiest thing in the world."

Jack took off running and the others followed. "Ironic that Smart built those power nullifiers to shut you down," Allegra told him with a smile as they ran through the tation. "You've got to love outsmarting the world's smartest man."

Jack smiled back as he led the group through winding corridors and up and down stairways in the station. He could hardly believe it, but Allegra was right. He had outsmarted Smart. The only question was, what came next? Was he really going to pull this thing off? Were all the right pieces really about to fall into place? Jack tried not to get his hopes up, but the odds took a big swing in his favor as he turned the corner and saw Jonas Smart walking down the hall ahead of him. Smart had two large duffel bags floating alongside him on HoverPads. Jack shot out an arm, and the group stopped short, piling up behind him. Alerted by the noise, Smart stopped and turned around, but saw no one there. Jack and the others were just out of sight, having quickly jumped back around the corner. *That was way too close*, Jack thought. They couldn't afford to be spotted now. Not when everything was going so well.

"This is it," Jack whispered, peering back around the corner. "He's even got the money with him."

Skerren leaned over Jack's shoulder to get a better

look. "A hundred million credits," he marveled. "Unbelievable."

"His ship is in the main dock," Allegra said as Smart went to a door marked HANGAR 17. "That has to be Obscuro's hangar."

Jack nodded in agreement as Smart keyed in a code and entered hangar 17 with his money in tow. Jack and his friends ran to the door as soon as it closed behind Smart. He had locked it behind him.

"Can you beat this lock like you did with the door in Gravenmurk Glen?" Skerren asked Jack.

"Yeah, I just need to wait until Smart gets far enough away from the door so the nullifier gets out of range."

Skerren nodded and quietly touched a hand to the door. Nothing left to do now but wait.

"Since we have a minute here, maybe we should talk about how we're going to play this once we get inside," Zhi suggested.

"What do you mean?" Skerren asked.

"Yeah, what are you talking about?" Jack asked.

"I mean, what happens if we go in there and see Obscuro already talking to Smart?" Zhi replied. "What do we do then?" He looked at Skerren and Allegra. "I know you guys have been after the rogue, trying to find out whatever you can about Glave and Khalix. Do we just wait until Smart's gone and then deal with Obscuro ourselves?"

"No," Jack said. "That's not good enough. We have to keep Obscuro from telling Smart about the virus. He finds out about that and it's game over."

"Jack, Obscuro's going to sell him that information sooner or later," Skerren said. "We can't outbid Smart for your secrets. No one can."

"Then we separate them by force if we have to," Jack said.

"By force?" Allegra repeated. "You're talking about assaulting a Circleman."

"A *former* Circleman," Jack corrected. "And we're not assaulting him; we're assaulting Obscuro."

"Because he's going to spill the beans on *your* secrets," Allegra said. "That's not going to look good, Jack. Smart will make sure of that, and he'll use that NewsNet of his to do it twenty-four/seven."

"As if that's any different from what's going on right

now," Jack said. "It'll only get worse if Obscuro tells Smart about the virus. We have to stop that from happening. Unless you guys have any better ideas, I don't see what choice we have here."

Silence fell outside the door of hangar 17. Jack's friends couldn't think of any other options either.

"We just need to make sure something good comes out of this," Skerren said. "Then it won't look so suspicious. We capture Obscuro and get the info on Glave and Khalix out of him. We put a stop to them—"

"And they provide the Rüstov tech that you and Trea need to stop the virus," Allegra said, finishing Skerren's thought. "That could work," she said, nodding. "That'd be perfect."

Jack's heart started beating faster. "It's gonna have to work out perfectly," he muttered. "If it's going to work at all." Before anyone could ask him to repeat himself, he straightened his back and looked at the door to hangar 17 with purpose. The nullification zone had passed, and his powers had returned. After Jack had a brief conversation with the door's locking mechanism, the light on the keypad turned from red to green. They were in.

The door slid open and the children crept inside.

Hangar 17 was an expansive, empty platform with only three walls. The fourth wall was made up of only the hangar doors, which were currently wide open. Powerful winds ripped through the room, loud enough to muffle the sound of Jack and his friends coming in, and strong enough to push them back on their heels as they entered. Docking equipment, tools, and cargo crates were strewn about the edges of the room. Jack and the others took cover behind them and escaped Smart's notice.

Smart was standing at the far end of the platform, staring out the open hangar doors as a cloaked ship came in for landing. Jack felt it approaching outside the hangar, but he didn't need his powers to spot the "invisible" vessel. Not when he was this close. The sound of its engines was unmistakable, as was the blurry, ship-size patch of air that was slowly descending toward the platform. Cloaking devices fooled only radar systems, not human eyes. After touching down, the ship dropped its cloak, and Obscuro emerged from its cockpit. Smoke trailed behind the Rogue Secreteer as he walked down the ramp toward Smart, his robes blowing in the breeze coming in from outside. Jack and the others did their best to listen in as they inched along behind the crates, working their way closer to Smart and Obscuro. It was unbelievable, but Jack's plan was working out perfectly. A combination of preparation, risk, and luck had put him precisely where he needed to be—right between Smart and Obscuro.

Obscuro reached the bottom of the ramp and stopped a few feet away from Smart. "The Rogue Secreteer, I presume?" Smart said to him.

"You may call me Obscuro," the Secreteer replied, offering a slight bow. "Pleased to meet you."

"I expect you are," Smart said. "I know I'd be pleased to meet someone willing to pay me a hundred million credits for a five-minute conversation. You are aware of what I expect in return for this money?"

"I am."

"And you are prepared to tell me what I want to know?"

"I am indeed."

"Good." Smart smiled, nodding. "It's good to know your greed has its limits," he added as he typed on his pocket holo-computer, moving the bags of money between him and Obscuro. "I was beginning to worry that you intended to hold out for more."

Obscuro put his hands up, appearing to wave Smart off. "I wasn't waiting for you to offer more money," he told Smart. "I was waiting for the SmarterNet to launch."

Smart looked up from his handheld device with a start. "The SmarterNet?" he asked. "What for?"

"Two reasons," Obscuro replied. "For one, I know you can't afford to spend a hundred million credits on me and my secrets, Mr. Smart. Not anymore. We both know there's no money in those bags. Don't bring them any closer."

Smart scowled. Obscuro's glowing eyes narrowed behind his mask and hood. Smart stopped the bags where they were. "And your other reason?" Smart asked with a hard edge in his voice.

"It's quite simple," Obscuro replied. "I know how the SmarterNet works. How it *really* works. Jack Blank isn't the only one with secrets, is he?"

Smart froze. He wasn't the type to show an opponent fear, or any other emotion for that matter, but Jack could tell that Obscuro had him scared stiff, and that scared

Jack. Something was wrong . . . something he didn't understand. Jack suddenly had a sinking feeling that he didn't really know what was going on. He wasn't seeing the big picture, and he worried that by the time he did, it would be too late.

"I don't need any more money," Obscuro continued. "I have my ship now. I'm ready to leave this place. What I want before I go are the access codes to your system."

"Why?" Smart squeaked out after a few moments. "What do you want with that?"

"Despite betraying my order, I remain a Secreteer at heart. My kind craves secrets like candy. Even far, far away from Earth, where the secrets uncovered by your device will be of no real value to me, I will still feel the urge to eavesdrop on this pale blue dot in the universe's starscape. Whatever remains of it. Call it whatever you want—an unhealthy compulsion, being homesick; perhaps it's both. The fact is, it doesn't matter what I want the information for. What matters is that it's a small price to pay for Jack Blank's secrets, and if that's not agreeable to you, I could always inform the people of Empire City what the SmarterNet really does."

Smart gritted his teeth. "I don't like being black-mailed," he said.

"No one ever does," Obscuro replied. "That's why it's so effective. Are you going to give me what I want, or shall I place a few calls to the city's independent NewsNets?"

"No," Smart said quickly. "No, don't do that. There's no need for that. You have a deal. You're right, it's a small price to pay."

"I thought you'd see it my way," Obscuro replied. "A simple note with the codes and the broadcast frequency on a piece of SmartPaper will do. Anytime you're ready."

Smart nodded to Obscuro and typed away on his hand-held computer. Jack looked over at Skerren, Allegra, and Zhi. "It's now or never," he told his friends.

Skerren nodded and drew his swords. "Follow me," he said. As Smart took a step toward Obscuro, Skerren charged out from behind a cargo crate. Jack, Allegra, and Zhi jumped out after him, quickly taking up positions between Obscuro and Smart. Allegra stretched out and wrapped Obscuro up so tight that he couldn't move.

"Get him out of here!" Jack shouted. Allegra struggled

to move Obscuro toward the door as Jack, Skerren, and Zhi stayed behind to hold off Smart and cover her escape. "Sorry, Smart. We're taking Obscuro with us," Jack said. "My secrets aren't for sale."

"Is that so?" Smart said with a laugh. "I don't think that's your decision to make, Jack, but I'm glad to see you showing your true colors once again. It's been too long. It really has."

"Don't try to stop us," Skerren said. "You're unarmed and outnumbered."

"Yeah, and your power nullifiers don't work on us," Zhi added.

Smart snickered with a cold, condescending laugh. "Silly boy. As if power nullifiers were the only weapons at my disposal. I'm afraid you'll find that I'm anything but unarmed, and as for being outnumbered . . . that is a matter of opinion. As Obscuro already surmised, there are no credits in these two bags."

Smart keyed in a sequence on his pocket holo-computer, and a swarm of gun-toting droids flew out of the floating bags. "Fire at will," Smart said evenly, and the droids began blasting at the children.

"Take cover!" Allegra shouted as she reached over to block a series of shots that were aimed at Jack. A burst of smoke erupted in Allegra's grasp, and suddenly the Secreteer wasn't her captive anymore. He was back in place next to Smart.

"You let him go?" Jack shouted in disbelief. "Allegra! What are you doing?"

"I was saving you!" Allegra fired back. "You were about to get hit!"

"And you *will* get hit unless you keep your distance," Smart said. "Allow me to introduce my SmartFire Sentinels, the latest in personal protection from SmartCorp. Get too close and they'll shoot to kill. Stay back, children, and don't interfere. With any luck, you'll only get wounded."

Jack didn't bother to thank Allegra for saving his life. He just kept moving toward Smart as she continued to block more shots that likely would have killed him if she hadn't been there. Skerren was also advancing on Smart and Obscuro, blocking shots with his blades. He sent a few ricochets back at Smart, and got close enough to slice a few Sentinels in two. Zhi was dodging blasts from

350

the Sentinels, trying to get closer as well. Trained in the martial arts since he could crawl, Zhi nearly equaled Skerren's fighting prowess despite his young age. Jack watched him deliver a flying karate kick that slammed one Sentinel into another. Meanwhile, Jack couldn't do anything but move back out of the Sentinels' range, which he reluctantly did after being urged repeatedly by Allegra. It was the only move. This close to Smart, Jack was powerless. The nullifiers were working as intended once again.

"Smart! The access codes, now!" Obscuro shouted.

Smart generated a sheet of glowing SmartPaper with the codes and held it up in front of him. "The information first," he told Obscuro.

"No!" Zhi shouted, getting in close enough to almost reach the piece of SmartPaper with the codes. He weaved under a Sentinel and shot his hand up, chopping the droid in half like he was breaking boards in the dojo. Unfortunately, another Sentinel blasted him from behind, and Obscuro grabbed him up by the collar. "Insolent whelp! Be gone!" The rogue threw Zhi sliding across the floor.

Zhi skidded right up to the edge of the platform leading out into the open air. His body slid out over the side, and he grabbed on to the ledge with his fingers.

"Zhi!" Skerren and Allegra yelled out, and ran to help him. Jack stayed rooted to the spot, his stomach sinking as Obscuro grabbed the codes from Smart's hands and leaned in to tell him what he wanted to know.

"No . . . ," Jack said, shaking his head. He had to put a stop to this. It was time to go to his contingency plan. His last resort. Jack didn't want to do it this way, but he was out of options, and he wasn't going to get another chance. Jack hit a button on his wrist communicator and shouted into it. "LOREM, NOW!!!"

"What?" Smart said, turning his head in surprise.

"*What?*" Allegra said as Jack's voice came ringing through her bracelet. Over at the edge of the hangar, she and Skerren were pulling Zhi up. Just as they reached solid ground, a purple Chinese dragon flew in and landed its massive body on the platform, blocking them off from Smart, Obscuro, and Jack. Lorem Ipsum was riding it. Her dragon swallowed up Smart's Sentinels in one gulp, but swung its tail out, sideswiping Jack's friends. Skerren, Allegra, and Zhi went flying into the wall.

"Lorem!" Jack shouted. "What are you doing? They're on our side!"

Lorem hopped off the dragon's back with a laugh, landing softly between Smart and Obscuro. She didn't seem to care that taking out Jack's friends was not part of the plan.

"Lorem?" Smart said, boggled. "Is that you?"

"Hi, Daddy," she replied, pulling her hair back out of her face. She was wearing one of Jack's communicator bracelets.

"Let's save the family reunion for later," Jack said to Lorem. "Shut Obscuro down before he talks!"

At least, that's what Jack meant to say. It took a few seconds for him to realize that he wasn't saying anything of the kind. He wasn't even speaking English. No matter what he tried to say, it kept coming out, *"Lorem ipsum dolor sit amet! Consectetur adipisicing elit sed!"*

"That's easy for you to say," Lorem told Jack, laughing hysterically.

He looked down and saw her hand touching his wrist.

Jack couldn't believe it. Lorem had double-crossed him!

"Lorem," Smart said. "You surprise me. Good girl."

"Thanks, Daddy," she said, smiling.

"Don't call me that," Smart replied in a curt tone. "Obscuro, you have something you wish to tell me?"

Obscuro nodded, and Jack looked on, horrified, as the Rogue Secreteer leaned over to whisper his secrets into Smart's ear. Jack watched as Smart's eyes grew wide, and then wider. Jack could say or do nothing to stop it. It was his worst nightmare, coming to life before his very eyes.

"This is beyond belief!" Smart said, pulling back from Obscuro in alarm. "I need . . . I need to get to my lab immediately!" Smart pushed past Jack, making a beeline for the door. Lorem hurried along behind him, turning back to offer Jack a callous explanation as she left. "Sorry, Jack," she said. "I know this wasn't our deal, but what can I say? I have my own plans."

As Lorem Ipsum closed the door behind her on the way out, Jack felt his world shatter. Things had gone about as wrong as they could possibly go.

"I have my own plans too, Jack," Obscuro said, placing a hand on Jack's shoulder after Smart and Lorem had exited the hangar together. "You should know my offer still stands. You're welcome to come with me when I leave." Obscuro motioned over at Jack's outraged friends, who were climbing over the back of Zhi's purple dragon and coming toward him. "It won't be safe for you here now," Obscuro told Jack. "Surely you know that."

Jack had to admit the Secreteer was right. Not only had one of his worst enemies just gained an impossible advantage over him, but he was almost certainly out of best friends to fight back with. He'd lied to them one time too many, and it had finally caught up with him.

"Your father gave me a message for you," Obscuro told Jack. "He said, 'Don't despair. We will be together again soon.'" Jack looked up at Obscuro, unable to say anything. "It's better you go with me and rejoin your family," Obscuro said, handing Jack a paper card. "I'll be leaving here soon. This will lead you to me when the time comes."

A burst of smoke shot up, and when it cleared, Obscuro was back in his ship, getting ready to lift off. Jack's friends surrounded him, wearing looks of shock and outrage on their faces. Unable to meet their gazes, Jack examined the card that Obscuro had just given him. It was blank. *That figures*, Jack thought. Everything had officially fallen apart. He was left with nothing, save for the knowledge that things could only get worse from here.

CHAPTER

20

The Prototype

Jack remembered Lorem Ipsum telling him that her gibberish touch lasted however long she wanted it to last. It was an aspect of her powers that made her especially dangerous, and one that Jack had been counting on to help his plan succeed—right up until the moment when Lorem had grabbed his wrist. Past that point, Jack's plan and any hope of success had gone out the window along with his ability to form meaningful sentences. He could hardly believe things had gone so horribly wrong.

Jack hoped that Lorem wouldn't add insult to injury

by dragging out the effects of her powers too long. As it turned out, he didn't know her very well at all. She dragged things out just long enough to rub salt in the wounds left by her betrayal. It took more than an hour for the Lorem Ipsum effect to wear off, which meant that Jack couldn't explain himself to his friends or offer any excuses for his actions.

When it came time to let Jack have it, Zhi was up first. He was kicking himself more than the others because he'd unwittingly made Jack's side deal with Lorem Ipsum possible by loaning him the purple dragon. "I don't believe this," he said. "I trusted you. I looked up to you. . . . You used me!" The purple dragon gave its master a confused look, like it didn't know what it had done wrong. Zhi stroked the dragon behind its ear, making it purr. "It's not your fault," he told the creature. "I never would have let you do this if I'd known what he had planned." Zhi turned back to Jack. "I only did it because you said you needed my help. This is how you pay me back? Where were you when I was hanging off the edge of the platform over there? Where were you when I needed *your* help?"

"We got all messed up listening to you," Skerren said

to Jack. "You never stopped lying for a second, did you? I asked you straight up if the spyware virus was the only thing you were keeping from us. You acted like you'd told us everything, but that was just an act. There's obviously something else going on here." Skerren shook his head in disgust. "You don't just keep secrets, Jack. You tell lies, and you tell them to your friends. I used to worry that you'd end up on the Rüstov's side in this war. Now that I know you better, I almost feel sorry for them if that's what the future holds. The only side you care about is your own."

Jack literally could not argue with anything Skerren said, even if he did disagree with the last part. It wasn't that he didn't care about other people. That was the whole reason he'd kept the spyware virus a secret to begin with, to protect the Mechas. Jack's mistake had come in trying to juggle the Mechas' secrets alongside his own, and letting his personal interests get in the way of solving the more immediate problem. It was that selfishness that had caused him to screw things up so badly and hurt his friends in the process. Jack didn't know just how badly he'd hurt them until he saw the look on Allegra's face.

"You made a bracelet . . . for her?" she asked, holding back tears. "For *her*?" Allegra looked at the bracelet on her own wrist as if it were something she'd once treasured that had been stripped of all value. She took it off and walked to the edge of the platform, ready to throw it out into the sea. She stopped herself just short of doing so. Why she stopped, Jack didn't know. He just knew that the pained look in Allegra's eyes would gnaw at him more than anything Skerren or Zhi had said that day.

"I want to know what Obscuro told Smart before he took off," Skerren said. "What is it? What else are you hiding?"

Jack tried to speak, but only gibberish came out.

"Don't bother," Allegra said, wiping her eyes. "Lorem scrambled him—he can't talk."

"Great," Skerren said. "That's perfect. We can't trust anything we did with him now," he told Allegra and Zhi. "There's something deeper at work here, and we don't have time anymore to figure out what. We wasted four out of five days listening to Jack, and he's still keeping secrets from us. Now we find out the SmarterNet has some hidden purpose too?"

"Should Smart be a suspect?" Zhi asked.

"I don't know," Allegra said. "We can't figure this out on our own. We need to tell someone what's going on."

"*We* don't even know what's going on!" Skerren said. "That's the problem! Jack hasn't shared that with us. And who do we tell? Our mentors? Midknight is off hiding who knows where and may or may not be a Rüstov spy! I don't know what to think; I don't know who to trust. . . . Gah!" Skerren blurted out, kicking over a tool chest that was sitting in the corner of the hangar.

"We'll tell the Inner Circle," Allegra said. "That's who we tell."

Skerren looked daggers down at Jack, and then nodded at Allegra. "Yeah, you're right," he said. "Let's go. I need to talk to Hovarth. Now."

Zhi had the other dragons come around through the open hangar doors, and he, Skerren, and Allegra all climbed onto their backs. "Find your own way home," he said to Jack, just before taking off. "We're done."

Jack watched his friends fly off in silence, leaving him alone in hangar 17. He made it back to Cognito later that afternoon, returned to his apartment, and sank into a couch in his living room, defeated. The Lorem Ipsum effect had worn off at last, but it was too late to matter.

Jack took stock of his situation after the debacle with Smart, Obscuro, and Lorem Ipsum. It was almost too horrible to wrap his mind around. Smart knew everything. *Everything.* Jack wondered what the old buzzard was waiting for. He'd expected the story to be all over the NewsNets by the time he got home. So far there was nothing, but it was only a matter of time. A SmartNews special report was sure to break in any minute. Tired and depressed, Jack just wanted to crawl into a hole and disappear. Trea had no intention of letting him do anything of the sort.

"It's about time you came back," Jack heard Trea say. He whipped his head around to see her walking out of his kitchen carrying three energy drinks from his refrigerator. "C'mon," she said on her way down to the lab. "We're all downstairs working."

Jack plunged his head into a pillow on the couch and sighed heavily. "You've gotta be kidding me," he grumbled, but she was already gone. Jack dutifully picked himself up and followed Trea downstairs. When Jack entered the lab, he found that things were not at all as he had left them.

Jack looked around, marveling at the miraculous transformation of his work space. There were no piles of anything on the floor. The lab was brighter. More spacious. It smelled better. His piles of computer components and Mecha parts were all separated by category and neatly organized into labeled bins. The surfaces of his lab stations were cleaned off and wiped down. The red-hot atomic-death chicken wings he had ordered the week before were gone, even though Jack was pretty sure there had been a few of them left in the container that were still good. He took a closer look and found that any leftover food lying about had been thrown into the garbage, and the garbage itself had been thrown out. The last time his lab had been this clean was the day he'd moved in.

Jack saw two of Trea's selves comparing notes and typing away at a computer terminal. The third was taking a break and gulping down her beverage at a lab station. "Wow," he said, looking around. "I didn't know you guys were still here."

"We never left," the three Treas replied at once.

Jack wandered around the lab, looking at the spotless countertops and organized bookshelves. "You've been busy," he said.

"You have no idea," the Trea behind Jack said. "What do you think? Everything is organized. There's a system now."

"I had a system," Jack maintained. "There was always a system."

The three Treas gave Jack skeptical looks. "You didn't have a system, Jack," one of the Treas at the computer terminal observed with a wry grin. "You had a breeding ground for bacteria."

"Exactly," the Trea next to her added. "You had a systematic avoidance of cleaning products. That's about it."

Jack frowned. He was in no mood to deal with his lab partner's triple talk.

"You ready to get to work?" the Trea behind him asked.

Jack shook his head. He had never been less ready. "Listen, Trea," he began, "I know what I said this morning, but I *really* don't think I can work on this thing right now. My head isn't in a very good place at the moment."

All three Treas stopped what they were doing and looked up.

"At the *moment*?" asked the Trea at the lab station. "You're joking, right? Your head's been somewhere else the entire time I've been working with you." She downed the rest of her drink and threw the empty can into the recycling bin, trading disappointed looks with her other selves along the way. "I'm not sure I can even really say I've been working with you at all. Jack, really . . . this is ridiculous. If you're not going to work on this now, when are you going to work on it? You've been putting this off forever. What's the reason this time? More running around with Skerren and Allegra?"

"No," Jack said. "No, I think that's over with."

The Trea behind Jack gave him a puzzled look, and he asked her to sit down with the others. Once she had, he proceeded to tell her everything that had happened that day. He told her about following Smart's trail to Obscuro, the fight in hangar 17, the deal he'd cut with Lorem Ipsum, and how it had all gone sideways. He told her how Smart knew all his secrets now, even the one he'd never told anyone but Stendeval, but he didn't tell her what that secret was. When he was finished, everyone was speechless. All three Treas were staring, captivated. "It's over for me in Empire City," Jack told them. "It's about to be, anyway. No one's going to believe a word I say after this comes out."

The three Treas took a minute to think about everything Jack had just told them, putting their heads together and discussing the matter quietly so Jack couldn't hear. Eventually one of them stood up. "You can sulk about what's happened or you can do something about it," she told Jack. "Nothing is over. Not yet," she added, cueing up displays of her work on the virus on multiple holoscreens around the lab. "You're going to need something to answer back with when your story hits the NewsNets. What if that something is the cure-code we've been trying to crack?"

Jack shrugged. "Wouldn't that be something?" He went over to the screens to look at Trea's work. "Too bad I don't have any ideas about what to do next with it."

"Take a look at what we've done so far. Maybe something will come to you."

That was when Jack noticed the Treas were all being

nice to him, even the abrasive T1, who usually got on his nerves so quickly. "Hey, which one of you is which here?" he asked. "Who's the supersmart Trea?"

"We all are," they answered in unison. Jack looked at them, confused.

"It's all about balance," one of the Treas at the lab station explained. "You and I were supposed to work together because two heads are better than one, only you were never here to help. That got me really mad, but eventually I realized I had all the help I needed right here. Three heads are better than two, so I pushed myself. And I grew. I found a way to spread out my intelligence across all my divisions," Trea said, motioning to her second and third selves. "I should thank you," she told Jack. "Your absence forced me to finally listen to Master Chi's lessons and find a way to balance my powers."

"That's amazing," Jack said, marveling at the evolution of Trea's abilities. Really, this new aspect of her power was something she could have done all along. She had just never tried it, despite the urgings of her teachers. It made Jack think of his own situation and all the guidance he'd ignored over the last year, trying to do things his own way. Jack cursed his stubborn nature and wondered aloud why good advice was always so hard to take.

Jack looked over what Trea had been up to the last few days, and he was stunned. The project had benefited incredibly from her fresh perspective and dedication. Trea had pored over all of Jack's work from the past year and done some of her own. She had organized it, added to it, reorganized it, and advanced it. She was looking for patterns. Ideas. Anything that might help stop the spyware virus. From the looks of things, she'd found one.

"I wrote a code language that should deactivate and uninstall the virus, but I've still hit a wall," Trea said. "I don't understand Rüstov technology well enough to go after the virus. We have to make sure the cure-code attacks the virus *only*, or the cure will be worse than the disease. I'm nearly there, but it's an unfinished sentence. I need you to fill in the blanks."

"But we're still missing the Rüstov tech we need for that," Jack said.

"And you know where to find it," Trea said. "What's wrong with you, Jack? Why are you avoiding this? You need to investigate the Rüstov parasite you have inside you. The answer could be right here in this room."

"I can't do that," Jack said.

"Why not?"

"Because I already tried it," Jack said. "And it woke up my parasite. I made it stronger, Trea. I heard its voice."

Trea gave Jack a look that told him she didn't want to hear any self-pity. "So what?" she said. "If your parasite is getting stronger, then you have to get stronger too. You don't have time to be afraid. As long as you're holding back, you're not growing your powers to the point that you should. That's not the only thing keeping you from curing this virus either. You're not focusing. If Master Chi taught me anything, he taught me how important it is to stay focused. You . . . you're all over the place."

"Yeah, well . . . I've got a lot going on," Jack said. He got up and went to the room in the back of his lab with the virus-resistant prototype. The three Treas followed. "You were right when you said I was afraid," Jack told them. "I'm afraid of failing and what that would mean for me and for everyone else." Jack sealed off the back room and opened the coffin, revealing his prototype.

Trea was so shocked that she pulled herself back into one piece. She leaned over the coffin, her eyes wide. "Jack, is that—"

"It's just a prototype," Jack said. "That's all I can think of it as at this point. I don't want to get my hopes up. Not yet."

Trea stepped back from the coffin. "More secrets," she said, shaking her head. "You *do* have a lot going on," Trea told Jack. "I don't know how you keep it all together."

"I don't," Jack admitted. "That's the problem." Jack looked at his chest, where he always imagined the parasite inside him to be. He was scared to death that unlocking that voice would lead to more danger for everyone, but the alternative was no better. "I have to do this, don't I?"

Trea nodded. "Good luck, Jack," she said. "I've done all I can. The rest is up to you."

Trea left Jack alone in the apartment. Once she was gone, he spent a short while going through his notes, which were now more her notes than his, before finally getting down to business. Trea was right. He would need something positive to come back with once Smart started broadcasting his secrets. A breakthrough on the virus was the only chance he had. It was probably the last chance the Mechas had too. Jack thought about the Rüstov spies Glave and Khalix, so close to achieving their goals. . . . He couldn't put this off any longer. It was time to do the hard thing, which, as usual, happened to be the right thing as well.

Jack powered down his lab and found himself a comfortable seat. He closed his eyes, took a deep breath, and reached out to open the very door he'd worked so hard to keep shut. The one that led to the Rüstov inside him.

CHAPTER

21

Bad Connections

Reaching out to the malevolent machine inside him was like diving into a whirlpool of subconscious thought. Jack was no longer in his lab; he was tumbling down a well, falling deeper and deeper into a mind hidden within his own. Even with his eyes closed, he felt the room spinning. It was noisy, too. The lab was quiet and still, but Jack heard a hundred voices speaking at once from a dozen different directions. He could feel it out there . . . the parasite. It was getting stronger. Bolder. More confident. After lying dormant for so long, the parasite was suddenly feel-

372

ing like its day had come, and it didn't want to waste the opportunity. Jack could feel it getting ready to say something. He tried to ignore it and focus on getting what he'd come for. Curing the virus, that was the only thing that mattered. He tried to ignore the parasite, but no force on Earth could have made the parasite ignore him.

Static filled the silent darkness, followed by the voice that Jack dreaded more than any other. It was a voice that sounded not much older than his own. Much like his voice, it had a quality that was aged beyond its years. "Well, well . . . look who's back," the parasite mocked. "After the way you ran off last time, I was afraid you weren't ever going to speak to me again."

"Shut up," Jack said, trying to stay focused. "I'm not here to speak to you. I'm here to study you."

The parasite laughed, and the volume of the static grew along with its amusement. "Just like last time," it told Jack, half muffled by white noise. "I hope you find what you need quickly. You don't have much time left."

Jack knew better than to take the Rüstov's bait, but he couldn't help himself. The parasite had gotten his attention with that remark. "What do you know about how much time I have?" he asked. "Time before what?"

There was a high-pitched noise, like feedback from a microphone. Jack winced as the sound stung his ears. "Ask . . . KSCCHHCH . . . father," the parasite said between bursts of static.

Now the parasite really had Jack hooked. The Rüstov's voice in his head was giving him a migraine, but he couldn't stop talking to it, despite the pain. "What about my father?" Jack asked. "Where is he? What do you know about it?"

The parasite's sinister laugh rang out again, this time much louder. After thirteen years under Jack's thumb, it was clearly enjoying the leverage it commanded at the moment. "You'll find out soon enough," it told Jack. "It's inevitable."

"Nothing's inevitable," Jack said. "I'll fight you. I'm going to keep fighting you."

"And you'll lose," the parasite replied. "I am meant for so much more than this. We are meant for more. The moment is nearly upon us. Glave is here now. Destiny cannot be denied."

"What destiny?" Jack asked, getting fired up. His head

was throbbing now. "There is no destiny! Stop talking in riddles. What's your plan? What's going on here?"

Jack's parasite snickered. "You'll see," it replied. "Everyone will see. What we've set in motion cannot be stopped by anyone. It's already too late. You're going to lose *everything*." The parasite's voice trailed off into static. The line went dead. Jack called out after it, but it was like listening to a radio that was tuned in to nothing. The Rüstov bug would say no more. The good news was, the pain in Jack's head was starting to subside.

Jack took a breath. The dead air helped clear his mind. He was getting distracted again, and he couldn't let that happen. The Rüstov was playing on his fears, trying to throw him off his game. Jack didn't have time to think about what the parasite had said. He had to focus on the task at hand. Jack pushed the parasite's taunts and warnings to the back of his mind and went back to inspecting the elements of his infection that he could see and feel. Jack's parasite would never voluntarily give him any help, and he didn't understand their technology well enough to control it by force, but he could still use his powers to look through it. Jack peered deep into the inner workings of the Rüstov nanobots swimming in his bloodstream. There were millions of tiny little microchips inside of him, each one with its own distinct circuits and unique codes. Jack didn't run away from them this time. This time he took as long as he needed. He became so focused that it would have been impossible to tell if the parasite had started talking again, because Jack had simply stopped listening. He was in a zone. Eventually he broke off the connection. After he got what he was looking for.

Back in his lab, Jack opened his eyes. He was sweating profusely. Outside, the sun was going down. Several hours had passed in what felt like mere minutes to Jack. He leaped out of his chair and turned on the machines in his lab. There wasn't a moment to lose.

Jack dove back into his work with renewed enthusiasm. He checked what he'd just learned against the data that Trea had left behind. Sure enough, he found a commonality between the prototype's circuits and the parasite's operating system almost immediately. Internal scans of the prototype revealed traces of the same Rüstov technology that was nesting inside Jack's own body. It was layered deep within the prototype's central processing unit, but it couldn't hide from Jack now that he knew what he was looking for. String after string of suspicious code jumped right out at him. Jack could see and hear it running commands on renegade applications inside the prototype.

"Gotcha," Jack said to himself. He'd found it. He understood what he was looking at now. After all this time he'd finally deciphered the language of the spyware virus.

Wasting no time, Jack fired up his tools and went straight to work attacking the problem. He labored for another three hours without breaking for food or drink. He'd been waiting to do this for more than a year now. This was the fun part. Goggles strapped over his eyes, Jack stared intently through a holo-magnifier as he burned the cure-code onto a microchip in a programming language never before written down anywhere.

The work came along easier than Jack had expected. Trea had already done half the job by creating a program that would deactivate the spyware virus; she'd just needed Jack to identify the malicious code and finish it off. Jack lost himself in his work, trying not to think about how much time he had wasted in getting to this point. The answer had been right there in front of him all along. He'd just never seen it before now. It was so simple and clear that Jack could hardly believe the virus had given him any trouble at all. Jack felt like he'd been struggling to remember the lyrics to a song, and then suddenly heard it on the radio and every word became clear. Now that Jack had picked up the virus's tune, its final verse was about to be written.

The finished microchip was a small silver square with the code burned onto it in the shape of a shiny green arrow. Jack took it from a robotic arm beneath the holo-magnifier. After a year of false moves and dead ends, he was holding the cure in his hands. An experimental cure, anyway. Jack wasn't about to start celebrating just yet. He still had to test it.

Jack sealed his lab door and opened up the coffin. It was time. Jack looked down at the prototype, fully appre-ciating the gravity of the moment. If it worked, what he was about to do was nothing short of extraordinary. Jack inserted the chip into the prototype's central processing unit and used his powers to make it run the code. The chip was programmed to tag every inch of the prototype's circuits with the cure and scrub its software until it was 100 percent virus free. After the cure-code reinitialized the prototype's operating system with a clean slate, it would need about ninety minutes to reboot and reload memory. All of this would take place while the prototype was in sleep mode. The moment of truth would come when Jack hit the power button and activated the prototype for the first time in more than a year. Jack looked over at the electromagnetic pulse he'd rigged up in case the cure-code failed. There was nothing left to do now but wait and hope.

After he'd done all he could in the lab, he went up to the roof for some fresh air. He found the *Knightwing* hovering overhead. Jack looked across the roof and saw Midknight and Noteworthy waiting for him.

"Hello, Jack," the veteran hero said. "We need to talk."

22

Uninvited Guests

Jack's stomach dropped.

"You!" Jack said, his voice apprehensive. "What are you two doing here?"

"Glad to see you, too," Midknight replied with a smirk. "Sorry to drop by unannounced, Jack. Couldn't be helped."

"Don't apologize, Midknight," Noteworthy said. "It's nothing the boy hasn't already done himself. Isn't that right, Jack?" he asked. "You seem to have developed a habit of eavesdropping." Noteworthy shook a finger at

Jack. "Very bad form. Caused us no end of difficulties."

"Everyone's looking for you," Jack said, backing away. "We told the Inner Circle what you were doing at the prison last night."

"I doubt that," Noteworthy replied.

"It's true," Jack said. "We told Virtua."

"Really?" Noteworthy asked. "What did you tell her? What exactly do you think we were doing?"

Jack didn't answer. It suddenly occurred to him that he had no idea what Midknight and Noteworthy had been up to at the prison.

"I think it's time we put our cards on the table," Midknight said, taking a step toward Jack. He had something in his hand. Jack couldn't see what it was.

"How did you find me here?" Jack asked. "It's supposed to be impossible to find someone in Cognito."

Midknight gave Jack a knowing smile. "'Impossible' and 'supposed to be impossible' are hardly the same thing," he replied. "I'm a detective, Jack. I find things out. You know that."

"Why were you guys trying to break Speedrazor out of jail?" Jack blurted out. His eyes were full of fear. "You want to put our cards on the table, fine. Let's put 'em all down. Are you Glave?" Jack asked Noteworthy. "Are you Khalix?" he asked Midknight.

Midknight's back stiffened, and he stopped dead in his tracks. *"Am I what?"* he asked, stunned.

"I saw you use your powers last night," Jack told Noteworthy. "I saw your weapon. The energy glave? Real slick, hiding in plain sight like that. We're on to you. I'm not the only one, either."

It appeared that Noteworthy was too appalled by Jack's accusation to even say anything. Midknight studied Jack's face to determine if he was serious or not. He stored whatever he had in his left hand away in his utility belt. "Jack . . . ," he said, shaking his head. "You know better than that."

Jack looked back at Midknight with a dead stare. "No, I don't. I haven't seen your face the whole time I've known you, Midknight. Why is that? Are you infected?"

Midknight folded his arms. "Of course not."

"Show me," Jack said.

Midknight let out a sigh and reluctantly unfastened the

straps on his helmet. "Even if you're not willing to take it on faith, with your powers you should be able to tell if there's a Rüstov parasite inside me. Inside either of us." Midknight removed his mask and stepped into the light. The only marks on his face were those left by age and combat. There was no Rüstov scar around Midknight's right eye.

"That doesn't prove anything," Jack said. "You could still be a collaborator. You both could."

"Collaborators!" Noteworthy exclaimed. "How dare you?"

"Clarkston, leave it alone," Midknight said.

"I will not leave it alone," Noteworthy said. "I didn't come here to be insulted by some Rüstov-infected boy. Listen here," he told Jack, "I don't care who you killed on Wrekzaw Isle last year. There's far more reason to suspect you than either of us. There always will be, as long as you've got that thing inside you."

"Clarkston, that's enough," Midknight said. "You're not helping the situation." The old hero turned toward Jack. "Neither are you, Jack. I don't know what makes it so hard for you to trust people, but if that doesn't change sooner or later, you're going to end up very lonely in life. We're not infected and we're not traitors. I thought you and I were friends, even if you did throw quite a monkey wrench into my plans last night. That's why we're here now. Because we need your help."

When Midknight finished talking, Jack officially had no idea what was going on. He didn't know what Midknight and Noteworthy were doing together, but after seeing the old hero's face, and listening to him talk, Jack believed him when he said they weren't in league with the Rüstov.

"All right," Jack said. "I'm listening. What do you need?"

Midknight nodded. "That's more like it. C'mere. I'll show you."

Midknight went back into his belt and produced the mystery object he'd been holding earlier. It was a small steel box no bigger than a walnut.

"You already know we've been working together," Midknight told Jack.

"It's an alliance borne out of necessity," Noteworthy said.

"It is," Midknight agreed. "A man in his position has access to a lot of information," he said, jerking a thumb toward Noteworthy. "For the last month he's been my primary source on Smart's latest invention."

"You're investigating the SmarterNet?" Jack asked. "There's something shady going on with it, you know."

"Thank you, Jack," Noteworthy said, rolling his eyes. "Whatever would we do without you?"

"It's obviously some kind of surveillance system," Midknight said, scowling at Noteworthy. "But no one knows how it works, and Smart isn't talking. That bothers me. It's been my experience that when someone guards a secret this closely, the truth is usually pretty damning. Wouldn't you agree?"

"Yeah," Jack said. "That pretty much describes my life for the last year. But what are you doing investigating Smart, with a Rüstov attack less than two days away? You don't think Smart's working with them, do you? 'Cause I made that mistake once already."

"I don't think Smart's working with the Rüstov per se," Midknight replied. "I just worry that in his haste to help himself, he might be helping them more than he knows. His launch timeline and Glave's attack deadline are too close together," Midknight explained. "Something is wrong. I'm sure it wouldn't surprise you to find out that 'the world's smartest man' has no idea what he's doing."

Jack shook his head. "No, it wouldn't. And there's definitely more to the SmarterNet than he's letting on. This afternoon Obscuro threatened to go public with the truth about the SmarterNet unless Smart gave him the access codes to the system."

"You saw this happen?" Noteworthy asked. "When?"

"What would Obscuro need with the SmarterNet access codes?" Midknight asked.

"I don't know, but you should have seen the scare that threat put into Jonas Smart," Jack said. "I don't get it. This is Jonas Smart we're talking about. People already decided against his way of doing things in the last election. They voted him out and shut down the SmartCams because they didn't like being spied on all the time. Now everyone's just taking his word that he won't do it again? It's like people have completely forgotten who they're dealing with. How is someone with his track record getting a free pass on such an obvious question like what his invention actually does? Why are people sitting still while he stonewalls them on that?"

"People have short memories. Especially when they're scared," Noteworthy explained. "The Rogue Secreteer's actions and the Glave and Khalix transmissions have got the people of this city remembering exactly why they're afraid of the Rüstov."

"People are lining up in Galaxis to leave the planet, and the ones who stay will put up with almost anything to feel safe again. Smart knows that better than most," Midknight told Jack. "He built the entire SmartCorp empire on that principle the first time around. He's as good as they come at striking fear into people's hearts, even if he doesn't have one of his own." Midknight shook his head. "He's a dangerous man when he's in power, and his ego won't let him accept being anywhere else. I've been investigating him ever since I first found out he was sinking all his money into one big project.

I knew it had to be his plan to get back on top. He lost his seat at the table once already. He'll do anything to regain power."

"Didn't you say the same thing about the Noteworthy family during your campaign?" Jack asked.

"I did," Midknight admitted. "I meant it, too. Clarkston and I don't necessarily like each other. We're just working together because sometimes the enemy of your enemy is your friend."

Noteworthy nodded. "I don't want to see Smart back in power any more than you two do."

"Exactly," Midknight said. "The intel for our last mission together came from Clarkston. My street connections picked up rumors about Speedrazor's plan to steal something important from Smart. It was his connections that cut through SmartCorp's front companies and identified the most likely target."

"The Intelligent Designs cargo train," Jack said.

"Very good," Noteworthy said. "Unfortunately, you blew up the cargo before we could find out what Smart was bringing in."

"Sorry about that," Jack said.

Midknight shrugged. "At least you managed to slow Smart down a few days. In the meantime I tried everything I could think of to find out what was on that train. I tracked down the rest of his gang in Gravenmurk Glen, but they were all brainwashed by the Secreteer and were no use to me. Next I went out into the Real World and infiltrated Intelligent's labs myself, looking for answers."

"What did you find out?" Jack asked.

"Nothing," Midknight admitted. "That was why I needed Speedrazor's help. Clarkston was there to help me break him out, and I was going to take him back to the Real World with me. The plan was to raid Intelligent Designs together and steal Smart's replacement for the SmarterNet component you blew up. No such luck."

"I don't get it. What's in the box, then?" Jack asked.

"The only thing Speedrazor could give me," Midknight said. "A blueprint of the technology he was trying to steal."

"He doesn't need to know all of this," Noteworthy said, losing his patience. "We don't need to explain ourselves to you," he told Jack. "We need you to tell us what this device does. Now."

Jack gave Noteworthy a tough look. If the Inner Circle's newest member was trying to intimidate him, his words were having the opposite effect. Jack didn't appreciate getting ordered around by the one Circleman he hardly ever saw and respected even less. "You know," Jack began, "if I had your money, I'd be able to afford some manners." Before Noteworthy even had a chance to respond, Jack turned to Midknight and asked, "Can I talk to you alone for a minute?"

"Of course," Midknight said. He followed Jack a few feet away from Noteworthy, who just stood there seething. On the other side of the roof, Jack motioned for Midknight to come closer. As he leaned in, Jack put his hand over his mouth and whispered, "Are we *sure* he's not Glave?"

Midknight let out a short chuckle. "Noteworthy?" he said, as if the very idea were ridiculous. "Why, because he uses that energy glave?" Midknight shook Jack off. "That's just a coincidence, Jack. The real Glave wouldn't be dumb enough to go around flashing a weapon with that very name every time he feels threatened."

"What if he's counting on you thinking like that?" Jack asked. "I don't know him that well, but he's definitely smarter than I thought. What if he wants to shut down the SmarterNet because it's going to expose Rüstov conspirators just like Smart says it will? What if he aligned himself with the Rüstov to get his family back into power?"

"Slow down, Jack," Midknight said. "Before we answer any of that, let's get a look at the evidence. A detective needs evidence to back up his theories or that's all they are. Theories." Midknight held up the tiny box with the SmarterNet data on it. "C'mon. Let's see what we've got here."

Jack agreed to do as Midknight said, and followed him back across the roof toward Noteworthy. Midknight handed Jack the box, and Jack activated it. A holographic blueprint projected itself into the air, displaying an incredibly complex and elegant design. Luckily, the blueprint was also very friendly. Jack asked the machine what it did, and it told him right away.

Jack's heart nearly stopped when he discovered the machine's purpose.

"Oh no," Jack said. "No!"

"What?" Midknight asked. "What is it?"

"Tell us!" Noteworthy said.

"It's a super-relayer-connector," Jack said. "A really strong one."

"A super what?" Midknight asked.

"Speak English, boy," Noteworthy said.

Jack ran his hands through his hair, trying to wrap his head around what he'd just learned and figure out how to explain it to Midknight and Noteworthy. "It's a computer signal broadcaster," he said. "The most powerful one I've ever seen."

"This little thing?" Noteworthy asked. "Really?"

"Jack, what does that mean?" Midknight asked. "I don't understand. What's the problem?"

"Midknight, this is bad. The SmarterNet goes way beyond surveillance. It's not just listening to all communications in the outside world. There's a meta-code hidden in the super-Wi-Fi signals this thing puts out. It links up every machine it touches on the same network so Smart can listen in. It *connects* every machine in the world, including everything right here in the Imagine Nation!"

"So the eyes and ears of every machine and every Mecha in this city become part of Smart's new spy network," Noteworthy said with a scowl. "I knew he was up to no good. This makes the SmartCam program look like child's play."

"You don't understand," Midknight told Noteworthy, his eyes growing wide. "This is bigger than Smart spying on people. It's bigger than Empire City."

"Way bigger," Jack said. "This thing goes out to the world. Smart probably thinks this thing is going to help sniff out Rüstov spies, but he doesn't realize what he's doing. He's just given the Rüstov the means to infect every machine on Earth! It's been running all day, and no one's got any idea. We have to stop it before the spyware virus goes global. We have to shut down the SmarterNet!"

"Spyware virus?" Noteworthy asked. "What spyware virus? Jack, what are you talking about?"

Jack let out an exasperated sigh. Noteworthy didn't

know anything about the virus yet. Jack was about to start explaining, when a massive explosion ripped through the night. The Empire City skyline lit up with fire, and sirens began to wail in the mechanized borough to the north. Machina was erupting in chaos.

It was already too late.

23

The Virus Unleashed

"I don't understand," Jack said as smoke began to rise up off the burning skyline of Machina. "We were supposed to have one more day."

"Looks like the Rüstov have moved up their schedule," Midknight said.

Sirens rang out across Empire City, and Jonas Smart's voice started broadcasting:

"People of Empire City . . . hear me now, and hear me well. The time has come to take up arms against the Rüstov once more. We are under attack."

The voice was coming from everywhere. Just like Obscuro's announcement four days earlier, this message wasn't just limited to the SmartNews channel or personal holo-screens. This broadcast was being projected all over the city: on the sides of buildings, on floating billboards, and on giant holo-screen projections that were being shot out of SmartNews image-casters. Jonas Smart's rallying call echoed through all six boroughs as he spoke, and the words IMAGINE NATION EMERGENCY flashed over and over on the screen below him.

Another round of blasts punctured the Machina skyline like bullets fired from a gun, and the screens cut to images of Mechas rioting in Machina. Jack, Midknight, and Noteworthy watched the anarchy unfold on-screen. The Mechas were tearing their borough—*and one another*—apart. They were picking up HoverCars and smashing them down on the MagLev roads. They were pulling recharge stations out of the ground and throwing them through windows. Jack looked on, helpless, as healthy Mechas tried to control their infected brothers and sisters. It was a lost cause. The few healthy Mechas left standing were either greatly outnumbered or falling prey to the virus themselves. The Mechas shouted epithets in the Rüstov language as they wrecked buildings, vehicles, roadways, and whatever else they could get their hands on. The senseless destruction was horrifying—even more so because it showed the people of Empire City exactly what an army of infected Mechas was capable of, in the most graphic manner possible. The Mechas were out of control. Worse, they were being controlled . . . by the Rüstov. Jack watched the chaos play out on the holo-screen and heard it in the air seconds later, like thunder following flashes of lightning. The storm he'd spent the last year dreading was raining down at last.

"What is this?" Noteworthy asked. "What's happening?"

Jack was about to explain, but Smart beat him to the punch. As the newsreel played on, the former Circleman's smooth, terrible voice laid over the images like a blanket of thorns. Noteworthy shushed Jack before he even got a word out. Midknight was fixated on the screen as well.

"These images are courtesy of the SmartNews Machina branch," Smart announced. "They will be confirmed, and no doubt duplicated by other NewsNets coming late to this story, but no one else in Empire City is going to tell you what I am about to. No one else in Empire City knows what I know, save for a young boy who isn't talking."

The picture on the holo-screen cut to an image of Jonas Smart speaking directly into the camera. The live feed showing the riot in Machina continued to play in a small box in the corner of the screen. Smart was not about to cut away from that scene. Not for a second.

"Less than a week ago we were all shocked to learn that a member of the Clandestine Order had gone rogue," Smart began. "So convinced was he of the Rüstov's advantage over us that he began selling off secrets so that he could flee the planet before their next attack. I for one was not at all shocked to learn that the primary source of the rogue's fears was a secret known only to Jack Blank."

Midknight and Noteworthy both cast dubious looks at Jack and then quickly turned back to the screen.

"It is no secret that I have never trusted Jack, despite his actions on Wrekzaw Isle last year," Smart went on. "I've gone through great pains to find out what he's been hiding ever since he first arrived here. This afternoon, at great personal expense, I finally acquired that information from the Rogue Secreteer. It is for this reason that I can tell you with absolute certainty that the riot in Machina is not a simple case of malfunctioning Mechas or some supervillain plot. This is a Rüstov attack, and Jack Blank is part of it."

Jack groaned and looked up at the sky. Everything he'd feared most was coming to pass. He paced the rooftop as Machina burned and his world fell apart.

"Today I learned about the Rüstov *spyware* virus—something you are seeing the effects of on your holoscreen now," Smart announced. "Once again our enemies seek to use our fellow citizens as weapons against us, only this time the deadly virus they have brought to bear is aimed at our Mecha population. The spyware virus lets the Rüstov see what they see . . . hear what they hear. The Rüstov can even take control of the Mechas and use them toward whatever ends they see fit. I'm sure you can imagine what ends they have in mind. What you may find hard to imagine is that Jack Blank knew about this threat more than a year ago and said *nothing*." Smart paused to let that fact sink in. "It's true. Just like every other creature infected by the Rüstov, Jack Blank is bound in the service of our enemy. The emissary who brought Jack here, Jazen Knight, was infected as well. Last year he and Jack led a team of Rüstov Para-Soldiers into SmartTower to try to kill me."

Jack spun around to look at the screen. "That's not true!"

"It's all true," Smart continued, almost as if he were rebutting Jack's outburst. "Jack Blank lied about the virus and covered it up. Then he and his Rüstov allies orchestrated a fake battle with Revile that he could win, so that he could endear himself to the people of the Imagine Nation. All the while he kept silent about the Rüstov's true plans, allowing the spyware virus to flourish. And it has."

"Because of your SmarterNet!" Jack shouted at the screen. He was seething. The parts of the story that Smart had right were bad enough, but he was jumping to conclusions to fill in the gaps, and twisting things to fit his version of history as he went along. He was also leaving out any part he'd played in creating this crisis, and he was smearing Jazen's good name while he was at it. This was going even worse than Jack had expected, something he hadn't thought was possible. Once again Jack was discovering new reasons to hate Jonas Smart.

"I warned you all, but no one listened. Telling the truth about this boy nearly cost me everything," Smart said. "Tonight I am vindicated, but what has ignoring my counsel cost this city?" Smart shook his head sadly. "We have long known that our enemy is clever, cunning, and, above all, patient. Clearly, that patience has served them well, but we have not yet begun to fight. I am calling on every citizen of the Imagine Nation within the sound of my voice to rise up and go to Machina now. Just as when a person is infected by the Rüstov they are no more, these Mechas are no longer our fellow citizens. They are tools of the Rüstov. We need to destroy them! Our very lives depend on it!"

A mighty roar rose up from Varagog Village, loud enough to be heard across the rooftops of Cognito. It was the kind of noise that made Jack think of pitchfork-wielding mobs getting ready to chase down the Frankenstein monster. "That's not good," Midknight said.

"Remember!" Jonas Smart called out. "*No one* can resist

a Rüstov infection. Only one person was ever thought to have succeeded in this—Jack Blank. After tonight it is plain to see he did no such thing. His treasonous act of covering up this virus has revealed him for what he truly is—a Rüstov sleeper agent. If you have any doubts left about that, allow me to dispel them by sharing with you his second, dark, dark secret, straight from the mouth of the Rogue Secreteer."

Jack closed his eyes and braced himself. *Here it comes,* he thought. Smart was about to reveal the truth about him and Revile. In a few seconds it would all be over. His fall from grace would be complete. Jack knew that spelled doom for both him and the Mechas. No one would listen to what he had to say about the virus after this.

"Ladies and gentlemen, Jack Blank is no ordinary Rüstov agent," Smart said. "He is quite literally the greatest threat the Imagine Nation will ever face. Today he is merely Jack Blank, but tomorrow, unless we stop him, this boy is destined to become . . . *lorem ipsum dolor.*"

Jack opened his eyes and looked up at the screen in shock. *Destined to become what?*

On the screen Smart paused, looking to be every bit as confused as Jack. Unsure, he tried to go on. "*Sit . . . amet?*" he said tentatively. "*Consectetur adipisicing elit?!!*"

Smart realized what was happening and turned to look behind him, enraged. That was when Jack noticed that Lorem Ipsum was standing right next to Smart. She had been there the whole time. "*Sed do eiusmod tempor!!!*" Smart yelled at her. He looked back and forth between her and the camera, furious, embarrassed, and helpless. "*Incididunt ut labore! Et dolore!!!*" he railed. "*MAGNA ALIQUA!*"

Jack couldn't believe his eyes—and ears. Smart couldn't talk! Lorem Ipsum had touched him right before he'd been going to reveal the big secret. He was saved!

Jack felt like he'd just dodged a bullet that had been fired at him from point-blank range.

Lorem laughed as Smart ranted and raved, speaking nothing but unintelligible gibberish. "That's what they all say," she snickered, gloating. She pulled her hair out of her face and looked into the camera. "Jack, if you're out there listening, I'm sorry about before. Like I said, I had my own plans." Smart grabbed Lorem Ipsum and shook her, but the ever-nimble girl twisted free, laughing as she squirmed out of his grasp. "I know my father," she said. "I knew the only thing that would drive him crazier than not being able to find out the truth about you would be finding it out and not being able to tell anyone."

She grinned as Smart lunged at her in a pathetic last-ditch attempt to do something. Anything. She dodged him, and he knocked into the camera. It rolled back into a wide shot that revealed Jonas Smart on his knees, defeated. "That's for locking me up in prison, *Daddy*," Lorem said to him. She turned back to the camera and stuck her face close up in front of the lens. "Your secret's safe with me, Jack." She gave a mocking, see-you-later kind of salute, and added, "This is Lorem Ipsum from Hightown, signing off. Good night and good luck, Empire City." Another explosion rang out in Machina. "Something tells me you're gonna need it."

Lorem reached toward the camera and turned it off. Screens all across Empire City turned to static. Jack still couldn't believe it. He wasn't dead yet. There was still time. He had to put it to good use before it was too late. He had just been given a second chance. A last chance.

He couldn't afford to waste it. It was time to stop the virus and prove which side he was on, once and for all.

"The SmarterNet," Jack said, taking charge. "That's what's accelerating the virus. It's spreading across Machina now, but it's going to go global. We have to shut it down."

"We?" Noteworthy sneered. "There is no *we*," he said, brandishing his energy glave. "I should kill you where you stand, you filthy interloper."

Jack didn't back down an inch. He was feeling confident, like something had just shifted and he was now riding a wave of good luck.

"Noteworthy, you step to me with that thing and you're gonna regret it. I'll use my powers to blow up every machine in this building before I let you stop me from doing what I have to do. I've got nothing left to lose. I don't even care anymore." It was a bluff, but it made Noteworthy think twice. Long enough for Midknight to step in.

"Let's everybody calm down," Midknight said. "Clarkston, you know better than to take anything Smart says at face value. Jack's big secret—whatever it is—isn't the

spyware virus. He told me all about that two nights ago in Gravenmurk Glen."

"You knew about this?" Noteworthy asked, flabbergasted. "How could you keep something like that from—"

"My question is, what was Smart going to say before Lorem put a stop to it?" Midknight asked Jack, ignoring Noteworthy.

"Never mind that," Jack said. "We don't have time for me to catch you guys up on every last thing. We have to find the Inner Circle and tell them what's going on. We're the only ones who really know."

"Some of us know more than others," Noteworthy replied. "We're not going anywhere until you tell us what Smart was going to say."

"It's got nothing to do with this!" Jack said. "The Rüstov are about to get their hooks into every single machine in the world if we don't stop them."

"Thanks to you," Noteworthy said.

"And thanks to Smart," Jack shot back. "No one else knows that, though. Think about it, Circleman . . . unless you want Jonas Smart to be the big hero here, you've got to act fast. Right now you've got thousands

of Rüstov-controlled Mechas rioting next to your borough. How long until that violence spills over that wall that Virtua built? As far as your people are concerned, the only person who was going to do anything to protect Hightown is Jonas Smart. He just got sidelined by Lorem Ipsum. You better pick up the ball and run with it, or come next election, you're going to find yourself out of a job."

Noteworthy seemed to be trying his best to find a reason to disagree with Jack, but it was hard to argue with his logic. Jack knew the Circleman would see things his way. Appealing to Noteworthy's good nature and sense of duty was a waste of time, but appealing to his self-interest and ambition? That was a surefire lock.

"Midknight, I need to get to Hightown," Noteworthy said. "Now."

Midknight stifled a bitter laugh and brought down the *Knightwing*'s entrance ramp. "Get in. Both of you," he said. "Incidentally, I think you've got quite a future in politics, Jack."

"This conversation isn't over, boy," Noteworthy said on his way into the *Knightwing*. "Not by a long shot."

"You don't have to tell me," Jack said. He climbed on board and closed the ramp behind him.

Midknight took his ship over the rioting borough of Machina on the way to Hightown. Jack, Midknight, and Noteworthy looked out in horror as waves of infected Mechas ran wild in the streets, smashing their home to bits. They were pulling down street signs and knocking down monuments. They were jamming steel girders into roadside data ports and starting electrical fires. Uninfected Mechas were running for their lives. They reached up at the *Knightwing*, calling out and waving their arms, desperate to be saved.

"We have to help them," Jack said, looking down at the trapped Mechas.

"No," Noteworthy told Midknight. "Keep going. They'll just take us down with them."

Midknight frowned. "He's right, Jack," the old hero said. "There's too many of them. We're no good to anyone if we're dead. We need a plan here."

Then, without any warning, every light in Machina went out all at once. A great whirring noise followed, like the sound of ten thousand power generators winding down simultaneously. Jack watched every Mecha on the street drop to the ground like they were puppets whose strings had been cut. The entire mechanized borough was suddenly as quiet as the grave, which for some unfortunate Mechas, it already was.

"What's going on?" Jack asked.

"You're asking me?" Noteworthy scoffed.

"Let's ask them," Midknight said, pointing up at the Hightown-Machina border, where Stendeval could be seen floating in the air next to Virtua. As Midknight brought his ship closer, an orange-white flash lit up the sky, and the rest of the Inner Circle appeared. They floated gently down to the ground surrounded by Stendeval's red energy particles. Midknight brought the *Knightwing* in across from them, setting it down on a plaza right next to the newly erected Machina-Hightown wall. A crowd of Hightowners was forming nearby.

"Midknight. Clarkston," Stendeval said as they exited the ship. "Please join us. We're going to need you both if we've any hope of stopping this madness before it spreads any farther. Jack, I'm glad to find you safe and in good hands."

"Be glad he's not in mine," Hovarth said. "You should know I'm very disappointed in you, boy. This disaster is your fault!"

"Not just mine," Jack said. "Jonas Smart has to share the blame in this too."

"What are you talking about?" Virtua asked.

"It's the SmarterNet," Jack said. "Smart built it to connect every machine in the world because he wanted a new spy network. That's what's spreading the virus so fast. Smart's machine sped this thing out of control."

"Is this true?" Hovarth asked Midknight and Noteworthy.

Midknight motioned with his hands. "We can't say for sure, but it makes sense," he replied.

"I'm afraid this information comes too late," Virtua told Jack. "The method of infection no longer matters. My people are already being taken over by the Rüstov. The virus is spreading too fast for us to deal with the infected individually."

"What happened to the lights?" Midknight asked. "Did the virus shut down Machina?"

"No, that was me," Virtua replied. "This morning,

based on Jack's work on the virus, I created a software update that all Mechas were required to download and install. It's a tracking program that scans all systems for computer code similar to what you provided me with. As soon as more than twenty-five percent of Mechas register that code, glitches, or any other aberrant behavior, a full-scale shutdown and reboot gets triggered. This affects every Mecha in Empire City, including me, so play close attention. Projo can broadcast my image only another few minutes before I shut down too. This is not a solution. I have only bought us time."

"Time for what?" asked Chi. "What do you want us to do?"

"The reboot is only temporary," Virtua replied. "We have ninety minutes at best. Hopefully it will be enough time for you to secure my borough and every Mecha in it so that we are not a danger to ourselves or others."

"Secure every inch of Machina?" Noteworthy said. "You're talking about tens of thousands of Mechas. What if we can't do it in time?"

Virtua turned to Stendeval. "Do you have enough reserve energy for an EMP?" she asked him.

Stendeval locked eyes with Virtua. He knew full well what she was asking. So did Jack. So did everybody. Stendeval nodded solemnly.

"Good," Virtua said. "If I or my people still pose a threat when we reactivate, you will use it. On all of us."

"NO!" Jack shouted. "Virtua, you don't have to do that! I have a cure-code ready! I have it in a beta test right now."

"It's too late for that, Jack," Virtua said. "We can't rely on experimental cures."

"And we're certainly not going to take your word that it *is* a cure!" Hovarth said.

Jack was about to defend himself against Hovarth's accusations, but Virtua cut him off before he even started. "We don't have time to argue. We have to prepare for the worst."

Midknight spoke up. "Virtua, you can't expect us to let you—"

"We will *not* be used as tools in the enemy's plan," Virtua interrupted. "Not again. If this is where the Mechas of Empire City meet our end, we will meet it without fear and we will keep our honor. If this is our fate, then so be it. All will know of our sacrifice, and none will be able to question our allegiance after tonight."

It was clear that it was no use arguing with Virtua. Hovarth put his hand on his heart and bowed his head to her. "I commend your selfless dedication, Lady Virtua," he said. "Your decision reflects a very Varagog way of thinking." Jack figured that was probably the highest praise that Hovarth knew how to give. Hovarth turned to Stendeval and the rest of the Inner Circle. "Before I was transported from my home, a crowd was forming outside Castle Varren, waiting for their king to lead them into Machina. Into battle. I'll lead them there still," Hovarth said. "We'll put their energy to good use and enlist their aid to secure the borough."

"Thank you, Hovarth," Virtua said. "I wonder if Circleman Noteworthy will be able to say the same about the crowd gathering on the Hightown side of this wall."

Virtua waved a hand at the growing mass of angry, scared Hightowners across the plaza. All eyes turned to Noteworthy. It was highly unlikely that he commanded the same degree of respect among his constituents that

Hovarth did among his subjects. "I can—I can try," Note-worthy stammered.

"This kind of work needs level heads, Clarkston," Midknight said. "If you can't control your people, and I'm not sure that you can, we've got to keep them out of Machina."

"That's going to divide our efforts," Jack said. "It will slow us down."

"We have no choice," Chi said. "We can ill afford to trade one unruly mob for another. The goal here is to quell the riot. My ninjas will guard the Hightown-Machina border, but it will take time for them to get here."

"I can help with that," Midknight told Chi. "You can use the bottom half of my ship as a transport. And I can help you lock down Machina," he told Hovarth. "I'll take the top half and round up every hero I can find, starting with Blue and Ricochet. They've been looking for me all day anyway. We'll get this done, Virtua. We've done the impossible before—with less time than ninety minutes, too."

"Aye," said Hovarth. Stendeval and Chi chimed in

with words of encouragement as well. For his part, Jack didn't like this plan one bit. As far as he was concerned, they were still ignoring the source of the problem. They had a plan for mopping blood off the floor without bothering to first stop the bleeding.

"What about the SmarterNet?" Jack asked. "We still need to shut it down and stop the spread of the virus. Can't you make Smart do that, now that we know it isn't just operating in the outside world?"

"We could," Stendeval said. "Unfortunately, thanks to Lorem Ipsum's gibberish touch, Jonas Smart won't be able to tell us where the signal is broadcasting from, let alone how to shut it off."

Jack threw his hands up in frustration. He hadn't even thought of that. He cursed the irony of it all. The same stroke of luck that had kept the truth about him and Revile under wraps was preventing them from heading off the Rüstov threat. It didn't help matters that it was his fault Lorem Ipsum had gotten involved to begin with.

"First things first," Midknight told Jack. "Even if we were able to shut down the SmarterNet, that still doesn't do anything to hold off the Mechas that are already infected."

"We can't just let it go," Jack argued. "There has to be something we can do. What if we knew the frequency the SmarterNet was broadcasting at? We could jam it."

"But we *don't* know that," Noteworthy said. "We have to deal with what we know. We have to use the EMP like Circlewoman Virtua said."

Virtua glared at Noteworthy. The rest of the Inner Circle did too.

"Obviously, I mean that as a last resort," he clarified.

"Obviously," Virtua said, giving Noteworthy another hostile look. Her face was scrunched up in anger and her color had shifted to a deep crimson.

"What can I do, then?" Jack asked, eager to help.

"You can tell us what Smart was going to say before Lorem Ipsum touched him," Hovarth said.

Jack should have been ready for that response, but he wasn't. Everyone looked at him, waiting for an answer. "Why—why does that matter now?" he sputtered. "Shouldn't we be focusing on the virus?"

"It's a matter of trust," Hovarth said. "Skerren told me

what you did today. If I can't trust you, then I don't want to fight alongside you." Jack didn't say anything. Hovarth shook his head in disgust. "You need to go home, lad. We'll figure out what to do with you later."

"Home?" Jack said. "But, no . . . I need to . . . You need me to—"

"I'm sorry, but Hovarth is right," Stendeval said. "You have to stay out of this, Jack, for a number of reasons. I know your heart was in the right place and why you did what you did, but we're going to have a devil of a time convincing anyone else of that right now. We can't deal with this situation and watch over you at the same time. There's a whole city full of people out there who think you brought this plague down upon us."

"They happen to be right," Noteworthy said.

Jack grimaced.

"Jack, listen to me," Stendeval said. "We can't afford to have anything happen to you. You're more important than you know, and it's far too dangerous for you to be out here right now. You're safe in Cognito. No one can find you there."

"Midknight did," Jack said.

"True." Midknight shrugged. "But I'm exceptional."

"Jack, please," Virtua said, her image flickering and fading. "Any time spent making sure you stay put is time that could be spent rounding up heroes to safeguard my people. I know you want to do something, and I know you did the best you could . . . but all you can do right now is avoid causing any more trouble. A hero has to put the needs of others ahead of himself." Virtua's image faded down to nearly transparent levels. She reached out a hand to Jack. It passed right through him like it belonged to a ghost. "I know you'll do the right thing."

Projo fell to the ground with a clang, and Virtua's image blinked out.

"Ninety minutes," Midknight said. "What's it gonna be, Jack?"

Jack hated the position he was being put in. Every piece of him wanted to go out and fight the Rüstov, but he couldn't very well go against what might have been Virtua's last words.

"All right," Jack said, looking down at his shoes. "I'll go home."

"I expected nothing less," Stendeval said. "Midknight, if you could?"

Midknight and Jack squeezed into the top half of the *Knightwing* and took off. Midknight dropped Jack off in Cognito and turned right around to go find help for the Mechas. As Jack watched the ship blast off into the night, he felt trapped and angry. He couldn't believe he was really going to sit this thing out. He knew Stendeval and Virtua were right, but that didn't make doing what they said any easier. It never had. Never once. The only thing that was keeping Jack in his seat was the fact that he didn't have any idea how to stop the SmarterNet, even if he were allowed to try.

Then Jack noticed a small white card he'd left on the coffee table earlier. The note he'd gotten from Obscuro. Suddenly it was no longer blank. The words that were now written on the card changed everything.

Jack grabbed his bag and went for the door. On his way outside, Jack reminded himself that he'd promised the Inner Circle only that he'd go home. He never said he'd stay there. Anyway, Virtua's definition of a hero was different from his own. Different from the one he'd learned from Jazen Knight, that is. Jazen had taught him that a hero is someone who tries to make a difference. A person who gets up every day and tries to make the world a better place. That was the kind of hero Jack wanted to be. That was the kind of hero he'd been trying to be all year. There was a chance he could still do that before it was too late.

24

Playing the Memory Card

Wearing a hooded zip-up jacket to help hide his once famous, now infamous, face, Jack ran through Varagog Village as fast as he could. Ordinarily, going into Varagog alone at night would have constituted an idiotic risk on his part, and doing so the same night he'd reclaimed the title of Public Enemy Number One wouldn't have been any smarter, but tonight it was. The village streets were empty. Almost everyone had followed Hovarth out of town into Machina. Still, Jack stuck to the shadows and played it safe. Breaking the rules and taking risks didn't have to mean being reckless. With a combination of stealth, speed, and luck, Jack reached his destination unharmed. The trick would be staying that way. Jack passed under an arch built into the great wall on Varagog's south side and ran down the steps toward the Flying Shipyards. Toward Hypnova.

Jack knew where he was going this time around. He didn't have to search every slip on the dock before finding Hypnova's ship. He just hoped it would be there, parked in her spot. Sure enough, it was. Jack ran down a rickety flight of stairs and saw the ship tied to the pier, sitting idle. Its black cauldron of purple flames filled the massive hot air balloon above it and held it aloft. Most of the ship's Mysterrii crewmen were asleep, scattered across the deck and tangled up in the thick maritime rope used for the hot air balloon's rigging. A few were up on watch duty, and they jumped out at Jack, yelling *"Razza frazza! Razza frazza!"* as he approached. Jack didn't ask permission to board. He ran right past the miniature sentries and jumped up onto the deck.

"Hypnova!" Jack called out. "Are you in there?" he asked, banging on the door of the cabin where they'd met during his last visit. "It's Jack! Jack Blank!"

The Mysterrii went absolutely nuts at Jack's intrusion. Suddenly they were everywhere, swarming Jack. He grabbed a mop off the deck and swung it around, trying to keep them back. There were too many of them, and they were too quick. The nimble little acrobats surrounded Jack, jumping down from the balloon rigging, springing out of trapdoors and portholes, and overwhelming him with their numbers.

"Hypnova!" Jack shouted as the horde of Mysterrii lifted him up off the ground and held him fast. "Hypnova, I need to talk to you! It's important! It's life or death!"

"You're right about that," a cool voice replied from the ship's top deck near the captain's wheel. "My crew is going to throw you overboard unless you can give me a good reason why they shouldn't." Jack looked up and saw Hypnova, as stunning as ever in her green and white buccaneer outfit. *Throw me overboard?* he thought. *Is she serious?* She certainly didn't look like she was kidding.

"I need your help," Jack blurted out, instantly regretting the words as they left his mouth. It was a dumb thing to say to someone who was looking for a reason not to kill you.

Hypnova laughed. "Not the answer I was looking for," she said. "I'm afraid that won't do it." Hypnova barked out a short command in the Mysterrii's language, and the little mummies holding Jack started over toward the edge of the ship.

"No!" Jack shouted, starting to get worried. "Listen to me! I didn't come here empty-handed. I have something you want too!"

"Really," Hypnova said, skeptical. "And what is that?"

"Redemption."

Hypnova studied Jack for a moment, and then told the Mysterrii to stop. "What are you talking about?"

"Redemption for what happened with Obscuro," Jack said. "He's leaving tonight. He offered to take me with him. He said it wouldn't be safe for me here after he sold Smart my secrets."

Hypnova gave Jack a curious look. "That's true enough. It isn't even safe for you here on this boat. But why would he offer you that? What does Obscuro care about you?"

"I don't know," Jack replied. "He said he feels bad about all this. He has a message from my father. . . . He said he could take me to him."

"I see," Hypnova said, her voice turning from curious to cold once again. "And if I help you escape this place so that you can be reunited with your father, it will redeem me in your eyes." Hypnova shook her head. "Not interested, Jack. Not at all interested." Hypnova waved her hand, and the Mysterrii started moving again.

"No!" Jack yelled out again, struggling in vain against the Mysterrii's grip. "That's not it. I mean redemption with the Secreteers!" Hypnova looked at Jack as if to say, "Go on." Jack did. Unfortunately, so did the Mysterrii. He was going to have to talk fast. "Hypnova, I'm sorry you got in trouble because of me," Jack said. "Really, I am! I would have said something before now, but at first I wasn't sorry. I was mad at you. I mean, you snuck around in my brain and stole my secrets. That's messed up. But I'm not mad anymore!"

Hypnova rolled her eyes. "Imagine my relief. If I may be so bold, what brought about this change of heart?"

"Look, it was my fault too, all right?" Jack said. "I get that now. If I'd been honest with everyone in the first place, there wouldn't have been any secrets for you to steal. None of this had to happen. If I hadn't let my fears get in the way of what I had to do, none of this *would* have happened! It's like they say, you don't blame a scale for its reflection . . . or a mirror for its weight, you know?"

"Sounds like you've got it all figured out."

"Hypnova, please! Make them stop," Jack pleaded. The Mysterrii now had him dangerously close to the edge of the ship. They were really going to do this.

"Get to the point, Jack," Hypnova said. "What do you mean by offering me redemption?"

"I mean Obscuro. I can give you Obscuro. I know where he is."

"And where is that?"

"It's hard to explain. I can show you, though. You have to believe me!"

"Why should I? Why should anyone believe you now?"

"If I'm lying, you can always throw me off the ship later," Jack said. He stopped fighting the Mysterrii as they neared the railing. He wasn't going to break free of them in time for it to make any difference. His only hope was convincing Hypnova to let him go. "I can take you to him," he told her. "I just need a ride. He gave me a card telling me where to find him. It was blank before, but it isn't now."

The Mysterrii raised Jack up to throw him over the side. "Hypnova!" Jack shouted out in a desperate shriek as they tossed him out into the abyss. He landed hard on the floor of a lifeboat that was tied to the ship's hull, less than five feet below. Jack's heart unclenched when he realized the trick. The other end of the boat filled with smoke, and Hypnova emerged from the cloud.

"Apology accepted," Hypnova said. "You're lucky I'm so forgiving. Obscuro gave you a memory card?"

Jack nodded and looked over the side of the little boat. Holding on tight to the edge, he looked down at the falls below and shook his head. That had been way too close.

"If you're lying to me, I still might decide to throw you off." Hypnova held out her hand. "Give it here."

Jack dug into his pocket and took out the card. He handed it to Hypnova. He thought her eyes were going to pop out of their sockets when she saw it. She gripped the card like it was a winning lottery ticket. It read:

Jack—

The time has come for us to take our leave. It is no longer safe for either one of us to remain, and somewhere deep in space there is a father who longs to see his son once again.

The following will lead you to me, but you must hurry.

15 N 27' 13.25"
144 E 50' 37.5"
10,000 ft.

Come alone.
—Obscuro

Hypnova looked up from the card to face Jack. "It really is from him."

Jack nodded. "I didn't know what the code was at the bottom, but I figured you would."

"It's longitude and latitude," Hypnova replied. "And

this third figure . . . altitude." She looked up at the sky. "He's close. We're practically there now."

"That's great," Jack said. "You think we can get back up on your ship now?"

Hypnova told the Mysterrii to help Jack up onto the deck. By the time he had climbed back up, she was already there waiting for him at the railing. Hypnova handed the card back to Jack. "It was never blank," she said. "It's a memory card. Secreteers use their powers to make people forget what's written on them until such time that they want them to be read."

"I guess Obscuro's ready for me now," Jack said as Hypnova helped him to his feet. "He won't be ready for you, though."

"I don't imagine he will be, no," Hypnova said. There was something in her voice that was still cautious, still untrusting. "What do you hope to get out of this, Jack? You have to know I'm not letting Obscuro get away this time. I have to capture him or kill him if I want the Clandestine Order to take me back. Even if I do manage to take Obscuro alive, the card says come alone. He'll know you betrayed him. You're not going to get to see your father if I come with you tonight."

"I'm not after information about my father. I'm after the SmarterNet access codes."

"An opportunity like this might not come to you again," Hypnova told him. "A chance to reconnect with your family . . . I know what that means to you. You're truly willing to sacrifice that?"

"Sometimes a sacrifice is the only move you can make," Jack said. "It's okay. I've waited my whole life for information on my parents—any kind of information. I've gotten that much out of Obscuro already. Just to know that my dad is even still out there is huge. That'll do for now. It'll have to."

Hypnova smiled. "Putting the needs of others ahead of your own. Sounds like you learned a thing or two in that school of yours after all."

"Better late than never," Jack said. "So we have a deal?"

Hypnova drew the saber from her belt and cut the tie lines that held her ship to the dock. "We have a deal."

The Mysterrii sprang to their stations, and the ship

took flight with the midnight wind. Hypnova set a course for the one place that apparently no one had bothered to look for the Rogue Secreteer—the crystal rock face of Mount Nevertop, ten thousand feet up in the air.

CHAPTER

25

The Rogue Revealed

Jack and Hypnova sailed off into the night, flying straight up along the rock face of Mount Nevertop. The crystal mountainside scrolled down beside them as they went, its cloudy white surface radiating a soft glow in the moonlight. Jack was rooted to the ship's railing the whole way, scanning the mountain intently. He wasn't quite sure what he was looking for. The coordinates Obscuro had written on the memory card put him somewhere around halfway up the mountain. What that said about Obscuro's hideout, Jack had no idea. Would it be easy to spot or hidden away? Would they find Obscuro hiding in plain sight, hanging out on the ledge of a cliff? Not likely, Jack decided. Obscuro's lair had to be tunneled into the mountain, like the pathway up to the Cloud Cliffs that Jack had walked, back on his first full day in the Imagine Nation. That was just a year ago, Jack thought. It might as well have been a lifetime ago. He kept looking for an opening in the mountain as Hypnova steered the ship up toward the ten-thousand-foot mark.

"I'm surprised to find you without your two friends," Hypnova said to Jack, trying to make conversation. "I thought you three were inseparable."

Jack grunted. "I guess you Secreteers don't know everything after all."

Hypnova raised a rankled eyebrow. "I thought you weren't mad at me anymore."

"I'm not," Jack said, taking the edge out of his voice. "You just made me remember something I'd rather not think about, is all."

Jack filled Hypnova in on his troubles with Skerren and Allegra.

"You have more important things to worry about,"

Hypnova said, dismissing the matter entirely. "They'll get over it."

Just then Jack's wristband communicator pinged. It had just come back online now that they were far enough away from Varagog for it to work again, and Allegra's voice cut in almost immediately. "Jack . . . Jack, are you there? Come in. It's me, Allegra."

Hypnova gave Jack a mocking smile. "What'd I tell you?" her eyes seemed to say.

Jack couldn't believe Allegra was calling him already. He thought for sure she would still be too angry to speak to him. He was happy, but the funny thing was, now he was nervous, too. "What do I do?" he asked Hypnova.

"Answer her," Hypnova replied, like it was the most obvious thing in the world.

Jack rolled his eyes. "Thanks," he said. He took a few seconds to gather his thoughts before hitting the button to contact Allegra. He'd never needed to do that before. Talking to his friend Allegra had always been the easiest thing in the world for Jack, but right there, at that moment, he couldn't for the life of him think of what he was going to say to her. He tapped a button on his wrist-band and called out her name.

"Jack!" Allegra said. "Finally! Where are you? I've been trying to reach you."

"Sorry," Jack said. "I couldn't hear you until just now. My wristband wasn't working where I was. No signal."

"Are you okay?"

"I'm fine. I'm fine, thanks," Jack said, warmed by Allegra's concern. "I was afraid you still weren't speaking to—" Jack stopped midsentence, hearing some commotion in the background on Allegra's end of the line. "What's that?" he asked her. "Where are you?"

"I'm in Hightown trying to keep a mob of crazy people out of Machina. Where are you? Don't you know what's going on? Didn't you hear Smart's speech?"

"I heard it," Jack said. "Everyone heard it. That's why the Inner Circle wanted me to stay home tonight."

"So you're home, then?"

"I was. Did they tell you that the SmarterNet is the reason the virus is spreading so fast now? Smart left that part out of his speech. I'm trying to stop it right now. I'm on my way back to the Rogue Secreteer, but that's . . .

435

Listen, forget about that for a second," Jack said. "Allegra, I'm sorry," he told her. "For everything. Really. I couldn't say it before because of Lorem, but you have to know how sorry I am about all of—"

"Wait, the Rogue Secreteer?" Allegra interrupted. "Obscuro? Jack, you're not leaving, are you? Don't go with him! You don't have to run away because of what happened, even if your father is out there."

"What? Allegra, I'm not going anywhere," Jack said. "I'm here with Hypnova. We're going to stop the virus."

"Hypnova?" Allegra asked. "I thought she hated us now. What do you mean the SmarterNet is spreading the virus? How are you stopping it? Where are you?"

"I'm on Hypnova's ship," Jack replied. "We're on our way up to . . . to . . ." Jack trailed off and looked over at the mountain. They were almost at ten thousand feet. "Hang on," he told Allegra. "Something feels weird."

"Weird?" Allegra asked. "Jack, you're not making any sense. What feels weird?" She kept asking questions, but Jack was no longer paying attention. High up on the mountainside he saw something, and what he saw was hard to see. There had been massive excavation work done on the rock face of Mount Nevertop, and a cloudy blur was visible within.

"Hypnova, do you see that?" Jack asked.

"I see it," Hypnova replied.

"See what?" Allegra asked, getting impatient. Distracted, Jack told her he'd call her back, and he shut off the wristband before she could say another word. Jack recognized that blurry spot on the mountain. That is to say, he recognized what had created it—a cloaking device, like the one Obscuro's ship had used back in hangar 17.

The cloak being put to use on the mountain was masking something much bigger than Obscuro's starship. As Hypnova's ship closed in on the blur, what Jack saw was a huge facility, built into the side of Mount Nevertop, far away from prying eyes. That location alone should have been enough security for anyone, but whoever had built this thing had added the cloaking device as an additional layer of camouflage just in case someone did happen to come across it. *What could be so important?* Jack wondered briefly. Only one thing came to mind. Jack's first guess was confirmed when he realized he was staring at the nerve center of a very big machine, and he wasn't picking up any vibes from it. In fact, his powers weren't picking up any vibes from anything at all, not even his wristband communicator.

"Holy cow," Jack marveled once he realized what he was looking at. "This is it."

"What?" Hypnova asked. "What is it?"

Jack shook his head. "I don't believe this," he said, blown away by his good fortune. "Hypnova, this is what I came here for. This is the SmarterNet!"

"Are you sure?"

"I'm sure," Jack said. "Obscuro is *at* the exact thing we need to shut down! This is too good to be true."

"I'm afraid you might be right," Hypnova said. "None of this adds up. His note to you . . . this place . . . What would he be doing here?" Hypnova pulled the ship into the massive chamber carved into the side of the mountain. The Mysterrii dropped anchor and began to tie the ship down. Hypnova looked around, uneasy. "I don't like this. Something's wrong."

Jack was barely listening. He was too busy staring at the massive transparent machine. If he concentrated, he could see it was there. Cloaking devices don't fool the naked eye. Jack was able to make out the basic size and shape of the SmarterNet because of the way light bends the wrong way on a cloaked object. It was hard to see in the dark, but Jack could tell it was a massive construct, big enough to walk on, around, and inside of. The SmarterNet was the size of an oil rig, a giant invisible machine, made even more invisible because of the nullifiers. Jack figured he couldn't shut it down, but he could still find its heart and rip it out. He didn't need his powers to smash the SmarterNet's control panel with a rock. That would do the trick, nullifiers or no. Jack was about to get out of the boat, when Hypnova grabbed him.

"Wait," she said, gripping his shoulder tightly.

Hypnova pointed at the floor of the cavernous chamber. A dead SmartCorp employee was lying there. A closer examination of the SmarterNet's general vicinity revealed several more dead bodies scattered about.

Jack got a bad feeling in the pit of his stomach. Hypnova was right. Something was definitely wrong.

"What is this?" Jack asked.

Floodlights switched on all around the chamber. "That's what I'd like to know," Obscuro called out. Jack squinted as his eyes adjusted to the light. When his vision cleared, he watched Obscuro step out onto an iron-grate walkway up near the ceiling. He hopped down onto the cloaked machine, which made it look like he was standing on thin air. His voluminous cloak flapped in the wind. "You were supposed to come here alone," he told Jack.

Jack looked up at the Rogue Secreteer. "I only came to get the codes to the SmarterNet," he said. "I didn't expect to find the machine itself here with you. What's going on, Obscuro? Did you kill these people?"

"Not personally, no," Obscuro replied. "But these things happen."

"That's how you rationalize it, then, eh?" Hypnova asked. "Collateral damage. More people who had to suffer for you to get what you want. People like Jack, like myself . . . like the order." Hypnova scowled and drew her sword. "It ends here." Without needing to be told, twenty Mysterrii drew knives from their belts as well. Jack had never even known they carried weapons. "After tonight there will be no more carnage left in your wake. Obscuro, your hour of judgment is at hand."

Obscuro nodded. "I see," he said as the Mysterrii began

to climb out of the boat and move toward him. "If I may have just one final moment. . . . You wouldn't begrudge a condemned man his last words, would you?"

Hypnova chortled. "By all means. Make them count."

"I will," Obscuro replied. He cleared his throat and issued a command in the Rüstov tongue. Hypnova heard only computer tones and static, but Jack understood it as an attack order given to forces that were waiting in reserve. Worse than that, he recognized the voice. He'd heard it before on Smart's recordings. Obscuro let out a chilling laugh as dozens of Rüstov Left-Behinds crawled out of the woodwork. Even with the armed Mysterrii at their side, Jack and Hypnova were greatly outnumbered.

"Obscuro!" Hypnova said, shocked. "What is the meaning of this? You've betrayed us to the Rüstov as well?"

The Rogue Secreteer's sinister, triumphant laughter echoed through the chamber. "You keep calling me Obscuro," he replied. He reached up and pulled back the hood of his cloak, revealing a face with a dark Rüstov scar around its right eye. "The name," he said, "is Glave."

CHAPTER

26

Glave and Khalix

Shock waves from the Rogue Secreteer's revelation punched through Jack's system from head to toe. He felt like he was waking up inside a crashing car. For a few scary seconds he was confused. Every synapse in his brain was firing at the same time, and he was thinking a million different things at once. Then, like a groggy rider in the passenger seat drawing focus on a wave of oncoming traffic, Jack understood the danger he was in mere seconds before impact. It was an understanding that came far too late for him to get out of harm's way.

Hypnova gasped at the sight of the unmistakable Rüstov eye. "You're infected," she said. "Obscuro . . . he never—"

"Obscuro is gone," Glave said. "That name is nothing more than a disguise that is no longer necessary." The Rüstov agent cast off his cloak. It fell away like a half-opened parachute plummeting down off the mountain.

"How . . . ," Hypnova started to say, then trailed off. Jack figured she was thinking the same thing he was. If Obscuro was infected, that meant his every move had been part of a Rüstov plot. Jack had to stop and think about how far back this went. The Rüstov had been manipulating everyone from the very beginning. He didn't know what that said about their plans, but he knew it wasn't good. The Rüstov had taken a Secreteer. They knew way too much.

"It wasn't easy," Glave said. "It took a long time to successfully infect a member of your order. Thirteen years, in fact, but I never gave up. And I never gave up on you, boy," he added, looking at Jack. "We didn't even know for certain that you were still alive until just last year, but I never stopped looking."

Jack scowled at Glave. *So that's what this is about,* he thought. The Rüstov wanted him, same as the team of Left-Behinds did last year. That's why Glave had wanted him to come alone. This was another attempt to steal him away and turn him into Revile.

"It was all lies, then, wasn't it?" Jack asked. "Just a trick to get me out here. You don't have any idea where my father is."

"Not *your* father, no," Glave replied.

Jack squinted at the Rüstov master spy. "What are you talking about? Your note said—"

"My note said 'there is a father who longs to see his son once again.' That part of the message wasn't meant for you. You simply assumed it was."

Jack opened his mouth to speak, and then closed it without saying anything.

Glave seemed to take great pride in Jack's befuddled state. "There are two of you in there, or did you forget?" he said to Jack. "I was talking about the father of the Rüstov *inside* you."

"The Rüstov inside me?" Jack repeated. "My parasite?"

"He has a name," Glave said. "He's called Khalix, and

444

he is the rightful heir to the Rüstov empire. I'm here to set him free."

Jack felt like he'd just been hit in the stomach with a sledgehammer. The realization that the chance to reunite with his father at any point in the future was nothing more than a false hope was bad enough, but this . . .

"No," Jack said. "That can't be right."

"You should be honored," Glave replied. "His father is the Magus. He has a great destiny before him. A destiny that's been put on hold for far too long."

"A great destiny," Hypnova said under her breath. She looked at Jack, her eyes full of fear. "He means . . ."

"That's right," Glave said, hopping down a level on the invisible SmarterNet. "Jack knows all about it. You both do. After all, you're the one who stole the secrets out of his head. Isn't that right, Hypnova?" Glave climbed up onto another iron-grate catwalk and walked a few more steps until he was standing directly across from Jack and Hypnova. The skin on his face was tight and dry, giving way to more rust and decay. Patches of Glave's hair were falling out clumps at a time. Jack wanted to smash his smug face in.

"I always knew the value of infecting a Secreteer would be impossible to match," Glave continued. "When the empire left this place years ago, I chose to stay behind to gather intelligence through strategic infection." Glave grinned an evil grin. "Obscuro told me things I never could have imagined. Things about the future . . . the glorious future." The Rüstov spy rubbed his hands together like a starving man sizing up a heaping plate of food. "Great things are in store for Khalix, Jack Blank. You're bound for glory, both of you. It's time for my prince to go home, and for me to receive my reward."

Jack couldn't believe what he was hearing. The parasite inside him . . . a Rüstov prince. In a way, he really was Rüstov royalty, just like the Left-Behind had said back on Wrekzaw Isle a year ago. Jack didn't bother to dispute Glave's claims any further. Like it or not, it all made perfect sense. It was the son of the Rüstov emperor who'd been tapped to one day become the empire's unbeatable soldier. It might just have been his imagination, but somewhere deep inside his mind, Jack swore he could hear Khalix laughing at him.

"I'm never going to be Revile," Jack said, unsure if he even believed it himself. "It's not going to happen."

"I'm curious . . . how do you intend to stop it?" Glave asked as Left-Behinds continued to arrive on the scene in greater numbers. "You cannot fight the future, Jack. We *are* the future. What you know about tomorrow merely confirms the empire's inevitable victory."

"The future isn't set in stone," Jack said, trying to find strength in Stendeval's words. "We make our own future."

"Indeed," Glave replied. "That's exactly what I've been doing for the last thirteen years. It's all happening exactly as I'd planned. Once I succeeded in taking a Secreteer as my host, the outcome was never in doubt. I started selling secrets to supervillains, knowing they would keep the heroes of Empire City out of my way while I worked to spread the spyware virus." Glave gestured to the cloaked machine behind him. "From Obscuro I learned the truth about the SmarterNet, the perfect delivery mechanism for the virus. I created a situation where I could gain access to this wondrous device and cast suspicion on you at the same time. Once all the pieces were in place, it took less than a week to cut the protection around you down to nothing. You people are so easy to manipulate. That is why your future holds nothing but death and defeat."

"You haven't won anything yet," Jack said. "We're going to smash that machine."

Glave shrugged off Jack's threat. "Be my guest. Even if you manage to succeed, you can't undo the work I've done here. The entire Mecha population of Empire City is infected. They're attacking the Imagine Nation on my orders, and this is not even the empire's first strike."

"What is it, then?" Hypnova asked.

"This," Glave gloated, "is psychological warfare at the highest level. I'm prepping the battlefield for the next invasion, sowing discord and confusion in the enemy's ranks. You people are your own worst enemy. I've got you fighting among one another already, completely oblivious to the real threat. This goes far beyond the Mechas. The SmarterNet is spreading the spyware virus to every machine on Earth. Surveillance satellites, communications net-works, missile silos . . . planes, trains, and automobiles—

even power tools and vacuum cleaners! Everything will work against you when the empire returns. You'll march with us on that glorious day, boy," Glave said, pointing a finger in Jack's direction. "Perhaps you'll even lead the charge. The Magus will have his son returned, and he *will* have his victory." Glave turned to the scrap-metal legion of Left-Behinds and gave the order to attack. "Take them."

The small army of Left-Behinds that had never stopped gathering behind Glave lurched forward, advancing on Hypnova's ship. Hypnova released the anchor and ordered her crew to take the ship out, but the Left-Behinds opened fire on the hot air balloon. The vessel went crashing to the floor of the chamber. As Jack and Hypnova staggered to their feet, the Mysterrii leaped into action, trying to keep the Rüstov from boarding the ship.

"He's right," Hypnova grunted as she snatched her sword up off the floor. "Smashing this machine won't stop the virus. It's already out there. It won't stop what he's done to us, either. Even if we cured the Mechas and the other machines . . . everything is suspect now. The trust is gone. He's already succeeded."

Jack stopped listening halfway through Hypnova's speech. He didn't hear anything after the word "cured." "Hypnova, that's it," he said. "That's it!" Hypnova looked at Jack like he must have hit his head too hard in the crash. "The cure," Jack explained. "I have the cure! I can't do anything about the trust, but I can stop the virus." Jack checked his watch. The ninety minutes were almost up. "Almost ready," he said. "If it works, we can upload it here and broadcast it to every Mecha. We can broadcast it everywhere!"

"Is it *going* to work?" Hypnova asked.

"I think so," Jack said, throwing up his hands. "I don't know. It's worth a shot, isn't it? Midknight showed me Smart's transmitter. It was advanced, but I got it. I understood that part of this thing." Jack looked up at the near-invisible SmarterNet. "I can do this," he said decidedly. "If I can use my powers, that is."

A Left-Behind jumped up at the ship's railing, right next to Jack. Hypnova spun around with her sword, slicing across the creature's chest, and then throwing an elbow into its jaw, knocking it off the ship. "Where is the cure now?" she asked without missing a beat.

450

"Uh . . . in my lab," Jack said, stepping back from the railing. "I ran it on the prototype. I can run it here, too. I just need the nullifiers shut down."

"Call your friends," Hypnova said, taking Jack by the wrist and walking him back toward the rear of the ship. "We'll take care of the nullifiers."

Hypnova started giving orders to the Mysterrii, and Jack called to Allegra on the wristband.

"Jack, what the heck is going on?" Allegra demanded. "It's getting bad out here. Midknight just called Stendeval. . . . He said they're not going to make it in time. Stendeval's going to have to EMP the Mechas."

"No," Jack said. "Allegra, you've gotta tell Stendeval to wait. Hypnova and I are at the SmarterNet right now. I can use it to cure the Mechas. At least, I think I can, but I need you to go to my lab and get the prototype. The cure-code is loaded onto its CPU. I need you to bring it here so we can broadcast it out."

"Bring it where?" Allegra asked. "Where are you?"

"Are you outside? Can you see Mount Nevertop?" Jack asked.

"Yes," said Allegra.

"Look up," Jack said, and he threw a heap of purple powder into the cauldron of purple flames. The bonfire flared up so fast it nearly burned his eyebrows off, but it lit up the night sky, illuminating the crystal surface of the mountain with a brilliance that was impossible to miss.

"Up there? How am I supposed to . . . ," Allegra started to say. Jack could practically hear her shaking her head in frustration. "Jack, there's no one here to help," she said. "All the heroes are in Machina. It's just me and the other students out here with Chi's ninjas."

"The other students?" Jack asked. "Good, you're going to need Trea to lead you to my lab."

"Jack, you're not listening," Allegra said.

Before Jack could say anything in reply, a metal hand grabbed at his shoulder. "Ahhh!" Jack screamed. He hit the deck, slipping out of his jacket as he dropped to the floor. On his knees, he turned to see a Left-Behind climbing over the back railing of the ship. It threw his jacket away and kept coming at him. Jack looked around for something to defend himself with and grabbed the only thing he could reach. It was the same mop he'd tried to hold the Mysterrii back with. Thinking fast, he stuck the mop end into the fire and then rammed the flaming torch into the chest of the Left-Behind. The Rüstov screamed as the flammable oils and greases on its machine parts lit up instantly. More Left-Behinds came crawling up the side of the ship, but Hypnova swooped back in, slicing two of them away with one swing of her sword, and kicking a third off the railing. She settled into position over Jack, guarding him.

"Allegra, I can't talk now," Jack said into his wrist. "The ship is crawling with Left-Behinds. I need your help. Please, go to my lab now. And listen . . . if we live through this, I'll tell you everything. I mean it. And if I don't make it . . . well, you already know how sorry I am."

There was a brief silence on the other end of the line. "I know," Allegra said at last. "I'm coming."

"Hurry," Jack said. "Please." He turned off the wristband and looked up at Hypnova.

"Well?" she asked him.

Jack nodded. "She's on her way."

"Good," Hypnova said, handing Jack a sword. "Because

so are they." She motioned toward the forward end of the ship. A squad of Left-Behinds was closing in. Jack heard a most unwelcome *ka-chuck* noise as the Rüstov soldiers cocked their weapons. Seconds later he ducked down screaming as the world around him erupted in a hail of bullets and a million splintery explosions.

CHAPTER

27

Melee at Mount Nevertop

"Cease fire, you imbeciles!" Glave shouted. "CEASE FIRE! Do you mean to kill your prince along with his host?"

The gunfire stopped. A few final shots rang out alone like the last lingering blasts on a string of firecrackers. Jack looked up, his ears ringing. Glave was still shouting.

"Do you want to explain to the Magus that you killed his son minutes before we were about to reclaim him?" the Rüstov spy railed at his men. "After we spent thirteen years looking for him? He's no good to us dead, you morons!"

455

The Left-Behinds grumbled like unappreciated work-ers, and then marched forward toward Jack and Hypnova, ready to take them by hand.

"They need to take you alive," Hypnova said. "We have that much going for us."

"Right," Jack agreed. "You know things are bad when that's the good news."

"Take pleasure in the little victories, Jack," Hypnova said. "Sometimes that's all we have." She threw open a hatch on the floor of the ship and pushed Jack toward it. "Get belowdecks."

"Not yet," Jack replied. Using the broadsword Hypnova had just handed him, he cut away a rope holding several barrels of flammable powder in place.

"What are you doing?" Hypnova asked.

"Using my environment," Jack replied as the heavy stores of fuel for the hot air balloon's bonfire rolled into the Rüstov, knocking them down like bowling pins. Jack looked up at Hypnova. "Not bad, eh?"

Hypnova didn't say anything. She wasn't even looking at Jack. She was looking at a trail of purple powder that had leaked out of one of the barrels as it rolled across the deck. Flames from the body of the Left-Behind that Jack had set on fire were inching ever closer to it. The powder ignited, and a thin line of fire blazed toward the barrels at the other end of the ship. "Get below," Hypnova said at last. "Now."

Jack cringed and went for the hatch. Hypnova followed close behind, racing down the ladder after him. The explosion rocked the boat with a force strong enough to rattle Jack's teeth and roll the ship onto its side. Hypnova and Jack were just fast enough to escape a burst of flames rushing over their heads, but went flying off the ladder on their way down to the lower decks.

Once the ship settled into place, Hypnova got up and walked across the wall—which, given the ship's current angle, was now the floor—and pushed the hatch open to see what was left of her ship. Half of it was blown apart. The other half was either on fire or soon to be on fire.

"My ship," was all she said.

Jack poked his head out next to Hypnova. He didn't know what to say to her. He was about to apologize, but decided this part wasn't his fault. Not really. The ship had been lost the moment the Rüstov had downed it. That

said, Jack couldn't deny that he had left a decidedly nega-
tive impression on Hypnova's life since having met her.
Of course, his life wasn't exactly smooth sailing as a result
of having her in it either.

"The whole ship is going to burn," Jack said. "We can't
stay here."

Hypnova grunted and took a step back, pulling the
hatch shut behind her. Jack jumped back to avoid getting
hit by the door. "I wasn't planning to," she told him. "Follow me."

Hypnova led the way to the stern of the ship, where she
took a chair and smashed out its ornate stained-glass rear
window. Jack figured she didn't see much point in trying
to preserve the ship's finer points now. He and Hypnova
kicked away the remaining shards of glass that were sticking out of the windowsill, and then they jumped through
it. The Mysterrii were waiting for them outside.

Glave was shouting at his Left-Behinds to find Jack. He
and Hypnova had a minute, maybe less, to figure out their
next move under the cover of the flames and smoke. Jack
got right down to business. "We have to shut down those
nullifiers before Allegra gets here," he said. "We can't

touch the SmarterNet, though. . . . We need it working for when they show up with the cure."

"*If* they show up with the cure," Hypnova said. "Assuming your cure works." She shook her head. "That won't be easy. We can barely even see the SmarterNet."

"Here, I almost forgot," Jack said, reaching into his bag to pull out two pairs of goggles. "Heat-vision goggles. I brought these to help spot Obscuro's cloaked ship. When I thought it was Obscuro, that is. Try them on." Jack handed one pair to Hypnova and pulled the other over his own eyes.

Hypnova shrugged. "It's better than nothing."

Jack agreed that the goggles' effect was far from perfect. He saw the SmarterNet glowing in clear shades of orange and red, but the cold crystal surface of the cavern registered as a deep indigo that blended seamlessly with the dark night. Getting around using heat-vision wasn't going to be easy. The fire produced a bright red glare that didn't help matters either. Jack tried flipping up one eye of his goggles, but the result was even more disorienting so he decided to press on with both eyes covered.

"Like you said, sometimes you've gotta go with what

you've got. I don't have any more for these guys," Jack said, motioning to the Mysterrii.

"That won't be necessary," Hypnova replied. "The Mysterrii's eyes work differently from ours."

"Good," Jack said. "Let's get to it. What do the nulli-fiers look like?"

"You know I can't tell you secrets," Hypnova told Jack.

Jack flipped up his goggles and glared at Hypnova. "You've gotta be kidding. You're not even a Secreteer anymo—"

"But I can smash any nullifiers I see," Hypnova inter-rupted. "And if you happen to notice what they look like in the process . . . so be it."

Jack calmed down and watched as Hypnova pointed at a gang of Mysterrii that was climbing up the side of the SmarterNet. The Left-Behinds tried to stop them, but the nimble and cagey Mysterrii still made it to the top. Jack watched as one of them ran at a tall, thin pole that was sticking out of the front corner of the rig. The little guy grabbed it and swung around. Another Mysterrii grabbed on to his feet as he passed by, and they both kept right on swinging. A third Mysterrii jumped on after that, and the pole finally snapped off under their combined weight.

The Mysterrii went flying through the air and into the arms of their comrades, who were hanging down from the catwalks like trapeze acrobats ready to receive their partners midflight. One of them was still holding the pole that they had broken off the SmarterNet. At the end of the pole was a metallic cylinder about the size of a coffee thermos, with a blinking red light at the top. The Mysterrii smashed it against the wall, and Jack felt a surge of power flood back into his body. It was invigorating, like a jolt of adrenaline snapping everything he saw into sharper focus.

It felt good, but Jack's powers weren't all the way back. Not yet. He knew how to get them back now, though, and that felt great. There were three more poles on top of the SmarterNet, one posted at each corner. Each one had a metal cylinder at the top like the one the Mysterrii had just smashed. "One down, three to go," Jack said. "Let's do it."

A fortunate gust of wind blew the black smoke from the fire toward the SmarterNet, and Jack and Hypnova followed the cloud and a wave of Mysterrii toward Jonas Smart's accidental doomsday device. Jack ran up a flight of stairs on one side, and Hypnova charged up a ramp on the other. He hadn't even reached the first landing before his path was blocked by Rüstov Left-Behinds. Seen through heat-vision, their organic body parts gave off a sickly lime green glow that clashed with the yellow and orange hues of their mechanical parts. If Jack had been able to use his powers, those mechanical parts would have been the Achilles' heel of every Rüstov on Mount Nevertop, but he had to take out the nullifiers before that would be the case. Still, Jack wasn't completely over-matched. He might not have been able to use his powers, but the Left-Behinds couldn't use their guns. They were both fighting with one hand tied behind their backs.

The Rüstov Para-Soldiers on the staircase lunged for Jack. He jumped back, and the lead Left-Behind fell face-first down the steps. It clutched at the banister to get up, and Jack thrust his sword into its heart. When that didn't stop it, Jack grabbed the breathing tubes and wires that ran into a mechanized pack on its back. Sparks went flying everywhere as the creature dropped to its knees. Two more Left-Behinds closed in behind the fallen Para-Soldier, but a trio of Mysterrii hopped over Jack's shoulders and landed on them. The Left-Behinds were still struggling to draw their guns when several more Mysterrii popped up over the exterior banister and held their arms fast. The Mysterrii raised their daggers and stabbed the Rüstov until they fell. It was so brutal that Jack had to turn away. When he looked up, the path was clear.

"Thanks, guys," Jack said, wincing at the sight of their handiwork.

"*Frezza frezza!*" one of the Mysterrii shouted back. "*Fez! Fez!*" it said, pointing onward up the stairs.

"Right," Jack said. The small but deadly creature's message was clear enough. Jack heard gunfire on the roof of the SmarterNet, and he followed the sound up in a hurry. The Mysterrii did the same, but they ignored the walkways and staircases, opting to crawl up through the guts of the great machine, climbing into vents, pipes, and any other openings they could squeeze themselves into. Jack kept going up a ramp that zigzagged its way up the SmarterNet's exterior like a fire escape. More Left-Behinds blocked the way, but Jack cut through them with the help of the Mysterrii, who kept coming out of nowhere. The Left-Behinds outnumbered Jack and his allies, but the Rüstov's numbers were no help to them fighting in such close quarters. Jack was starting to feel more and more optimistic about their chances, which was perhaps why Khalix started piping up—Jack's parasite wanted to take some of the wind out of his sails. At least Jack hoped that was what was behind Khalix's sudden bold streak.

"Just give up already," the Rüstov prince said inside Jack's head. "Every one of these Para-Soldiers will gladly die for me, and my father has a million more where they came from. You know we'll never stop. Why prolong the inevitable?"

Jack froze in place. Khalix's words sent a chill up his spine. Not so much because of what he said, but rather because Jack could hear him in the first place. "Is this going to be a regular thing with you now?" Jack asked in as brave a voice as he could muster. "Chiming in with little comments all the time?"

"You've only got yourself to blame," Khalix replied. "You're the one who let me back into your life."

Don't let him get to you, Jack told himself.

"Tough talk from someone who's done less than nothing for the last thirteen years," Jack said out loud. "What, you're a big man now because Daddy's coming to your rescue? I never had that. That's why I'm stronger. That's why I'm going to win." Jack did his best to sound convincing. He could hear what Khalix said, but not what he thought. Jack hoped their connection worked the same way from the other side. Jack concentrated as hard as he could, trying to shut Khalix out. He hoped that willpower alone would be enough to do it without his powers. He didn't have time to think about his parasite right now. He had a job to do, and there were too many Left-Behinds trying to stop him, not to mention the ruthless spy behind all this—Glave.

Jack made it to the top of the SmarterNet and saw several Mysterrii lying on the ground, unconscious. He hoped they were just unconscious. Across the roof Glave was busy choking the life out of one of them, but he dropped him once he saw Jack. "There you are," Glave said with a satisfied smirk on his face. "You should have run, boy. That would have been the smart thing to do."

Jack steeled his spine and slid his goggles up so he could look Glave in the eye. "I haven't done the smart thing all year. Why start now?"

There was a blast of black smoke where Glave was standing, and before Jack could even blink, the Rüstov agent was standing at his side. "Why indeed?" he asked as he grabbed Jack up off the ground.

Jack was cursing himself for so quickly forgetting about the Secreteers' abilities, when another smoke cloud erupted from the ground, this time right in front of him and Glave. There was a sound like fabric whipping through the air as somebody kicked Glave in the face and then moved quickly behind him, striking the Rüstov spy so hard that Jack almost felt bad for him. Almost.

Glave fell hard, dropping Jack. When the smoke cleared, he saw Hypnova standing over him. She threw her cloak over her shoulder with a very businesslike gesture and took a moment to admire the blood that now decorated the little gold spikes on the metal glove she wore on her right hand.

"You have much to answer for, Agent Glave," Hypnova said without looking up. She said Glave's name like the word itself was poison in her mouth. She drew her sword and pointed it at him. "I'm going to use this to ask the questions. Now get on your feet. I want to kill you properly."

Glave rose to one knee and wiped blood from his lip. He scowled at the sight of it and spit it out. Glave looked so filled with rage, Jack thought his eyeballs might explode. Instead, a cloud of black smoke exploded all around him. Hypnova flapped her cloak and vanished in an equally dark cloud. Seconds later they met in the sky above Jack. Hypnova swung her sword down at Glave. He pulled two black daggers from his belt and crossed them in front of his face to block her steel. The two Secreteers blasted around the chamber inside clouds of black smoke, fighting in the sky, on the mountain's crystal ledges, and on the catwalks surrounding the SmarterNet. Their blades clashed repeatedly as each one did his or her best to kill the other.

Meanwhile, one of the Mysterrii that Glave had strangled was slowly getting up. "*Ooofah,*" it said, rubbing its head and neck.

Jack went to it. "Are you okay?" he asked.

The Mysterrii shook him off, pointing behind Jack. "*Razza frazza!*" the Mysterrii said. "*Razza frazza!*" Jack turned and saw more Left-Behinds staggering onto the roof.

"Right," Jack said. He dug into his bag and took out an explosive charge. "Can you climb that?" he asked the Mysterrii, pointing at one of the three poles with a working nullifier. "I need you to put this up there," he said, hoping the creature understood him. "This . . . ," he repeated, holding up the charge, "up there!" The Mysterrii snatched the miniature explosive out of his hand and went for the nullifier.

Jack headed over to the other side of the roof, away from the advancing Left-Behinds. He looked over the side of the SmarterNet and saw that the levels below were swarming with more Rüstov. He was trapped on the roof, and up here the Para-Soldiers had plenty of room to fight. Jack had to take out the nullifiers fast. There was an explosion across the roof, and Jack ducked down. Tiny bits of metal from the blast dug into the back of his neck, but it felt great because of the boost of energy that came with it. His Mysterrii friend had just blown up the second nulli-

fier. Two down, two to go. Jack looked up at the nullifier in front of him. He couldn't reach it. He checked his
bag. There was only one more charge. After that he was
empty. Jack considered activating the bomb's timer and
throwing it at the nullifier up on top of the pole, but he
was afraid he might miss. He looked around for something else he could use to hit his target, and saw more
Mysterrii climbing up the side of the SmarterNet. One of
them disarmed a Left-Behind on its way up and handed
its gun to Jack.

"That'll work," Jack said, dropping his sword for a considerable upgrade in firepower. "Thanks."

Jack took aim at the nullifier, pulled the trigger on the
Rüstov machine gun, and blasted the nullifier to bits. The
kickback from the weapon sent him flying across the roof.
When he skidded to a halt, he looked up, right into the
eyes of a Rüstov Left-Behind. He threw his arms up and
blasted the Para-Soldier, screaming the whole time.

As soon as he stood up, another Left-Behind ripped
the gun from his hand and punched him in the stomach, sending him reeling. Jack didn't get the chance to
appreciate any good vibes brought on by the elimination

of the nullifier he'd just shot to pieces. He was too busy staggering across the roof, sucking wind. He collapsed back in the same spot he'd been standing in when he'd first fired the Rüstov gun, which was a good thing. When the Para-Soldier that had hit him grabbed him from behind, Jack was able to pick up his sword and stab it in the chest. Jack clapped his hand around the Left-Behind's shoulder and shoved the sword in. The Rüstov swung its arms wildly and knocked Jack across the roof. He landed in the corner next to the last remaining nullifier.

Jack rubbed his head where he'd been hit. Above, Hypnova and Glave were still thrashing about in the sky, vanishing and reappearing in bursts of smoke again and again. Glave and Hypnova were locked in each other's grips like wrestlers.

"You're wasting your time," he heard Glave tell Hypnova as he tried to drive a knife into her neck while she struggled against him. "You saw the future in the boy's memories, just as I did. You know how this is going to end."

"You still . . . have to make it happen!" Hypnova grunted, and she leaned back all the way, taking Glave down with her in a spiral dive that allowed her to spin out of his grip. Glave's knife went flying away through the air. Hypnova and Glave separated. The Rüstov agent hovered in the air with a furious look in his eyes.

"*I'm* not going to make it happen," Glave said, gnashing his teeth. "He will," he added, pointing at Jack.

Jack scrambled to his feet as Hypnova charged into Glave once again. He'd worry about them later. A few feet away a Left-Behind with a sword sticking out of its chest was headed for him. Two more Para-Soldiers were right behind it. As the Rüstov advanced on his position, Jack backed up to the ledge of the SmarterNet, with the last nullifier directly above him. Just like the other one, it was out of his reach.

The Left-Behinds closed in, and Jack took a step back. There was nothing behind him to step on. He dropped off the top of the SmarterNet, catching the roof with his fingers to keep from falling all the way down. Almost immediately he let go and dropped down again, this time catching himself at the next level. His bag caught on a piece of the SmarterNet, so Jack threw it off his shoulder. It fell away and landed on the ground, empty. Jack's last explosive charge wasn't in the bag anymore. It was right where he had left it—crammed into the wiring on the back of the Left-Behind he'd stabbed in the chest. Jack had set the explosive on a delay to avoid getting blown up himself, and it just so happened that the Left-Behind carrying it was standing right below the last nullifier.

The explosion on the roof was just big enough to take out the three Left-Behinds and the pole supporting the final nullifier. The blast also had enough kick to shake Jack loose from the side of the SmarterNet.

The pole with the nullifier fell down to the floor of the chamber, and Jack was right behind it. He bounced off the fire-escape-style ramps on the side of the machine and hit the ground hard. Jack rolled over and let out a groan. Everything hurt, but he didn't have the option of staying down until he felt better. At the moment, the Left-Behinds were all still inside the SmarterNet, and Jack knew that moment wouldn't last. He had to finish this before it passed altogether.

Jack no longer had his sword or any backup. Hypnova and the Mysterrii were all otherwise engaged with the enemy. He had to go it alone. Jack had no idea where the last nullifier had landed, but he could track it down using his powers, or lack thereof. He still couldn't access his machine-controlling abilities, but he did feel a fuzzy connection to them with three of the four nullifiers gone. Jack could feel where the dead zone canceling out his powers was coming from. He was in the back of the chamber, with the SmarterNet in front of him. The power-draining signal was coming toward him. The nullifier had to be out there in front of him, somewhere right in front of his face. He threw away his goggles and got up to look. Less than a minute later, he saw it. The nullifier was halfway up the wall, precariously balanced on a rock ledge on the side of the cavern. Jack grabbed some wall and started climbing. As he went up, the Left-Behinds started jumping off the sides of the SmarterNet and pouring out of its access ramps. Jack tapped his wrist to get an update on Allegra's status. "Allegra, where are you guys? Close, I hope?"

Much to Jack's surprise, someone else answered the call. "I'm afraid I'm not privy to Allegra's whereabouts at present," Stendeval said.

"Stendeval?" Jack asked. "Is that you? What's going on?"

"It's all right, Jack," Stendeval said. "Allegra gave me her bracelet so we could be in direct contact once she arrives at Mount Nevertop. Unfortunately, I can't join you in this fight. I have to conserve energy for the EMP, if necessary."

"Stendeval, you don't need to blast the EMP into Machina when the Mechas reboot," Jack said, climbing. "We have a chance. I have the cure."

"An experimental cure," Stendeval said.

"I have a good feeling about this one," Jack said. "I don't know if it will work, but there's a chance. A good chance."

"There is also less than ten minutes' time before the Mechas wake up. Innocent lives are at stake on both sides of the Machina-Hightown border, Jack. This isn't just my decision to make. I gave Virtua my word that I wouldn't let the Rüstov use her people against the Imagine Nation again."

"You have to give us time," Jack said, looking below him to find several Left-Behinds gathering at the base of the rock wall. "Promise you'll give me the chance to fix this."

"Like you promised me you'd stay in Cognito?"

Stendeval asked. Jack didn't say anything. "I will do what I can. That is all I can ever promise anyone."

Jack frowned. "That'll have to do. I'll check back with an update as soon as I can. Wish me luck."

Jack continued to climb, and the Left-Behinds followed him up the wall. He picked up the pace until he heard a scream on the roof of the SmarterNet behind him. He paused to get a look at what was going on, unable to tell if the cry had come from Hypnova or Glave. Jack watched as a stream of smoke went flying off the top of Smart's machine and crashed into the floor of the chamber. A black cloud spread out at the point of impact, and Jack hoped it would be Hypnova who would be revealed as the victor when it lifted. No such luck. The smoke dissipated, and Jack saw that Glave was the one left standing. The Rüstov agent looked up at Jack, and then at what Jack was after.

"No . . . ," Glave said, and burst into a cloud of smoke. A trail of black smoke fired up across the chamber like exhaust from a rocket, headed toward the ledge with the nullifier. Jack's head spun back around, and he made a frenzied last push to beat it there. He was almost upon it. He kicked down at Left-Behinds below him as they clawed at his heels, and pulled himself up onto the ledge, his objective just a few feet away. The second he got there, Glave materialized in front of him and grabbed the pole with the nullifier at the end. He held it with both hands like a staff, and Jack leaped for him, grabbing the pole and trying to wrest it from his hands. They both went tumbling down the wall, rolling toward the cliff-side edge of the cavern. Jack didn't think twice about the danger involved. Falling off the mountain was the least of his worries. If Glave was able to keep the nullifier away from him, it was all over anyway.

"Jack . . . ," Glave grunted, struggling with Jack on the floor of the cavern. "Stop . . . you're going to—urkk!"

Glave shut up as Jack kicked him in the face. Jack had gotten turned around in the fall and was able to hold on to the pole with one hand, with his feet pressed up against Glave's chest. He planted one foot on Glave's shoulder and kept right on kicking with the other. After enough kicks the pole slipped from Glave's fingers and Jack went flying backward too fast to stop himself.

"NO!" Glave shouted as Jack's momentum carried him out and over the side of the cliff.

Jack didn't scream. He was too scared to even breathe. He felt every ounce of oxygen leave his body, and the world slowed to a crawl as he fell. It was like someone had hit the pause button and he was having an out-of-body experience watching himself slip away . . . watching as the ledge pulled back from him . . . but that wasn't right. The mountain wasn't moving. *He* was. Jack was falling out into the night, completely helpless, and the second that realization hit, the world sped back up, spinning out of control.

Jack screamed as the fear rose in him, stampeding through every inch of his body. He saw the nullifier falling alongside him. He hadn't even realized he'd let it go. His mind was everywhere. Jack heard Stendeval calling out from his wrist communicator.

"Jack? Jack!" Stendeval cried. "What's going on?"

Jack heard Khalix screaming in his head. He was in no shape to shut him out, not while he was falling to his death. Jack took a breath and screamed again, his arms and legs flailing as he raced toward the ground. Then a stream of glowing light rushed past him. And then another. Then he was caught.

"Gotcha!" a voice in the night called out as a hand clamped down hard on Jack's wrist. Jack's stomach jumped into his throat as he reversed course with a jerk and started going back up.

"Wha?" Jack mumbled in a dumbfounded daze as he tried to figure out what was happening. Above him he saw Zhi's glowing dragons flying up through the night sky. Jack's mind was racing. He wasn't dead. He was caught. Caught! By a dragon rider!

Jack looked down as a blue dragon came up below him, and he saw Allegra riding it. She'd made it. And she'd brought the cavalry. Jack drew focus on the dragons above him and saw Skerren, Trea, and Zhi. They were all there.

"Allegra!" Jack shouted, half laughing, half tearing up with relief. "You made it! Oh, man, I can't . . . thank you! Thank you so much!" he said, still getting over the shock of it all. "Did it work?" he asked. "Did you get it? Did you get—"

"The prototype?" asked the man holding on to Jack. "Yeah, they did." Jack was pulled up and set down on the dragon. "Rebuilt and better than ever, thanks to you."

Jack knew who it was before he even saw his face. Even so, he still said, "Holy cow. . . . I don't believe it."

"If that were true, I wouldn't be here," the prototype replied.

Jack shook his head and smiled. This time his eyes couldn't hold back the tears welling up inside them. "Am I glad to see you, Jazen. You have no idea."

CHAPTER

28

The Comeback

Emissary Jazen Knight, also known as the virus-free proto-type, pulled his dragon up to join the others that were hovering in the air above him. He and Jack's fellow students parked their flying beasts in the clouds across from the mouth of the cavern housing the SmarterNet, just out of the Rüstov's firing range. They came to a stop, and Jack stared at his friend, his mouth agape. Jazen's presence there was his doing, but Jack still couldn't believe his eyes. Jazen Knight, the person who had brought him to the Imagine Nation and had died saving him from the

Rüstov last year . . . He was right there in front of him. He was back.

"The cure . . . ," Jack said. "It worked. You're here."

Jazen smiled. "I'm here. I don't know how you did it, but you brought me back, Jack. You saved my life."

"Yeah, well . . . I owed you. You saved my life plenty of times. Just now, for instance."

"Eh," Jazen said, waving his hand. "Who's counting?" Jazen opened his arms wide and hugged Jack. Jack wrapped his arms around Jazen's back and held on tight. He held on as if he would have fallen down into the darkness if he'd dared to loosen his grip even the tiniest little bit. For a kid who'd never known any family, Jack felt like he'd just gotten his big brother back. When he finally let go of Jazen, he wiped his eyes and looked at the other dragons that were circling around him. His fellow students—*his friends*—were all there.

"You came," Jack said. "You all came. Thank you."

"We didn't come for you, Jack," Skerren replied. "We came because we were needed."

Jack swallowed hard and looked at Skerren. "Maybe. But I was the one who needed you. So thanks either way."

"What's the situation here, Jack?" Allegra asked.

"Where's the SmarterNet?" Trea wanted to know. "Allegra said you found it."

"It's in there," Jack said, pointing at the giant hole carved into the side of Mount Nevertop. "You can't see it from out here. It's cloaked. The SmarterNet is broadcasting on a global frequency," Jack told the group. "It's sending the spyware virus out all over the world. We have to transfer the cure-code from Jazen's system into the SmarterNet's mainframe and send out our own signal. Otherwise the Rüstov are going to control every machine on Earth, and every Mecha in Empire City is going to die."

Jack's classmates contemplated the enemy forces that had gathered at Mount Nevertop. Glave and the Rüstov fighters were all lined up on the ledge, watching as Jack and his friends formulated their game plan from a safe distance.

"Unless we stop them," Jazen said.

"Can we do that?" Zhi asked. "Can we transfer the code?"

"Jack can," Allegra said.

"Right, I can . . . ," Jack started to say, and then he trailed off, turning toward the mountain with a startled look. "No," he said, frowning. "I can't. Not yet."

"What are you talking about?" Skerren asked.

Jack didn't say anything right away. He just stared at the mountain. Jack couldn't believe it, but something was still blocking his ability to speak to the machines in the crystal cavern. The last nullifier from the roof had fallen down off the mountain, far out of reach, but Jack's powers still weren't fully back.

"There's one more nullifier in there," Jack said.

"Nullifier?" Jazen asked. "You mean Smart's power drainers?"

"Yeah. He uses them everywhere now," Jack said, squinting at the cloaked SmarterNet. His powers had risen against the weakened nullifier zone enough for him to feel out the details of Smart's machine. Enough to almost see it, even while cloaked, but not enough to control it. The dead zone blocking his powers was still there in front of him, but it was more focused now. Jack could feel with pinpoint certainty where the last nullifier was. "It's there inside the SmarterNet," Jack said. "In its core.

We have to take it out before I can feed the cure-code into the system. I need you guys to keep Glave and the Left-Behinds off my back long enough for me to get to it."

"Glave?" Trea asked. "He's here too?"

"He's here, all right," Jack said. "He's the Rogue Secreteer."

"What?" Allegra exclaimed, nearly losing control of her dragon. The creature roared as it bumped into the other flying serpents, and Zhi tried to steady it.

"I don't understand," Zhi said. "Glave is the rogue? How?"

"Jack, that can't be . . . ," Trea said.

"It's true," Jack replied. "He's infected. Obscuro is Glave's host. The whole thing with him was just a Rüstov plan to turn us against one another so they could spread their virus . . . and so they could get their hands on me."

"Why go through all that? Why do they want you so bad?" Skerren asked, scowling at Jack. "I want an answer. Before we go in, I want the truth."

Jack took a deep breath and looked at Skerren. "They want me because I'm next in line for the Rüstov throne." Skerren's eyes grew wide in shock. "It's true," Jack told his friends. "I'm the heir to the empire. The Rüstov prince is right in here," he said, tapping his chest. "They think I'm going to win the war for them."

"Are you?" Skerren asked.

"Yes," Khalix said, taunting Jack in a voice only he could hear. "You are, Jack. We are, whether you like it or not. You can't fight the future."

"No," Jack told Skerren. "And if you'll fight with me, I'll prove it to you. But I need your help. I need you to finish this with me. Please."

"I'm ready," Allegra said.

"I'm more than ready," Jazen said, pounding a fist into his palm. "Let's do it. I've never wanted to hit anything so bad in my whole life."

Jazen kicked his heels into the sides of his dragon and dove down at the floating mountain, with Jack riding shotgun. Trea, Allegra, and Zhi charged after them into battle. Jack looked back and saw that Skerren was coming too. He was the last one in line, but he was coming just the same.

One of the Left-Behinds started shooting again as the dragons raced toward the cavern. Jazen and the School of Thought students took evasive action as some of the other Para-Soldiers raised their weapons to fire. Glave ripped the gun out of the first shooter's hands and kicked him off the side of the mountain. "How many times do I have to tell you morons?" he shouted as the trigger-happy Para-Soldier fell screaming. "Don't shoot at the emperor's son!"

The other Left-Behinds lowered their weapons, and then scattered as the dragons swooped in, swiping across the ledge with their tails to clear a path where Jack and his friends could land. The cavern was too tight a space for the dragons to fly in, but they were still able to knock several Left-Behinds out to join the one that Glave had thrown away. Jack and his friends dismounted their dragons and confronted the enemy head-on.

Skerren leaped off his dragon high up at the roof of the crystal cavern and cut loose a series of stalactites that were hanging off the ceiling. Each one that fell landed with a deadly impact, impaling Left-Behind Para-Soldiers and crushing them where they stood. Skerren rolled his landing to come up in a fighting stance, slicing away at more Rüstov fighters. He was taking on large groups, moving toward them without pause, as if he were the one who outnumbered them. Apparently he had gotten over his reservations about this fight. Trea immediately split into what looked like three T2s upon entering the crystal chamber. She punched Left-Behinds and made holes in them, doing damage right alongside Skerren. Her three selves working together were a force to be reckoned with.

Glave started waving his arms and yelling at his men as the tide of battle turned against him. The Rüstov spy grabbed a gun off the ground and thrust it into the arms of a random Left-Behind. "What are you waiting for?" he shouted. "Them you can shoot!" he said, pointing at Skerren, Zhi, and Trea. "Fire your weapons! Kill them!"

As soon as the Left-Behinds primed their weapons and turned toward Jack's friends, the Mysterrii descended upon them from above. They had inched their way across the cavern using the crystal stalactites like monkey bars and now dropped in on the unsuspecting Para-Soldiers. The Mysterrii saved Skerren's, Zhi's, and Trea's lives, disarming the Rüstov and buying the children just enough time to take cover behind crystal stalagmites and the flaming wreck of Hypnova's ship. The Left-Behinds started throwing the Mysterrii off their backs and out over the ledge of the cliff, and Zhi sent his dragons down to catch them.

Meanwhile, Jack, Jazen, and Allegra broke for the SmarterNet, racing against time to reach its core and the supertransmitter waiting inside. Jack and Jazen led the way. Jack's connection to machines, fuzzy as it was because of the last lingering nullifier, allowed him to see the SmarterNet well enough, and he knew Jazen's mechanical eyes would have no trouble getting through its cloaked state. Allegra still bumped into near invisible walls and low-hanging equipment as she followed Jack and Jazen, but she kept herself in a semifluid state on the way through and avoided getting hurt. The Rüstov soldiers guarding the SmarterNet tried to stop them, but Jazen ran through them like a Mecha possessed whenever they got in his way. He literally tore into the first one he came across and ended up ripping off its bionic arm without even meaning to. He stopped to look at the severed metal arm and then at Jack like he didn't know his own strength.

"I gave you a few upgrades." Jack shrugged.

"I can see that," Jazen replied. "Very nice work." Jazen slammed the wounded Para-Soldier into the wall, swinging the severed arm like a baseball bat, and pressed forward.

Jack, Jazen, and Allegra continued to fight their way through the SmarterNet, pushing the Rüstov back. They had just made it to the second level when Stendeval checked in with an urgent message. "Jack, the Mechas are about to wake up. We have minutes left, maybe less. I need to know where you stand."

"You have to hold off!" Jack shouted into his wrist. "We're almost there. Jazen is here with me—it worked! Do you hear me, Stendeval? The cure-code works!"

"Which way, Jack? Up again?" Allegra asked as she shot an arm across the floor at a Left-Behind, pushing it back.

"This way!" Jack shouted. "Don't go up, go in!"

Jazen punched his hand into a Para-Soldier's stomach and started ripping out wires. It tried to shoot him, and he turned its gun around at another Left-Behind that was coming up behind it. Stray bullets shorted out the SmarterNet's cloaking device.

"Be careful!" Jack told Jazen, pushing the gun down

and away from Jazen. "No shooting in here. We need the SmarterNet intact."

"Sorry, Jack," Jazen said. "I think I've been in storage a little too long." Jack shook his head and pointed the way toward the SmarterNet's core. Jazen dropped the gun and kept moving.

Outside, Jack's friends were starting to get overwhelmed. Jack could hear it in their voices as he made his way through the SmarterNet.

"Zhi!" Skerren shouted. "Bring the dragons back around! We need them to breathe some fire on these guys."

"They're all still down with the Mysterrii," Jack heard Zhi say. "Besides, my dragons don't breathe fire."

"What?" Skerren shouted. "What kind of dragons don't breathe fire?"

"Jack, we'd better hurry," Allegra said. "It's getting ugly out there," she added, looking below her.

"We're here," Jack said, running down a short flight of steps to a landing at the center of the SmarterNet's middle level. It was a small circular platform with a waist-high railing that looked out on the crystal chamber. Jack looked around at the platform and saw thousands of wires, cables, and gauges all surrounding a bright beam of red light the size of a lamppost. His powers felt nonexistent next to it. "This is it," Jack said, spotting the super-relayer-connector component Midknight had shown him a blueprint of earlier that night. It was sitting on a computer console at the base of the red light, safe under heavy bulletproof glass. That was just fine. Jack didn't want anything bad happening to that transmitter. The nullifier was a different story.

"What's that?" Allegra asked, pointing at the red beam of light.

"That's info-light," Jack said, his eyes darting around the SmarterNet core. "Concentrated data packaged into a ray of light for the fastest data transfer possible. It's the SmarterNet's signal."

Allegra reached out to touch the red info-light beam. It made a hissing noise when she touched it, like butter melting in a frying pan. "Ah!" Allegra cried out, pulling back her hand.

"Don't touch it!" Jack said to Allegra. "Allegra, a 'concentrated ray of light' is just another way of saying 'laser beam.' This one here is the largest data ray I've ever seen."

"Now you tell me," Allegra said, rubbing her hand.

"Stay focused, guys," Jazen said. "We're about to have company."

The staircases leading down to the SmarterNet's core level were filling up with Left-Behinds. Jack, Jazen, and Allegra were backed into a corner with no way out. They had gotten this far by staying mobile, but now they were stationary, and it was only a matter of time before the Rüstov's numbers overwhelmed them.

"Find the nullifier, Jack," Jazen said.

"I'm trying," Jack said, his breathing getting more and more rapid. "It should be right here. I can feel it, but I don't see it. The only thing I recognize in here is the super-relayer-connector transmitter."

"The what?" Allegra asked.

"Never mind," Jazen said. "As long as he knows what that means, I'm happy." A Left-Behind rushed Jazen and slammed into him like a battering ram. Jazen grunted as he got forced back a few steps, but he spun the Rüstov around and pinned its arm behind its back until Jack heard something break. The Left-Behind cried out, and Jazen kicked it back the way it had come. Allegra shot two arms up the opposite stairwell like spears, sinking them into the midsection of an approaching Para-Soldier. Still, more of them were coming. They stepped right over their fallen comrades on their way to the core.

Down on the floor of the chamber, Jack could see his friends were in an equally desperate position. Looking over the railing as he scanned the area for the nullifier, he saw Skerren completely surrounded by Left-Behinds. He was swinging away with his swords, but the Rüstov outnumbered him ten to one. Trea was in a similar predicament. Two of her divided selves were standing over an injured third self, fighting Rüstov and trying to hold their ground. It wouldn't be long before they ended up like Zhi, whose arms were being held from behind by two different Left-Behinds. He was kicking away at the Rüstov in front of him, trying to keep them from getting ahold of his legs, but his chances didn't look good.

"Jack, hurry!" Allegra said, fighting back more Para-Soldiers at the gateway to the SmarterNet core. She had spread out her body into a shield, trying to block the way in on her side, but the Rüstov were pushing her back. Frantic, Jack kept looking around the SmarterNet's core for the last nullifier.

"I don't get it," Jack said. "The nullifier signal is coming from right here. It should be right in front of us. It should be—"

Jack cut himself off midsentence and looked up at the red info-light laser. "Jazen!" he said, pointing. Jazen understood what Jack was thinking without needing to hear a single word, and he immediately threw his hand into the path of the laser.

"Arrghhh!" Jazen screamed as the red light burned him, but he didn't pull his arm out. He reached around inside, fighting through the pain. Finally Jack saw him tighten his grip on something inside the beam and pull back, hard. Jazen's half-melted hand ripped out a tall metal cylinder from the center of the red laser.

"That's it!" Jack shouted. "That's the nullifier."

Jazen crushed the nullifier in his ruined hand. "That *was* the nullifier," he said.

Jack's eyebrows perked up as power flooded back into his body like a river of energy. "Outstanding," he said with a smile. Jack reached out with his powers and froze the joints of every Left-Behind on the mountain with a single thought. He got them just in time.

Down below the core, Skerren, Trea, and Zhi were all left blinking out looks of surprise and relief as the Rüstov fighters attacking them turned into statues. Skerren and Trea both relaxed from the defensive stances they had taken up against blows that were no longer coming, and Zhi squirmed his way out of the grip of his Rüstov captors.

Skerren looked up at Jack with approval and scraped his swords together as he walked around a motionless Left-Behind. The alien invader struggled to move against Jack's will, but it was no use. The creature was helpless.

"I'm going to enjoy this," Skerren said, and struck down the Rüstov. Trea and Zhi followed his lead, dismantling the Rüstov forces piece by piece.

A crackle-static noise came out of Jack's wrist as Stendeval checked in for the last time. "Jack, the Mechas are awake," he said. "They're awake and they're coming over the wall. We're losing control at the border. I'm sorry, but I can't wait any longer. I have to act."

"Don't!" Jack said. "I'm going to transfer the cure right now. I just need thirty seconds more. It's right here in Jazen's head."

Just then a plume of smoke shot up on the platform,

and Glave appeared next to Jazen. "This head?" he asked, holding a gun to Jazen's temple. "I'm sorry, but I don't think you have thirty seconds."

"No!" Jack said. Obscuro was a fresh host for Glave. He didn't have enough mechanical parts yet for Jack to freeze in place. Glave smiled and pulled the trigger.

Nothing happened.

Now it was Jack's turn to smile. "I'm sorry, I don't think you have any idea what I'm capable of when there's nothing blocking my powers."

Glave's face fell. He looked at the useless pistol in his hand and dropped it to the ground. "I'm not going to lie to you," Jazen told Glave. "This is going to hurt."

Jazen couldn't have known how right he was. He grabbed Glave by the head and flipped him over his shoulder, throwing him across the platform to the other side of the SmarterNet core. Glave came down upon a golden sword as Hypnova appeared beneath him, looking tired and bloody but not beaten. Hypnova hoisted Glave up on her steel until she was face-to-face with the Rogue Secreteer. "I hate to do it like this—coming out of nowhere," Hypnova said. "I really did want to kill you proper." Hypnova pulled her sword from Glave's stomach and pushed him out over the railing. "Oh well," she said as Glave fell to the ground like a sack of flour.

"There goes your ticket home, Khalix," Jack muttered under his breath. The Rüstov prince had no answer for him. "Now for the virus," Jack said, and reached for Jazen. He put one hand on Jazen's head and one on the SmarterNet's super-relayer-connector. "All right, SmarterNet. You're about to become the emergency broadcast system. . . . This is not a test."

The SmarterNet's info-light signal changed from red to green as Jack replaced the virus code with the cure-code. He turned up the power, and the green laser beam burned right through the roof of the SmarterNet core and up through the levels above it. The info-light signal rose up into the night sky, illuminating Mount Nevertop with a brilliant emerald glow.

"Stendeval!" Jack called out after a few seconds. "The cure-code is live. What's happening down there? Is it working?"

The line was silent. Then a sound like static came through, but only for the briefest of moments. It wasn't static. It was air whistling through grinning teeth. "Yes, Jack," Stendeval said in a voice so warm Jack could practically hear the smile on his face. "It's working. The Mechas are coming out of it. It's over."

No sooner had Stendeval confirmed the cure-code's delivery than Jack started to feel it himself. His mind fell in tune with the SmarterNet's signal as it went out across the world, interacting with every machine everywhere. All across the Earth, Jack could feel the Rüstov spyware virus dying. But Stendeval was wrong. It wasn't over. Not yet. There was still one more thing he had to do.

CHAPTER
29

Moment of Truth

"Stendeval?" Jack said into his wrist. "Now that you don't have to fire that EMP anymore, you think you've got enough juice left to get the Inner Circle and a few other people up here? I've got something I need to get off my chest."

Stendeval's voice came over the line after a brief silence. "Are you sure, Jack?" he asked.

"I'm sure," Jack replied. "They're ready. And even if they aren't . . . I am."

"As you wish," Stendeval said. "And, Jack?" he added. "I'm proud of you."

"Me too," Jazen said, patting Jack on the shoulder. "We all are."

"You might want to hold off on singing my praises just yet," Jack replied.

"What are you talking about?" Jazen asked.

Jack directed his answer at Allegra. "I told you that if we made it through this I'd tell you everything." A series of red energy particles started to spiral out of the air down at the floor of the crystal chamber. "It's time."

There was an orange-white flash of light, and Stendeval, the rest of the Inner Circle, Jonas Smart, Lorem Ipsum, Ricochet, Midknight, and Blue all appeared in the cavern. *That was fast,* Jack thought. He and the others left the core and went down to greet them.

As he came off the steps, Jack saw Skerren bow his head to Hovarth for a moment before going back to dressing the injured Trea's wounds. "How's that feel?" he heard Skerren ask.

"Better," she answered, a slight smile creeping onto her lips. "Thanks."

"What's going on here?" Hovarth demanded, looking

around at the dead Left-Behinds and his battle-worn protégé in confusion. "What is this?"

"This is the SmarterNet," Jazen replied, stepping forward so the others could get a look at him. "It's Jonas Smart's fantastic invention that nearly gift-wrapped this whole world to the Rüstov. Impressive, isn't it?"

Jonas Smart sprang forth with his finger in the air, shouting, "*Lorem ipsum dolor sit! Amet consectetur! Adipisicing! Elit!*" Lorem laughed while he ranted and raved, speaking nothing but gobbledygook. Smart got frustrated and started yelling at her instead, not that anyone understood him.

Jazen let out a surprised laugh at Jonas Smart's unintelligible tirade. "I suppose that's one way of putting it," he said. "What's with him?"

"Jazen?" Virtua asked, before Jack could explain. Projo the image-caster zoomed forward, and Virtua's image followed slowly behind him, squinting in disbelief. "Jazen Knight?"

"In the flesh," Jazen said with a wave. "More or less," he added, noticing he was waving hello with his melted hand.

"Partner? Is that really you?" a deep voice squeaked out in shock. Ricochet and Midknight stepped aside so Blue could get a better look at his resurrected friend. He inched up toward Jazen, looking like he was coming up on a ghost he was afraid he might scare off. "Am I seeing things?"

"Hey, Blue," Jazen said, and smiled. "Long time."

Blue reached out and poked Jazen's shoulder as if to confirm he was real. "You . . . you're back?"

"Yep, and I'm ready to go back to work," Jazen said. "You don't by any chance know anyone who's looking for a partnerphhh—"

Jazen wheezed out a groan as Blue took him up into the kind of bear hug that puts bears to shame. "Easy, big fella." Jazen laughed, wrapped up in Blue's hug with his feet dangling in the air. "You're gonna bust me up all over again."

Jack smirked. "For the record, Blue? *This* is how I wanted to tell you about Jazen."

Just like Jack before him, Blue took his time letting go of Jazen Knight.

"If he's here," Virtua said, pointing at Jazen. "That

502

means it worked. Jack's cure worked." She looked up and down her arms like she was inspecting them for traces of the virus.

"It worked." Jack nodded. "The spyware virus is gone for good."

"So you say," Noteworthy replied. "How do we know that for sure?"

"We were all just in Machina, Clarkston," Midknight said. "We saw what happened when that green light went on in the sky. The Mechas all regained control of themselves."

"Did they?" Hovarth asked. "Perhaps that is what we are meant to believe." Virtua flickered, and Hovarth turned to her, saying, "It's not that I don't trust you or your people, Virtua. You have conducted yourselves with honor. Jack, on the other hand," Hovarth continued, shaking his head. "You lied about the virus once already, boy. And you were *supposed* to go home. Why should we trust you now?"

"Because I'm about to cop to something way worse than the virus or sneaking out," Jack told Hovarth. "Trust me, no one who would admit to what I'm about to say has any reason to lie about anything else. Once you hear it, you'll understand that the virus is the least of my worries. And yours."

Allegra tugged at Jack's elbow. "Jack, maybe you don't have to do this."

"What?" Jack said, furrowing his brow. "I thought you wanted to know everything."

"I did," Allegra replied. "But you're scaring me with this. I was thinking . . . maybe it's better if some things stay secret."

Jack shook his head. "The truth is gonna come out sooner or later," he told Allegra. "Smart already knows it. Lorem can't keep him gibberished-up forever."

"Actually, I can," Lorem Ipsum chimed in, prompting Smart to unleash an angry, babbling rant. It was like he was stress testing his vocal chords, trying to find the maximum volume he could reach. Jack watched him go on, seriously considering Lorem's offer.

"No," Jack said at last. "Thanks, but no. That would just be running away from the problem again, and I'm done with that. Let him go," Jack told Lorem. "There won't be any point to keep him like that once I get this out, anyway."

"For you, maybe," Lorem replied. "I like him better this way."

Chi gave her a stern look, giving an order with his eyes. "Lorem, release him," he said.

Lorem Ipsum shrugged and said, "You guys are no fun at all."

She snapped her fingers, and Smart took in a giant breath, like a drowning man breaking through the water to get air. "Finally!" he said. "Don't listen to another word this boy says! He's been lying to us this whole time. He's been working with *them*! It's just like I said from the start. He's nothing but a filthy—"

Blue picked Jonas Smart up by the collar. "You're gonna want to choose your next words very carefully," he told him. Blue gave Smart a menacing look and tightened his fist until his knuckles popped. "Don't forget, I'm not a cop anymore. Just a private citizen with a major bone to pick."

"Are you people going to let this brute threaten me like this?" Smart asked the others, struggling to get free of Blue's viselike grip.

"Blue has a point, Jonas," Stendeval said. "Jack has the

floor right now. If I were you, I'd wait quietly. Your turn will come, I'm sure."

"Not necessarily," Blue said. "I'd still like to hit him, if that's all right with you." Blue's loyalty forced a smile onto Jack's lips, followed by a short outburst of air from in between them. Under different circumstances it would have been the start of a laugh.

"Thanks, Blue, but I've got this," Jack replied. "It's like you said, I gotta face it. Once I get out in front of this thing, it won't have any power over me anymore." Jack waved his hand at Smart like he didn't matter. "He can't do anything but tell people my secrets. If I go ahead and tell them myself, he's got nothing left to threaten me with."

Blue nodded and set Smart down on the ground, at which point the former Circleman made the extremely smart decision to keep his mouth shut. He sulked as he pulled down on his suit jacket, smoothing out the wrinkles left by Blue's giant mitts.

"You're not a cop anymore?" Jazen asked Blue quietly on the side.

Blue shook his head. "You've got a lot to catch up on. Go ahead, Jack."

Jack looked over at his fellow students, Skerren and Allegra in particular. "I owe you guys big-time for riding to my rescue like you did. I know I didn't give you much reason to put yourselves out there like that. I've had too many secrets for way too long. I know that secrets are part of life in the Imagine Nation, but if I've learned anything over the last year, it's that secrets keep people apart. I thought maybe they could keep people safe, too, but it turned out that my secrets did just the opposite. And somewhere along the line they turned into lies. You were right about that," Jack told Skerren. "There is a difference between secrets and lies, and I think it's time that turns one into the other. All year long I had a million opportunities to tell the truth, but I always kept my mouth shut. I changed the subject, avoided questions, and ran away. I took the easy way out, and all it did was make things harder. I've gotta tell you, I'm tired of it." Jack shook his head. "I'm tired of going it alone. Allegra, I know you were angry with me for trusting in Lorem and not in you, but the truth is I didn't trust anyone. And I'm sorry about that. I could have stopped all this before it started if I had."

"I don't believe this," Skerren said, shaking his head

507

with a frown. "You mean to say there's something else besides the bit about the Rüstov prince?"

"Rüstov prince?" Hovarth said. "Where?"

"Right here," Jack admitted, pointing at himself. "It's my parasite. You've heard his name before. It's Khalix. He's trying to talk to me right now, and it's all I can do to keep him out of my head, but that's just part of it. I only found out about him tonight. The rest of it I learned the night Jazen died. The night I faced Revile." Jack felt the group tense up. Mentioning Revile tended to have that effect on people.

"Last year you all asked why he came here to kill me, and I said I didn't know. That was a lie," Jack revealed. "He told me why right there on the roof of SmartTower. The truth is he came to kill me so I wouldn't ever grow up to become him."

Jack's words hit the group like an invisible shock wave knifing through their bodies. People straightened their backs with startled jumps, blurted out stunned exclamations, and leaned forward with astonished eyebrows stretched up as high as they could go. Only Stendeval and Smart remained still. Smart was frowning, clearly upset that he wasn't the one to reveal the true nature of Jack's dire future.

Jazen was the first to speak. "What?" was all he was able to say.

"You heard me," Jack said. "I'm him. I'm Revile. At least, I might be . . . one day."

There, Jack thought. *I said it. It's out there.* He felt a weight lift up off his shoulders, but not all the way off his back. That part was out of his hands and completely dependent on the group's reaction. One thing Jack knew for sure, there was no turning back now.

The admission was met with more silence. This time Virtua ended it. "Jack, that doesn't make sense," she said. "Revile was fully grown during the invasion, thirteen years ago. You were just a baby. What you're saying . . . it isn't possible."

"No one would be happier than me if that were the case," Jack said. "But I've had to rethink my definition of 'possible' ever since I got here. Revile was here for the same reason back during the invasion. Only difference is, back then he was trying to kill me when I was just a baby. Revile comes from the future," Jack told the group. "It's a future where the Rüstov win the war, and he . . . or I . . . we're the reason for their victory. The Rüstov kidnapped me so they could turn me into the ultimate supersoldier killing machine. Revile told me all about it." The words were coming to Jack more easily now, spilling out of his mouth without any filter. It was almost like someone else was speaking. "Revile said he helped them kill planet after planet until eventually he couldn't take it anymore. He regained control of himself and came back here on a time-travel suicide mission to change his past—our future. He came back to kill me, and Legend stopped him. He ended up killing Legend instead."

"Jack, this can't be right," Jazen said. "Are you sure this isn't some kind of Rüstov trick?"

"It was me, Jazen," Jack said. "I saw the face behind the mask. I heard the voice. It was me."

"So . . . you killed Legend?" Noteworthy asked.

"I didn't kill anyone," Jack said. "That wasn't me fighting Legend during the invasion. Not yet, it wasn't. I'm thirteen years old. I haven't done anything but fight back."

"Still, the prophecy says you'll lose that fight," Hovarth countered.

"It's not a prophecy," Jack told Hovarth. "It's a possibility. An alternate future that may or may not happen. Stendeval told me—"

"It won't happen as long as we don't *let* it happen," Hovarth interrupted. "I'd prefer to be sure. When a seer has a vision of the future like this in Varagog, we take the matter very seriously."

"It's not like that," Jack said. "There's no 'seer' here unless you count me. This is science, not magic."

"All the more reason to be afraid," Smart cut in.

"What did I tell you about opening your mouth?" Blue said.

"The future is real!" Smart said, hustling away from the angry blue giant as fast as he could. "I know! Half of my inventions come from the future. And this vision of the future is backed up by events from our own past! Legend is dead, is he not? If Revile's words are untrue, who killed Legend? How else could Revile have even come to be? This future *must* happen. Jack must become him. The Rüstov prince is talking to him, fighting to control him! He freely admits it! He knows! He puts us all at risk with his selfishness. He could have saved us all by letting Revile kill him, and he chose not to."

"Of course I chose not to," Jack said. "I'm not gonna lie down and die for the Rüstov."

"You mean like Legend did? Like Virtua was willing to? You put yourself ahead of us," Smart accused. "You hid the truth about the virus, and only acted to stop it once I exposed your secrets!"

"It was the secrets you kept about the SmarterNet that nearly spread the Rüstov virus all over the world," Jack shot back. "They played you, and you don't even know it. Anything you got from the Rogue Secreteer, you got from the Rüstov. Obscuro was infected by a Rüstov spy named Glave. That name ring a bell? You did exactly what they wanted you to do, going on TV and getting everyone to fight one another while they moved their plan forward. The Rüstov count on people like you to tear us apart and make us weaker."

"You're just trying to shift the blame away from yourself," Smart said. "You're the one they're counting on to defeat us."

"I think he's going to be the one to defeat *them*," Stendeval interjected into the conversation. Everyone turned to Stendeval, waiting for him to back up his statement. "If you want to persecute this boy, you might as well persecute me. I knew Jack's story before he did. I knew it when I hid him away during the invasion, and I knew it when I watched over him in the Real World. I was the one who told Emissary Knight where to find Jack so he could bring him home. None of this happened by accident. I knew it all."

"You knew about this?" Noteworthy asked. "You knew about Jack's future, and still you brought him here? How could you do that? And why am I the last one to find out about *everything*?"

Stendeval looked at Noteworthy like a teacher being patient with a student who isn't trying very hard to understand the lesson. "I once met an accomplished poet and thinker who said, 'What lies behind us, and what lies before us, are small matters when compared with what lies within us,'" he told the wealthy Circleman.

Noteworthy looked at Stendeval like he was speaking another language. "What the devil is that supposed to mean?" he howled. "What lies within him is the Rüstov prince!"

"There's far more than that inside of Jack," Stendeval replied. "The only future I believe in is the one that we create. Jack's future is in his hands, and from what I know of this boy's courage and resolve, the Rüstov are going to regret making him part of their plans."

"And you know best, do you? Is that it?" Smart asked Stendeval. "There you go again, making decisions on your own that affect all of us. Your ego puts us all in danger."

"That is quite a statement coming from you, Jonas," Stendeval replied.

"The whole of the Inner Circle should vote on what's to be done with Jack," Smart fired back. "It's not for one man to decide for himself behind closed doors. The people of Empire City deserve to know what's being done about this. Every Circleman here needs to make it clear where they stand—with Jack, or with the Imagine Nation."

"The Circle already voted on Jack's future. Last year," Chi said. "You were there."

"I wasn't there," Noteworthy cut in. "And I'm willing to bet that none of this was discussed back then. Jonas is right. This affects all of us, not just Jack. We have to do what's best for *all* the people of the Imagine Nation."

"Aye," Hovarth agreed. "The Imagine Nation must come first. For the good of our great land—to protect our *future*—Jack Blank has to die."

No one said anything for a long half minute. Jack realized Smart did have something to threaten him with after all, and he was seeing it play out here. He hoped that someone else would step up and take his side, but there was nothing but silence. That's when Jazen Knight spoke up.

"Cowards," the emissary spat out, eyeing the silent assembly with contempt.

Hovarth's head snapped up to look at Jazen. "What did you say?" he asked in a slow, smoldering voice.

Jazen didn't flinch. "I called you a coward, Lord Hovarth," he replied. "This is the Imagine Nation, not the Assassin Nation. You ought to be ashamed of yourself."

Hovarth drew out his giant battle-ax and stepped toward Jazen. "No man talks to me that way and lives."

"I've been dead once already," Jazen said. "It wasn't so bad," he added, stepping forward to meet Hovarth chest to chest. Blue got in between them and pulled his partner back. Stendeval and Chi got in front of Hovarth. Jazen never stopped talking.

"They tell me I've been gone a year, but you'd never know it listening to this conversation," Jazen went on, getting louder after Blue let him go. "Sounds to me like we're right back where we started!" He looked down at Hovarth, Smart, Noteworthy, and everyone else who'd held their tongues when the warrior king of Varagog had called for Jack's head. "You all claim to represent the interests of the Imagine Nation, but you don't even understand what makes this place worth fighting for. This is the land of possibility . . . of hope . . . of courage! There's no place left on Earth like this, and if you harm this boy, it's already gone. The true greatness of the Imagine Nation isn't found when times are easy; it's there when the moment is hard and we rise up as one to meet the challenges we face. When we cast aside differences and triumph together in a way we never could when standing apart. That's how we beat the Rüstov the first time. That's what we need to do now. In case you hadn't noticed, Jack saved the world tonight . . . from the Rüstov! You've got it backward," Jazen told Smart. "Either you're with Jack or you're against the Imagine Nation. You all need to decide where you stand on *that*."

When Jazen finished talking, the only sound that remained was the wind blowing through the mountain air. His words hung there in the silent crystal chamber, daring to be challenged. There were no takers.

"I didn't really save the world," Jack offered up. "Not alone." All eyes turned back to him. "I didn't stop the virus by myself, even if I thought I had to. It was Trea's work on the virus that made the cure-code possible," Jack said, giving his lab partner the credit she deserved. "It was you guys fighting the Rüstov so Jazen and I could send the cure out through the SmarterNet," he added, looking at Hypnova, the Mysterrii, Skerren, Allegra, and Zhi. "And it was you guys." He pointed at the Inner Circle, Midknight, Ricochet, and Blue. "Trusting one another and working together to keep the peace in Empire City and save lives. It wasn't easy, but we did it. Everything Jazen just said, we did that here tonight. We did it together. The Rüstov are so cynical. They think they can beat us by turning us against one another, but we're better than that.

We're smarter than that. At least, I hope we are. Don't let them be right about us," Jack pleaded. "Please?"

Jack was spent. After everything that had happened that night—from the disasters the Imagine Nation had just narrowly avoided to the disaster that this conversation had become—he had nothing left. And now everyone was just staring at him. He was desperate for something to take the focus off him.

"Well?" Jack asked. "Somebody say something."

Nobody did.

Jack's eyes fell on Allegra. She was staring at him. "Allegra?" he asked her. "What do you think?"

Allegra hit him with a look he couldn't read one way or the other. Next to her Skerren stared him down with cold eyes that left nothing to the imagination. He walked over to join Hovarth, whose expression had yet to soften since he'd been called a coward by Jazen. Neither his nor Skerren's reaction came as much of a surprise, but Allegra . . . Jack stayed focused on Allegra. As Jack fixed his eyes on her, he realized that he was afraid of what she might say, more than anyone else there. He didn't know what he'd do if Allegra turned her back on him too. Jack's shoulders tightened as he waited for Allegra's answer.

Allegra opened her mouth to speak. "I think . . . ," she began, then cut herself off. "I think . . ." She paused again. Then she smiled. "They *aren't* right about us. We are better." Allegra reached out a hand to Jack. "Together."

Jack's entire body unclenched.

But as Jack reached out to take Allegra's hand, he saw it. Glave's body was no longer lying where it had fallen. Then Jack felt it. The ship from hangar 17 dropped its cloak in the airspace across from the SmarterNet. It fired two missiles from underneath its wings. Jack looked up in terror when the new machines in the area broke through onto his internal radar. He'd been so focused on the conversation that he hadn't even noticed them until it was too late. He grabbed Allegra's hand and stepped out in front of her, throwing his other hand out toward the two rocket-fueled killers that were flying right at him. No, not at him, he realized. In the split second he had to read their targets, Jack saw the missiles were aimed at the SmarterNet. The Rüstov were trying to kill the cure-code's broadcast. He managed to turn away one missile, altering its flight path to shoot past the mountain harmlessly. The other one crashed into the sidewall of the chamber. A fireball filled with a million crystal shards rushed down toward Jack and the others like a wave of flaming shrapnel. "Down!" somebody shouted. Jack didn't know who.

Everything went black.

CHAPTER

30

The Fifth Day

"I told you, Jack," a smug voice purred in the darkness. "I told you it would end like this." It was Khalix. Jack recognized his voice as soon as it faded in. There was no more static surrounding it. It came in crystal clear.

Jack felt tired, like he'd woken up an hour too early after going to bed several hours too late. He wanted to rub his eyes, but he couldn't find his hands. He couldn't feel or see anything. It was a little bit frightening, but he was in no immediate pain. If anything, he felt like he was floating in an endless void. He was nothing but a thought. Nothing but an idea.

"Where are we?" Jack heard himself ask.

"Right now? Just passing Jupiter's twenty-third moon," Khalix replied. "It's quite a view. You could get up and take a look if you were awake, but we can't have that."

Jack searched his memory, trying to piece together what was going on. The last thing he knew, he was trying to cover Allegra as the missile struck Mount Nevertop. The fire and glass were raining down. . . . He was unconscious. That had to be it. "This a dream," Jack decided. "I'm dreaming."

"There's no dreaming in cryo-sleep," Khalix told him. "You're sedated for the journey back to Rüst. Of course, that's no reason we can't still talk, you and I. We can talk about *my* dreams . . . ," the Rüstov prince mused. "They're finally coming true."

A cold wave rippled through the void, rolling over Jack as he realized Khalix was telling the truth. Flashes of memories hit him like snippets of film flapping through a projector onto a theater screen. Glave's men coming off the starship, surprising the wounded Inner Circle . . .

Left-Behinds dragging his body out from underneath the crystal rubble. . . . He remembered the dazed, helpless feeling of being loaded onto the ship before it took off.

They finally did it, Jack thought. *They got me. . . . I lost.*

There was nothing Jack could do about it now. There was no one left to help him. He was all alone. Caught in the void, Jack felt like gravity suddenly grabbed hold of him, pulling him down backward into a black hole. His heart would have been racing if he could have felt it beat. He would have been hyperventilating if he could have felt himself breathe, but none of those feelings existed in this place. There was only his mind, racing around in a circle like a hamster on a wheel.

"That's right, Jack," Khalix said, perhaps sensing his fear. "It's time. Time for both of us to claim our destiny. Your power . . . our technology . . . we're going to make an unbeatable team. Only now, *you're* going to see what it feels like to be trapped in this body. The last thirteen years have been yours," Khalix said. "The future belongs to me."

The future.

Khalix's words echoed through Jack's mind, and then

something clicked inside his head that slowed the pace of his descent into fear and despair. It was something Stendeval had said:

The only future I believe in is the one that we create.

Stendeval had told everyone that he was counting on Jack to defeat the Rüstov. That his courage and resolve would make the Rüstov regret they'd ever heard the name Jack Blank. Jack grabbed on to that thought and held on to it like it was a life preserver. "What lies behind us, and what lies before us, are small matters when compared to what lies within us," Jack told himself.

"What's that?" Khalix asked, and Jack realized he'd said that last part out loud. At least, he'd said it in a way that Khalix could hear.

"Bring it," Jack told the parasite, throwing down the gauntlet.

Khalix was silent for a moment. Jack felt like the royal parasite was surprised.

"If you want to scare me into giving up, you're gonna be disappointed," Jack continued. "I'm not afraid of the future anymore, Khalix, no matter how bad it looks. You still have to make it happen. Bring it on," Jack said again.

"We'll see who's still standing when tomorrow finally comes."

"We . . . we will, Jack," Khalix replied, his voice catching a moment on the first word. "We will, indeed."

Khalix kept talking, but Jack stopped listening. He dropped back, deep into the pit of his own mind, and did his best to ignore his other half. For better or for worse, they were stuck with each other for the rest of this long, crazy ride. Jack thought about the fight ahead of him. He hoped that he'd be strong enough to win it. He'd find out soon enough.

The future was about to begin.

ACKNOWLEDGMENTS

If you're reading this, it means that the second book is done. I'm not going to lie to you. . . . Part of me has no idea how that happened. I am never going to complain about writing like it's a job, but really . . . this was a tough one. For a second novel, this book came with some pretty big firsts.

This was the first time I've ever written anything with a deadline. In the past I've never had any pressure to finish a book, other than that which I put on myself (significant pressure, to be sure, but still a very different feeling). This is also the first book I've written since becoming a parent, and I can assure you that any free time I used to have for writing is very much a thing of the past. I am writing these lines while my son sleeps, and I fully expect to be interrupted any second now. Add to that the stress of a daily commute to New York City, a real job at MTV, and the madness of spring break in Acapulco, and you've got a very busy, very memorable year in which I somehow, someway produced a book. Luckily for me, this year also produced one last notable first: Today is November 1, 2010, and the first day of my life as a full-time writer. It's a new adventure for me, and the fulfillment of a lifelong dream. So here's to the new chapter in my life, and to the people who made *these* new chapters (in Jack's life) possible:

My agent, Chris Richman, whose sage advice on writing and the business of writing has never steered me wrong. Thank you and the entire Upstart Crow team for your tireless efforts on my behalf.

My editor, Liesa Abrams, who sees the Imagine Nation as clearly as, if not more clearly than, I do. Your careful guidance and keen insights helped me grab a tiger by the tail and shape this story into the one I was trying to tell. On top of that, you are just an awesome person to work with. I am lucky to have you and everyone at Aladdin on my team.

Chris McCarthy and Carlo DiMarco at MTV, whose flexibility and understanding with my schedule made it possible for me to get this book written in the first place. I want to thank you and the whole mtvU crew for your support and friendship over the years. I am really going to miss seeing you guys every day.

My wife, Rebecca, whom I love like crazy. I've said it before, and I'll say it again: I may be a guy who always has one foot in the Imagine Nation, but you make sure I always have one foot in the Real World, too. I don't know where I'd be without you.

My son, Jack, who has changed my life in every way possible, and I wouldn't have it any other way. You never fail to bring a smile to my face, and your mom and I love you very much.

And finally, I have to thank you—the readers. Thanks to everyone who picked up a copy of the first book, and maybe even liked it enough to come back for more with this book. I hope you enjoyed Jack's latest round of adventures. I am going to do my best to keep you all entertained for as long as I can. Thanks again, and I'll see you back here next year for the third book.